The nurses' phone rang, the odd double ring that announced an outside call. A moment later Carla called out, "Dr. Lynch, it's for you. Line two."

I picked up the receiver, spotting a smear of blood on one cuff. Rolling up the sleeve so it wouldn't show, I said, "Lynch here."

"Got your message." When I said nothing, Mark prompted, "About the kid and his kidnapped sister?"

"Oh, yeah. It's been a busy couple of hours." I rolled the other cuff to match. The tough doctor looked.

"I talked to the kid, Wayne Edward. This claim he's making, about the sister being kidnapped by the foster father. It didn't happen, okay?"

"Okay, but—"

"So back off."

I held the phone out and stared at the receiver as if the device had lost its mind. Or its manners. Mark was still speaking, so I put it back to my ear.

"—don't mean to be a typical cop, but I'll handle it. I know what's going on with these girls and I don't need you to—"

I put the phone back on the hook. Hanging up on a call was something like number twenty-four on Miss DeeDee's list of things a real lady never did. I wasn't a real lady. "Men. Stupid, dumb, idiot men." Then I clarified to myself, "Man. Stupid, dumb, idiot man." And then I thought, did Mark say these *girls*? What girls?

GWEN HUNTER

GRAVE CONCERNS

MIRA®

MIRA

ISBN 0-7783-2006-5

GRAVE CONCERNS

Visit us at www.mirabooks.com

Printed in U.S.A.

There are all kinds of heroes, all manner of bravery, all sorts of inspiration. A hero, brave enough to look your fears in the face. You have inspired me. With respect, I dedicate this book to Micki Glenn

ACKNOWLEDGMENTS

Though I drew on Chester County, South Carolina, and its hospital blueprint for inspiration and information, Dawkins County, its citizens, its employees, its hospital and patients are entirely fictional. I have tried to make the medical sections of *Grave Concerns* as realistic as possible. Where mistakes exist, they are mine, not the able, competent and creative medical workers in the list below.

For medical help:

Laurie Milatz, D.O., in South Carolina
Susan Prater, O.R. Tech and sister-in-love,
in South Carolina
Watson Wright, coroner in South Carolina
Marc Gorton, registered Respiratory Therapist,
in South Carolina
Tim Minors, paramedic, in South Carolina
Barry Benfield, R.N., in South Carolina
Susan B. Jacobs, R.N., in South Carolina
Jason Adams, M.D., in South Carolina and Florida
Earl Jenkins, Jr., M.D., in South Carolina
James Maynard, M.D., in South Carolina
Robert Thomas, M.D., in South Carolina
Eric Lavondas, M.D., in North Carolina
Isom Lowman, M.D., in South Carolina
Mark G. Kimble, D.C., P.A., in South Carolina

Daniel S. Shapiro, M.D.
  Associate Professor of Medicine, Pathology
  & Laboratory Medicine
  Boston University School of Medicine
  Director Clinical Microbiology &
  Molecular Diagnostics Laboratories
  Boston Medical Center
Randall Pruett, Fran Jackson, Joan Strait
and Sonya Pearson—co-workers in the lab.

As always, for making this a stronger book:

Miranda Stecyk, my editor
Jeff Gerecke, my agent, who wisely told me to write
a medical thriller.
My writers group for all the help in making this
novel work. Thanks for bleeding all over its bits
and pieces.
My husband, for answers to questions that pop up,
for his catching so much in the rewrites, and for
his endless patience.
My mother, Joyce Wright, for editing as I work.

And to all the wonderful people who have let
me use their names in the writing of this series:
Fazelle Scaggs, Dempsey Ann, Hybernia, the
Fairweathers, Orinada, Trellie, Blevin, Steven Stone
and all the rest. Thank you!

AUTHOR'S NOTE

About Dawkins County:

Most doctors who commute to the small county hospital where I work are scheduled for weekend coverage of the E.R. Upon hearing of the small population in the mostly rural area—less than 50,000 people—they expect to experience a restful weekend with a rare car accident and perhaps a sore throat or earache. Instead they find an incredibly high incidence of alcoholism, drug use, teenage pregnancy, sexually transmitted diseases, heart and liver disease, unvaccinated children with childhood diseases not seen in this country for decades, diseases acquired through contact with wildlife, farm animals and poor water in the few well systems in the outlying areas, farm and industry traumas, people hit by trains, and on and on. Most leave feeling shell-shocked. Long-timers like me just grin and say, "Wait till next week. It'll be worse!" An often-heard phrase in the E.R. is, "Oh honey, I could tell you some stories...."

About Rhea:

So many of you have fallen in love with Dr. Rhea-Rhea Lynch. I love her, too! For me she is as alive as I am, as full of angst and energy, pathos and joy. Though Rhea and I are nothing alike, and she is fully fictional, I would recognize her if she walked into the room. I have heard the same comment from many of you.

For those of you who have asked, Rhea ages one year for every three books. After book three she will be permanently listed in her mid-thirties. And no, I don't yet know how her romantic life will turn out! I am as ambivalent as Rhea about the men in her life!

Thanks to your help, Rhea will be around a long time! (And yes, I pronounce her name RAY, like a ray of sunshine—though she would hate that comparison!)

About the practice of medicine:

Our knowledge of medicine is evolving so fast that even the finest doctors have a hard time keeping up with the changes. When you read any medical novel, many of the procedures used by the characters will quickly become outmoded, outdated and be put out to pasture! I hope you will keep this in mind when you read the Rhea Lynch, M.D., series! As to mistakes—yep, I make 'em, and all mistakes are mine, not the knowledgeable professionals who help with research! Mea culpa, in advance!

About the Author:

If you wish to learn more about me, please visit www.gwenhunter.com, or go to my author's page at www.mirabooks.com. I will answer any letters that come via e-mail through my Web site or snail mail through the publisher as quickly as possible. And please remember to include a return address!

Thank you all!
And enjoy!
Gwen Hunter

Prologue

As an E.R. doctor I've seen a lot of patients die—pass on, as we say in the South—but some deaths are worse than others. Much worse. Some stay with you, tainting dreams and nightmares for years afterward. Dreams that start with a bang and drag you into them feetfirst and screaming, like a roller-coaster ride in a fun house on Halloween. Or dreams that start slow and build slower, and then suddenly you're buried deep and unable to breathe. The dreams that were left after Deacon blew into Dawkins County were like the second, slow and miserable, gathering into fierce and biting terror, roaring over me in a dark wave.

Change comes to all of us—change of jobs, addresses, lovers, friends, thought processes, beliefs and hopes. A strong person deals with the changes, rocks with the waves, bends with the winds, all that pseudo-psychobabble garbage. Dr. Phil and Dear Abby stuff. Me? I guess I'm getting pretty good at change. In some ways, I'm even starting to expect it, like it, roll with the punches. But the change that some people experience can be more transformation than the average person can withstand and survive. Maybe.

1

IT'S MY HOUSE, I'LL WHINE IF I WANT TO

I shifted on the hard front window ledge of my little bungalow-style house. The wood cut into my thigh muscle and ground against bones higher up. It was uncomfortable, but not enough to make me move away from the ice-cold window glass. In the background, the CD player flipped to a new disc, a remix of oldies.

"Oh, Girl," came through the speakers over my head. Motown. Soft and rich and so full of broken soul it made me want to cry. Motown. The music my mother had listened to when she was on the downside of a manic-depressive swing, halfway through a bottle of Jack Daniels Black Label, one new man or another kicked out of the house and her party friends sent home. Motown. I should change the music. Put on a little seventies rock or pop. Maybe a little Carly Simon or Doobie Brothers.

But I didn't. I wasn't going to let my mother's response to music color my appreciation. Motown was my mother's crutch, not mine. I liked Motown. Always had. The window was frigid against my arm and the ledge had pressed a wedge of numbness into my flank. I should do something. Be industrious. Clean house, maybe.

Several boxes of clothes waited behind me to be sorted

and put away. I was in desperate need of undies; the elastic on several pairs had come totally off. For only the second time in my life I had tossed a handful of them into the trash. My stock was so low I might be driven to hand-wash some or buy more. There were underclothes in one of the boxes, I was almost sure. And I would rather dig those out than go shopping. I had lived in this house for nearly two years, and I still hadn't unpacked completely. The only things I had unearthed from the boxes behind me were several sweaters, some T-shirts, boots and a burgundy down-filled coat that was too warm for Southern winters. The coat was left over from my three-year residency stint in Chicago, a place where winter comes early and stays late.

The song changed to ''BetchaByGollyWow'' by the Stylistics. Okay, maybe there was a strain of self-pity in my thoughts to match the music, but then I was PMSing, so I had an excuse. I could indulge for a moment. It was my house, I could whine if I wanted to. I grinned at the thought. The only thing that would have completed my totally female mood would have been a pound of dark chocolate and a half gallon of Bryers Fudge Ripple ice cream drenched with Kahlua.

At the thought of real chocolate, I think I actually sighed, but the sound was covered by the music. All I'd had in the house was no-brand hot cocoa, the kind with hard little marshmallows floating in it. It wasn't exactly Godiva. I sipped at my cooling mug, unsatisfied.

I wasn't a particularly introspective person. I didn't spend hours rehashing conversations that had gone wrong, or the fact that I got into the slowest line at the checkout and then got a surly employee instead of a smiling one, or that I had a flat tire while driving in a gale at rush hour. I didn't even agonize over personal decisions that had turned out bad.

Medical failures, of course, were a different matter. I

spent untold hours and days trying to figure out why I had lost a patient or why a particular medical procedure had not been successful. I was a contract doctor in a small rural emergency room and failure on the job was not acceptable to me. But worry over personal stuff? No way.

Looking down the road, I spotted Miss Essie trotting along, until now the one constant in my life. She was part of the changes I was facing. Miss Essie had helped raise me, but suddenly she'd left behind her slippers and her kitchen, had practically stopped baking, and had taken up with the Internet and e-mailing herb-loving friends. She had bought expensive walking shoes, power walking five miles a day. Moving like the Energizer bunny dyed purple, she vanished through the bare bones of the leafless trees. It had been over a week since my last loaf of fresh baked bread.

Yeah, I was whining. Dang.

In the distance, just visible through the December-dead tree branches, a county cop car pulled into a neighbor's drive. Soon after, another joined it. The CD changed to the Chairman of the Board, a soft pain of lost love. I rocked myself on the window ledge and watched the activity up the street, feeling intrigued in spite of myself. I put the cold cocoa mug on the window ledge and leaned closer to the glass, my breath making two little spots of condensation. Stoney, the cat who had adopted me, jumped to the window ledge beside me and sniffed at the mug. Unimpressed, he walked up my leg and settled, curling tight against my waist.

Five minutes later, the county coroner pulled in behind the cops and someone started rolling out crime scene tape. Crime scene tape wasn't used for natural deaths.

Maybe I had just found another reason to avoid unpacking or shopping. It looked as if a neighbor had been killed. Straining like any rubbernecker at a roadside accident, I gawked up the street. And tightened all over.

I heard the strange pop-crack just under the beat of the bass from the speakers. Though I hadn't heard the sound in ages, I recognized it instantly. The sight of cops at a dead run from the house, sliding under the crime scene tape and behind their squad cars, was the clincher. Gunshots. I shoved the cat from my lap, jumped from the window ledge and ran for the kitchen. Grabbing my medical bag off the counter, I locked the doggie door at the rear of the house to keep the dogs inside, and ran back to the front.

I was just in time to hear someone bang on my door, five pounding hits, followed by the sound of multiple sirens approaching. Cops and ambulances, two of each, raced past my front windows and pulled across the street into the neighbor's yard. My dogs were barking wildly, racing from front entrance to back in alarm. More sirens in the distance. More gunshots. Five more thumps on the door.

I wrenched open the front door to see Miss Essie in her purple jogging suit, dark skin ashen with alarm, an arm raised to pound again. "Somebody hurt. You get yourself over to help, Missy Docta Rhea." Cops shouted in the near distance, and fainter, the sound of screams, I recognized the sound of pain. "But you take care," she said, shaking my arm, her eyes wide. "You hear me? You don't get yourself *shot!*"

I eased out between the noses of my two excited dogs and shut the door. I could hear them whining through the heavy wood. "I'm always careful, Miss Essie."

She snorted in disbelief. I grinned at her and shrugged. Our backs to the door, we waited several long minutes. No further shots sounded; no one was returning fire. Screaming, however, continued. One-handed, Miss Essie pushed me toward the neighbor's yard. Before I could change my mind, I kissed the air near her cheek and took off up the street.

I had felt chilled sitting against the window, but a sudden

hot sweat broke out on me as I ran, my Nikes slapping the pavement. Still no gunshots. I couldn't spot any cops; EMTs weren't huddled at the back of the units. No one was in sight. It must all have ended while I was getting my bag. Except for the screaming. A high keening, like an animal newly caught in a trap. Panic and pain. Increasing my pace, I turned to the left and jogged up the low hill.

A puff of dry dust erupted beside me. A pop-crack sounded almost simultaneously. To my left, I caught a blur of someone running, and had an instant to tense before impact. With a single, massive blow, I was airborne. We hit the ground hard. Breath exploded out of me. Electricity zinged through my back. We rolled into a slight depression, his body half-crushing, half-protecting me, over and over, into the ditch. I lost my bag. Felt a shoe come off partway.

"Are you out of your freaking mind?" he shouted into the back of my head. "You could have been killed."

When I didn't respond, he rolled me once more, glaring into my face. I struggled, pushing, shoving at him half-frenzied, and he eased back a bit, his eyes still furious. Air hissed into my lungs, painful but wonderful. My chest spasmed once, fiercely, starting at the weak place near my spine, radiating agony across my back, then down into my legs. Tears fell as my body reacted to the impact and the loss of breath. I gulped, sobbed once.

"Don't expect me to say I'm sorry," Mark Stafford said, his tone rancorous.

Who cared about his apology? I shoved at his chest, still fighting for air. He eased his weight off me, holding himself up with his arms. After a moment he added, "Knocked the breath out of you?"

I nodded frantically, concentrating on the second breath, which shuddered along my bronchial tubes, an exquisite pain. Then the third. Finally a deep intake of cool December air brought with it a sense of relief. I wasn't going to die, which I knew intellectually, but try convincing your body when it can't breathe.

My back spasm eased. I felt stinging down my side where a rock had bruised me as we rolled. A cramp in the thigh that had gone numb on the windowsill. A sharp pang between my shoulder blades where we'd landed and he hadn't cushioned my fall closely enough. My fingers tightened on his arms.

Mark wasn't even breathing hard. A flying tackle through gunfire and he wasn't even winded. It ticked me off.

"Did I hurt you?"

I nodded, my breathing deepening, taking on a slower pace. My heart thudded in my ears. He gentled his arms around me, cradling me.

"It's still better than being shot." He brushed the hair out of my face, his fingers harsh on my skin. Flicking. Angry green eyes met my tear-filled ones.

"Why?" I gasped, the sound squeaking out with the air.

"Kid is still shooting. We got a team going in, but it's not secure yet. Idiot."

I shook my head. "No." My voice was starting to steady. "Why?"

I felt him grow still over me. A collecting sort of stillness, like a runner tightening just before the sound of the shot starting a race. His eyes blazed into mine. I knew he wanted to roll over me and leave me in the dirt rather than answer. I could feel it in the tension of his body, see it in his eyes as the fury slid away, replaced with something else. The cop look. That flat, barren expression they must teach in Cop 101.

"You mean Skye." His tone was dead, almost as harsh as his fingers on my face. His green eyes had gone cold. "Why did I sleep with her? Or why am I denying the baby is mine?"

"Either. Both," I managed to answer. I wiped the tears

away on the back of one sweatshirt sleeve. I was crying because I had taken a fall, not because I hadn't seen him in four months, and I didn't want him thinking I was. I made my tone as cold as his. "Why didn't you come back that night?" My voice was almost my own again, as distant as the look in his eyes.

"Because when she picked me up from your house, she told me she was pregnant." Mark's voice was expressionless, empty, unyielding, like his body lying against mine.

Skye McNeely was petite, with green eyes and brown hair streaked with blonde. A crime scene tech who had a crush on Mark. And she was six months pregnant, claiming Mark was the father.

He had denied it. There was a paternity suit pending. It had made the rounds of the county gossip mill for months. I waited, staring into his face. He had grown a beard. I wondered if it was as soft as it looked. I kept my hands motionless on his arms, his jacket clenched tight.

"I slept with her one time. While you were in the hospital after you got stabbed. While I was so pissed off with you for…" He stopped, took a breath. I could feel it against my bruised ribs. "When I thought we were over. When I thought I couldn't even look at you again, because every time I did I remembered you made me kill Taylor Reeves."

The breath caught in my throat at the expression in his eyes. It was fierce, hurting, like that of a wounded animal. In an instant it was gone, his face blank. "The kid can't be mine. *Can't* be. It was way more than six months ago. I used protection."

"Like that's never failed before."

"It isn't mine. It. Can't. Be."

"So. You were pissed off with me and you went out and boinked the first thing that flashed you some skin?" I didn't use other less ladylike words. My mama would have been proud on her sober days. "That's real honorable."

Mark jerked as if I'd slapped him. Maybe I had. Honor was important to well-bred Southern boys. His eyes went flat green, like jade in a dim room. His skin flushed, muscles tightening as if to move away. I clenched my fists on his sleeves and pulled him even closer, our mouths almost touching. But it wasn't gentle. I could see his bared teeth behind the beard.

It wasn't the way I had intended this conversation to go, not the way I had envisioned it for the last four months, but a captive audience was better than any of the scenarios I had visualized. My ex-boyfriend couldn't get away. But I could see in his eyes that he wanted to. The cop look wasn't enough of a barrier to his emotions as he needed. Another gunshot sounded. I jerked hard. Mark didn't even flinch.

I growled, "And why didn't you come back? You owed me an explanation, Mark. And my key back. At least that."

"You're not getting your key back," he snapped, tightening his arms at my back. "I have to fix this, Rhea. I didn't want you dragged into it."

"I am dragged into it. The whole putrid, obscene mess. First you're dating an E.R. doc, then you're the father of a co-worker's child. According to the local wags, you were doing both of us at the same time." It sounded coarse and crude. I meant it to be.

The screaming became a heaving squeal from inside the house. *And this little piggy ran wee-wee-wee, all the way home.* Strange, the things that cross your mind when you're huddled in a ditch with a man you might love, and bullets are flying overhead. Another gunshot sounded.

Mark ignored it. This time so did I. A tic began beside his mouth. "I know. I'm sorry."

The words surprised me. Mark was sorry? We had covered a lot of ground in these few seconds. The last night he had left my house—the night a fire raged in Dawkins

County, destroying two homes and damaging four others, scorching acres of pastureland and taking twenty acres of dry timber—I had given him a key to come back. To come back to my bed. It was to be a first for us. A first time. A beginning of something stronger, something better.

But he hadn't come back. Hadn't called. Hadn't returned my calls to him. And then the rumor broke. He had gotten a co-worker pregnant. Mark Stafford, straight arrow, a Beau in a world of Bubbas, had done the unthinkable and then denied paternity.

He said he wasn't giving my key back. What the heck did that mean? Wordless, I searched his eyes. His hold had gentled on my face, fingers tender, as if he had been denying himself a touch he craved and wanted to feel just that little contact with me. I was suddenly aware of our legs intertwined, his hips pressed against mine. I flattened my palms against his chest, pushing him away. It wasn't entirely effective. Something about men having better upper body strength. His mouth dropped and touched my lips. I jerked my head to the side, so angry that I wanted to hurt him. His radio crackled.

"Cap'n, we're ready to go in."

Mark slid to one side, his legs still draped across mine, his eyes on my hostile ones as he found his radio. He looked amused, mocking and resigned all at once. "I'll send someone back for you. This time, stay down till you're needed." Into the mike he said, "Go."

And he was gone, leaving me lying in the ditch, my body aching from the impact of the fall. Bruised from rolling into the shallow depression.

2

YOU SHOULD HAVE LET ME PLAY DOCTOR

I dropped my head back, not moving. The air was dry and cool, not really cold, but it felt colder after the warmth from his body. There was a sharp *bang* from the house. More shots sounded, different this time. Deeper, maybe a shotgun. Shouts, excited cursing. Cops at a scene. The screaming went on, now little breathy sounds with a rough edge, as if the screamer's throat was raw. I hadn't thought about the screamer while Mark's body was pinned on mine. The sound had been continuous.

I raised up and rolled until I was on my stomach, eased through the dirt of the ditch until I found my medical bag. It was on its side but still closed, the clasp somehow having withstood the impact of being tackled. Swiveling again, I pulled the Nike back on and retied it. I was covered with dust and dirt, my navy sweatshirt filthy.

Worse, my back wasn't happy. I had been stabbed not so very long ago; rehab had done what it could, but I was weak at the wound site. Stupidly, I had reinjured myself lifting one of my dogs when she was wounded. I'd saved her life, so it was worth it, but the pain now was not good. A third injury to the same spot could mean scar tissue. Degeneration. I breathed slowly to ease the discomfort.

The shots stopped. Voices changed pitch, more angry, less on edge, less the near-panic of moments before. I knew it was over, but I stayed in my ditch, waiting until Mark's "all clear."

After four agonizing minutes, I heard running footsteps and lifted my head. It was Jacobson, a county cop I knew from the E.R. Stout, mid-thirties, Jacobson had reached the zenith of his career, still in uniform, still driving country roads. He loved what he did, though—you could tell by the excitement on his face. Adrenaline high. "Cap'n says EMS needs you." He dropped down, offering his hand as I slowly rose. I was pretty self-sufficient but wasn't above accepting help, not when I was bruised and achy. I took the hand and let him pull me to my feet and haul me out of the ditch. My back zinged with electricity again. I ignored the sensation.

"What do we got?" I asked.

He answered as we half jogged. "Neighbors heard a gunshot. One cool one on the scene when the first man got here. The guys didn't do a thorough enough job securing the scene. Shooter was in the closet in his bedroom. Came out firing. Coroner is down. GSW to the upper right quadrant. EMS says sucking chest wound. Small caliber round, most likely a .38. They're working on her."

A cool one was a dead body, GSW was a gunshot wound, and upper right quadrant described the location of the wound, high on the right side of the chest. A sucking chest wound meant the bullet had left a hole to the outside world when it entered or exited, and air was sucking in with every breath the patient took. It was a dramatic wound, but easy to treat on the scene and seldom life-threatening, if treatment was fast enough and internal bleeding not too extensive.

I nodded as we neared the house. "Entrance and exit wounds?"

"Both. The exit is the nasty one, of course. But they can't get Betty to shut up. Full-blown panic attack. She won't let anyone near her."

"Betty's the one who was shot?" I brushed the grit and dust off my grubby jeans and sweatshirt as we moved.

"No. Betty's the new coroner's assistant. A real rookie. I think this is the first time she's seen blood." He sounded amused, with the kind of "little woman's having an attack of the vapors" tone used by big he-men at police scenes. "It's sure the first time she ever got shot at."

"And they want me there to do what? Use my womanly ways to calm her down?" I could hear the edge of sarcasm in my voice. If Mark had called me up out of my nice comfy ditch for that, I'd remove his privates in an orchiectomy. Without anesthesia.

"Or give her a sedative. Whatever it takes." Jacobson glanced at me from the corner of his eye. He was baiting me. I ignored the look.

"I'll give the sedative."

We entered through the back, climbing up three steps to a small stoop. The rear of the house was secluded, all windows covered with shades and drawn draperies. But the back door was propped open and cops were opening windows in the kitchen and the dining room as we passed through, shoving back the drapes, letting in light and air. A strange scent hung in the house, vaguely electrical, slightly burned. Underneath it all was the scent of fresh feces. Either someone's bowels had released from fright, or the corpse's had in death.

The front of the house was still dark and no one opened windows there to let in air and light. No one moved anything. It was a crime scene. I stopped and knelt by my bag, pulling out a paper coat and latex gloves, paper shoes to cover my own. PPEs—personal protective equipment. It was to protect me from any blood or other bodily fluids and to keep me from contaminating the scene. I had never been at a crime scene, but I knew enough about what not to do.

Mark came out of a bedroom and nodded. "Body's in here. Betty's in there with the coroner." He nodded left and right with the directions, cop eyes firmly in place. Ignoring him, I turned toward the patients. The screaming went down a notch, now sounding muffled, more like the little piggy who had none.

Betty was curled under a table just inside the living room, her arms around her legs, her face buried in the curl of her body. "Anybody give her a paper bag to breathe in? Start a line?" I asked the room.

"Can't get her to hold still for it," a female voice said from the darkness. "Her limbs are clamped tight and we can't get her to relax."

"Well, pick her up and take her outside."

"How?" Jacobson asked over Betty's howls.

"Just pick her up by the elbows and knees and carry her." How hard could it be? But I didn't add the last part. He-men didn't like to hear a tone suggesting they weren't all-knowing and all-seeing.

Jacobson and another cop lifted the table off Betty and picked her up as I suggested. The screaming decreased as she was toted through the house. "Put her in the sun, give her a blanket to ward off shock and keep someone with her," I called after them. "If she passes out, let me know." Betty would be a lot easier to handle if she passed out from hyperventilating, but doctors aren't supposed to wish for that sort of thing—not out loud, anyway.

My eyes had adjusted to the near dark and I found a cluster of bodies on the far side of the room near the Christmas tree, lit by a single strand of lights. I picked my way over, taking in details as I moved. The new coroner had taken office in late August when the person elected to the job had resigned because of his wife's health problems. Appointed to fill out the term, Anita Yarborough had then run for office and won.

Normally a take-charge sort of woman, now she was lying on an ambulance gurney, its legs knocked down so the gurney was close to the floor. Her shirt was off, her right bra strap cut away, and a bandage the size of a waffle was stuck on her upper chest, sharing skin with EKG leads attached to a heart monitor. Smeared blood was drying in whorls on her chest and stiffening in the waistband of her khakis. She had an IV in the left arm at the AC—the elbow—along with a blood pressure cuff, while the right arm was in a sling, secured snugly at her waist. The EMTs were razzing her, and Anita was razzing back as they raised the gurney to full height and locked the X-shaped legs in place. The carpet beside the gurney was soaked through with blood.

"You never struck me as the satin bra type, Anita, honey," Carla said, adjusting the IV pole attached to the gurney. She grunted as she bent past her paunch.

"Not purple satin, anyway," Hybernia Boyle said. Hybernia was new to the area, a paramedic with several years of experience. She was petite compared to Carla's moderate bulk, an African-American body builder with well-defined biceps that stood out even in the dim light. Anita's bra looked black with all the blood. I would never have known it was purple.

"Especially not with pearls." Carla pulled the stretcher-back up to a sitting position.

"Yeah, I guess I can see the satin, but the pearls…and them little push-up pads?"

"You and Rupert had big plans for tonight? A little play-by-play?"

Anita grunted. "Yeah, and you two put a big damper on

my love life. Rupert will not be happy you cut off my bra. It's his favorite.''

"Rupert and you can play doctor tonight in the real setting.''

"Fun and games? Strange sexual practices on public property?'' I asked.

"Hiya, Doc,'' Carla said, her eyes a turquoise green in the dim light. "You want to take a look? We got slightly decreased breath sounds on the right.''

"Sure. Hi, Anita. What happened, how you feeling?'' I bent over her with my stethoscope and pressed the bell to her upper left quadrant, the side opposite the wound. Her heart rate was rapid, over 90, but the heart itself sounded clean—no rubbing, no clicks, no skipped beats. The heart monitor was showing a normal sinus rhythm.

"Just freaking peachy, Doc,'' she said, her voice breathy and pain-filled. "Kid shot me by accident. He was aiming at a cop. You gonna fix me up so I can keep my date tonight?''

"I think you might be having that date in your hospital room,'' I said, "but no playing doctor. You need a medical license for that. Breathe.'' The EMTs chuckled automatically. It wasn't much of a joke, but things seemed funnier in tense situations. The breath sounds on the left were normal. "Again,'' I said, moving the bell high and low as she inhaled and exhaled. "Again.'' All normal, except for a single soft sighing sound I couldn't identify.

When I moved the bell to the right side, however, there was a difference. The breath sounds had a resonance to them, almost an echo. I heard the left lung moving but not the right one, the sound echoing through the air and blood that had replaced the lung. The lung had collapsed. I remembered that soft sighing sound. As I listened, the heart rate sped up. Breathing sped up. The human body wasn't designed for air to enter between the ribs. Sometimes when a lung collapsed, it was sudden, like now. I had actually heard the lung caving in.

"Doc," Anita said, her eyes getting larger, then squinting with pain. "Doc, something's happening."

The standard treatment for a sucking chest wound was a Vaseline-gauze dressing and a special cellophane covering that sealed around the wound. On battlefields, soldiers had been known to stuff a clean pair of socks into a sucking chest wound to stop the air flow. If the lung collapsed, however, a chest tube and suction were necessary, not something I wanted to do in the field. Ambulance units didn't stock chest tube kits. Instead, there was an emergency treatment I could use.

"Blood pressure? O2?" I asked.

"BP is 140 over 102. Oxygen at four liters, pulse-ox shows 95 O2 Sat, and a rate of 97. Ringers running in a 14 Jelco IV, high-flow," Carla said.

"Pulse-ox is dropping. Ninety," Hybernia said. Her voice held a note of warning.

"I think we have a right lung down," I said calmly. The heart monitor showed signs of distress, the rate up to 103. "You got another 14 Jelco?"

Carla turned and placed the EMS tool kit on a nearby table. She opened the big beige-and-orange plastic carryall, while Hybernia got out alcohol swabs, gauze, tape.

"Start another line. We have any crepitus?"

Hybernia pressed around the patient's shoulders with the flat of her hands. "Not earlier, but we do now," she said. Crepitus was noise in the tissue, in this case caused by the presence of air up under the skin. When pressed, Anita's flesh crackled, like bubble wrapping. I placed my hands beside Hybernia's dark ones and pressed as the paramedic stepped back. The sensation was like squishing Rice Krispies between heavy layers of cloth.

"Anita, your right lung has collapsed. Air and blood

pushed it shut by filling the space between the lung and the chest wall,'' I said, keeping my statements and vocabulary basic. ''I need to make a way for the air to escape so the lung can reinflate. I need to cut away the rest of your nice bra, and put a needle in you. And it's gonna hurt.''

''Do it,'' she said. Her voice was raspy with pain and lack of air. ''Get them out of here, though. I'm not a public display.''

I glanced behind me. Three cops in suits stood there watching, two with narrowed eyes and crossed arms, one taking notes. I hadn't seen them until my eyes adjusted. I knew they were not about to leave the victim. She had become part of the crime scene. Something odd, though— they looked like Feebs. What would FBI be doing at a local homicide? ''How about a drape?''

Carla draped Anita's breast area with a blue sterile drape as Hybernia repositioned the sling and cut off the bra. So much for her husband's favorite purple push-up.

I had no sterile gloves, only the regular latex ones I was wearing. ''Betadine?'' I asked.

Hybernia held up a handful of Betadine swab packages, each package holding two swabs and sterile cleanser. When I nodded, she ripped open two packages and held them toward me. Across the gurney, Carla tied a rubber tourniquet around Anita's arm beneath the elbow and cleaned the entire area with alcohol wipes as she looked for a likely vein for a second IV.

I took two Betadine swabs from the first packet and swabbed the side of her chest, between the fourth and fifth ribs in a circular motion, starting at the point where I would insert the large needle, and working my way out. Tossing away the two swabs, I took two more from the second packet and repeated the process. It was as sterile as I was going to get.

''One more,'' I said to Hybernia. She tore another packet

and I took the swabs, cleaning the fingers of my gloves before taking up the huge needle and wrapping one end in sterile gauze so I could get a firm grip on it.

"Anita, slow your breathing down," I said. "You're going to be fine." My gaze narrowed to the place I wanted on the patient's chest. My left fingers pressed firmly, flattening between the ribs, shoving fat and tissue taut. I could feel air there, just beneath the skin. It crackled.

With my right hand, I positioned the needle over her chest, its point between the first and middle fingers of my left hand. "That's it. You're doing fine. Now, take a breath and hold it." As the motion of her chest stopped, I shoved the 14 Jelco in. Anita hissed air through her teeth as the large needle pierced her flesh. She grunted with pain. Air blew out through the end of the needle. I could feel it even through my gloves. "Got it."

Anita gasped again as Carla inserted a second—make that third—IV needle down low in her hand and popped the tourniquet off. "Talk about strange sexual activities, bet you guys are great dominants." Anita's voice was less breathy, but held an edge of shock. "You wear leather and studs off hours?"

"I prefer red stilettos and garters to whips and chains," Carla said, taping the IV in place. I mirrored her actions as I secured the Jelco on the chest wall with gauze and tape. Air continued to blow out, relieving the stress on Anita's heart and left lung. I could hear a blood pressure cuff inflating.

"Me? I like whipped cream and baby oil. Course, if I changed over to dog collars and leather, I could make better money than I do working in the medical profession," Hybernia said as she repacked the EMS carryall.

"Money? My favorite subject," Carla exclaimed. "Maybe we could work together. You do the whips and I'll do the sharp, shiny objects."

Anita laughed, as she was meant to. I watched Carla hang the IV bag and open the fluid valve wide.

"We could call ourselves the Maniacal Medics, specializing in needles and rubber." Carla popped the tourniquet in the air as if to demonstrate.

"Though I hate to interrupt this fascinating banter," I said, "pulse and O2?"

"Sat is back up to 92 and pulse is steady at 108. Blood pressure is still up, 150 over 110. Likely due to stress."

Because I agreed that the patient was stressed enough to cause a rise in blood pressure, and because a rise was actually better than a drop, which might signify shock and blood loss, and because the EMS guys—gals—had done everything right to stabilize the patient, I nodded and stepped back. "Take her on. Hope you feel better, Anita."

"Hang on, y'all," Anita said. "Doc, I need a favor."

"I'd rather not give you pain meds until you reach the hospital."

"I'm not asking for pain medicine." She grimaced as she adjusted herself slightly on the gurney. "I need a new assistant coroner. I hereby deputize you."

"No way," I said quickly.

"Too late," Carla said with an evil grin.

"Betty's lost it. She can't do it today. At least not alone," Anita said. "And Bobby Ray Shirley hasn't been released by his doctor to return to full-time duty." Her voice was growing raspy and I could see the pain in her eyes. Tendons in her neck were standing out and the heart monitor was showing an increase in the heart rate. Anita was stressing out and I wasn't helping.

Bobby Ray Shirley had suffered a heart attack at the end of summer. I remembered that a replacement had been brought in at that time. I didn't want to mention the other assistant's name, but I had to ask. "What about your other assistant? The one you got when Bobby Ray went in for his cath?''

"Skye McNeely is six months into a difficult pregnancy, and is only available off and on. You can do it. Just get the cops to help you. And Betty, if she calms down enough. Paperwork is on the dining room table.'' She pointed a finger toward the dining room.

"I do not want to be an assistant coroner.''

"Tough," Anita said. "You should have let me play doctor.''

"And you should pick your friends better,'' Carla said.

"I beg your pardon?''

"It wasn't Anita's idea to make you assistant coroner. It was that cop. Captain Mark Stafford.''

An orchiectomy would not be enough. I'd kill him. I really would.

3

HIS AND HER READING MATERIAL

I had never been on a crime scene and I was terrified I would mess up, overlook something, forget something. The only good aspect of the job was that no matter how I might botch it, no one would die. Gallows humor. I kept it to myself.

Betty was outside in the yard, receiving medical attention from the other pair of EMTs. Her screaming stopped suddenly, as if someone had finally broken down and slapped her. That was technically assault, though, and not something a medical professional would do if there were witnesses. Of course, in a small county like Dawkins, there was a good chance at least one member of the emergency team was related to Betty and simply took matters into his own hands. That old "I'm my own second cousin" line wasn't always a joke here. It was reality.

I was standing in the doorway to the master bedroom. The space was too small to call a master suite, though it did have its own bath off to the side. The queen-size four-poster bed was on the far wall, between two windows, the spread, sheets and a blanket, wadded at the foot of the bed. The body on the blue floral mattress was male, nude, seriously overweight, about mid-fifties. He had lower teeth missing; it looked like the incisors and at least one molar. He was also missing a left eye, part of his sphenoid bone, and had a hole on the right side of his head, well behind the temporal bone. If it was suicide, he had held the gun far back on his head and fired forward. He hadn't died right away. In fact, from the look of the sheets, he had taken his time dying. Had gone out kicking and screaming. Well, kicking, at least.

The room smelled strongly of feces and marijuana, old beer and cigarette smoke, unwashed male and dirty sheets. On the bedside table was a Ziploc bag holding what looked like marijuana, an ashtray overflowing with butts, and drug paraphernalia: paper clips twisted into roach clips, a bottle that looked like a bong, partially filled with water, though it had been hand-painted with daisies and a black-and-white cow. The mirror over the dresser was also painted in that style, with the addition of bunnies. Very arts-and-crafts looking. Martha Stewart wannabe. The furniture was dusty and piles of clothes covered every surface, including the floor. No way to tell if they were clean, but I wouldn't have bet on it. A stack of *National Enquirers* lay on the floor at one side of the bed. A carton of cigarettes and a stack of girlie magazines were on the other side. His and Her reading material. Cute.

I walked around the bed to the right side and looked closely at the wound. I had taken the requisite pathology courses in medical school. I knew the wound had a contact mark, but it wasn't perfectly round. The gun had been held at an angle as it was fired. An angle from behind. Not a suicide. And the fact that the gun had been held from the back, close to the skull, indicated that this wasn't an accident. You didn't accidentally hold a loaded weapon to a man's head and fire. Well, not if you were sober. I'd seen dumber things, but this didn't look like one of them.

I heard movement in the doorway behind me. "Who shot him?" I asked, not taking my eyes from the body.

"Foster kid living with them," Mark said. "Kid claims the guy was abusing him and his sister. The sister disappeared. Claims he was trying to get the old guy to tell where he had hidden her. Claims the gun went off accidentally."

"Okay. Maybe you do," I said softly, walking closer to the bed.

"Do what?"

"Accidentally hold a loaded gun to a man's head and shoot him. You believe him?"

"He lawyered up before I got to him."

"And?"

"Weirder things have happened. But yeah, I do."

"Why?"

"Before he shut up, he kept saying, 'Now, I'll never find her,' over and over, like he was really afraid he'd lost his sister. Felt guilty for letting her down."

"He'll need medical treatment if he's been abused."

"It's Social Services' problem. Not yours."

I jerked my eyes to Mark. He was standing in the doorway, arms crossed, that cold, heartless cop look on his face. I felt anger rise, hot and fierce. "I'm a doctor. I work on the living. Just what exactly is my job?"

"I understand you're the new assistant coroner. Pronounce him, so I can take pictures and get the investigation under way." The tic beside Mark's mouth was back, but nothing at all showed in his eyes.

"He's dead," I said distinctly. And if my tone added *you imbecile,* well, that was okay by me.

"And?" Mark's eyes flared with cool green flames.

"And unless he's got an extra arm between his shoulder blades, I don't think he did it to himself." Sarcasm. A girl's best friend.

"Thank you, Dr. Lynch, for your cooperation and help-fulness. Guys, get in here."

I shoved past Mark and went out into the light.

At the back door, I ripped off the PPEs and dropped them into a trash bag the cops had placed there. My protective clothes were now officially part of the investigation. Yip-pee. I grabbed a stack of likely looking papers from the dining room table and went out into the sunlight.

Someone had brought an EMS unit into the backyard, the doors of the ambulance thrown wide, the gurney on the grass nearby. Cops and EMS guys wandered around. Betty was sitting on the ground, dripping wet, her arms still around her curled legs. It looked as if someone had thrown a bucket of water over her. The treatment must have worked. She was silent.

I knelt near her. "Betty? I need you to get up off your butt, come back inside the house and show me how to do the necessary paperwork to document this scene." I didn't mean to sound so demanding, not really. But I wasn't hav-ing a good day.

The woman slowly lifted her head. Betty was maybe my age, short, a few pounds overweight and out of shape. Her eye makeup had rained black streaks down her pale face; her lips were slightly blue. Shivers ran down her body and goose bumps were tight on her arms. "Go away," she whispered.

"No."

Betty's eyes widened.

"Guys!" I called. Gus, an EMT I knew well, jogged over. "She refuse medical treatment?"

"Yep." Gus knelt near me, folding his lanky frame. "In no uncertain terms."

"Well, get her a blanket, start an IV and get some O2

on her. She's getting shocky. And if she still refuses treatment, strap her down and take her to the hospital.''

"You can't treat me if I say no," Betty said, her voice growing stronger.

"In my opinion, you are not in your right mind. You are therefore no longer capable of denying treatment. You may have had a psychotic break from the emotional trauma of the shooting. I'm going to see you get the help you need.'' I was lying through my teeth, but maybe she didn't know it.

Gus grinned and called to his partner.

"You can't do this," she said.

Actually, I could, but it might mean a lawsuit, an expense I didn't want. "Try me." I was bluffing, but I was good at the doctor look.

Betty folded, her face crumpling. "If I finish the paperwork, will you just let me go home?" Tears fell, winding through the caked mascara. "I just want to go home."

"You finish the paperwork and show me what to do, you can leave. You prove to me that you are not in your right mind, I'll strap you down, stick needles in you and haul you off.''

"I'm not going back in there, though. And you can't make me.''

I figured I had the best deal I was going to get. I stood, took a blanket from Gus's partner and draped it over Betty's shoulders. "You fill it out, you show me how to do it right, and you can go home.''

"Okay. I'll do it." Her voice sounded faint, tiny, wounded. I should have felt like the big bad wolf, but I didn't. I had a thing about whiny women. Hated 'em.

"Doc, can you talk to the woman over there?" The sheriff's deputy looked down at me, where I was sitting in the dirt, his expression uncertain. "It's the man's wife. Without a coroner, and with Betty so upset, we got nobody to talk to her. She knows the man inside is dead, but…''

My eyes followed the cop's jutting jaw.

The next of kin was an underweight, gray-haired woman, holding herself across the middle. She was crying, dressed in a long plaid smock and loafers, white socks and a heavy sweater. Despair was apparent in her posture, in the misery on her face. It was easy to see that she had been informed of the death inside. I didn't want to become part of this coroner situation any more than I had to. I glanced at Betty.

''Don't look at me. No way,'' she said. Her face was still streaked with blackened tears, like a tarry candle melting, and she was still wet, so I had to agree she wouldn't be the appropriate person to deal with the grieving. She looked like a mourner herself. ''Here.'' She shoved a sheaf of papers at me.

In the pile were forms entitled Authorization for Coroner's Autopsy, Permit for Removal of Deceased, Investigative Report, and Death Certificate. Papers that allowed the cops to do their jobs under the law, as well as papers the family had to sign. No choice. I sighed and stood, brushed the dirt off my jeans once more. I'd get Mark Stafford for this. Somehow, I'd get him. ''What's the name?'' I asked the cop.

''Nila Pendergrass. Mrs. John Earle Pendergrass. The wife.''

I wondered if Nila knew her husband had been accused of abusing the children. Tramping across the winter-dead grass to the woman, I identified myself and offered my condolences. Asked after the family's choice of a funeral home. Did a version of the line I used in the hospital when I had to tell a family there had been a death. A passing. Mrs. Pendergrass was more receptive than many I dealt with, but then, perhaps she had been standing on the lawn watching the proceedings for long enough to become a believer. Family disbelief was the hardest emotion for a doctor to combat—disbelief that death had made a stop at their door and taken off with a loved one.

Mrs. Pendergrass rocked and moaned as I spoke, but seemed to accept that the death was real. I patted her shoulder, wrote down the name of the funeral home, one of three in town, all owned by the same family. Everything was going smoothly—or as smoothly as death ever can be—when Nila looked up at me. It was the first time I had really focused on her face, which was rounder than her thin frame suggested, shiny with tears and free of makeup. She looked angry, or perhaps scared, more so than grief-stricken.

"The officers say that miserable lying boy is the one who shot my John Earle. Say's he claims my John Earle was molesting his sister and him both. Ain't true. My John Earle never touched a hair on them kids' heads except in love."

"Uh…" My doctor repartee had just reached its limits. What was I supposed to say? Fortunately Nila Pendergrass didn't need anything in the way of encouragement. The expression on her face was bitter fury. Her eyes sparkled with it, her lips tightening in a harsh frown that added years to her age.

"He come to us with the girl, who done run off and shacked up with a boy. Probably end up pregnant or with AIDS or something other. He come to us with her and he ain't been nothing but trouble. In and out of detention at school. Playing hooky. Toking up, stoned half the time, and likely as not doing drugs harder than that, too. Real trouble. Both of them. He'd lie to protect hisself. He'd lie just for the hell of it. Bringing dope into the house." The tip of her tongue flashed lizardlike, licked her lip fast, her gaze sliding away.

It sounded as if she was trying to lay a case for the bag of marijuana beside the master bed belonging to the kids. Mr. Pendergrass was going to be protected at the kids' expense. As assistant coroner, did I have the right to say so? Probably not. I settled on, "Well, ah, thank you, Mrs. Pendergrass. I'm all done. If you have any questions you just call the coroner's office and leave a message. We'll get back to you." And I scuttled back to the dirt patch where Betty still crouched. She was grinning, enjoying the conversation.

"You gotta love it, Doc," she said.

No, I didn't. I didn't even have to like it. I glanced back over my shoulder at Mrs. Nila Pendergrass, who was being led away by a neighbor, her shoulders shaking, the neighbor's arm around her scrawny waist.

The state of South Carolina is set up under the coroner system, whereby the coroner is elected by the populace, then takes special classes for a minimum of sixteen hours. At least three of the most populous counties have graduated to the medical examiner system, where a forensic pathologist handles all the jobs of the coroner, as well as doing posts-mortem and screenings to determine cause of death. With its population of fifty thousand, and its mean household income in the low twenties, Dawkins was still under the coroner system. Lucky me.

The paperwork was pretty straightforward. Names, date, next of kin. A separate form for having the body shipped to the forensic pathology lab in Newberry. And I didn't have to hang around Mark. He stayed inside with the body; I stayed outside with Betty and the cops, who were waiting for a juvie officer to show up. The sun was shining, the temperature was rising into the fifties. All in all, it was a beautiful December afternoon in Dawkins County, South Carolina.

In a small county, there was no special jail for an underage killer. There would have to be other arrangements made. For now, the boy sat in a sheriff's unit, all the doors open, his hands shackled behind his back, his head hung

forward, hiding his face. A stout woman in a business suit
sat sideways in the driver's seat, her sensible gray pumps
firmly on the ground, hands clasped between her knees. A
detective, slender, sandy haired, stood at the back of the
car, smoking, one foot on the bumper. He looked cold in
the thin rumpled suit coat. I didn't recognize him. A new
man on the job?

The chilly December air carried sound well, and now that
Betty was calmed down enough to sound human and not
piggish, I could hear the boy's high-pitched voice as he
talked to the female cop. I knew that he had asked for a
lawyer, so I figured this was just comfort, not interrogation.

"She called," the boy said. "That's how I know she
ain't dead." He ducked his blond head, the breeze catching
his too-long hair and sliding it across his scalp in wisps.

"Called you?" The woman's voice was soothing, ma-
ternal. I was sure she was a cop, though I didn't recognize
her.

"Yeah. It was last Wednesday, just after I got home from
school. Phone rang and I got it. She said, 'Wayne Edward'—that's my name, Wayne Edward—she said, 'Wayne
Edward, I ain't coming back. I'm staying with Deacon. I
don't love Vance. I love Deacon.'"

"Well, maybe she did run off with Deacon. You said
she was getting presents in the mail. Perfume, candy.
Maybe she had an anonymous admirer." The cop's voice
was reasonable, calm, faintly curious—just enough to keep
him talking, though not enough to make the boy realize he
was talking to a cop. So maybe it was an interrogation. I
left the paperwork in Betty's shaking hands, stood from my
crouch beside her, and made eye contact with the detective
standing behind the cop car. He had dropped his foot from
the bumper and I could see him clearly. He looked like a
Feeb. It was the suit. Wrinkled, but way better than what
a local investigator could afford. He shifted uncomfortably

and straightened his shoulders, glancing at the woman. Was she a Feeb, too? Why were FBI agents interested in a local boy who had shot his foster father? What was going on here?

"But that's jist the point. Whoever sent her that stuff was anomenous, not nobody named Vance. You ask me, I think it was Mr. Pendergrass, but it didn't work, 'cuz Beata is in love with Tory Stevenson. And she don't even got classmates named Deacon and Vance. I know 'cuz I called her best friend, Kendra, and asked." The boy sniffed, shivered in the chill air and hung his head even lower. From the distance, I could see spots of bright color on the shoulder of his T-shirt. Blood?

"Mr. Pendergrass made her call and say that stuff, 'cuz he was making her do sex with him. I heard 'em. And she tole me." Wayne Edward, his hands bound behind his back, sniffed hard against the tears and mucus, rubbing his face against one bony shoulder, smearing the mess beneath his nose. "And the boy she wants to do sex with is Tory, but he won't look at her twice, so Mr. Pendergrass took her and hid her away. And now I'll never find her. Not never."

I stared at the Feeb, raised my brows, crossed my arms, saying in body language that this might not be quite kosher and he had a witness. The man frowned, blew out smoke-filled breath, flicked the butt down and crunched it beneath his heel. Shaking his head, he called the woman away. The boy didn't seem to notice, but he fell silent. I could hear birds chirping in the winter air.

It hadn't been an interrogation, not exactly, but the kid hadn't had a lawyer handy. Anything you say can and will be used against you in a court of law. Wasn't that part of the Miranda rights? Did it hold true even after someone asked for a lawyer? And what if the cops listened and then didn't use the information to convict the boy? I couldn't answer that question, but the Feeb's annoyed face as he turned away let me know he, too, thought a line had been crossed.

Appearance of wrongdoing could be just as dangerous to a cop's career as the actual wrongdoing itself. Mark's words came back to me from the one time he'd visited me in the hospital after I was stabbed. He had been put on administrative leave until a special board cleared him of possible charges in the death of the man who was trying to abduct me at the time. Dumb rules, I had thought then. Now I wasn't so sure.

When the cops were out of earshot, I returned to Betty and her unsteady penmanship. I'd started to kneel in the dirt next to her when I spotted something unexpected.

The coroner in Dawkins County had no official transport vehicle. Bodies were carted by ambulance from crime scenes to the morgue at the small rural hospital where I worked, and then on to Newberry for postsmortem, if needed. Body bags may not have been commonplace in some ambulances, but county equipment and personnel often did double duty here. Coroner assistants used their own personal vehicles for transportation to crime scenes, arriving when they could.

Hence, the person I saw waddling up the drive from the road was not entirely unexpected. Skye McNeely, holding her belly with one hand and applying pressure to the small of her back with the other, trudged uphill in a maternity jumper and sneakers she couldn't have tied herself. Skye had put on at least fifty pounds with her pregnancy, all in her boobs and her butt, and of course the huge beach-ball shape out front. It was a contemptible reaction, one I would never admit to out loud, but I was happy to see her looking less than perky and svelte. I was also happy to spot her first, so I could get away.

Coward? Me? Coward, catty, contemptible… Yep, a

pretty fair evaluation of me today. Oh, yeah, let's not forget the whining. "Enough of the paperwork done to ship the body?"

"It's all there. Can I go home now? I'm cold and wet and," Betty raised her voice so the EMS crew gathered a few feet away could hear clearly, "I need to call my Gramma and tell her about the unexpected shower I got in the cold air, that might could give me the pneumonia. And how my own cousin did the drenching."

One of the crew turned away laughing. The sun was in my eyes and so I couldn't have said later who it was. Probably a good thing, considering the interrelated family structures in the county. Hear no evil, see no evil.

"You go on home and take a hot bath, Betty," I said. "I'm sure you'll be okay."

"Easy for you to say." The pudgy woman braced herself on a hand and pushed to her feet.

I made it safely down the driveway and back to my house before Skye could spot me. I wasn't certain of her possible reaction to seeing me, but somehow the thought of me on her turf at the same time and place as Mark didn't conjure visions of smiling affability. I was a confirmed coward. I was outta there.

4

IN THIS RINKY-DINK HOSPITAL?

Night had fallen when I pulled out of the drive in my little BMW Z3. I left the dogs running loose in the yard, yipping as I drove away. They could get back in through the doggie door, there was plenty of water inside and in the creek out back, they had been well fed and I had a twelve-hour shift to pull at Dawkins County Hospital.

A deer crossed the road in front of my car, legs prancing in the headlight beams. Dawkins was a mostly rural place, acres of fallow, furrowed farmland, dairy farms, lots of cattle farms and pig farms, dozens of small horse farms, several poultry farms, and even a few of the exotic—one llama farm, one ostrich farm, a few goatherds and a vineyard. And Dawkins was home to more deer per capita than any county in the Southeast. Deer-versus-car was fast becoming the most reported accident on both city and back roads, as the hungry deer searched for new grazing land. Even the extra hunting allotted for bow and doe days had not made an appreciable impact on the deer population. Except for man, there were no predators left to keep the herds down, and the numbers were exploding.

Dorsey City—DorCity to the locals—glowed on the horizon, city lights bright against cloud cover that was moving in. The moon, already curtained behind a thin cloud layer, was nearly full as I pulled off Starlight Lane and headed in to work on a cold December Thursday night.

My job had changed in the last few months, the hours I worked dropping back to the 168 a month I was originally contracted for. I had been working far more than the seven days on, seven days off, twelve hours per shift for which I had been hired. Dawkins County had pulled in a couple new doctors for the odd shifts, and I now found myself with more time on my hands. Not necessarily a good thing for a woman who was having fits of PMS and unusual chocolate cravings.

I could fix that easily enough by agreeing to work a few twelve-hour shifts a month at the new hospital under construction on the state line. It would be fast-paced work, being in charge of the majors unit of a huge emergency department in a large teaching facility. I would get to use skills that had been atrophying in the boonies. I admit I missed the speed, the sheer wonder of a well-trained trauma team in the heat of an emergency. I missed the first-rate, cutting-edge equipment available to MDs in a big trauma center, the numbers of medical professionals a doctor could draw upon. But my first love was the little six-room, eight-bed, one doctor, two RN per shift emergency room in Dawkins. It had quickly become home and I wasn't really looking for new employment. Not just yet.

I parked in the doctors' parking lot, grabbed my starched lab coat from the passenger seat and my heavy carryall, and jogged into the E.R. through the ambulance air lock. It looked as if nothing was happening; I loved shifts that started out like this. Though I had slept for five hours in the afternoon, I had been hoping for a quiet, peaceful night.

Waving to the group of nurses gathered at the desk, I moved quickly up the hall to the call room. It was freshly made up with clean sheets, extra towels, a blanket or three.

I tossed my stuff on the bed and glanced in the mirror over the sink. Black eyes stared back at me. Scruffy, short black hair curled around an oval, olive-skinned face, and my mouth was a little too wide. No perky, blond beauty here. I pushed away from the sink and padlocked the door after me.

Moving up the hall to the door leading to the extralarge bathroom that was part of the miniscule suite, I padlocked it, too. There had been a few occasions in the last year when unauthorized people had gotten in. Now I carried a key and two locks with me when I worked nights, for protection. Slipping into the understarched lab coat, I jogged slowly back to my department, worn navy scrubs and long-john T-shirt soft against my skin beneath the rough coat.

There were two patients waiting for me in the E.R. when I entered again. The numbers of nurses had decreased, the shifts having changed in the few minutes I walked the halls, and the desk was almost deserted. A tech was sitting at the low side of the desk doing paperwork from the previous shift, while the doctor I was relieving sat at the high side doing the same. A nurse was in the drug room counting pills for the thrice-daily inventory. The other nurse was in the fracture room, evaluating one of the two patients there. Walk-ins, not real emergencies. That was great by me.

Feeling better than I had in weeks, I propped my elbows on the nurses' desk and dropped my chin into my hands. "Dr. Wallace," I said, half formally.

"Dr. Rhea-Rhea." Greenish eyes twinkled at me from nearly my height. At around five-ten, I was tall, and even sitting in the high bar-stool-type chair, Wallace Chadwick could look me in the eye. He nodded his dark-skinned head, tilting a close-cropped pate my way. "Good day today. Saw only about twenty-five patients. Nothing major except an MI we flew out to Richland Memorial. The two now are brand-new and all yours. Still awaiting report on them."

"Thank you very kindly."

"I hear you're the new assistant coroner."

I sighed, stood straighter and swiveled, keeping my weight on one elbow. "Bad news travels fast. How'd you hear?"

"Cops told me when I treated the shooter."

"Boy? Blond, maybe thirteen, on the small side?"

"That's the one." Wallace handed me a chart on Wayne Edward Geter, age twelve. "He'd been pretty badly abused by the old guy. If it was me, I'd a shot him myself. Kid may be back tonight, if the pain meds wear off."

Remembering the adolescent boy in the sheriff's car, I raised my brows. He hadn't looked terribly much in pain this afternoon. "Pain meds for what?"

"Warts. Perianal. Worst case I've ever seen. Kid may need some reconstructive surgery, too, for a partially prolapsed rectum."

I propped the chart on the desk and scanned it. Without being so blunt, Wallace was telling me that the boy I had glimpsed had been repeatedly raped, and now had genital warts. I shook my head. Maybe because I had avoided the foster care system by the skin of my teeth when my mother died young, I felt a special tug on my heart. "Foster kids don't have much in the first place, then to get abused in the foster home…"

"Yeah. This county has some great foster parents. Wayne Edward got dumped on one of the few bad ones. And it was all recent damage. No chance any previous foster-care giver did it. Cops changed some thinking when I told them, and they may be looking at charging the wife. Anyway, the kid's hurting. I got him scheduled for a consult on the warts and prolapse in Columbia next week. Because he's a prisoner, he'll get first-rate medical care courtesy of the county. It was all pretty tough on Zack, though."

"How's that?" I looked up from Wayne Edward Geter's chart at the change of subject. Zack was a nurse on day shift. And then I remembered. His daughter had disappeared last month, precipitating a two-county manhunt. When she reappeared four days later, she had been with her new boyfriend. Couldn't understand why anyone had been worried. "Mina came home, didn't she?"

"Yeah, she came home. Pregnant and infected with chlamydia and herpes."

"Ouch."

"Double ouch—now he learns that the father of the baby could be any one of three or four boys she was partying with. He's real torn up."

There were many days when I was happy to have no children. "They keeping the baby?"

"I don't know. Mina wants an abortion. The hospital is providing counseling, but Zack's family is pretty religious. There is a difference of opinion," Wallace said, pursing his lips. The last sentence said a great deal about the situation. "Anyway, when the kid comes in, abused, talking about his sister who disappeared, it was tough on Zack. He went home early in the afternoon, but he'll be back tonight at eight for a graveyard shift. You up to playing psychiatrist?"

"Think a bucket of cold water over his head would work?" I hated counseling unless it was just listening. I could listen with the best of them. "I saw that method used today to great effect."

"Oh? Are you doing a paper on it?" He grinned.

"I could." I pursed my lips, pretending to consider the suggestion. "I could title it 'Panic Attacks and an Effective Emergency Home Remedy.'" I explained the situation with Betty at the crime scene earlier in the day, making small talk as Wallace grabbed a small canvas bag from the floor beneath one of the computer screens. Together we walked toward the air lock doors.

Behind us the EMS scanner blared to life. "Dawkins County, this is unit 67. Dawkins County, this is unit 67." The EMT was shouting into the mike, sirens screaming in the background.

Wallace paused, turned and came back in, the air swishing around us as the doors slid together. "This sounds bad."

I nodded, listening, angling back to the E.R. Wallace followed. I was already considering my assets, and what I might need in a real emergency.

"This is Dawkins County, go ahead unit 67." The nurse answering was Coreen, her voice soft and controlled. She was a newbie, with less than a year's experience in an emergency room, but she was learning fast. The other nurse on duty, Ashlee Davenport, appeared at the desk.

"We are inbound, code three, with a multiple GSW, white male, estimated age mid to late thirties. BP is 60 palpated. Pulse irregular at 120. Patient is intubated, on 100 percent O2, two lines established with large bore needles." He paused and took his first breath. "Estimated time of arrival three minutes. Patient is shocky and has lost massive amounts of blood."

"I want to know about the wounds. Where and what caliber?" I asked. I watched Wallace drop his canvas bag back under the nurses' desk and roll up his sleeves. Looked like I had help for this one.

"Ashlee," I said, "get me two units of O neg blood down here stat. Respiratory, lab, more hands. Let's consider this a full code. Thanks," I said, taking paper and plastic PPEs from Wallace. Still talking as I listened to the conversation between Coreen and the EMT, I shook out the long blue gown and shoved my arms down the sleeves of the personal protective equipment needed at any bloody scene. A passing nurse slipped a face shield over my head and I adjusted it in place.

Over the monitor came the news that my patient had been shot in the chest and abdomen with a 9 mm semiautomatic handgun. Three entrance wounds, two exits.

"I want a CBC, urine, start 2 units stat and cross four more, ABGs and lytes, occult blood of stool. Everybody in protective clothing. Get the surgeon on call on the phone, and make a call to Medic for flight times. I want two more lines—large bore Jelcos. Get a chest tube kit ready—make that two kits," I amended as I listened to the scanner, "and I want a femoral line. Tetanus and ancef. Get X ray here for portables. Tell them they need extra hands. Don't let anyone else go home. Get me the supervisor. Did I leave anything out?"

"If you did, we'll figure it out as we go along. Looks like a hot time in the old town tonight," Ash said.

"That's my line," I said, watching the blond nurse open the trauma crash cart.

"I'm adopting it."

"Help yourself." People poured out around us. A lab tech handed me paperwork for the uncrossed blood beneath her arm. I scrawled illegibly across the sheet and pointed at Ash. "Get these started the second he's on the table. Trendelenburg since there's no head wound." I turned to Wallace, his face appearing malformed behind the plastic face shield. "Airway or circulation?"

"I'll take his head, airway and breathing."

"Chicken."

"You want me to take the bleeding just 'cause you're a girl?"

I said something very unladylike and Wallace laughed. "I'm technically off the clock, so you get the fun parts."

"Yeah? If the rounds took out the lungs you may get more than you bargained for."

"Dr. Lynch?" I turned to Coreen. Her brown eyes appeared tinged with yellow in the fluorescent lighting. "My cousin called me on my cell phone. Thought you might want to know. It's a cop."

"What's a cop?"

"The guy in the ambulance. The one they're bringing in."

"Thanks." I thought I spoke, but no sound came out. Mark was a white cop in his thirties.

The ambulance entrance crashed open. Police officers ran in, pulling a gurney. Blood was everywhere, thin and bright red. An EMT rode the patient, doing CPR. I slammed down on my reactions and directed my focus tightly on the patient. Just the injured body in front of me. Not someone I cared for personally.

The patient was wearing MASS trousers, fastened with Velcro and fully inflated to force the blood in the major extremities up into the body. Tattered uniform pants were in place beneath the MASS trousers, one bullet hole visible in the cloth.

His bare chest was so smeared with blood it looked as if he'd been painted. Bulky bandages were taped over three sites on his chest and abdomen. Officers applied pressure at each site, bare hands and uniform sleeves coated with scarlet.

The cop's face was obscured by the ambu bag pumping air through the tube down his throat and by the EMT's large hands. Other bodies worked feverishly, masking my view. But the cop was bearded. A blood-caked fringe peeked out on the jawline.

My chest ached when I tried to draw a breath. I closed my eyes to force concentration, but opened them when the room seemed to heave beneath my feet.

"Move him on three!" Hands gripped the blood-soaked sheet beneath my patient. *Beneath Mark?*

"One, two, three." They heaved. The flaccid body flopped to the E.R. stretcher. The gurney was shoved away. Voices babbled around me.

"I've got blood in the airway. Get me a trach kit."

"The anesthesiologist is here."

"Sandra? You want this?"

"I'll take it."

"Watch it!"

"Blood going. Got a cuff inflated around it. Starting second unit."

"No pulse. Nothing on the monitor," I whispered.

"Someone start chest compressions again," Wallace said, and an EMT began CPR again.

My gloved hand, holding my stethoscope, found the man's chest, touched the flesh. My eyes lifted. Met Mark's. He was standing beside me.

My hand holding the stethoscope bell trembled and pulled away. I remembered to breathe, blinked against sudden tears. I turned away so he couldn't see my reaction as I placed the bell of my stethoscope back on the bloody chest. It took a long second to hear chest sounds, find my voice. "What happened?"

"Charlie Denbrow's wife caught him in a…compromising situation in the back of his patrol car while on duty. Pulled his gun and shot him."

"And the other partner to this compromising situation?" My tone was steady, cool, professional. My hand no longer shook. Inside I ached and quivered. I took another deep breath and my chest still hurt.

"Dead at the scene."

"I suggest that you call in the medical examiner. I can't leave here to go pronounce her."

"Him."

"Say what?" I could hear squishing sounds in the chest cavity with each compression. The cop's chest was full of blood. Considering the location of the wounds, I had to guess that one round had hit the inferior vena cava or the descending aorta. Every shot was midline between crotch and breastbone. The guy was dead and didn't know it.

At a major trauma center, one with a major trauma emergency department and a well-trained surgical-trauma team waiting on hand, maybe he could have been saved. Maybe. But even there I wouldn't put any money on it.

"The compromising partner. Him."

"I have a pulse," someone said. Chest compressions stopped. "Sinus rhythm."

"Wallace, listen to this," I said.

Wallace placed his bloody stethoscope bell on the patient's chest.

"You hear it?" I asked.

"Got ABGs and lab work drawn," a woman said.

"Yes. I hear it." Wallace cursed and looked up. His eyes slid past me to the doorway. "Statler?"

"Present."

"We got a problem tailor-made for you."

I stepped toward the head of the bed and Dr. Statler eased into my place. I hadn't seen the surgeon amid the press of helping hands. Leaning over, he settled his own stethoscope bell on Charlie's chest and listened. "Quiet, please," Statler said. The room grew still, the silence marred only by the whoosh of air being pumped into the patient's chest.

Statler leaned in farther. His starched white lab coat was instantly smeared with blood down the front and across one sleeve. I was still slightly shocky, noticing small details too clearly, and the room seemed colder than only minutes earlier. But I was functioning. Doing my job. And the patient wasn't Mark. It wasn't Mark.

I looked down into the patient's face. Beneath his bloody beard I could see what looked like a scratch and little nubs of something, a lesion just starting beneath the skin. There was another on his chest, larger and better defined, at an old injury site.

"Bullet got his descending aorta," Statler said.

My eyes jerked to the surgeon's face. The EMTs and nurses sucked in a communal breath. A thrum of electricity shot through the group. The cops looked up, eyes wide, most not knowing what the statement meant, but all sensing something bad. Real bad. Mark went rigid. His hands fisted. Mark understood the words. Charlie might as well be pronounced dead on the table.

When Statler spoke again, he seemed unaware of the tension his words had created in the room. He sounded ruminative. Considering. The world seemed to slow down. "Sandra? Do you still have that heart-lung bypass machine you were showing off?"

"You got to be kidding. You want to use that here? In this rinky-dink hospital?" Sandra growled. "I got him trached. I need a film for placement."

"We have a crew still on the premises. Only way to save him is to take him off his own circulatory system and repair the damage. We could take a vein from his leg."

"Forget it. This guy's dead. We don't even have time to do the scans to pinpoint the damage. There's no microsurgery capability here. Surgery would take all night and we'd still lose him. No. No way."

A portable X-ray machine purred into place. The people at the foot of the bed rearranged themselves, others helped to put a slab of film behind the patient. "Ready to shoot. All out as wants out," the X-ray tech said. No one moved except to put on lead aprons that were hanging on the wall. The cops didn't bother, their expressions still frozen.

"If we attempt nothing, he's dead." Statler glanced at his watch and nodded slowly. "Yes. Surgery tonight. Right now. If you please."

Sandra spat a curse. But she stood and stormed from the room, heading toward the surgery department. The cops blew out a single breath. Someone swore, his tone relieved.

Wallace met my eyes, his brows lifted. *Here? In this rinky-dink hospital?* his gaze echoed. I shrugged. It wasn't my call. And the patient wasn't Mark. I was still feeling small aftershocks and trying to decide what my strong reaction had meant. Mark wasn't lying on the table dying. I couldn't get my thoughts around that truth.

"We need about twenty units of blood. I want four going at all times until we get him on the heart-lung machine and the cell-saver," Statler said, referring to two machines, one that breathed and pumped blood for a patient, and one that collected, washed and recirculated blood lost during surgery.

One cop slapped another on the back and laughed in relief. The technicians around us were careful to avoid eye contact with any officer, as that could give hope to the hopeless.

"I need the arterial blood gases," Statler said over the laughter.

"Here's his first set of ABGs," a voice said. A female hand passed the report to Statler. "He's A positive. I have ten units of O and six of A in the lab. I need someone to coordinate trips to Columbia to the Red Cross to pick up more."

"Done," Mark said. He turned to Statler. "He's one of ours. Anything you need, you got."

Statler kicked the brakes off the E.R. stretcher. "Let's roll, people. Dr. Lynch, I'll need someone to call in the other surgeon on call. I believe it's Dr. Derosett."

"He's that new Muslim guy, ain't he?" a voice asked.

"Don't want a Muslim working on Charlie. Terrorists, every one of them."

Without pausing, Dr. Statler looked down his thin, patrician nose and shoved the E.R. bed forward. "Devin De rosett is a surgeon, and a good one. You want your friend to live? Stop being such redneck idiots."

I watched which cops turned away, which ones turned red and which ones smiled. Good for Statler. I didn't know the stuffy old guy had it in him.

"I'll scrub in and help where I can," Wallace said, following down the hallway.

"Thank you. Perhaps you might wish to call Pearl. The surgery may indeed take all night, if he makes it through the surgery at all, and your wife might object. How many units are hanging?" Statler's voice echoed down the hall way.

"Two. Starting the third one now."

"I'll call OR and tell them you're on the way," Coreen said. "And I'll call Dr. Derosett."

"Thank you, my dear. Dr. Lynch, a pleasure as always. Wallace, shall we?"

I waved a bloody hand at him. If Statler wanted to try to save this guy, he could have at it. I put his chances at about half a million to one. And I was being generous.

The stretcher was suddenly gone, leaving thin line of blood where the wheels had tracked, and cops staring after it.

5

I THINK I SOCKED HER

Sheriff Gaskins bustled into the trauma room, thick black nose hair twitching. His usual laughing face was wreathed in a concerned frown, his hairline peeking out from beneath the cowboy hat he wore pushed back on his head. "Dispatch just informed me. What do we have going on here? And why wasn't I notified one of my men was shot? Has his wife been contacted?" Gaskins glared around at the cops.

I stepped back into the room and watched the tableau unfold. In South Carolina, the sheriff is the highest elected law-enforcement official in a county. Gaskins was a political being, through and through, always conscious of his office and his image. No one answered him. No one moved. The cops looked away. No one wanted to tell C. C. Gaskins that one of his men had been shot on the job while having sex with another man. The media would have a field day.

Sensing the unease, C.C. glared. "Who's supposed to be out running patrol? Is the entire city and county police force in this one room?"

Mark took his arm, offered to give a report and led Gaskins out into the hallway. The sheriff left cowboy-boot footprints in his officer's blood. Over a shoulder, Mark nodded to the cops. *Get back to work. I'll call you,* was the message in the gesture. A line of cops followed the two men out.

"Rhea-Rhea?"

I met the dark eyes of Eddie Braswell. He was smeared with blood from hands to shoulders, and splattered with blood everywhere else.

I took Eddie's arm and led him away in the short stream of technicians and nursing personnel, my posture mimicking Mark's and the sheriff's. Nurses followed us out. I thanked someone who spread out a layer of sheets to wipe our feet on and to absorb the blood from the shooting.

Peeling off the PPEs, I trashed them behind the soiled utility door. I was still shaken, but it was safely hidden inside, where all the nasty emotions should be kept, out of sight from the general public. It was a belief that had been pounded into me throughout childhood by my best friend Marisa's Aunt DeeDee. I took a deep breath and shuddered only slightly. Besides, doctors aren't supposed to cry. It's bad for the image.

"You need a shower," I said to Eddie. Eddie Braswell was Marisa's stepson, which made him my responsibility in some kind of weird way. Marisa wasn't blood kin, but she was my best friend, closer than any family I had. Her people were my people—family, as far as I was concerned.

"I think I'm evidence." His voice was hesitant, breathy with shock, his eyes wide with images only he could see. "I think I have to preserve myself for a while."

"Why's that?"

"I saw the whole thing. I took the gun away from Charlie's wife and called in the shooting. I tried to stop the bleeding." He looked down at his blood-soaked body and back to me. "He's gonna die, isn't he?"

"Yes." I let him absorb that for a moment. It was cold and hard, and I didn't try to sugarcoat it. Why bother?

Eddie had been there the whole time. "I'll get you some scrubs. You can shower in my room and change. Just keep the bloody clothes for evidence."

"The surgeon thinks he can save him."

"Surgeons always think that." I slung my stethoscope around my neck. "They're born with a built-in God complex. They have to be, in order to cut open a human being and play around inside, rearranging the body parts. Doesn't mean they really are God.

"I'll be back in a sec," I said to Coreen. She nodded, her dark-skinned face shining with perspiration. There was a smudge of blood on one cheek. "Check your face. Blood." I pointed.

Eddie and I walked down the hallway, our footsteps almost silent. Finally he said, "The God complex thing doesn't wash. Why did the surgeon really take Charlie to surgery? If he can't be saved, why bother?" A nurse passed, her mouth tight, her eyes tired.

What could I answer? *For the thrill of trying? Because the thought of losing isn't part of a surgeon's mindset? Because there's a new piece of equipment on-site and Statler gets a chance to play with it?* Reluctantly, I replied, "Because there is a chance, however slim." Uncomfortable, I changed the subject. "Why were you at the scene? I understood that the guy was having sex with another man in the patrol car."

Eddie mock-punched me. "That's my Rhea-Rhea. All tact and consideration."

I actually laughed, and some of the gloom I was still feeling fell away. I looked at Eddie and remembered the kid he had been, wide-eyed and joyful, on horseback at Stowe Farm, skinny legs whapping into the sides of a big pony. And I remembered the same kid only a year past, pale and underweight, dark eyes haunted, a confused teenager into drugs and in trouble with the law. Now Eddie was healthy, robust, his brown hair skinned back, short with blond spikes, a tattoo of a snake curling around one wrist. Taller than I, he exuded confidence, that peculiarly male boldness that said he was ten feet tall and bulletproof. He shrugged.

"And that means what?"

"It looked like a routine traffic stop. I know Charlie, so I pulled over a ways up the street to wait it out. Thought I'd see if he wanted to get a burger on his break. Charlie got the guy out, made him assume the position. Cuffed him and put him in the back of the squad car. Then something went weird." Eddie wiped his hands on his trousers. The dried blood cracked but didn't come off. "Charlie climbed in after him. Or maybe was pulled in after him. I turned off the radio and rolled down the window. Anyway, up pulls Gabby, Charlie's wife, and she climbs in, too, and I hear hollering. Then shots. I ran to help. Pulled Gabby off Charlie and took the gun. I think I socked her. I guess that could be trouble for me, huh?"

"I doubt it," I said, keeping my tone neutral, my eyes focused on the door ahead. I opened it and pulled back a sheet hiding a rack of scrubs, then handed Eddie a set of mismatched extra large and a red biohazard bag. "Go on."

"I called for help on Charlie's radio. Started trying to stop the bleeding. It seemed like ages, but the cops were there in maybe two minutes, the EMTs in maybe four. I had help. It just wasn't enough."

"Charlie's uniform pants were belted around his waist when he was brought in. Was the other guy dressed?"

Again Eddie tried to clean his hands. "Yeah. Why?"

"Pants belted and zipped?"

"Yeah." Light was dawning in Eddie's eyes. "Just like Charlie when I pulled him from the car."

"Last I heard, it's real hard to have, ah, homosexual intercourse with both parties' pants belted in place."

Eddie slowed and turned bewildered eyes to me. "Charlie's wife was yelling about having sex. About catching them at it. And Charlie's face was in the guy's lap. I saw that. But maybe…"

"Maybe he got shoved there?"

"I guess I should tell someone." He looked back the way we had come.

"You'll get the chance. Probably the rest of the next twenty-four hours. You better grab a shower while you can."

Eddie shrugged again and faced forward. "Yeah. Guess so."

"So, how do you know Charlie? Last I heard, he was on the crime scene team. He came to my house once, when I had a problem with a possible intruder. Drove my car to make sure there wasn't a bomb underneath." The sudden realization of who the patient had been rolled over me hard. I knew the guy. He wasn't Mark, but I knew him.

"He got bored. Wanted to work a case or go back to patrol."

"And?"

"I'm working part-time at the LEC for Mark Stafford while he does paperwork to get my records as a juvenile sealed and any outstanding charges against me dropped. I met Charlie there." Eddie looked at me from the corner of his eyes. "Then Stafford wants me to go on to school in criminal justice. I think I might do it. I think I might like CSI work, you know? A forensic scientist."

No, I didn't know any of that. I hadn't been around Mark in months and had no idea that he was working with Eddie Braswell, and I had no idea that Eddie wanted to be a cop. Life was weird. "I think that's great, Eddie. You got your GED yet?"

"Passed by a mile." He grinned happily. "I guess you

know Mark made me move in with Miss Essie till I get my life straightened out.''

No, I hadn't known that, either, but before I could formulate a reply, my beeper went off, just as I unlocked the door to my room. The E.R. extension was displayed. I handed Eddie the keys, not sure what to say about Mark taking an interest in his life. It felt strange. "Take a shower. Bag your clothes. Lock the door when you get through.''

"Thanks, Rhea.''

"Anytime.''

"Hey, Rhea?''

I paused with one hand on the door.

"You been to see the kids lately? Rheaburn's making this stuck-in-one-place crawling motion. Lynnie started saying 'mama' Monday past. And Marisa, well, she needs company. I know you're working too much to be there every day, but I think she's lonely.''

I softened, the thought of Risa and my godchildren bringing me a hint of calm. I took a deep breath. "I'll get out there this weekend. Promise.''

Eddie gave me this little *chick-chick* sound from the side of his mouth, accompanied by a gun-firing motion with his bloody left hand.

I jogged back to the E.R., still feeling out of sorts and not quite focused. My back hurt with each motion. That was a worry, but more so was the feeling of not being quite all there. I kept seeing the body on the gurney, an EMT straddling him, pumping the two-handed CPR motion of roughly a hundred beats a minute. *Not Mark. Not Mark.* He had dumped me, so why did it matter? But it did matter, it mattered a lot, and I had to figure out why.

Zack was in the E.R. when I got there, looking calm and relaxed, not as if he had a teenaged daughter in trouble at home. Tall and slender, he handed me an old chart and a new one on the same patient. Wayne Edward Geter, age twelve. The boy accused of shooting his foster father was back, and in pain.

"Two others patients who were waiting decided a building filled with cops was more detrimental to their health than their complaints, and left. You just have the one."

"Thanks." I paused. "You okay, Zack?" It wasn't exactly Freud or Jung, but for me it was pretty good.

He nodded, his face tightening for a moment. "I'm fine. Into every life there falls a little rain."

"Is that the Bible?"

"More or less." Zack nodded, his close-cropped hair glistening in the lights, his dark skin gleaming.

"Wasn't the Holy Land a desert?" When he nodded, I said, "Rain is a blessing in a desert and only a little ever fell."

Zack looked as if I had come up with some profound new wisdom. I hadn't, I was just quoting Miss Essie, but it must have meant something to Zack. He continued nodding as I turned away and entered my patient's room.

A uniformed detention officer stood against the counter, his hands resting on his gun belt, his eyes on the wall until I entered. Then he looked me over carefully.

"I'm Dr. Lynch. Uncuff him, please."

Without comment, the officer uncuffed the boy, who lay on his side in an uncomfortable position, adult-size orange jumpsuit rolled up at his ankles, feet bare, a pair of yellow flip-flops on the floor beside the bed. With perianal warts, sitting could be painful, and lying on his back might be just as bad.

I had a sudden image of this boy being tormented by his foster father, and my rush of anger at the vision was scalding. The boy's face was tear-streaked with misery, and snot burbled beneath his nose. I looked away, breathing deeply, fighting my rage, controlling it, tamping it down. Pendergrass was dead. He couldn't hurt this child again. Handing him a tissue, I pulled a stool close to him, my back to the cop. "I'm Doctor Rhea-Rhea. You want to tell me about it?"

"I killed a man." The young prisoner tossed back his too-long blond hair and blew his nose, wiped fiercely, leaving red streaks beneath his nostrils and across his face. "And now I'll never get my sister back. I don't know what he did with her. I can't find her if I'm in jail. I was so *stupid*." He socked the mattress beneath him. "Stupid, stupid, stupid."

"Are you sure he took her?"

Wayne looked up at me. "Who else woulda?"

"I don't know. Maybe someone else."

"Stupid cops want me to believe she run off." It was what I had been about to suggest. I shut my mouth on the words. Wayne lifted blue eyes to me. "We was in this together. Always. Beata'd a never left me. Not never."

"Bee-a-da-ud?"

"Beata. My sister. It means happy."

"Ah." After a moment I asked, "What does your family call you? Wayne? Ed?"

"Wayne Edward. Both names. After my daddy's daddy and my mama's daddy. They're both dead. My mama's in prison. My daddy run off."

The words sounded as if they'd been spoken so often they had lost all meaning to the speaker. They made me want to cry for him, but I knew this kid would hate me for any tears. He'd hate my sympathy as much as I hated the man who had abused him. My rage tried to squirm free, but I held it, mastered it, took several small breaths to keep it under control. "Are you hurting, Wayne Edward?"

"Yes, ma'am. Pretty bad."

"I'll give you something for pain."

"But you're gonna have to look at me, you know, down

there. Ain't you?'' He turned red, his fair skin beet-colored instantly.

I thought about it. Legally, I should take a look. Morally was another matter. This boy had been abused enough. "Are you bleeding down there?" Wayne Edward shook his head. "Just burning?"

He nodded. "Bad. Hurting something fierce."

"Can you wipe a tissue back there to make sure about the bleeding?" I passed him a clean tissue and showed him how to hold it. "The other doctor left good notes. I may not have to examine you."

"You know why I'm sick?"

When I inhaled, my breath shuddered, but my voice was steady. "Yes. I know."

"Does everyone know?" The beet shade deepened to scarlet.

"It's illegal for any doctor or nurse to tell anyone what you have or how you got it. It's illegal for anyone to know unless you tell them."

"Really?"

I nodded.

"Good." The red receded slightly as I turned away. Wayne Edward stuck his hand gingerly through the front opening of the utilitarian jumpsuit and swiped slowly across the tortured skin. When he brought the tissue back out, it was covered with serous fluid, but no blood.

"I'll get you some medicine. Some topical stuff for where it hurts on the skin and some to take like a pill. Can you swallow a pill?" At his nod, I added, "You can put this salve on the skin where it burns." I offered some packets of antibiotic ointment. It wouldn't kill the virus that caused the warts, but it might halt a secondary infection before it started. "I'll get the cops to bring the ointment to you anytime you need it." I looked up at the detention officer. "*Any*time. Understand?"

"Yes, ma'am." The officer was looking away, but he had heard me.

"And the pills you can take every four hours if you need to."

"Thanks, Doctor. I 'preciate it. But...I still killed my sister." The tears started to fall again. "'Cause if I can't find her, she's dead. What if he has her underground? I seen that on TV one time."

"Are none of the cops listening?" I glanced at the officer. Unless he had no peripheral vision at all, he saw me, but he didn't turn.

"My lawyer said not to talk to them." He shrugged. "But I guess there's one or two maybe listening,"

"Well, maybe you should keep talking to that one or two—with your lawyer present, of course. Cops can find people a lot easier than teenaged boys can." And I'll call Mark and ask him to go talk to you, I thought, but kept that to myself. I didn't know if my asking Mark for favors would help the boy or make matters worse. I dredged up a smile and left the room.

Calling the LEC, I left a message about Wayne Edward with Mark's voice mail. At the latest, he'd get it in the morning. It was the least I could do. Almost literally.

The night was slow for the first hour after Wayne Edward left, only a couple of infants with viruses, a case of pelvic inflammatory disease and a car wreck with minor injuries. Nothing to sink my teeth into. Nothing to keep me from dwelling on Wayne Edward and his missing sister and their awful experience in foster care. I didn't think too much about the man Wayne Edward had shot. Dead is dead and maybe the man deserved what he got. It was a blood-thirsty thought, not one I was comfortable with.

Of course, it was only quiet until I wanted to take a break and eat dinner. That was an invitation for the EMS radio to go wild. I had just reached into the fridge for the meal packed for me by the hospital kitchen when I heard the words, "Dawkins County, this is unit 351. Dawkins County, this is unit 351." The ambulance siren was blasting in the background.

"Dawkins County. Go ahead unit 351," Zack said.

I peeked around the doorway. Zack was bent over the radio, pen in hand, taking notes. Maybe I wasn't a psychologist, but it looked as if my words of wisdom had helped the man settle a bit. He looked pretty good, more stable.

"Dawkins, we are inbound with a twenty-two-year-old white male with small caliber GSW to the upper right arm, entrance and exit wounds, arterial bleeding controlled at the scene by family member. Vitals are as follows—BP 145 over 98, respiration 22, pulse 115, with regular sinus showing on monitor, pupils E and R. One IV via large bore needle at left AC running normal saline."

"ETA?" Zack asked.

"Two minutes out, Dawkins."

"Three-five-one, has law enforcement been notified?"

"Affirmative, Dawkins. Detective and marked units on the way to the E.R. Unit 352 is on the way in also, Dawkins, carrying a second vic."

I heard the amused tone even over the scratchy reception. Zack must have picked up on it as well because he said, "Confirm, second victim?"

"Confirm. Victim of…altercation. With same family member who controlled arterial bleeding at site."

This sounded interesting. With this many patients, though, we should have heard something on the police scanner. I glanced over and discovered it was off. "Zack, ask them if the second victim shot the first victim." Grinning, Zack repeated my question.

"Confirm that, Dawkins." The paramedic was laughing. Enjoying his job.

"Patient to trauma room bed one. Dawkins 414 clear," Zack said. Turning to me, he said, "I assume you want the second patient in fracture room, separated from the first patient?"

"Oh, yeah. And maybe the family member in police custody." I dropped my unopened dinner back into the fridge, turned on the scanner and washed my hands.

"You want any special equipment, other than gloves and face shield?" Zack asked.

Before I could reply, the radio blared again. "Dawkins County, this is unit 352. Dawkins County, unit 352."

Zack sat back down and answered the call, a fresh page for notes at his side.

"Dawkins, we are inbound with a white, thirty-two-year-old male, signal 22 and possible 24 with multiple signal elevens. Victim of an altercation. Please note that the signal 22 could not be corrected at scene." There was humor in this medic's voice, too, and the sound of muted screaming in the background. I drifted closer and could feel Coreen behind me.

The medical signals were codes that meant the patient had a dislocated joint and a possible fracture, and multiple contusions. In other words, he'd been beaten up. And the laughter by the emergency personnel likely meant they thought he deserved it. "Because of patient's signal 40, we were unable to start an IV and are unable to provide reliable BP. Pulse is 145, respiration is 30, first BP on arrival was 175 over 120. Pupils are equal but constricted with possible signal 45."

"Zack, ask if they have a paper bag. Or rebreather mask."

Zack repeated the question. The EMT said, "Affirmative, Dawkins. But unable to use at this time.'' In the background, I heard something crash. Zack was grinning widely.

"Can they get any information about the patient? Allergies, past medical history?''

"Negative, Doc,'' the EMT said. Zack had pressed the Transmit button down and I was effectively speaking to the medic myself. I took the mike and sat in Zack's place. "Patient is unable to respond. No family at the scene. Patient's ID was provided by officers and the patient's driver's license.''

I sighed. I had a hysterical, possibly drugged-up, beaten-up patient, one known to law enforcement on sight. "Is the patient in police custody?'' I asked, releasing the Transmit button.

"Affirmative, Dawkins.''

"Great. Just freaking lovely,'' I muttered. I depressed the button and said, "Patient to fracture room on arrival. Dawkins 414 clear.''

6

STUPID IDIOT SHOT ME

Behind me the ambulance doors swished open and two EMS guys wheeled in, one applying pressure near the head of the gurney, both walking with that odd, hunched-over gait the lifesaving types adopt when working on the run. My GSW patient was a good-looking kid, even through the green plastic oxygen mask he was wearing over a face glazed with pain. I followed the gurney to the trauma room, checking the monitors as we moved. His BP and pulse had both come down since the report and he looked remarkably calm for someone who had been shot. I knew he was twenty-two, but he looked closer to twelve, long and skinny, his feet and ankles hanging off the gurney, one bony elbow on the railing, a shock of dark hair hanging across his forehead.

I stood back and watched as the EMTs, Carla and Hybernia, and two cops moved him off the gurney and onto the E.R. stretcher. He gasped in pain at the motion but didn't cry out, just pressed his lips together until they turned white. The heart monitor sped up for a moment.

"I'm Dr. Lynch," I said to take his mind off his discomfort. "What's your name?"

"Levi Cordell." His face twisted into a grimace as Hybernia adjusted the sling on his right arm. "And before you ask, it's Thursday night, I'm twenty-two and this is Dawkins County E.R. I'm in my right mind."

I smiled. The kid had an attitude but he was well-spoken. "Tell me what happened."

"My brother and Wicked Owens and I had just installed a new security system in Pucky's Guns and Things," he said, his words a staccato narrative. "Tested it out and it worked perfect. Wicked left—it was his bowling night—and we're driving out of the lot when this guy roars up in an old beat-up Ford pickup. It had a brown front left fender with no headlight and no tailgate. I remember it clear as if I had taken a photo of it. Anyway, he takes off into the place. Leaves the truck running.

"My brother, who thinks he's still in the Delta Force doing Special Ops in the Middle East, slams on the brakes, does a skidding 180 and takes us back to the shop. There's gunshots all over the place and he just has to do his commando thing and go in after him."

While he talked, I moved in and eased the sling off his arm, working around Carla, who was applying pressure proximal to the wound. The bandage was secure, with large amounts of dressing packed into the entrance and exit wounds. Zack lifted a face shield over my head and I bent at the knees to allow him to adjust its Velcro closure on my forehead. He handed me an open packet of sterile gloves on their folded autoclave paper and I pulled them on.

"Idiot," the kid continued. "He could have just waited. The alarm worked perfectly. Cops were on the way. But, no. He has to commando the place. And I have to be stupid and follow him." The tone was filled with self-disgust.

Carefully, I lifted the dressing and looked at the entrance wound. It was clean and smooth, but very discolored where the blood was collecting beneath the skin and deep in the

tissues. I lifted the arm gently and Levi interrupted his narrative and hissed once, softly.

"I'm sorry. I have to check the exit wound. That means
lifting it."

"Okay. You want me to go on? Or was my soliloquy
just to keep my mind occupied while you tortured me?"

I smiled and examined the exit wound. It was considerably less neat, with a jagged tear where the bullet came
out. "Both, actually." I glanced up at Carla. "Ease off
pressure, please."

As she relaxed her hold, the blood seeped, bright red,
from the wound. Then it spurted, hard and fast. It hit my
face shield as I jerked back reflexively. "Pressure," I demanded, and her gloved hand clamped down again. Out in
the hallway, I heard screaming and cursing and sounds of
a body hitting something. I didn't bother to turn around,
just pulled off the bloody face shield and tossed it into the
sink.

"And?" I asked the kid.

"And the stupid idiot shot me."

"Your brother the commando, stupid idiot?" I asked as
I rewrapped the bandages holding the dressing in place and
checked for a pulse in his wrist.

"No." The kid grinned weakly, his lips slightly gray. He
looked a mite shocky. There was no pulse in the wrist at
all, and my patient's hand was turning cool and blue. "Not
my brother the commando idiot. The would-be-robber idiot.
My brother takes him down in about two seconds with four
really cool moves. He's in no danger from the other guy's
weapon, because it's trapped under Eli's arm. But it's
pointing right at me as I come in the door. I take a hit and
then Eli has to take care of me."

I twisted my body back to the wall to turn up the oxygen,
and gestured for a nasal cannula. The grin was still there
as I removed the mask and replaced it with little green tubes

inserted in his nose. A silly grin, delight underlying the shame he felt for getting shot. The kid had a serious case of hero worship.

"Saved my life."

"Undoubtedly," I said. "It looks like the bullet hit the major artery in the upper arm. How does it feel? Not the wound, but the arm and hand."

"Cold. Like it's asleep."

"Zack, call in a surgeon, or see if Derosett can take a breather from the Denbrow procedure. This patient needs an anastomosis and a good evaluation of tendons and nerves, just in case."

The kid's dark eyes widened. "You can't fix it here in the emergency room?"

"Nope," I said. "Make a fist. Good. Do this." I showed a pinching motion with my thumb and forefinger, then moved my fingers side to side and spread them out and back in. The kid repeated all my motions, still talking.

"I have to have surgery?"

"Yep. The surgeon will need to even-up the ends of the artery and sew it back together. The artery in this part of the arm is too small for a nip and tuck. Once damaged, it has to be repaired very carefully or it won't heal." When he started to protest, I added, "You can go to surgery for a quick half-hour procedure, spend a couple nights in the hospital and maybe be gone in forty-eight hours. Or you can sign yourself out against medical advice, go home without the procedure and die. That's the worst-case scenario. Best case, if you go home, is you lose the arm. Your choice."

The kid snorted. "You sound like my brother."

"I'll take that as a compliment. Cops'll want to talk to you. Zack, let's get a CBC, Type and Screen, PT, PTT, and an X ray of this arm to make sure the bullet didn't take a bite out of the humerus," I said, ordering a battery of tests to make sure he hadn't lost a lot of blood and was a good candidate for surgery. "Get a urinalysis, too. ETA on the surgeon?"

"Ten minutes. Derosett's free. Second string OR crew will take longer."

"You got any family we need to call?" I asked.

"Only my brother. And the cops were detaining him at the scene. Of course, that won't stop him. I give him another five minutes and he'll be here. Cops would have to arrest him to keep him away. And then he'd probably not go with them conscious." That hero worship again.

I patted his leg. "No other injuries?" I asked.

"Only to my pride."

"Last I heard, injured pride doesn't bleed and won't kill you."

I stepped aside and let the techs draw blood and offer papers to sign. My next patient was in the fracture room, and he didn't sound very happy to be there. I did a quick bit of paperwork. When I had no other legitimate reason to avoid the hysterical patient, I entered his room.

When I pushed my way between three emergency medical techs and a cop, my patient was throwing himself against the railing, back and forth, side to side, and wailing with the motion. His right arm stuck out at an obtuse angle, bent back high. The underside of his arm was fully exposed, chest bruised from his thrashing. His face was bruised, his lip busted and bleeding. He had two black eyes and one knee looked as if it was swollen.

Four moves, the kid had said. Impressive. Or very dangerous. "I'm Dr. Lynch," I stated.

With the first word, the patient threw himself across the bed and grabbed my lab coat in his good fist. "Give me something for pain!" he roared.

I jerked back and squealed, the sound remarkably like a small pig being stepped on by a farmer. Or like a grade school girl might make if a boy showed her a spider. I swallowed the sound.

My coat was wrenched in his fist. He jerked me hard, tried to drag me closer. I half squealed again, unable to help myself. I was trapped.

The EMS guys and the cop jumped in and liberated me, but were laughing so hard they were pretty ineffectual. Free, I stood in the corner, the coward's place, and glared at them all. Which only made the EMS laugh harder.

"Very funny, guys. Leather restraints and sheets around his chest," I said. When Zack stuck his head in the door to see what the commotion was, I added, "Cath UA and UDS and X ray of his shoulder, knee and facial bones. Get me some Versed, two mils IV, up to ten until relief. I'll try a closed reduction in a bit, but keep some Romazicon handy to reverse it if he stops breathing." Which might be a good thing, I thought. But I didn't say that aloud.

"Will do, Dr. Rhea."

"Drugs!" the patient screamed. "I'm in pain, damn it!"

"I'll bet you are," I said.

He called me a name that had an EMS guy suddenly on top of him, putting a knee to the patient's chest in retaliation. "Shut your nasty mouth!" he ordered. The man on the gurney gasped out a breath and grew still for a moment. It made me feel amazingly warm and comfortable all of a sudden. The guys could tease me and laugh all they wanted, but no drunken GOMER could. GOMER, as in Get Out of My Emergency Room—a patient who was either a druggie looking for a free fix or a compulsive visitor to the E.R. or an emotionally needy patient wanting sympathy. Or an abusive patient wanting to prove he was in charge of his world.

I tapped the EMT's arm. "Ease back. He can't breathe." To the patient I said, "What's your name? Pain medication's on the way."

After a moment he gasped, "Art Stinson."

"What drugs are you on, Art?"

Instead of answering, he told me where to go and to have unnatural relations with my mother at the same time. I shrugged and walked out of the room, letting the men secure and restrain him and start an IV. As I closed the door, Art Stinson was gasping with pain and cursing God, the world and me in particular.

Respect and consideration from a grateful patient. Ah, the benefits of eleven years of higher education and the desire to help others.

At the nurses' desk, three men lounged, two in the uniform of the Dawkins County sheriff's department and one in plain clothes—black slacks, white shirt smeared with drying red and brown blood, black loose jacket thrown over one shoulder. A leather holster, empty, wrapped around his chest. He was speaking.

"—Security Service, out of Ford County and South Charlotte. You can call Hugh McLerner of Bank of America to verify my credentials, or Wicked Owens, if that's easier." Wicked was a local boy who ran a security service favored by many of the county physicians. The cops nodded when he dropped the man's name, and wrote the information in their reports.

From behind, the man didn't look much like a security specialist, who I had figured would be a little out of shape and nerdy, like his brother. This man looked taut and still, a coil turned once too tightly. I had no doubt this was the object of worship by the kid in the trauma room. His brother had said he was a commando in the Delta Force, which was army, if I remembered correctly. I moved closer and paused. "Excuse me…"

He turned smoothly at the words, chocolate-brown eyes tight in an unsmiling face, as if he had been aware of my presence and waiting for me to comment. Without my asking, he pulled out ID and a business card and held them to me. I took them, glancing at the words *Symtech Security Systems* and *Eli Cordell* below that.

He shifted on the balls of his feet, angling his body to mine, his gaze direct. His words, though, were aimed at the men beside him. "My company designed the security system at several Bank of America branches and we're doing the new hospital opening off I-77. We design and install hardware and software for computer security systems and video surveillance." When no one replied, he added, "My brother and I take on small jobs when necessary, and when the money's right. Puckey's Guns and Things was a job between jobs as a favor to Wicked. That's it, guys. Check me out. Wicked's still at the bowling alley, I'm sure. I'm going nowhere," he stated to the cops.

"You're Dr. Lynch?" he asked me. His eyes were focused tight on me. The intensity of his gaze was almost unnerving. I didn't wear a name tag, but he knew who I was, anyway.

I nodded. "And you're the hero, commando, stupid idiot?" Oh, God. I hadn't meant to say that. Squeal like a little girl just once and it takes the sense out of you for a minute or two. But Cordell didn't seem to notice.

"Right." He flashed a half smile, mouth still tight, his eyes flicking to the room where his brother's stretcher had been. It was now empty, the kid was probably in X ray. "Right," he repeated. "I guess. But it wasn't supposed to go down that way. I forgot for a second that Levi doesn't have military training. I took the guy down without thinking about him coming in behind me." He shook his head, his expression grim. He had a day's beard on—a scruffy black brush that was oddly appealing. "And a second was all it took. Is he going to be all right?"

"Yes," I said. The cops wandered away to the far side of the nurses' desk, giving us some privacy. "You did a good job on the bandage and stopping the bleeding. We have a surgeon available on-site. He'll need an arterial repair to save the arm, though.''

"But he'll have use of it?"

"Barring complications, yes."

"You got a place I can shower and change? The cops want my shirt. Evidence."

Glancing down, I saw the white shirt was stuck to his skin with blood, matted black chest hair visible through the thin fabric. "There's a lot of that going around tonight," I said without explanation. "I'm sure the nurses can find you something." I handed the card and ID back to him but he took only the ID, leaving the business card in my hand.

"Keep it," he said, his eyes still tight on mine, the almost-smile still hovering on his mouth. "It has my cell number on it. You may need to contact me about Levi."

I blinked. Slipping past him, I tucked the card into my scrub shirt pocket. Had he just made a pass? While his brother was in danger? But when I glanced back, Eli was getting directions to the X-ray department and a place to clean up from Coreen. I was forgotten, as if we had never spoken.

Okay. No pass. But I suddenly understood the attraction that a dangerous male had for the female psyche. The man was definitely interesting, in a menacing sort of way, the way Mark had been when we first met—dangerous and predatory. Instantly I recalled the moment when I'd thought the bloody body on the stretcher was Mark. The memory zinged through me, an electrical charge of fear. I caught my breath, shook myself mentally and went back to work.

After X rays and a drug screen that showed three categories of illegal drugs, I was ready to try a closed reduction of Art Stinson's shoulder. The Versed had been administered and he was sleeping soundly, his mouth blowing little puffs of air as he breathed. Zack was monitoring the patient carefully. Art was pretty well medicated already and if he had made the bad mistake of choosing drugs that reacted negatively with the Versed, he might stop breathing totally. Then I'd have to keep him alive till the corrective med worked. Lucky me.

Art had been firmly secured to the backboard atop his stretcher. I pulled off my lab coat and stretched my own shoulders and spine as I studied the position of the patient's arm and his X rays. Nothing in the shoulder appeared broken on the films just dislocated. A conspicuous hump was situated between Art's collarbone and shoulder tip, deforming the shoulder. An anterior dislocation—painful, but easy to repair if your patient was drugged or agreeable to being worked on. Art Stinson was pleasantly unconscious.

EMS guys and two cops stood at the door. ''Okay, guys,'' I said, lowering the stretcher rail. ''Let's lift the backboard to the floor. Get him rolled slightly to his good side so I can get a firm grasp on his arm and we'll go for the closed reduction.'' Art murmured in his sleep, probably cussing, which seemed to be his lingo of the night.

The men positioned themselves around the stretcher and gripped the hand-holes in the red-painted board. On three, they heaved up and over, lowering him to the tile. Art was still dream-cussing, though he was too drugged to know what was going on in the room. And his eyes were swollen so badly from the beating, he couldn't have opened them even if he'd been conscious. His blood pressure and pulse were normal, so I knew the meds were working and he was out.

Standing, I put my foot in his armpit and grabbed his arm above and below the elbow. Steadily, I pulled the arm out and forward. Nothing happened. I took a deep breath and heaved. Art was trying to come around, his breath making little strangling sounds, and still nothing happened. The shoulder was going nowhere. I relaxed my grip and stepped back, walking around the stretcher, breathing deeply.

"Okay, one more time," I muttered. With one foot on his chest, I grabbed the arm again and hauled back with all my strength. My spine pinged with warning pain that I ignored. Art choked and screamed. Beneath my instep, the bone bumped back into place. Art shrieked with pain and relief intermingled, coming half-awake before dropping his head, asleep again. I stepped away and nodded for the men to put him back on the stretcher. "You can take your backboard, too. We're done here for now."

I looked at Art's X rays while pulling on my lab coat. He had a lot of swelling on his knee, but no obvious broken bones, and his facial bones seemed fine, which was a near miracle considering the swelling and bruising around his orbits. I made a mental note to get an orthopedist to check him out in the morning. He had called me a bitch, but doctors weren't allowed to react to verbal abuse from patients. We still had to see to their care. Oh yeah, lucky me.

The nurses' phone rang, the odd double ring that announced an outside call. A moment later Carla called out, "Dr. Lynch, it's for you. Line two."

I picked up the receiver, spotting a smear of blood on one cuff. Charlie Denbrow's blood. Rolling the sleeve so it wouldn't show, I said, "Lynch here."

"Got your message." When I said nothing, Mark prompted, "About the kid and his kidnapped sister?"

"Oh yeah. It's been a busy couple hours." I rolled the other cuff to match. The tough doctor look.

"I talked to the kid, Wayne Edward. This claim he's making, about his sister being kidnapped by the foster father. It didn't happen, okay?"

"Okay, but—"

"So back off."

I held the phone out and stared at the receiver a moment

as if the device had lost its mind. Or its manners. Mark was still speaking, so I put it back to my ear.

"—don't mean to be a typical cop but I'll handle it. I know what's going on with these girls and I don't need you to—"

I put the phone back on the hook. Hanging up on a call was something like number twenty-four on Miss DeeDee's list of things a real lady never did. I wasn't a real lady. "Men. Stupid, dumb, idiot men." Then I clarified to myself, "Man. Stupid, dumb, idiot man." And then I thought, did Mark say these *girls?* What girls?

7

MISSING GIRLS, BOTTOM BUNKS AND GATORS

An unfamiliar man in a starched lab coat stood at the desk when I left the break room. He was tall and lean, wiry-looking. "Dr. Lynch, here's your resident," Zack said as he wheeled a patient into the observation room.

I looked at the man blankly. "Todd Sinclair," the stranger said, his grip firm and his clear, blue eyes as direct as his handshake. "Second-year resident."

"Call him Cowboy, Dr. Lynch," Coreen said in passing, her slight form moving like a sailboarder between the bodies of law enforcement and EMS. "He's a real live cowboy, too. On a cattle ranch." She tossed the words over her shoulder.

"Whatever," Todd said in a slow West Texas accent, flashing blinding white teeth, a top incisor crooked over its neighbor. "I'm easy."

"Cowboy. Am I supposed to know about you?" My impression was that he was in his thirties at least, way too old to be a second year, with tanned skin, tousled, damp blond hair, and blue eyes wreathed in strong lines. He had an outdoor face, unlike most residents, who were tradition-ally pasty-white from working sun-to-sun. They usually lived in the dark, like vampires, or at least under artificial illumination.

"Wallace Chadwick hired me to pull a few nights. I'm at CMC, so he wanted me to work with you part of a night, to check me out before I fly solo."

Residents were doctors, in the sense that they had completed medical school and had their MDs, but they were taking what could be called post-post-graduate work in a hospital setting, usually with a doctor over them. It looked as if that doctor was me.

It was late in the residency year, so Cowboy would either spend his shift asking questions to verify his knowledge and confirm his method of treatment—typical second-year resident technique—or would spend his time challenging me about standard treatments, practices and techniques, trying to catch me up on something I didn't know, and further his own expertise at the same time—third-year resident methodology. Residency was supposed to be half competition, half training. I liked competition and the responsibility of teaching, but it would have been nice to know it was coming.

"Dawkins, this is unit 351. Dawkins, unit 351. Trauma Pediatric Code," the paramedic said. It couldn't be too bad. Her voice sounded almost calm. "Trauma Pediatric Code."

"At this hour?" Coreen asked. "You're just bringing us all kinds of fun tonight, Dr. Lynch."

"This is my fault?" I asked, picking up the mike.

"Must be. Since I started working here, every night with you is busy. Making me earn my sign-on money."

"Take the call?" I asked Cowboy, holding out the old-fashioned microphone.

"Sure." He walked over, gait as lanky as his frame, and sat, pulling out a PalmPilot for notes as he took the mike. "This is Dr. Sinclair. Go ahead."

I was impressed. My PalmPilot was in my pocket but I

never used it. Instead, when I needed to make patient notes, I grabbed a stray Bic pen and one of the scraps of computer paper the nurses left lying around. Cowboy might look like he'd just stepped off the ranch, but he was no Luddite. I fingered my PalmPilot. Were the batteries still any good?

"Dawkins, we are in transport with a seventeen-year-old white male, compound fracture of left femur, victim of hit and run, van-versus-bicycle. Bleeding controlled, contusions and lacerations present. No other visible deformity." The EMS guy gave normal vital signs for physiological and neuromuscular tests, ending with, "Patient is in full spinal protocol, with two large bore IVs, and two liters of O2 via nasal cannula."

"Keep fluid at KVO," Cowboy said. I approved. The kid wasn't bleeding, his blood pressure was normal and there might be a head injury. No need to give fluids wide open. "ETA?"

"Fifteen minutes. Incident took place down near the Lancaster Line."

Cowboy looked at me. "Room upon arrival?"

"Trauma one."

He pressed the Transmit switch. "Trauma one upon arrival."

"Dawkins 414 clear," I instructed.

Cowboy repeated the words and set down the mike.

"I appreciate that," Coreen said, sticking her head out of the drug room where she was counting pills. "Most doctors won't even pick up that thing."

"I was standing right by it. I even know how to answer phones," Cowboy said.

"Good doctor. Smart doctor," she said, in the same tone she might have used cooing to a pet dog. "You take after Dr. Lynch, then."

Cowboy glanced at me. "Orders?" I asked.

"Ortho on-site?" he responded.

"Not in this little one-horse town."

"Get an orthopedic surgeon on the phone and make sure we have two units of O neg blood ready to transfuse on admission if needed," he said to Coreen. "We have a compound fractured femur on the way."

"Will do. The OR crew on call is going to love us tonight," she said.

"The surgeons, too," I said. "But most of them are young enough not to need sleep. Hope you don't mind, but I'm going to eat while you work," I said.

"Help yourself. I can depend on the RNs if I need anything?" It was a polite way of asking if the crew tonight was any good.

"Implicitly."

Dinner in the foam container looked particularly unappetizing—cold turkey and congealed gravy with a scoop of dressing and grease-slimed, overcooked green beans—so I grabbed an egg-salad sandwich from a vending machine. It was actually fresh and not six weeks old and stinky. It went down good with a Coke and a package of raspberry flavored, cream-filled cake fingers from another machine—my favorite food groups, caffeine, simple carbs, sugars and fats. I opened them all and ate in the break room, an edible heart attack and diabetes in plastic wrap.

The ambulance was late and I finished my meal uninterrupted, then made a quick trip to the call room and freshened up. I reached the E.R. just as the teenager was brought in, moaning and grunting in pain. Standing back, I nodded to Cowboy to take over. It was hard not diving in, but my enjoyment tonight would have to take a back seat to the resident doing his job.

I watched as the EMS crew brought the patient in and transferred him to an emergency stretcher. The teen was shocky, and I watched with approval as Cowboy checked the IV lines himself and turned the fluid up a bit. Still not

wide open, in case of a head injury, but enough to coun-
teract the shock.

"Melanie. You gotta help Melanie," the teen was mumbling. Coreen reassured him that he was fine. The patient
windmilled his arms in panic and the EMS crew finally
restrained the patient's arms, so he couldn't fight. The
mumbling slowed and he looked slightly dazed. "Melanie?"

Cowboy gave orders for appropriate blood work and
started assessing the patient, searching for abnormalities in
skeletal and neuromuscular structure, while nurses took
care of stripping the teen. The blood-soaked jeans had been
cut half away at the scene and the surgical scissors made
quick work of the denim remnants. That changed when the
blades started on the tee.

"Oh, man, no. Not the shirt." The kid came fully awake
as the scissors snipped into the jersey. "I'm not hurt in my
chest," he said. "Not the—stop. *Stop!* Not the shirt. Oh
man. Why you got to cut off my shirt? This thing is a
classic. Stop!" No one listened. I heard Zack telling him
there was no way to get the shirt off because of the IVs
and spinal protocol. He was sorry. Placating. But the
T-shirt was a total loss. "You should be helping find Melanie. Leave me alone." Tears fell from the outer corners
of the patient's eyes.

"What's your name?" Coreen asked.

"Ollie Miller. Oliver Cromwell Miller, but I go by Ollie."

"How old are you, Ollie?"

"You already asked me that. The van didn't hit my head,
just my leg. When are the cops gonna get here?" He tried
to raise his head against the restraints and sandbags. "I saw
the guy. He took Melanie."

I looked up quickly and Cowboy paused in his assessment. What was this?

''They chased us down the road, rammed me, and one of them took her. Threw her in the back of the van. I couldn't get up to stop them. But I got a real good look at one of them. SOBs got away in a dark green utility van. Took Melanie with them.'' Someone jarred his leg and the patient gagged, gurgling with pain.

When his discomfort subsided a bit, I moved toward the head of the stretcher where he could see me. ''Have the cops talked to you at all?''

His eyes rolled toward me, pupils constricted in the bright lights. ''Yeah,'' he said. ''Right after they got there. Before the ambulance drove up. SOB was crazy. He thought I was some guy named Vance. And he took her. I don't think the cops believed me at first, but her bike was right there. Ahh!'' he yelped, and the cussing began.

I glanced around for a police presence. The hallway in front of the room was empty. An uncertain disquiet settled on me. This was bad. A kidnapping and no cops?

And then I remembered Mark's words from his insulting phone call. ''I know what's going on with these girls....'' A cold chill settled on my flesh. What did Mark know? What was going on? What girls? After hanging up on him, I couldn't exactly call back and demand an answer. Miss DeeDee would have said I reaped what I sowed for not practicing the proper social niceties. Of course, Miss DeeDee thought murder was appropriate, as long as one was polite about it.

After seven minutes and twenty seconds, Cowboy had determined that the only obvious injuries were numerous contusions and the patient's femur, hidden beneath a heavy, bloody dressing. Blood had been drawn, and urine and stool had been tested for blood and found negative.

The second-year resident was fast, which was good, but he kept asking for tests and procedures that Dawkins didn't offer, and showed his displeasure when he was told no, which was bad. He wanted a FAST sonogram done, and was irritated when he couldn't get one. A FAST was a Focused Abdominal Sonography for Trauma test. It bounced ultrasound waves into the patient's abdominal cavity and showed bleeding, air or anything that shouldn't be there. It was a screening test used only in three hospitals in the Carolinas: Duke, Carolina's Medical in Charlotte, Richland Memorial in Columbia, S.C. Dawkins was regional, small and not exactly on the cutting edge of medical treatments and practices, not for machines that cost tens of thousands of dollars.

But the teenager's vital signs were stable, temp normal, the X-ray tech was ready, and the orthopod was on the way in. Quick work. I was impressed with Cowboy Sinclair.

I stepped out as the X-ray films were taken. Two uniformed cops I vaguely recognized met me. About time.

"When will you let us talk to Ollie?" the shorter cop asked.

"He'll have to go to surgery, but we'll get you in as soon as possible."

The cops exchanged a look. Frustration. Anger. Adrenaline overload. Too much testosterone. "We sure as heck can't wait until after surgery. We need to talk to him first. His girlfriend was kidnapped by the hit-and-run. We got a description of the guy and the van circulating in the county, but we need more. He might remember the license plate by now or something they said that would allow us to ID them."

"Lots of victims remember stuff after the event," the other cop said. "We got an investigator on the way, but if our witness is going to surgery, we got to talk to him before he's sedated. Come on, Doc. Give us a break."

I knew they were right. Every minute that passed after a kidnapping decreased the likelihood that the victim would be found before he or she was killed. "I'll see you get to him as soon as the X rays are done."

"Thanks, Doc," they both said.

I motioned to Cowboy, who was standing by Ollie. When I got his attention, I pointed to the cops and then to his patient. Cowboy nodded. A minute later, he waved the cops in. I was uneasy about the whole situation, my fingertips tingling in a warning I didn't understand. Just in case I needed them later, I wrote the officers' names into my PalmPilot. And I was pleasantly surprised to find the batteries were still good.

The night didn't get any better, the slow shift I had hoped for metamorphosing into a forty-five patient tour-de-trauma. The five hour nap I'd had after being made assistant coroner was nowhere near enough to prepare me for the nonstop hours.

Two hours after Ollie went to surgery, I was closing up a laceration on an eight-year-old when I heard a noise at the door. Pausing with the ethilon gripped in my gloved hands, I looked up.

Eli Cordell was watching from the hallway, his trim form motionless—not the stillness of an ordinary human being with life beating in his flesh, but utterly, wholly still. Deceptively quiescent, the way an alligator rests mute and stationary just before it rips the belly out of a young deer.

I looked back at my patient and continued the automatic motions of my hands. But I was still seeing Eli against the doorway, an image burned into my eyes. He was leaning one shoulder against the wall, his arms hanging, clean cuffs folded back to expose several inches of tanned forearms covered in straight black hair. One thumb hooked in the waist of black jeans, fingers dropped across the buttons. He wore black leather lace-ups, like the combat-style boots cops wore, feet crossed at the ankle, one knee bent.

He was watching me, his eyes intense, his lips turned up at the corners with that hint of amusement I wasn't sure he really felt. Wide shouldered, slim waisted. Not an ounce of fat on him, as if he trained hard every day. There were strands of white threaded through his dark hair, putting him in his late thirties.

I finished up, smiled at the half pajama-clad, half street-clothed mother and patted the child as I pulled off the sterile drapes. "She'll be fine. You might want to put her on the bottom bunk, though. Sometimes kids go through phases of restless sleep like this, and a short fall is preferable to a long one. Next time it might mean something worse than a few stitches to the scalp."

"We'll do that, Doctor. Thank you. Kimber, you tell the nice doctor thank-you," her bloodied mother said.

Kimber stuck out her bottom lip and scowled through disheveled blond hair, which made me laugh, and I patted her thigh again. "You'll be fine, Kimber. And you'll grow out of such restless sleep in a year or so."

"I don't *like* the bottom bunk," she stated. "I can't sleep in it."

"A mattress on the floor, then," I suggested. When the scowl became a glower, I shrugged and ducked out of the conversation. Besides my breakup with my former fiancé, John Micheaux, there was a second reason I had no children. There were times I had no idea what to say to them.

I pulled off my blood-smeared gloves, tossed them and washed up at the sink. I was inches from the unmoving man dressed in black and I found myself uncomfortably aware of him. "Mr. Cordell. How's your brother?" I asked, not making eye contact while I shut off the water and pulled towels to pat my hands dry.

"He'll be fine. He just came out of surgery," Eli said, his voice a soft burr of sound. "To quote the doctor, his hand is nice and pink and he has a pulse. He didn't lose a lot of blood, so he should be able to go home day after tomorrow or the next day. He'll have to be careful while it heals, though, and the surgeon mentioned that I'd need to learn how to wrap the arm to give it support while the artery mends.''

It sounded like a succinct course of treatment, and I agreed as I twisted open a jar of Bag Balm, the heavy, greasy cream created for chapped cow udders that was kept in the E.R. in winter for human use. Finally, I looked up at Eli Cordell. His eyes were black and piercing, focused entirely on me. As if I were the only being in his entire world. My breathing did something weird deep inside me in that moment and I looked away, thinking of the deer and the alligator. I remembered the Bag Balm jar in my hand and smeared a glop on. ''That's good. And it's all because of you. You did a good job at the scene.'' My voice was calm and even, and didn't reveal that my heart was racing. I glanced back at him, like that deer in the instant it spotted the gator.

He nodded, a subtle incline of his head. My stomach did a slow somersault, and the thought of Mark washed through me. Mark, who had slept with Skye. Mark, who wasn't really part of my life anymore… I realized I was staring again and warmth instantly flooded my face. I wasn't sure, but I might be blushing.

I inclined my head in return, not certain what I was saying, but knowing I was saying something with the motion. Fortunately, the EMS radio blared to life. I was saved by the bell. Sort of. It was one minute to four in the morning.

8

GOURMANDS, BREAST MILK AND FAVORITE DISHES

Satisfied that everything was under control and that EMS had stabilized the patient they were bringing in, I pulled the two other patient charts and looked at the status of each. But something was nagging at me, keeping my attention divided. Something about Ollie, but I couldn't figure out what.

Over the course of the next hour, Cowboy and I took care of an acute belly pain, turning her over to a surgeon for a probable ruptured appendix. Sent home a head trauma with a negative CT scan and no symptoms of brain injury. The green-haired, multiple-pierced kid had banged his head falling from a skateboard in the middle of the night. His mama needed a sedative, maybe a whole medicine chest of them, to deal with the teen, who was rebelling, big-time. They needed serious family counseling and a whole new method of communication, but that was beyond my job description as an E.R. doc. I wondered how my friend Marisa would deal with her own children when they hit their teenaged years. Her decreased verbal communication skills had to mean trouble in the distant future.

As the pierced teen went out the air-lock doors to the parking lot, it hit me what was bothering me. It was something Ollie had said. Something about Vance. I had heard that name recently. Vance who? My fingertips were still tingling, as they did when something important was hanging there inside my head, but I was so tired I couldn't catch it. I'd get it eventually, but I was worried that I needed it now, not later.

We worked steadily for another hour, directing the necessary codes, overseeing the treatment of each and every patient. Cowboy Sinclair worked up a patient, then brought his course of diagnostic testing and treatments to me for approval. The method allowed me to learn both his level of diagnostic skills and his personality.

The doctor was methodical, smiled often and spoke on a level tailored for his patients. He asked questions and listened to the answers, then made sure he was clear in his comments before he left a patient's room. Cowboy was a great communicator, but he needed to speed up a notch or two if he intended to work at a high-volume, fast-paced medical center. How he could do that and still not compromise his interaction with the patients, I didn't know. After his residency, he might be best suited to a small E.R. like Dawkins, where he could have the luxury of a slower tempo.

I decided I liked Cowboy. He was easy and relaxed, and I heard him cracking jokes with the nurses, telling them a story about his grandmother, a full blooded Apache. Cowboy I could take home to Miss Essie. He was housebroke, as Miss Essie had once said about the rare approved date brought home by Marisa back in her high school or college days. Being housebroken was an enormous compliment. I wasn't always sure *I* was considered housebroken, but I was family, which counted for far more.

At 5:37 a.m. the phone rang and it was for me.

"Dr. Lynch here."

"Rhea-Rhea!" a cheerful voice said.

"Risa!" I checked my watch again in surprise and then understood. "Which twin was hungry this time?"

"Rheaburn," she said softly. "He's always hungry."

I could hear suckling in the background. "He takes after your father, the gourmand."

Risa chuckled, but when she spoke, her tone was loving. "Breast milk is still his favorite dish. We miss you."

"I miss ya'll, too. I'll be there tomorrow if at all possible. I hear the kids are crawling. You got a gate up at the head of the stairs?"

"Yes." She paused and I knew she was trying to say something that she had no words for, not since her injury. "Tomorrow? Promise," she said instead.

"I'll be there. I saw Eddie today. He's this grown-up man now." I told her all about Eddie and how he had helped at a police scene. Marisa had completed three years of medical school and could follow everything that had happened. And she was clearly proud of her stepson. When I hung up, I was smiling. Silly how a two-minute phone call could lighten my entire day.

At 6:30 a.m., the EMS radio blared again, alerting all to the incoming patient. Cowboy took the call. This time, however, we were prepared, the police scanner already warning us of the problem in the DorCity limits. "We got a fourteen-year-old white male," the EMS said. "Bus-versus-pedestrian. Nonresponsive at the scene, tubed and IV. Pupillary at two to none. Hematoma on left temple at 10 centimeters. Patient was posturing at the scene, reflexes decreased on both sides, but left side showing measurable and increasing improvement at scene and in transit."

The kid had been smacked by a bus; that alone was scary, and I considered flying him out from the scene. The hematoma and almost nonexistent pupillary response, along with the posturing at the scene, suggested a concussion and possibly brain damage. Posturing meant his body was in spasm, turning in on itself, but the improvement was an indication for the good. The EMS guy continued shouting, the siren wailing behind his voice. Cowboy was taking fast notes on his PalmPilot.

"Deformity of left lower arm, contusions at left hip and thigh. BP is 100 over 59, pulse 74. Transporting with full spinal protocol," the EMT said.

Deciding we could keep this one, I said, "Keep fluid at KVO," requesting the lowest rate of IV flow. "ETA?"

Cowboy repeated my comment and question.

"Twelve minutes."

"Trauma room on arrival," Cowboy said. "Dawkins 414 clear."

I pointed at Zack. "Phone the pediatric specialist on call and tell him we have a Trauma Peds Code coming in twelve minutes. Get him in here stat." Without waiting to see him follow my order, I spotted Coreen. "Call CT in and tell them they have a Peds trauma head scan coming in less than thirty. Nonresponsive. Hematoma on left temple."

Coreen nodded, pecking at the computer keyboard as she dialed eight digits. Multitasking like a son of a gun. I was impressed.

The radio blared again. "Unit 478 to Dawkins County, Trauma Code. Trauma Code," and I heard Zack pick it up.

"Dawkins here. Go ahead, unit 478."

"We got a forty-nine-year-old Hispanic male, no English, conscious and appears to be alert, but not enough Spanish to determine person, place or time," the paramedic shouted. "Suffered a twenty-plus-foot fall onto concrete and a couple concrete blocks. Compound fracture of the right humerus with massive bleeding, ineffective pressure applied at the scene by bystanders, now controlled. Flail chest, possible pelvic injuries, bloody urine. Patient was wearing a helmet and no obvious head injuries noted. Pupils equal and reactive."

"Small favors, that," I murmured.

"Obvious deformity to right lower leg and left knee. BP is 183 over 94, respirations 24 and shallow, pulse is 115 with regular sinus showing on monitor. Two IVs via large bore needles at right AC and hand."

"Breath sounds?" Cowboy asked.

"Decreased over flail ribs. Small amount of crepitus noted on right side," the EMT shouted, as if the mike was suddenly too far from his mouth. "Permission to call in Medic for flight directly to CMC?"

Cowboy looked at me, uncertain. I took the mike and the chair he vacated. "This is Dr. Lynch. Approve you call Medic flight to trauma center. Call us if you need anything meantime. Dawkins 414 clear."

I looked up at Cowboy. "It's better for the patient if he can get directly to a trauma center. We could handle that level of injury, but he'd need to be flown out anyway once we got him stable. May as well decrease the time to the trauma center by an hour or so."

Cowboy nodded, but I could see he was disappointed. Adrenaline junkie, just like all E.R. docs. Addicted to excitement.

The outer doors blew open and four EMS guys shoved a stretcher into the trauma room. The boy lay flaccid on the stretcher, one EMT pumping an ambu bag, handing it over to the respiratory tech as the wheels were locked in place. I took the pupillary and airway position at the head of the bed. Two E.R. doctors, three nurses, the X-ray tech and the pulmonologist who was making rounds when Coreen found him on the ICU, all converged at the EMS gurney and, on a count of three, we lifted the boy's backboard to the E.R. stretcher. It was 6:45 a.m., a great time for an injury of this sort—twice as many hands on-site to evaluate and assist. But man, it had been an awful night. Wallace and Dr. Haynes, the pediatric specialist, joined us. Wallace looked fresh and happy to be on the job, not as if he'd been in the OR all night. I was exhausted and hungry but still had this emergency to attend to.

Before I blocked them out, I glanced at the rest of the trauma team. Cowboy was at the circulation and bleeding position near the kid's waist, while an orthopedic surgeon searched for skeletal deformities and tested reflexes on both arms and legs. Nurses were starting new IVs and cutting off the rest of his clothes. Haynes stood at the stretcher's foot, watching.

The patient's airway was secure, the ET tube taped in place. Earpieces of my stethoscope in position, I listened to the patient's chest as the respiratory tech pumped the blue ambu, breathing for him twelve times a minute. He had a strong, regular heartbeat, equal breath sounds on left and right, no rubbing, no odd little clicks, meaning the endotrachial tube appeared to be well-placed, not lodged in the esophagus, and the boy's respiratory system was functioning, though not under his own power. His heart sounds were nonremarkable. Around me, EMS personnel and nurses exchanged equipment, the EMS stuff for the hospital stuff.

Using my Maglite, I checked the kid's pupillary response. His pupils were sluggish on the right, unresponsive on the left. I didn't like that at all. I checked again. No change. I called out my findings to Coreen, who was taking notes. "Patient is posturing both sides, hyperreflexive on the right," Haynes said.

"Type and cross two, coag workup, and get me two new IVs," I said, ordering blood cross-matched and the patient's coagulation system checked for abnormalities. "Blood gases, cath a urine, and CBC."

A nurse was already cleaning the patient's penis with Betadine for a catheter. The urine was clear and yellow as she pulled a small amount for a urinalysis and released it into a tube for transport to the lab. As she poured, she let a few drops land on a long, narrow plastic stick with reagent pads on it. The pads changed color to denote specific results in human urine. Beside her, a lab tech was drawing blood and labeling the tubes.

Cowboy called, "AC and carpal pulses nonremarkable." He and Haynes switched places. "Femoral, popliteal and plantar pulses nonremarkable on left. Concur with hyperreflexive on right."

"One hundred ten over 70, pulse steady at 85. Rhythm strip run and…normal sinus—O2 saturation is ninety-eight on four liters of oxygen. Rectal temp 99," someone said.

"Urine blood negative," the nurse said. "No protein."

Coreen nodded again, taking everything down for later review. No one could be expected to remember everything in an emergency, so one person was always responsible for taking detailed notes of what was done to the patient and when and why. It usually wasn't a nurse—they were needed for other things—but the job was getting done and I approved.

The patient suddenly went into spasm and reached up to his face, fighting the ET tube. He was coming to and in a state of panic.

"Versed and Norcuron," I ordered. I needed to get him paralyzed so we could work. It was 6:59 a.m., fourteen minutes since arrival. Blood gas and CBC results were put in my hand. Nothing unexpected there. Gases were normal, blood was in normal range.

"Now this is when you need a FAST," Cowboy said as the nurses injected the two drugs through the IVs, to temporarily paralyze the patient. No one responded. We knew it, but most hospitals had to make equipment decisions based on money at hand and yearly budgets, and another ultrasound wasn't high on the list this year.

"Ready for X rays?" I asked.

"Everybody not in an apron out," the X-ray tech called as she swung an X-ray arm over the patient. "Head, C-spine and lumbar, pelvis, both legs and arms?"

"Go for it," I said, agreeing to order what amounted to a full body X ray.

While the X rays whirred, I stepped out into the hall. Wallace followed. "Sinclair seems competent. What do you think?"

"He's good. Woo him for here. He'll need a slow-paced environment."

"That was slow?" Wallace asked in amazement.

I didn't usually mention the speed of bigger, better equipped hospitals, especially to the long-time physicians on staff, but I made an exception, glancing at my watch. "It's been over fifteen minutes. In a trauma center, all this would have been done in half the time. And he'd have had a FAST. Now he'll need a belly CT to rule out something that could have been done in five minutes for less than a third of the cost."

Wallace sighed.

I turned to the desk and Ashlee standing there. "We got a patient rep here?"

"What do you need?" she asked.

"Personal effects need to be bagged, I need to know if CT is ready for him, and I need to know about family."

"I can bag his stuff, and the family is outside doing paperwork. CT is ready and waiting."

"Thanks. Get the family for me?"

"Right away, Dr. Rhea."

I stepped back into the trauma room and did a quick evaluation. Twenty minutes since the patient came in. He was stable. "Where are we?" I said.

"X rays done. Five to ten minutes on developing," the X-ray tech said.

"Five hundred milliliters of saline in, stool is still negative for blood, rectal temp is 99.2," said one voice.

Another took up instantly. "We have 117 over 53, with pulse 132 and O2 sat of 100."

A third voice said, "Sixteen French OG tube is down, stomach contents brown and normal."

"Decrease the oxygen," I said. Turning to the pulmonologist and Dr. Haynes, I murmured, "Looks like you came in for nothing." They shrugged and left together.

Twenty-seven minutes after the bus accident victim arrived, I scanned all the boy's X-ray films and pronounced them negative—even his skull and the deformity noted to the patient's leg at the scene. No broken bones after being whapped by a bus. Amazing. But his reflexes and pupils were still not responding normally. I feared the neurological changes might not be temporary, but could reflect more permanent brain damage. I should have flown this one out to a neurotrauma center, even though he'd had improvement at the scene.

"CT's here," Ashlee said.

"Take him down," I said. Coreen kicked the brake loose on the stretcher as Zack tossed a blanket over the patient's nude body. I looked around and spotted Ashlee with a group of women, a bag of personal effects in her hand. She nodded me over.

"This is Dr. Lynch. She's the best we have."

I was?

"Doc, this is Kevin's mother and two sisters."

I smiled, nodded to each and gave them the news, the good first, then the bad. "Kevin shows no broken bones. His heart and lungs seem to be fine. However, he may have a concussion and possibly a hematoma on his brain where his head hit the bus or the street. Did either of you see the accident?"

"No. No one did. We heard the tires screech and a thump

and we came running,'' the youngest said. "Kevin was on the ground by then, up under the bumper.''

"Not under the tires?'' I hadn't noted any tire tread marks on him.

"No, ma'am. The tires didn't hit him, just the bumper.''

"Do you know what I mean when I say a hematoma on his brain?''

"That's like a bruise, but worse,'' the older woman said. "I watch *ER*. Are you saying my baby's got brain damage?'' Tears gathered suddenly in the outer corners of her eyes.

"I know this is scary.'' I took her hand in mine. She gripped hard, steady tremors running through her fingers. "Yes, it's possible that he may have brain damage. He was fighting, though, and that's a good sign. In fact, he was fighting so hard we had to give him a drug to temporarily paralyze him so we could keep him safe.''

The woman sucked in a deep breath.

"They do that, Mama. Don't worry. They might even have to give him something to make him unconscious to keep his brain from swelling. That's normal, right?'' she asked me.

I smiled. "Right. Are you a nurse?''

"I took CNA training in high school. Then all the local hospitals stopped using certified nursing assistants. I'm working in a nursing home and going to school now to get my RN.''

Everyone wanted to be a nurse. The money was good, but the hours could be brutal on a family-oriented person. "Good. You can help keep your mama calm and ask the right questions. I'm going to ask Ashlee to take you to the CT department now so you can be near Kevin. Then we'll decide what to do later. If he has an injury, he'll be flown to a trauma center where a pediatric neurology specialist or neurosurgeon will take over. Good luck.''

Kevin's mom nodded and turned away.

9

A GOOD BELLY SCRATCH COULD HEAL THE WORLD

It was still dawn as I left the E.R., shoulders aching, feet throbbing and my brain mired, as if stuck in sticky red mud. My car was parked under a security light, the black paint gleaming. A form was leaning against the passenger door, booted feet crossed at the ankle, arms crossed over his chest, his head down, leather jacket unzipped. I recognized Eli Cordell and slowed my pace. Stopped. I never asked the hospital security guard to see me safely to my car. Maybe that was a mistake.

Eli raised his head and met my eyes in the dark. My stomach did a weird slow-motion roll-over thing and I wasn't sure what I was feeling. It could be a symptom of viral onset, but I didn't think so. I had a feeling it was closer to a flight or fight reaction. He stood, moving with a grace that was all muscle and training, tucking both thumbs in his waistband. He was like a cat, watching me. Waiting.

When he realized I wasn't coming closer, he said, "Have breakfast with me."

"Why?"

"Because you want to," he said without a smile.

"Bite me." I hadn't planned the words. Wouldn't have

said them if I had taken time to think. I have a big mouth sometimes.

He laughed, his eyes deliberately misinterpreting my comment. "I was thinking more along the line of nutritious breakfast foods—you know, filled with vitamins and minerals and protein. You haven't eaten anything since that revolting egg sandwich. You can't tell me you're not hungry."

Something crawled along my skin at his words. He had been watching me? "Did you stick a hidden camera in my department?"

"I know how to find out things. And I have talent for not being noticed when I don't want to be. It's what I'm best at."

"And that's supposed to make me feel what?" I wasn't sure if he was teasing. Was he a stalker, waiting to slit my throat over sausages and grits? Had he been watching me while I worked? This was creepy. Had I scratched myself at an inopportune moment?

"Don't worry, I wasn't stalking. I didn't watch you eat the whole thing, only the last little bit. You're cute when you eat egg and Twinkies together." He almost smiled a real smile. "Have breakfast with me. I need to talk about Levi and the proper level of rehab care. I need a good nurse or physical therapist recommendation, because he's going to fight rehab tooth and nail. Besides, you know you're hungry."

He was right. I was. And I was startled at the desire I felt to agree, one that had little to do with Levi's rehab needs or even my own nutritional insufficiency. This man reminded me of Mark when I'd first met him. A man with a dangerous aura, before I discovered the teddy bear beneath. And before I discovered Mark's susceptibility to blondes with pert breasts.

I didn't want another Mark. I didn't want to be hurt again. "Another time," I said.

"I make you nervous." His voice had dropped, a burr of sound.

"Yes. You do." I didn't mention that my physical reaction to him was just a bit unnerving, but somehow I was afraid he already knew that.

The amusement was back on his face, in his voice. "Interesting." He moved away from my car, into the shadows of the physicians' parking lot. "Nervous could be a good thing. Keeps you alert. I'll ask again."

And he was gone. It was only after I was in my little car that I remembered the silence as he moved into the darkness. His booted feet had made no sound. Downright eerie.

The sun cleared the clouds over my shoulder as I drove home, encountering locals as they converged toward schools and jobs in Charlotte and Columbia. I enjoyed the road beneath the tires, the Z3 zipping around larger, slower vehicles with ease, the wind noise hollow against the rag-top, barely heard beneath the Christmas oldies I was listening to at full volume. The mellow voice of Elvis came over the speakers, singing "Blue Christmas," reminding me that I would be alone again this holiday season. What a depressing thought. But when the King started in on the line, "You'll be doing all right," I remembered what had been nagging at me all night.

Vance. Ollie said the hit-and-run driver had called him Vance. When Wayne Edward Geter's sister had called the house, she had said something like, "I'm staying with Deacon. I don't love Vance. I love Deacon."

Okay, it would be a huge coincidence. Unless someone named Deacon, or someone who was a deacon, was taking young girls. Unless there were a lot of girls missing. I knew the media, though. Something like that couldn't be kept quiet for long. So there wasn't someone named Deacon who was taking young girls and calling strangers Vance. No way. But Mark had told me to butt out, using the tone that said he had a case going and I was in the way.

My fingertips were itching. I rubbed them over the leather steering wheel cover, the grain smooth under my hands. It had been a long time since my fingers itched, and this made two—three?—times in a little over one day. They itched when there was trouble brewing or when I was on the brink of perceiving something important. I turned down the radio.

Digging in my bag one-handed, I found my cell phone and punched speed-dial for Mark's cell number. I hadn't dialed it in months. It felt weird hitting the keys. Weirder still when Mark snarled into the phone, "What?"

"No *Yeeeellow?*" I asked. Mark used to answer the phone "Yeeeellow." Now it was, "What?" When he said nothing, I added, "It's Rhea."

I could hear the faint intake of breath. Surprise. Maybe pleasure? "Rhea?"

"Yeah. Got a minute?"

"Sure." He sounded cautious. I didn't blame him. After all, I had hung up on him.

"You remember the shooting when you got me sworn in as assistant coroner?"

"I didn't swear in or at anybody." He sounded defensive and grumpy and maybe a little sleepy.

"Okay, but it was your idea, don't deny it."

Mark sighed. "Rhea. What do you want to know?"

I zipped past a cement truck, between two vans, and slipped in behind an SUV going twenty-six miles per hour as we approached a school. "Wayne Edward Geter said his sister had called the house after she disappeared. She said something about, 'I'm staying with Deacon. I don't love Vance. I love Deacon.'"

"What about it?" The tone was guarded, but something

had Mark's attention, and he wasn't telling me to mind my own business.

"This is what I would have told you last night, if you hadn't been so irritating and copishy. I heard him talking to a plainclothes policewoman, and a plainclothes guy was listening in. They both looked like FBI, which I thought was weird. Anyway, last night I had a hit-and-run victim. He said a guy in a van had rammed him on purpose and then kidnapped his girlfriend. And the kidnapper called the boyfriend Vance. It's probably on the news."

"Yeah?" Mark's interest was sharper, keener. And he didn't want me to know.

I wondered why. "Yeah."

After a short silence he said, "I got tied up last night and haven't heard a report. So who was the patient?"

"So it is important!" I said, pulling onto the bypass to avoid school traffic.

"It could be. So who was it?"

"Can't tell you."

"Rhea." He sounded as if he might cuss. And Mark seldom said a foul word in front of a woman. Mark had indeed been a Beau in a world of Bubbas, or at least he had been until Skye got her claws into him. I wasn't likely to forget Skye.

"I can't. Patient confidentiality. But you can call the cops who came to the hospital. Hang on." I dropped the phone in my lap and zoomed back into the middle lane. Again driving one-handed, I felt around in the darkness of my canvas bag until I found the trusty PalmPilot. Hitting a few keys, I found the cops' names. Jeff Rozicki and Frank Choquay. Not Southern names, though the cops had Southern accents.

I picked up the phone and gave Mark both names. "You know 'em?"

"I know 'em, but they're probably off shift by now." He made that sound as if it was my fault.

"I don't know how to get them, but I guess you could call dispatch."

"Gee. What a good idea. Even though I'm a cop, I'd have never thought about that possibility."

Heat shot through me at his tone. "You know, since you impregnated your co-worker, you have been acting like an ass." I thumbed off the phone and dropped it into the bag. Miss DeeDee's rules broken twice. I was in danger of becoming poor white trash. "Men." Sometimes having a quick retort was inordinately satisfying. And being able to hang up on him again made it even better.

A few minutes later, I picked up the phone and dialed the dispatch operator at the Dawkins Law Enforcement Center. While I was turning into my driveway, I left a voice mail message for Officer Choquay.

"This is Dr. Lynch. We talked last night when the kidnap victim's boyfriend was brought into the E.R. I just thought of something that might help. Would you or Rozicki give me a call at my cell number?" After I recited the number, I hung up, popped the car in first, set the handbrake and crawled out into the balmy morning.

The dogs met me at the door, both yawning sleepily and offering to lick all the icky hospital smells off me. I made them settle for licking my chin, and completed the ritual with a belly scratch. For the dogs, not me—though I sometimes thought a good belly scratch could heal the world. I could see UN officials sitting around the concentric rings in Geneva giving each other a communal belly scratching. It would be hard to declare war against someone who had scratched your tummy.

I answered my cell before turning the key in my lock. "Good morning. Belly scratching are us."

"Uhhh, I'm trying to reach Dr. Lynch?"

"Officer Choquay. Sorry. This is me. Just greeting my dogs."

"Oh. I got six labs and two bird dogs myself. Whatchyou got?" As I entered my house, we talked for several minutes about the merits of dog breed specialization versus mutt smarts. Finally Choquay said, "So, what can I do for you, Doctor?"

"I'm just curious. Are there statistics on the number of runaway girls from each county who don't come home on their own and remain missing, and if so, have the numbers increased recently?"

"Yeah, the statistics are correlated each month, but not by my department." Something in his tone alerted me. He wasn't telling me something. But then, there was nothing to hide. No reason why he shouldn't tell me any particular thing. Maybe I was just tired. It had been a long night. I shrugged the thought away and I told the officer about the coincidence of the name Vance.

Choquay did a very strange thing. He stuttered an entire line. "Well, I don't know what…I don't know what…" He paused. More formally, he said, "I'll turn your concerns over to the detective in charge of the case. Thank you, Dr. Lynch. Anything else?"

I was silent for a long moment, standing in the dim morning light of my kitchen. Finally, I asked, "They didn't get her back, did they?"

"No, ma'am. They didn't. But we're still looking."

"Good luck," I said, and hit the key to end the call. *Good luck.* Such a pathetic line.

But something was going on. Something about missing girls.

10

THEM THROBBIN' MAN-THINGS AND HUGE BREASTS

Dawn had glared with a false promise of heat, but the temperature was dropping. Typical December. Tomorrow it could be back into the seventies or it could be freezing. Warring mountain and coastal trade winds and shifting pressure systems made weather prediction tricky in South Carolina.

The dogs went nuts, running back and forth through the small bungalow, nails clicking and scratching on the hardwood floors, as I shrugged into cold weather running gear. Lycra tights under sweatpants; running bra; T-shirt; sweatshirt; windbreaker; insulated gloves, socks and running shoes; water bottle and cell phone—all the accouterments of the modern exercise addict. Belle and Pup seemed to think they were small dogs, unaware that they knocked me off my feet regularly. Belle is a hip-high mix of setter and lab, with a curly black coat and amber eyes. A found prize. Pup is part Belle, part yellow lab and part moose, or maybe part bull. He's huge, as if someone had taken a yellow lab and given him growth hormones till he got twice as big as nature intended. Pup is also the smartest dog I have ever met. I didn't see Stoney, who, catlike, abhorred exercise of any kind.

After a long session of stretching my tight muscles, the dogs and I ran through the trees behind my house, along the creek, angling toward a cow pasture decimated by the fire last August. It would be spring before the life came back, before the green sprouted and birds and wildlife returned, and then only if the drought ended. Some of the trees might not be dead, but it was impossible to tell. They were uniformly scorched, blackened, lifeless.

The cows stayed away.

Pup and Belle ran silently beside me, no leashes necessary, though I carried one with three hooks, just in case I had to secure the dogs. If there was an emergency, like another fire or an encounter with a poisonous snake or rabid dog, I'd leash them to each other and to me. I don't take any chances with my dogs.

The air was cold, hurting my teeth, pulling skin taut. The world smelled sour and burned. I worked my arms hard with each step, moving them forward and back with exaggerated motion. My back hurt, the pain constant and jarring. Stretching as I moved, I tried to ignore it. I had learned to live with the discomfort, but it was worse today after twelve hours spent bending over patients.

We ran hard, feet pounding, the dogs leaving me only twice, once when I paused to drink from my water bottle and again when a dead animal called to them from the brush. I slapped my thigh, and they bounded back, wearing twin expressions of woe. ''No rolling in stinky dead animals,'' I reminded them. Belle huffed with disgust. Pup just looked over his shoulder with longing.

After my usual five miles, my exposed skin flushed and red, cheeks burning with cold, we slowed and turned toward Miss Essie's house. The dogs barked and ran ahead, traveling the short stretch from me to Miss Essie's winterized herb beds and back three times. As they gamboled, I cooled down, walking and stretching again before I reached the back deck.

Her dark face was wreathed in smiles as she opened the door and hugged me. "You save that woman what was squealing like a pig?"

For a moment, I had no idea what she was talking about, then I remembered Betty. "No, I actually worked on a quiet patient while EMS took care of the screamer."

"Well, you done good," she said, patting my arm, letting me into the warmth of her kitchen. The wonderful aroma of freshly baked bread surrounded me. I think I said a prayer of thanks as I walked to the sink, poured and drank a glass of water to replace more of the fluid I used on the run. Over my swallows, I listened to angry voices.

"It ain't a religion, Miss Essie." In the kitchen, Arlana stood with her hands fisted at her waist, one knee cocked out, her head doing that side-to-side swivel no white woman could ever quite manage. "It's a way of decorating." She was wearing stretch Lycra tights that ended mid-calf, a stretch Lycra top and oversize T-shirt. Her hair was done in cornrows, blond streaks braided through and gold beads dangling off the ends. There was no makeup on her cocoa-skinned face. "You said I could decorate any way I want, and I want this particular balance."

"Ain't gone be no feng shooie in this house and that the end of it." Miss Essie threw one end of her purple shawl over one shoulder to punctuate the statement. "You want breakfast, Miss Docta Rhea?"

"It's pronounced *fung shu-ay,* not *feng shooie.* Tell her, Rhea," Arlana demanded.

Miss Essie lifted her head, steely eyes darting from the angry girl to me.

At the moment, I would have sold my left pinkie for a piece of homemade bread, and getting on Miss Essie's bad side wasn't one of my goals. I sniffed appreciatively at the fresh raspberry-coffee scent and filled a warm mug with the sweet, milky beverage. It was bliss. I sat at the table and pulled over the jar of preserves, slicing into a loaf of sourdough bread.

"Rhea?" Arlana warned.

"You're on your own till I get fed."

"You a selfish woman."

"Yes, I am," I agreed as I slathered summer strawberry preserves over the fresh bread. "Selfish and hungry and smart enough to keep my mouth shut."

"You ain't *never* been smart enough to keep that mouth shut," Arlana said.

The taste of warm yeasty bread and strawberries exploded and my mouth watered even as I gulped down another bite. She was right, but I wasn't going to tell her so. "Heaven," I said around the mouthful. "Miss Essie, you are one of God's angels. Honest."

Miss Essie made a *harumphing* sound in the back of her throat. Disgust mixed with a hint of pride. "Slow down. You gone choke."

"Yes, ma'am. This is wonderful." I took another bite on top of the first two.

"Rhea? You tell her about feng shui." Arlana's foot started tapping. That was a bad sign. "Tell her it's not about spirits and the devil."

I swallowed, putting down the bread, politely waiting to take a fourth bite till I was finished speaking. But it was hard. "Feng shui is used as a decorating tool, Miss Essie. It's got nothing to do with spirits. It's more about balance and energy."

"Spirits *is* energy." The old woman narrowed her eyes at me. "Jist because Arlana my great-grandchild don't mean she always right."

"More like the spirit of the human soul," I suggested.

"I got God's spirit in me. What need I got for feng shooie?"

"It makes the room look bigger. More open," I said.

Miss Essie looked from me to Arlana. "She ain't hanging no statues on my walls, none a them fertility idols with throbbin' man-things and huge breasts that look so full they be ready to split."

I nearly choked. Quickly I hid the reaction behind my cup of coffee till I could speak without a grin. Raspberry coffee burned my tongue, helping forestall the incipient giggling fit. Miss Essie might take laughter personally, and I wanted more bread. After a moment, I managed to say, "I think feng shui would clash with the throbbing, ah, man-things and huge breasts." *And* I said it with a straight face.

"Did I hear something about big breasts?" Eddie rounded the corner, a tall bare-chested teenager, a T-shirt and damp towel in his hand. "What's a man got to do to get in on this conversation?" Water sparkled in his short hair; khaki pants hung beltless on slim hips. "Come on, what was that about big boobs? I know what I heard."

"You ain't no man. That skinny rib cage look like a starved dog. Anyway, to be part of this talk, you got to be a woman," Arlana said.

"No, thanks. I couldn't handle the weight gain, the chocolate cravings or the emotional swings."

"You put on a shirt, boy," Miss Essie warned. "Show some manners. I taught you better than that."

Silenced by their conversation, a bit dazed, I bit into the bread again. I had no idea paradise came with entertainment.

Arlana swatted him, her open palm smacking his bare back.

"Ouch." He laughed and twisted away. "Or the level of violence."

"I'll show you some violence." Arlana's eyes were spitting sparks. Eddie snapped the towel at her and dodged away from her hand as she smacked at him again. I cut another piece of bread, onion flavored this time, with jalapeño jelly to slather on top. This was fun.

"You just a royal pain, white boy. And while we talking pain, you get into my CDs again and I'll pack my things and take off, like Elorie and Natasha Curtis, and not come back. Leave your skinny white butt listening to country music and Miss Essie's wise woman sayings all by yourself."

"Just let me know when. I'll help you pack, fill your car with gas and check your tires. You know, all the manly stuff you girls can't do."

Arlana ran around the table again, trying to pinch him. Eddie quickly outpaced her, tucking his backside out of reach. I bent my elbows in close to my sides so I wouldn't contribute to the disaster waiting to happen.

"Elorie and Natasha not come back yet? They not call?" Miss Essie asked. When Arlana answered no and squealed, running down the hall with Eddie in hot pursuit, she sighed and shook her head. "They sisters," Miss Essie said to me. "Been gone for too long, near bout a year. I hear about them from the church. Those girls missing. What Arlana say, 'bout both them packing and taking off? They didn't. They jist took off and din' take nothing with them. Din' tell they people they going. Jist up and disappear. They mama so afraid." A frown pulled at her mouth, the wrinkles angling down, a harsh line from nose to chin. "Specially when she find some jewelry and such hid away, like some man might give. People talking. Trouble here, and it brewing strong."

Head still shaking slowly, as if she grieved, Miss Essie poured herself a cup of coffee in her favorite purple mug. "They not mine, but I fear for them. Fear deep and cold like the grave. I hope nothing bad happen them girls. Hope no one took them. This an evil world. Evil. The Lord letting Satan run free now in the last days, and we all in danger, most of all God's people.''

"I'm sorry, Miss Essie." I remembered Beata Geter, another girl the cops thought had run off. Unconsciously, I rubbed my fingertips along my thighs to ease the faint tingling in them.

"I know Natasha from school. They went off with some man they just met, I betcha." Arlana darted back into the room, dodging left around the table.

"They been took!" Miss Essie said, her tone dark with warning. "Took by some evil. And I hearing they ain't the only ones."

Chilled by Miss Essie's warning, I thought about Beata's phone call and the name Vance. "Did they call back home at all?"

"Nope, not a word," Arlana said. "But I know them girls. They took off before and stay gone almost six months. They be back again this time, too, when they money run out. Now you stop worrying, Miss Essie, it ain't good for you, you hear?" Arlana demanded. "Ain't no evil. Jist two girls what may act good in church and all, but on the street, if a man want 'em, all he got to do is give 'em something lacy, black and sexy, or some jewelry or some such, and they all over him." She looked at me pointedly, her certainty making my fingertips stop itching. "All over him *together*."

"My kinda women," Eddie said, again herding Arlana into a corner at the sink. He snapped her hard with his towel and she screamed and lunged at him. Miss Essie caught both their arms, bringing them up short.

"You chil'rens make nice. We family now."

The words echoed in the sudden silence. The two teens eyed one another doubtfully. Arlana pursed her full lips and turned her head away.

Growing up, the only thing I'd had that approached a real family had been Marisa's loving but formal relatives, and I had watched the Stowes from the outside. I had never been part of a family like this one. Hadn't even seen one like this. I bit into the onion bread, spicy sweetness burning my mouth.

"Family! And ain't gone be no breasts and no man-things hanging on the walls in this house," Miss Essie said firmly. She gave their arms a small shake and let them go.

"I'll be nice if someone will tell me about the big boobs," Eddie said from inside the T-shirt he pulled over his head.

"What you grinnin' about, Rhea?" Arlana demanded. "You think decorating this house is funny?"

"Not exactly," I murmured, careful of my life and health. To Eddie, I explained, "Miss Essie didn't want any African fertility goddesses in the house. Apparently Arlana told her feng shui involved fertility idols."

"I did not. I told her we could go one of three ways—with an open plan based on feng shui, an African theme, or eclectic."

"I tole you, I ain't giving up my gas stove."

I hastily bit into the bread. Communication problems were in full swing. Or maybe it was the generation gap.

"*Ec*lectic. Not *E*lectric."

"And that mean what?"

I spoke up when Arlana spluttered in frustration. Clearly they had been over this ground a time or two too many. "It means a lot of different styles, whatever makes you happy. It means you can mix your favorite chair with a new table, and old dishes with good china."

"Well, why didn't the child say so?" Miss Essie slapped the kitchen cabinet with the purple drying rag. "I like purple. Lots a purple. All shades, like that purple ribbon on the Christmas tree." She nodded to the dining room, a sliver of which I could see if I bent back and craned my neck. The room was decorated for the season, the tree swathed in royal colors of purple and hung with purple ornaments. "I can get that with electric? And still keep my gas stove?"

"Yes, ma'am," Arlana said, narrowed eyes on me. "You can get it."

"And ain't none a this decorating gone interfere with your nursing school?"

"No, ma'am. I'll do it over Christmas and on weekends. After class."

"I like that open space thing. Don't like clutter, stuff on every shelf. Jist no feng shooie and no man-things and breasts."

"Arlana can do that. Can't you, Arlana?" I lifted my mug in a half toast.

Arlana nodded once, slowly. "Yeah. I can get down with that."

"What about the big boobs? I like big boobs. Don't I get a vote?" Eddie chimed. He almost sounded bereft and lost, his face like a kid who had been denied candy, but a mischievous twinkle spoiled the effect.

"No breasts," I said, laughing. "Sorry."

Eddie mock-sighed and cut a slice of sourdough bread. "A man can't get any respect in this household. Good bread, Miss Essie," he said through the mouthful of yeasty heaven.

"Don' talk with you mouth full. You neither," she said, swatting me with the towel.

"What did I do?" I took another slice of bread, afraid I was about to lose privileges.

"You talk with you mouth full when you first started. I didn't tell you then. I telling you now."

"Yes, ma'am," I said, relieved. Family was difficult for the uninitiated. Having been raised in a single-parent household, when that single parent had suffered from untreated bipolar disorder and was a raving alcoholic, had left me severely challenged in such situations. But perhaps it made me appreciate real family more when I saw it. I had thoroughly enjoyed the last few minutes, and only part of that enjoyment had been the food.

In my peripheral vision, I saw Miss Essie fold the towel and turn her back to me. When she spoke, her tone was odd, almost diffident. "I baking a few extra loaves of bread today. Onion, cheese, two yeast bread. You take them to Miss Risa and the twins when you go see her."

I looked up from the bread at the timid tone. Miss Essie was many things, but insecure wasn't one of them. Arlana's eyes squinted in warning, her mouth turned down saying *no*, and I knew what the warning meant.

After a moment I said, "Come with me, Miss Essie. You haven't been out to Stowe Farm in ages."

"And I ain't gone go tomorrow. I busy."

I sipped coffee. Arlana made a dramatic motion with one hand and I inclined my head to show I understood. Eddie's face was closed, his gaze tight on the preserves. Eddie was Marisa's stepson, and was likely caught in the middle of the battle going on between Miss Essie and her…rival. Taking a deep breath, I said, "Miss Essie, Auntie Maude—"

"You don' say that woman's name in this house!" Miss Essie said, her voice hard, too loud.

Miss Essie had never raised her voice to me, even when I was twelve and she caught me raiding her kitchen at night, stealing, a hungry child who didn't think to ask. I lowered my coffee mug to the saucer with a loud click.

"That English woman come here and take my babies away from me, move my Missy Risa to the farm, when they all should still be here, *in this house!*" Miss Essie stood staring at me, her face ravaged with grief, the towel twisted tight in her hands.

"I'm sorry, Miss Essie," I said, a vague shock sliding down my spine at her tone.

"You should be. You help Missy Risa get that woman over here from England. I still so mad at you I could jist 'bout spit."

It was suddenly clear why there had been a lot less bread in my life lately. I stared at the loaf, putting two and two together. Miss Essie was more than just a little mad at me. She was mad enough to spit.... How dumb could I be?

Suddenly Miss Essie slipped her arms around my shoulders. I hadn't seen her come up behind me. "I'm sorry, chile," she sighed. "I didn't mean it. I jist so fearful and angry I can't stand it no more. I striking out when there no need. Hurting the people I love best."

Relief flooded through me. I blinked back unexpected tears, unable to speak for a moment.

"I fearing for Elorie and Natasha. I know you not responsible for that English nanny woman out to the farm. I know Miss Marisa make you get her. I know how that child is when she get something in her head. Ain't no stopping her. Even now, when she ain't so much herself no more. I jist an old woman, given to fear and fancies and missing my babies."

I patted her arm, slipping my own hands along her forearms in an abbreviated hug. "It's okay. I understand. And I never would have found a nanny for the twins if Risa hadn't demanded it. You know that, I hope."

"I know that. My Miss Risa love me. But that don't mean I going out to that farm while that English woman still there. I is still a mite stubborn."

I almost laughed at the understatement, but remembered

the onion bread before the laughter escaped. All might not be right with the world, but it felt pretty great at the moment. I had onion bread, family entertainment and a good hug.

11

TIME WASN'T COOPERATING

The rest of the morning disappeared in slumber, my face buried in the slightly dank pillow. It was past time to change sheets, but Arlana hadn't been over in a few weeks to earn a little extra cash by cleaning my house, and she hadn't remembered to tell me to change them, either, so I hadn't bothered.

It was midafternoon when I woke, so groggy my eyelids felt as if they had been glued shut while I slept. Stoney was curled up on my chest, purring, his nose butting my chin. At least he wasn't sitting on my face. I managed to get one eye open, only to have him bat the lid with a paw to tell me it was time for lunch.

"Yeah. Okay. Stop that," I said, rolling stiffly out from under him and out of bed. "You promised to mouse for me. Or catch moles. That was the deal." Stoney yawned at me, bored with old contracts. "Now you're acting just like a man, not listening to me and still expecting me to feed you, sleep with you and meet all your social needs," I grumbled. Before I did anything else, however, I fed the animals and poured fresh water. The ancient pipes thumped as they expanded.

My house was brick, with a covered porch across the

front and down one side. It was old, probably built in the forties, with few modern conveniences until the last owners had upgraded it. In order to sell it, at a time when the market in Dawkins County was limp, they had agreed to all sorts of improvements inside and out, and I had new tile and countertops in the kitchen, new insulation in the walls and floors, new windows, new doors and locks, new paint and ductwork underneath. Except for the plumbing, it was as new as it could be, considering the house was built decades ago.

The public rooms all opened to one another, the kitchen flowing into the dining room, into the living room, into the Florida room on one side and the hallway on the other. The bedrooms opened to the hallway, the master bedroom with its own bath, and the two guest rooms sharing a bath. It was nothing spectacular, but I really liked my little place.

To shake off the jet lagged feeling, I changed into jogging clothes, stretched hard and went for a run, leaving Stoney practicing yoga moves on my pillow. The dogs loped beside me, all three of us glorying in the unseasonably warm sunshine. The weather had turned back to autumn, with breezy temps in the seventies. We ran a slow five miles, turning away from the fire damage and moving along the bare path beside the creek. After an hour I felt better, though my back was not holding up well. I hadn't stretched long enough before hitting the trail. I could feel a pain starting in my mid-thoracic region, radiating up my right arm and down my right leg with each jarring stride. The idea of living with the pain for the rest of my life wasn't pleasant, but the physical therapist had done about all he could with the severed muscles and nerves around my kidney. Now only time could decrease the effects of the injury. And so far, time wasn't cooperating.

When I got back home, four loaves of warm bread were sitting on my kitchen counter. There was no note, but I knew they were from Miss Essie. It was her way of reminding me that I was delivery gal for the Stowe Farm today. A fast shower later, the dogs and I were heading deeper into the countryside.

There isn't much room in a BMW Z3. It is a two-seater with just enough space behind the seats to stack four loaves of bread, if the ragtop is up. But the dogs never seemed to mind the cramped quarters, crawling back and forth from floor to passenger seat, knocking the leash out of sight, noses stuck out the partially lowered window to catch strange scents. Their excitement made the Z3 smell like a kennel, but it was always worth it to see Belle and Pup take off across the fields at Stowe farm, playing tag.

The farm is six hundred acres of fields, pasture, timber, barns, outbuildings, ponds, lakes and creeks, and the crumbling remains of sharecropper houses. And of course, there's the Stowe farmhouse. The house is two-story redbrick with a wraparound porch and a low-pitched roof covered with slate shingles. A new wing was built on the back of the house twenty years ago. It held a work area with spacious laundry facilities and a large sunroom with a breakfast area on the first level, as well as a sundeck above, reached only by a dumbwaiter and two doors on the second floor.

The house came into view as I drove slowly down the pea-gravel road, passing between twin stands of pecan trees. When I was a kid, I had thought I was coming to visit a mansion owned by the richest people in the world. Summer vacation had taken on a totally different meaning at the farm. I had left behind my drunken mother with her increasingly outrageous behavior, her weekly parties, séances, mood swings, TV preachers and buying sprees, to discover a world of trees, space, horses, people, freedom and joy that I had never known existed. It was still one of my favorite places on earth, my love only slightly tempered by knowing that Miss DeeDee had bought it back for Marisa after she made a killing on the stock market.

Miss DeeDee was Marisa's aunt, a criminally psychotic, one-time socialite, now a resident of a three-star psychiatric institution. Even locked behind padded bars, Miss DeeDee had made a fortune on the stock market at a time when others were losing their shirts. She had bought the Stowe family farm back for Marisa and the twins. A guilt-gift to try to make up for injuring Marisa, giving her brain damage that would never completely heal.

I parked behind the house, let the dogs loose and watched as they took off at a dead run for the barn, looking for something interesting to roll in. In front of the barn, a sparkling black SUV was parked, the back hatch open. As I headed to the house, I saw a tall man in khaki pants and a work shirt leading a lame horse around from the back of the barn. The animal was huge, over seventeen hands high. Red-brown with two black socks and a black mane, it had a rough, almost three-legged gait. Tying the horse's halter to a hitch, the man leaned over the horse's neck, his hands moving down the central spinal ridge. I couldn't tell what he was doing, but the horse had his ears perked up and he looked happy, so I didn't think the man was a vet. There wasn't enough equipment for him to be a ferrier. I nodded to him and moved away, watching the dogs run toward the lake.

Miz Auberta met me at the back door. Auberta Edwardina Lindsey had been the housekeeper back when I was a girl, and had been rehired by Marisa the moment she decided to move to the farm. Miz Auberta was a little redder, a little skinnier and a lot faster than she had been in my childhood, having joined Weight Watchers and begun dying her hair fire-engine red when she turned fifty. Marisa also claimed she had a tattoo, but Auberta never mentioned that to me. She smiled the same wide smile, said the same words in greeting that she always had, and patted my back in welcome.

"You just come on in and make yourself at home." She took the bread and made appropriate sniffing sounds. "Onion loaves! Miss Essie called to say she was sending these out. Why that stubborn old woman won't come out here is beyond me."

I wasn't about to list all the reasons for Miss Essie's attitude. Instead I said, "How're Marisa and the twins?" Rheaburn and RheaLynn were named after me, my godchildren, the only infants on the face of the earth who were really perfect.

"I hollered at Miss Marisa when I seen you drive up. Twins are down for a nap, thank God. Rheaburn and Lynnie may have been awfully little at birth, but they caught up mighty fast. That Rheaburn's crawling all over. Got into the bathroom today and pulled the tissue off the roll and emptied out the trash can. Had a used tissue in his mouth by the time I caught up with him. And Lynnie was sitting at the door cooing at him, like she was giving advice. I bet that one's gonna be a talker, my little Lynnie."

Miz Auberta would know, if like recognized like. I didn't have to respond, as the housekeeper rambled on. She had decorated the kitchen for Christmas. A garland hung over the big stove, and a small fiber-optic Christmas tree glimmered with variegated colors.

"I do love having babies in the house again. My own youngest grandchildren are in high school now, and they both plan to be teachers, making college plans, can you imagine it? I sure raised a smart group of grandkids, though I have no idea where they got the genes. Must be from their mothers, 'cause my boys sure ain't bright." Auberta prattled on, cutting a loaf of onion bread and handing a slice to me on a paper towel, then wiping the counter down with the hem of her long apron. I tuned her into the background, as I had as a kid.

In the kitchen, the coffeepot was gurgling, something was bubbling on the stove and the emergency scanner was buzzing softly with the sound of the dispatcher fielding complaints and delegating officers and ambulances where they were needed. Like many in rural areas, Miz Auberta was an emergency scanner addict, listening to the unit to keep her perpetually up-to-date on county activities. Marisa and I had listened at her door when we were children and knew the unit ran even at night. Before Marisa came down, I heard officers and EMS dispatched to a Signal 025, a person trapped; a Signal 016, a burn; and a Signal 044, an overdose. Typical complaints, but an awful lot of them, as if yesterday's busy night was still in full swing. And though Miz Auberta hadn't stopped talking, I knew she hadn't missed a thing.

"Miz Auberta, you know anything about some girls missing in the county? Maybe heard anything over the scanner or at church?"

"Lord, honey, there's gossip all over, but I haven't heard anything unusual in particular." She paused, stirring the pot on the stove. "Course, there's been some unusual police codes lately. Some 10-100s and a few 10-38s. Don't know what they mean, 'cause they aren't on my copy of the county list." She turned sharp eyes to me. "What do you know?"

"It's not what I know, but what I'm beginning to suspect." I shook my head. "If you hear anything, will you tell me?"

"You know I will. And you do the same." As if to seal her promise, Auberta turned the scanner's volume up a hair.

Marisa ran down the service stairs to the kitchen, her steps sounding both firm and light, graceful and surefooted. She swung around the corner, one hand on the door casing, her blond hair in a ponytail that floated out behind her, her jeans-clad legs almost dancing. "Sunshine!" she sang. "You are my sunshine!"

"Risa!"

She grabbed me and spun me around, and though I hated being called Sunshine, I found myself giggling with her, like we had done as girls. Normally I detested women who giggled. It was so infantile. But with Marisa, all rules and biases were put aside.

"You look better every time I see you. Miz Auberta says the twins are asleep."

"Little angels," she said happily. "Girls day out?" It came out as "Gursh day out?" Marisa had suffered a neurological injury that left her with permanent speech impairment. She hadn't exactly lost the ability to speak, but the part of her brain where language was stored and processed was damaged. She was still going to physical therapy, and there was some hope a new neurosurgical technique being developed at Duke Medical might offer some future improvement. But for now, communicating with Marisa could be challenging for me and frustrating for her. Marisa knew what she wanted to say, but except for simple phrases and songs, the words weren't there.

"Not again, already," I said, leading her to the loaf of bread Auberta was slicing. "Last time it was a facial, a massage, a pedicure and a manicure. Miz A, you should have seen people's faces when *I* showed up at work, all glowy and dewy, with painted nails. I thought Anne and Ash would pass out in the hallway." I had felt stupid all night long, sewing up patients with mauve-tinted nails pressing against my latex gloves.

"You should wear makeup. Gal like you with beautiful skin should capitalize on it."

"Day spa in Ford," Marisa said, meaning the largest city in nearby Ford County. "European facials and salt scrubs."

She stumbled over the words, but I got the gist. Then she gave a mischievous grin. "Waxing."

"Not on me. No way. You talked me into that once, and once was enough. I learned my lesson." I took a second slice of onion bread and settled at the big table beside her. Addressing Miz Auberta, I said, "My eyebrows had second degree burns—my skin blistered, peeled, and hurt all week. And how Marisa was able to stand a bikini wax I don't know. It's medieval torture."

Marisa giggled and looked up at me, her laughter fading when she saw the bread. "Miss Essie?" she said, her tone plaintive.

"Still being stubborn. Auntie Maude?"

"Sleeping. Twins up all night." Marisa sighed and ate her bread in silence. Auntie Maude was a recent addition to the household, a retiree from the British Home Office. The older woman was perfect for Marisa—crisp, demanding, gentle, and full of that uniquely British starch that gave her an air of authority. Nothing startled or astonished Auntie Maude, not after years traipsing all over the world in the service of the U.K. government. Unfortunately, Miss Essie couldn't be in the same room with her without trying to reenact the Revolutionary War.

"So who's the guy outside with the horses?" I was hoping to distract Marisa.

Putting out iced tea for us, Miz Auberta said, "We got a lame horse, so twitchy no one can ride him. Last week he took to kicking every time one of the stable boys touched him, and he never done that before. Vet says he's fine. So I got my chiropractor to come take a look."

I took the slice of onion bread out of my mouth without biting down. "You've got to be kidding. On a horse?"

Miz Auberta laughed. "You ever be in pain and walk out of the chiropractor's office pain free, you'll get over that attitude. My chiro has a subspecialty in vet work."

"You agreed to this?" I asked Marisa.

She shrugged. "Need to sell horse. Get…ponies…for the twins."

"They're eight months old." I managed to keep the incredulity out of my voice.

"Hard to find…Welsh…ponies." Marisa stumbled over the words. "Get 'em trained like I want. Girls day out when?" So much for distracting her. "And shopping."

"Yuck." All day in a chair, being slapped and greased and wrapped in weird things, then on to shopping. "A fate worse than death," I groaned. With Marisa, shopping was never a hit-and-run deal. And she didn't mean Wal-Mart. She meant hours in an upscale, high-priced mall where women in starched lab coats offer to scent the wrists of passersby and every department store has it own internal specialty shops. It made me want to shudder.

"Please?" There was laughter in her tone and the pleading was entirely fake. Marisa had always been determined to make me into a proper Southern woman, loving all the things she did. Spas, massages, pampering, and above all, shopping.

"You girls should go." Miz Auberta added her opinion. "Have a day of fun."

I sighed, outmaneuvered. "How about Monday?"

"Call Shirl?"

"Yeah, okay. Shopping where?"

Miz Auberta put a sale flyer down in front of me. I finally realized they were ganging up on me. Call me dense. "Christmas shopping in Pineville and SouthPark. She's been about to make me crazy, wanting to go. But I can't drive like I could once. I refuse to drive in Charlotte traffic. Not no more, bad as it's got."

"Okay," I sighed. "Monday for torture day."

"Lake," Marisa demanded, standing.

"You do know that I know you use this brain injury thing to get your way," I said baldly.

"It works." Marisa laughed that tinkling Southern-belle laugh of hers. When I joined in, I sounded a bit like a mule braying.

"Sure. Let's walk to the lake. Long as you don't make me fish." I knew I sounded sulky. A day spa, shopping and fishing all in one week would have been too much.

"I like to fish." When I glared, she sighed, her blue eyes shining. "Okay, I promise. Just talk." The look in her eyes implied that she had news to give me. Not good news. I wasn't particularly adept at comforting people with bad news, and I cut a hunk of the onion loaf to give me something to do with my hands and mouth.

We walked toward the lake, where the dogs were splashing in the convoluted game of tag they had devised. Belle sank her teeth into Pup's tail, turned and ran, whipping her way through trees and brush and up under the deck. Pup followed, catching her, and returned the favor. They never drew blood, the huge teeth simply working like a human hand. Marisa pointed and laughed. Words weren't really necessary. Never had been, between us.

Marisa and I took off our shoes and sat on the edge of the pier, passing the onion loaf back and forth, breaking off chunks to eat as we dangled our bare feet above the chilly water. It hadn't been cold enough to make the water frigid, but the small lake no longer held the warmth of summer. The sun heated us where it rested on our backs. The smell of dank water, manure, hay and Marisa's Chanel Number 9 combined pleasantly. Ducks that didn't fly south for winter honked and paddled toward us, hoping to be fed. I relaxed completely, bad news to come or not.

We chit-chatted as best we could. Finally Marisa got around to the reason why she wanted the private talk.

"Steven has…" She paused and started again. "Divorce is final."

I wanted to jump up and dance, but I figured that might hurt Marisa's feelings. She had loved Steven Braswell from the first moment she saw him. She was grieving over a divorce she'd never wanted. Personally, I thought it a wonderful thing that the obsessive-compulsive, cheating, wife-neglecting, slimy son of a slug was out of Marisa's life. Instead of saying that, though, I murmured, "I'm so sorry, Marisa."

She tossed a few crumbs onto the water. Ducks swam over and snapped them up. "He's getting married. To Sarah."

I looked away from the pain in Marisa's face. Steven had been having an affair with Sarah Gibbons during the time Marisa was attacked and injured. As far as I knew, he had never seen his children.

"I hope she gives him herpes."

Marisa laughed, the kind of snorting laugh people make when they are halfway between tears and laughter and laughter barely won out. I laughed with her and tossed more crumbs to the ducks. Belle and Pup came bounding after the waterfowl and the birds half flew, half swam away from the dock, honking loudly, quickly outdistancing the barking dogs.

"Well, I do. And she might. If you cheat once, you might cheat again." I thought of Mark and Skye. Was I talking to myself, too?

Marisa shrugged, but when she spoke the plaintive tone was almost gone. "I liked being married."

Humor had worked the first time, and it was a safe refuge in this unfamiliar conversational territory. "I know. You were an old married lady for a lot of years. You miss the regular sex."

Marisa laughed and looked at me evilly. "Yes, but I like shopping more."

"You would."

With the birds gone, Pup sprang to the dock and settled against Marisa, his massive head in her lap. He was as much her dog as mine, and sometimes couldn't decide where he lived, on the farm or with me. Every time I left, I had to wait for the big dog to choose whether to stay with Marisa or come with Belle and me. I knew one day he would decide to stay on the farm. Belle and Smokey and I would be just three then. Marisa stroked the dog's ears slowly and they both sighed happily.

Half an hour later, Marisa looked at her watch. "My baby's up now. Come on."

We moved toward the house, scuffing our bare feet in the dead grass. The horse with the limp walked around the barn, his irregular gait less noticeable than before. The dogs ran and barked shrilly, using us as pivot points in the game of tag.

Back inside, my beeper went off, just as Miz Auberta's scanner blared a Signal 009—dead at scene, no transport. I knew before I looked that I was being paged by the police for my new job as coroner. Yep. The LEC number was displayed on my pager. Dang. I hated dead bodies almost as much as I hated day spas and shopping. And this had started out as a pretty nice day, too. A good nap, a couple of runs, made Marisa laugh, found out old Steven Braswell was finally out of Marisa's life. And now a dead body to spoil it all. I called in.

The Law Enforcement Center dispatcher gave me directions to the scene, which wasn't far from Risa's.

"What do I have?" I asked.

"Black female, badly decomposed," she said. "The FBI and the task force decided it didn't fit the profile and told me to call you."

Task force? Profile? Profile of what? My fingertips were already tingling. "Okay...I think. Let them know I'll be about twenty minutes."

"Ten four." She hung up. Moments later I heard the scanner inform Unit 214, which was Mark's call number, that the assistant coroner had an ETA of twenty. What was the FBI here for? And what profile?

Something was going on in the county, something that had been kept off the scanners and out of the media. I remembered the strange Feeb at Wayne Edward Geter's arrest, and Mark's interest in the name Vance. I remembered Beata, Miss Essie's Natasha and Elorie, Ollie's girlfriend, taken following a hit-and-run. Mark's words—girls were missing.

I stuffed the rest of the onion bread into my mouth, chewed and drank down the iced tea. Hugging Marisa, I let myself out, promising all the while to come see the twins later, to call Shirl and to plan for Girls Day Out on Monday. Yuck.

Calling the dogs, I loaded them into the passenger seat and drove the back way out, past the barn. The chiropractor was again leading the bay horse. The animal did not look the least bit vicious, and he was not limping. The head stable hand stood watching, scratching his bald head, his cowboy hat gripped in his fist. I was needed at the crime scene, but curiosity won out. Leaning out the window, I was glad I remembered the old man's name. "What's up, Malachi?"

"Miz Auberta told me 'bout this guy here and how he could fix Jesup, and be danged if he didn't! That horse been gimpy over three weeks, and look at him now."

The chiropractor walked toward us, leading the docile horse. The dogs pressed inquisitive noses out the window. Malachi moved to the big animal and the chiropractor halted. I watched as Malachi ran his hand along the horse's back and up, then repeated the motion with greater pressure. The bay flicked his ears in curiosity, stamped once and snorted.

"I'll be a monkey's uncle. Would you look at this? How's he to ride?"

The chiropractor murmured something and Malachi laughed as the doc moved to the bay's left side and vaulted onto the horse's bare back. The bay sidestepped once and turned an inquisitive eye to his rider.

Turning to me, Malachi said, "Ain't no one been on this horse in six months. Mister—I mean, Doc—you got a minute to take a look at a couple other horses? And there's an old dog what's half-lame, too."

Thinking about the pain in my own back, I rolled up the window, let out the clutch and pulled away. Like Jesup, I was experiencing pain that no one had been able to relieve. It was mostly low-level, but there were times when it was bad. Like today, when I pushed the clutch.

Though I had never been to one, I had patients who swore by chiropractors. I couldn't think how being jerked around till my spine popped could be good for me. But what if someone could help me? I had my records, X rays, surgeon reports of the damage, physical therapist's final discharge notes. It was something to consider.

As I drove, I speed-dialed Shirl, but Dr. Adkins was not in her office. I left a message about Girls Day Out with her service. Maybe, if I was real lucky, she'd be too busy to spend the day getting rubbed and wrapped and plucked and cut and steamed and painted. Yuck.

I pulled into the field, my black Z3 covered in a layer of road dust. The dogs were so excited they were trying to climb into my lap, crawling all over one another, hoping to get a better scent. They smelled like dog and lakewater.

Sour and stinky. "Get down. Belle, be good. Pup, no!" I got a lick across my cheek for my trouble.

Strapping on the three-way leash, I let the dogs and myself out of the car. Each dog's collar was hooked to one end of the leash, and the third end clipped to my belt loop or wrapped around my wrist. They might rip my jeans or yank me off my feet, but they weren't going to get away. There was a single hoop at the knot where the three leashes joined, and I grabbed it now to control the dogs better. Getting the file folder marked Coroner Forms out of my trunk, I slammed it and moved to the crime scene tape.

There were three county sheriff cars, a crime scene utility vehicle, an ambulance, a rescue squad truck and three POVs—cars owned by private citizens, like me. A group of men and women stood inside a wide area of short scrub cordoned off with yellow crime scene tape.

"You brought *dogs* to a crime scene?" Mark shouted over at me. He sounded mad. "Put 'em back in the car before you contaminate the site," he yelled as he strode over. All the other law enforcement types looked up from the ground, Mark's tone attracting attention and making me angry all at once.

I tightened my grip on the loop as the dogs recognized Mark and tried to reach him, barking in excitement. My dogs liked Mark. Stupid animals. "I was out with the dogs when I got the page. And no, I won't put them back in the car." Of course the dogs would contaminate the crime scene. Probably roll on the body if they got half a chance. I *had* been stupid, but I wasn't telling Mark that.

"Are you out of your mind, woman?" Understanding the angry tone, Belle whined, looking back and forth between Mark and me. Pup jumped at Mark, hoping for a treat.

"I am perfectly sane, Captain Stafford, and unlike you, I am also polite. I can tie up the dogs." Mark took a breath to reply, but shut his mouth, stopping whatever he had been about to say. We stared at each other. A tic started in Mark's right cheek. I figured the tic was my fault, but I didn't back down. I glared as good as I got.

"Doc can tie her mutts up at a tree, Cap'n," a reasonable voice said. "I got a bowl she can use for water."

Without looking, I put the voice with a name and nodded. "Thanks, Jacobson." Mark stomped off. "What's going on here?" I asked the other cop.

"Other than the captain acting a mite riled? We need someone to do the paperwork on a body. Got a black female, tentatively identified as Ida Lomattie Brakefield, been missing for six weeks."

"Natural causes?"

"Don't think so, Doc. Hard to say for sure. There's tire tracks in dried mud nearby, like somebody drove up and dumped the body. And Ida was last seen with a man in a truck, driving away from a bar. Suspicious." Our feet swished in the parched grass as we angled to Jacobson's Crown Vic. "There's scavenger disturbance of the body and the scene. Bird feed and rat bait. She's too far gone to tell what killed her."

"Dried mud? The last rain was weeks ago."

"Yep. Six weeks ago, about the time Ida disappeared."

I nodded and turned over the dogs to the cop, letting Jacobson take them to a place where they could sit in the sun and watch the humans. Carrying the file folder, I crossed under the crime scene tape and walked toward the body on the ground. The cops were making jokes about the corpse, waiting for me to do my job so they could do theirs.

There are many ways to describe a body that has been dead awhile, left in a field, open to air, scavengers and what heat there was in the season. None of them are poetic, and only a jaded cop can make it sound funny. Reminding myself how much I hated dead bodies, I curled my lip up at the stench and went to work.

12

IT'S FRIDAY NIGHT. WHY WOULD I HAVE A DATE?

I filled out the necessary paperwork to bag-and-tag the body and get it off to the forensic medical examiner in Newberry. And though I hung around for an hour, I found out little about the FBI and nothing about the task force. Mark wasn't in a talkative mood and the other cops seemed to think it was my fault. Go figure.

There were only three things of interest I heard at the messy scene. First, Charlie Denbrow was still hanging on after the surgery to seal up the holes in his chest and abdomen. Second, the investigator in charge of determining what he and the other man had been doing in the car when Charlie's wife shot them had begun to reconsider the homosexual aspect. Eddie's report about the cop's zipped and buttoned clothing was making waves. Gabby Denbrow's allegations were suddenly being looked at in a different light. The brass were real hush-hush about it all, which—oddly—seemed to please the street cops. And last, Skye McNeely was in early labor and had been admitted to the hospital.

No mention was made of why Mark Stafford was not at the hospital with Skye. What did that say about him? That he was standing true to his contention that he wasn't the baby's father? Or that he was avoiding his responsibilities? I had no way of knowing.

When I got home, my message light was blinking with a call from Cowboy. *"Afternoon, Doc. A couple friends and I are getting together for a movie. If you like action flicks, meet us at Pineville at the AMC at four. We'll do burgers after. Unless you got a hot date or something. Page me with an answer."*

"Me, with a date?" I asked Stoney. "It's Friday night. Why would I have a date?"

Stoney opened one eye as if considering my question, and closed it, as bored with my love life as I was.

It was almost four now, but that was what fast cars were for. I paged Cowboy with a yes, grabbed a bag, ran a comb though my shaggy hair, spritzed on perfume to hide a faint wet-dog-decaying-corpse smell and ran for the car.

Under ordinary circumstances, I didn't much like driving fast, but action flicks were a personal favorite and there were three out I wanted to see. I busted every speed limit on the way to Pineville, paid my way in, bought a tub of popcorn and a drink big enough to swim in, and jogged to theater twelve. I made it just as Cowboy was about to give up and leave me to find his friends in the darkened room.

"Trailers are playing now. Move it, Doc."

"Rhea," I said, as he took an elbow and guided me into the dim cavern and up the stairs about halfway.

"Rhea, meet Howard and Maggie." After a couple of quick how-do-you-dos, the movie started and I settled in, happily crunching popcorn, my drink in the holder in the chair arm, the popcorn tub passed around. Matt Damon lit up the screen as the falsely accused cop gone rogue to prove his innocence. Lots of action sequences, lots of big screen special effects and stunts, even a surprise ending. Except for the dead body, it had been a perfect day.

After the movie, we stopped in at the Steak & Shake,

ordered high-fat food and shakes and did the get-to-know-you thing the way only doctors do. Medical small talk, bonding over weird stories and odd cases we had actually seen, and the even weirder ones we had only heard of. Foreign objects discovered in body cavities was the primary topic. I probably won the storytelling contest with the one about the snake skeleton discovered in the guy's bladder. What can I say? People are weird.

As we waited for food, Howard proclaimed himself "African-American, happily gay, and actively but safely looking for Mr. Right. Nice to meet you, Rhea Lynch. And in case you're wondering, no, I don't do foreign objects." The comment was right on target and we all laughed.

Maggie was a wunderkind—a twenty-one-year-old genius with a better than 4.0 grade point average all through school, a photographic memory, a gamine face and a crush on Howard to which he was oblivious.

Like Cowboy, Howard and Maggie were second-year residents working at the parent hospital of Carolinas Health Care Systems in Charlotte. All were single and all were tired, with that bone-deep exhaustion of residents everywhere, the effect of too much caffeine, too many hours without sleep, and a diet composed of fast foods and gallons of really bad coffee.

Cowboy was the glue that brought the group together, a down-home Texan in boots, ancient and threadbare jeans, a year-round tan and a real cowboy hat, with an authentic sweat line around the band.

"We're all single, tired and lonely, if we happened to find time to think about it," he explained to me at one point. "Too smart for some crowds, too unhip for others, and we don't own the right clothes to do the bar-hopping thing. And, ma'am, we are seriously in need of relaxation. We don't fit in anywhere else, because all we can think about is the last patient we saw with blood spurting, tire tracks across his abdomen or an ax sticking out of his head. Other residents go home to wives or family. All we got is each other. It's Friday night. We'll fall asleep on our feet, but we'll do it together.'' The three musketeers clinked oversize shake glasses at that and I joined in. I remembered what it felt like. And this felt like home.

At eight-thirty—a late night for residents—with a cold front blowing in, the little party broke up. Howard and Maggie claimed study needs and laundry time. Of course, if Howard had said he needed to go rob a bank, tattoo his nose, amputate a body part or jump off a bridge, Maggie would have followed right along. The guy had to be half-blind not to notice her crush. They drove off together in an old Honda.

Cowboy followed me to my car, claiming he was too wired to go back to his apartment. "Let's go for a ride on my bike,'' he suggested.

Suddenly uncomfortable that I had missed a signal, I backed up to my car and crossed my arms. I hadn't had a date in so long, I had forgotten what it was like. Had forgotten what it felt like to have a man around who was interested in me for something other than my doctoring skills. But this hadn't felt like a date. Blunt as usual, I said, "Is this a date?''

Cowboy put his old hat on and seemed to think awhile. "Well, I reckon I'm too broke to date, ma'am. And maybe too old to date. For sure too tired to date. When I find Miss Right, I'll likely skip the preliminaries and just propose. So, no, it's not a date.'' His uneven teeth flashed in the dark. "Unless you find that insulting. In which case it just became a date, Dr. Lynch, ma'am.''

"No date, thanks anyway,'' I said. "We could just be friends.'' I grinned at the line, and so did he, his eyes crinkling at the corners.

"You like bikes?''

"As in two wheels, a cute basket between the handlebars and playing cards stuck in the spokes?"

Cowboy quirked his lips in a half smile and nodded to the lean, black, predatory, sex-on-two-wheels machine across the parking lot. "More like that."

I didn't much like motorcycles, but Cowboy's motorcycle told me something about him I hadn't noted before. Maybe I should have reconsidered on the date aspect. I dismissed that idea immediately. He wasn't my type. No chemistry. Not like the chemistry I had glimpsed in the chocolate-brown eyes of Eli Cordell. The thought startled me. Where had that come from? Besides, Cowboy didn't date and I had no desire to be proposed to tonight. "Nope," I said. "Not much into motorbikes."

"Horses?"

"Haven't been on one in years."

"Music?"

"Love it," I said.

"Well, see, common ground already. Country?"

"I can stand it. I like jazz, oldies, salsa, seventies soul and rock-and-roll better."

"Skip the jazz and I think we can cement this friendship over music."

We shook on that and it felt good. I hadn't made a new friend in ages, and this could be the beginnings of a lasting one. I had a certain talent for making friends, the kind you kept for years, not just the casual work-with-you kind. I shuddered with cold as the wind picked up. Cowboy took the keys from my hand and opened the car door, motioning me inside. "Turn it on and let it warm up," he suggested.

I complied. The engine whirred hard in the cold. Icy air blew out of the vents. "Cowboy, you ever hear about chiropractors working on horses?"

"Sure. On my place back in Texas, I used to have the local doc come out when there was a problem I couldn't track down. And I take my sister to one now and again, when she falls barrel-racing and wrenches something. Of course, my sister isn't a horse." I could hear the humor in the comment, but his face was hidden now, backlit by a streetlight.

"Glad to hear it. Am I the only person on the face of the earth who hasn't heard about chiropractors and horses?" I held my hands to the vents as the air turned tepid. I should have worn a coat. "My best friend had a doc working on one of her horses today and it was like this miracle cure."

Before Cowboy could answer, my beeper went off. It was Miss Essie's number. Cowboy crawled into the car's passenger side while I dialed, and the heater kicked in, a blast of warm air circulating. Eddie answered.

"Rhea?" His tone sounded strained.

"Yeah, Eddie. You need something?"

"They just called me to emergency assist at the LEC. You know a kid named Wayne Edward Geter?"

"I know the name," I said. The abused kid who had shot his foster father.

"A prisoner shot a guard at the LEC, opened three cells and took off with Wayne Edward. We got six prisoners still missing," Eddie said.

"Wayne Edward's been kidnapped?" I asked, confused.

"Not exactly."

"What happened?"

"They were trying to transfer Wayne to a facility in Columbia and he went nuts. Grabbed an officer's gun and tossed it to another prisoner, who gut-shot Gerald Chambers. From there on things get a little confused."

I remembered Gerald Chambers. He was white, thirtyish, married with two kids and wildly ambitious. Gerald wanted to be more than a detention officer, he wanted to be a cop. So far, he hadn't had the brains to accomplish his goal of carrying a big gun and driving a cool car with flashing blue lights. He had recently let himself be injured by a patient he was supposed to be guarding at the hospital, and she'd gotten away. Not the brightest of men, but not someone I would want to see hurt.

"Okay. But why are you calling me? Do they need me at the hospital?"

"No. Wayne Edward and this other guy, Graham Cornwell, are together. Cornwell may have killed a woman a few weeks ago. He was just locked up tonight. They stole four-wheelers and are heading toward the farm. I knew you would want to know."

My heart shot into my throat. Eddie meant the Stowe Farm. Where Marisa was. "Have you called Miz Auberta?" *I've got to go,* I mouthed to Cowboy.

"She's gone for the night. That nanny-woman answered. She won't let me talk to Risa. Wayne's a juvie but he's gone over the line. They're treating this like he's an adult. Armed and dangerous, and the man he's with is worse, a three-time loser. There's a manhunt in the works. They're calling in the dogs and a helicopter. And I got to go help out at dispatch, so I can't go check on the farm." I thought instantly of Ida, the woman found dead in the field. Her body had been discovered not that far from Stowe Farm. My fingertips started to tingle. I scrubbed them across the rough fabric of my jeans.

"Malachi?" There had to be someone nearby.

"It's Friday night. Drunk at the Cattleman's Lounge."

"I'm on my way." I shooed Cowboy out of the car. He stood, watching me, the passenger door held open. "I'll call when I get there, Eddie. How long do I have?"

"Look. It isn't likely that Wayne Edward is heading to Stowe Farm. Marisa's probably fine and I'm spitting in the wind for nothing. But they were spotted heading southeast. Stowe Farm is the only thing out that way until you hit

I-77. They could be a third of the way there by now, if they took hunting trails. They've been riding for something like twenty minutes.''

My heart clenched. I figured Wayne Edward was along for the ride and the other guy was leading the way. But what did Graham Cornwell want and how badly did he want it? If a habitual felon got to an isolated farm and found potential hostages, would he take them? It wouldn't be the first time there were deaths in the county for similar reasons. "Don't worry. I'll be there soon."

I ended the call and threw the Z3 into gear, quickly telling Cowboy what had happened.

"I'll follow you," he said. "You might need help."

"Sure. After all, you're a cowboy and cowboy's can do anything."

He just grinned at my sarcasm, ripped off his hat and sprinted for his bike.

"You get left behind and I won't slow down to let you catch up," I shouted. True to my word, I left him in the parking lot and sped for the 485 access ramp. Why was Wayne Edward heading toward the Stowe Farm? That was nowhere near his foster home. And if they passed the farm and reached I-77, then what? It wasn't as if someone was going to stop for felons in prison orange thumbing on an interstate. They needed a car. They needed hostages. A hot sweat started under my arms, down my back. They needed hostages.

I was at the I-77 turnoff before Cowboy caught up with me and flashed his lights, black helmet catching my tail-lights. It was a fifty minute drive to Stowe Farm driving sixty-five miles per hour. For the third time today, I didn't obey the posted speed limits for the trip across state lines, and I sped up a good ten miles an hour more when I turned off I-77.

Perhaps my speed was contingent on the helicopter that

hovered on the Dawkins County horizon, a light trained on the ground making small circles. Perhaps it had something to do with the fact that when I called Marisa, Auntie Maude wouldn't let me talk to her. Perhaps it was just the way my fingers itched. Whatever the cause, I wanted Marisa safe. Maybe the nanny thought she was protecting Marisa, but Auntie Maude and I had a harsh discussion coming, not one she would win by lifting her patrician British nose in the air.

I whipped onto the pea-gravel drive, still traveling too fast and fishtailed for about twenty yards before getting the small car under control. I cussed crudely in the privacy of the car, banged my fist against the steering wheel and brushed at tears that burned and made the nightscape blurry. Cowboy's headlight flashed across my car, steady and controlled. He had slowed down and made the transition more smoothly. The house and grounds were lit up like an amusement park on the low hill. We sped toward the back of the house and I skidded to a stop, dust billowing around me. Running to the door, I banged with my fist. In the distance, I heard gunshots. Dogs barking. They were close.

A light flicked on, illuminating Auntie Maude in a frowsy flannel gown, a look of mild outrage on her face. When she opened the door, I shoved my way though, cut off the lights and threw the door wide to admit Cowboy. "Marisa! Marisa, get down here!" I shouted. I felt around in a drawer and found the flashlight that was always kept there for emergencies. Handing it to Cowboy, I said, "Check the house and see that it's locked up. Cut the lights."

"Yes, ma'am." When he whirled, heading toward the front of the house, his duster coat swirled out behind him in the flashlight's glow. Very Clint Eastwood. I was oddly comforted by the sight. I rammed my hand down on the array of security-light switches, throwing the grounds into darkness.

"Mistress Rheane Rheaburn Lynch! What *is* the meaning of this?"

Moving in the dark, I clicked on the scanner in the kitchen. "When I call Marisa I *will* be put through—immediately. Marisa!" I shouted again.

"Rhea? What?" Marisa stood at the foot of the back stairs, her blond hair unbound, her feet bare on the cold floors, a white nightgown and robe clutched at her throat. A princess to be saved, a heroine in an old novel.

My throat clenched, and when I spoke, the words were rasping. "Did you know this woman is screening your calls from family, even when they tell her it's an emergency?"

"Auntie Maude?" Marisa's eyes were round, her face pale.

"There is nothing so important as rest and a stress-free environment for a young woman such as she."

"Marisa's not an invalid," I said, talking too loudly, shutting the back door and keying the dead bolt. I got my tone under control and continued. "Marisa is not stupid or unable to deal with problems. Marisa had an injury to her brain that affects speech, not one that affects IQ. Marisa, where're your daddy's guns?"

Marisa ran for the library and unlocked the doors with a key she took from a bureau in the hallway.

In the South, especially the rural South, guns may be as much a necessity as a right. On farms, packs of wild dogs, feral cats, rabid animals, injured livestock and all manner of other problems are often best handled by a gun, especially in a county with no animal control department. In our teens, Marisa and I had been given lessons by Miss DeeDee, that included how to clean, load, fire and handle a .32, a .38, a 9 mm semiautomatic, a hunting rifle and a single shot shotgun. I didn't like guns. I hated guns. I routinely put people back together after they got shot up with guns. But I wanted them right now. Bad guys were on the way.

Marisa opened the locked gun cabinet with a second key, hidden in a book. I remembered the hiding place, the same place her father had kept the key, and Miss DeeDee after him. I pulled the heavy draperies closed and flicked on a small lamp.

"What do you want?" Marisa asked. The excitement seemed to clear her speech.

Looking over the country arsenal, I discounted the hunting rifle. It had been part of Aunt DeeDee's training, but with a couple of angry, frightened cons on the loose, I wanted stopping power, not precision. I reached around Marisa and pulled out the handguns and the shotgun, explaining about the jail break and the two men heading this way, the helicopter on the horizon, the gunshots in the distance.

"Well, why didn't you say so," Auntie Maude said, exasperation in her tone. "Give me the 9 mm. I am familiar with that weapon, thanks to a Yank I, ah, dated in '72 in a certain Eastern European nation where the ambassador found himself in a spot of bother."

That was a story I wanted to hear. But later. I opened the separate area in the bottom of the gun cabinet and took out ammunition.

As I spoke, Cowboy entered the room and stopped for a moment just inside the door. I glanced up to find him standing still as stone. After a second he spoke, his voice soft, a bit rough. "Place is locked up. I'll check the barn. Is anyone else on the premises but us?"

"No one," Auntie Maude said, "except for the twins upstairs."

He took the .32, loaded it and left, telling Auntie Maude to keep the lights off and lock him out. The woman followed and I heard locks snapping as I loaded the two other handguns and the shotgun. When the weapons were all loaded, I handed Auntie Maude the 9 mm, Marisa the .38, and I took the shotgun. "Safeties are on," I said, cutting the last lamp before moving back into the center of the house.

The scanner was scratchy with dispatch issuing orders and information being relayed from the field. It was bedlam out there. An officer was down, reported shot. Then he was not shot, just suffering a broken wrist. A patrol unit was overturned in a pond, the officer trapped. Then it was disclosed he was just wet and embarrassed, his unit submerged. The chopper was giving locations only his pilot could see. The men on the ground were yelling for information no one could give. No one was listening. Three times I heard Mark's voice; once, he mentioned Stowe Farm.

Overhead, a helicopter roared, low to the ground. Lights moved across the lawn as if searching. Where were they, the two escaped prisoners? On the house lawn? I strained to see orange forms in the shadows. The chopper banked, its lights on the pecan trees at the drive. Gunshots sounded far-off, pops beneath the chopper noise. Were we in as much danger from gun-happy cops as from escaped prisoners?

Upstairs, the twins began to scream, dual cries of fear and anger. I met Marisa's eyes for a moment. She was terrified but she didn't head for the second-floor nursery, Aunt DeeDee's training holding over a mother's need to comfort.

I grabbed my cell phone and dialed the county dispatch number. When Eddie answered, I shouted, "There are people at Stowe Farm—three women, two babies and a man in the barn—who belong here. The man's wearing a duster, not prison orange. Please tell your guys in the helicopter not to shoot him.''

''Calm down, Rhea,'' the dispatcher said. ''The officers are out there to protect civilians, not to hurt them.''

''Right. Like no one's ever died from friendly fire before.'' Terrified, I hung up. *Where was Cowboy?* What was taking him so long? Over the scanner, I heard the dispatcher pass along my warning about the number of civilians and the man in the duster, but the words were overridden by other communication traffic.

At some point, Auntie Maude had changed clothes, and was now wearing dark pants and a dashiki tunic. Very colorful. Very orange. When this was over, I'd have to tell her the color choice was not a good one. Marisa had found slippers and fastened her robe. The pearl buttons gleamed in the faint light.

I took a place at a window that gave me a view of the rear grounds and part of the barn as well as the front lawn. Marisa moved to the curving front stairs and sat, her robe billowing. Auntie Maude took a stance at the bottom of the back stairs, where she could see both the back and front doors, and cover me. She was wearing stout shoes and had thrown a sweater across her shoulders against the chill. A portly woman with a fleshy face, she made an incongruous picture in the dashiki and sweater, holding the gun.

Outside, I could see Cowboy moving, dark against the white of the four rail fence. Horses milled and moved, raising dust that caught the moonlight. The lights in the woods seemed closer. I thought I could see forms moving in the distant brightness, headlights bouncing.

I wasn't certain that the searchers in the woods had heard the dispatcher's warning about a man in a duster, so I dialed Mark's cell and told him about Cowboy. Instead of replying, Mark cursed as he hung up, a word so foul his mother, Clarissa, would have fainted. Must have been the stress of the moment. A nighttime chase, like a video war game but with real guns and real bullets, tended to bring out the worst language.

"Who are the brigands?" Auntie Maude asked, her tone almost cheerful.

"A kid who shot his foster father and a man with three felony convictions. The kid I'm not worried about, but Graham Cornwell may have killed a woman and then gut shot a detention officer. Cornwell may not be someone we can reason with."

"I once reasoned with a tribe of headhunters in the Congo. I am quite good at reasoning, as the fact that I still possess my head should attest."

Another good story, for when we had the time. "Why didn't you let me talk to Marisa?"

"You didn't give me a good reason. Miss Marisa had the headache and had taken to her bed early."

"Oh." I looked back at Marisa. "You okay?"

"I'm fine, Rhea-Rhea. Thank you very much for asking."

Something in the courteous phrase struck me as funny, and I laughed, the sound harsh. We were a sight, a group of Old West homesteaders fending off the bad guys, in dashiki and sweater, nightgown and slippers, jeans and an old shirt. The helicopter flew over again and sped off. Cowboy appeared at the back door, knocking, and Auntie Maude let him in. He found me quickly in the ambient light and looked around, spotting us all. "Barn is fine, but I let the stock out into the front pasture. They were getting spooked by the chopper. They'll be better off running free. And the ruckus is coming from the back." He turned to Marisa, barely visible in the dark. "Todd Sinclair, ma'am. Anything I can do, you just say so."

"Thank you," Marisa said, "for your kind offer." Words relearned in a rehab for just such an occasion.

We waited in the dark after that. The helicopter didn't return. Far off, we could hear engines. Dogs. Men's voices. Gunshots.

13

WAS COWBOY HOUSEBROKE?

In the next silent hour my cell phone rang three times. Miss Essie wanted reassurance, though how she knew there was a problem I had no idea. I gave her platitudes and promised to call when the excitement was over. Shirl phoned, demanding to know what was going on and why she and Cam hadn't been invited to the party. Miss Essie had called her, demanding that she "do something about the mess her babies done got into." Cam Reston was staying over for the weekend and they were bored. Shirl and Cam were both doctors and adrenaline junkies, and thought gunshots and escaped convicts in the woods smacked of entertainment. Finally, long after the gunshots faded away, Mark called.

"We got 'em," he said without preamble.

"It's over," I said to the others. I clicked on a lamp and put down the gun. The sudden light was too bright, glaring. Marisa set her weapon on the stairs and went to check on her babies. Auntie Maude followed. Cowboy gathered the weapons and began removing the shells. "What happened?" I asked Mark.

"Graham Cornwell crashed his four-wheeler into a twenty-foot gully and broke his legs. The kid stopped at the top and just waited. We caught up with them about fifteen minutes later, about a half mile from the farm." Mark was still breathing hard, anger underlying his words.

I ignored the anger as part adrenaline, part exhaustion, part frustration over the fact that Skye was still in the hospital. "Where were they headed?"

"Don't know. We figured they wanted hostages, but the kid said something about a graveyard. There aren't any graveyards near here. We got a negotiator talking to him. But y'all are okay now. Tell Marisa the county is sorry about the mess we made back near Little Amber Lake." The anger seemed to dissipate as he spoke, leaving a hint of amusement. "We'll get the patrol car out and repair the damage to the dam."

I laughed. "You hurt a dam?"

"One of the guys was trying to take a patrol car down an old logging road. Said he hunted down it and it was plenty big enough. It wasn't. His unit spun out, took down some scrub trees, landed in the lake, knocked out the overflow valve and hit a concrete support for the old earthen dam. No risk of downstream flooding—not with the drought—but we got one wet and irate officer. We need to get a state engineer in to check out the support. And the county may owe Stowe Farm some water if the drought doesn't break."

"I'll pass it along," I said dryly. "You okay?"

"Just tired. I'm too old to find this sh…ah, stuff, fun anymore."

"Go eat some doughnuts, drink a pot of coffee and debrief your guys. It'll get better in the telling."

"It always does. So who's the guy in the duster?"

"A real live cowboy. A doctor friend from the hospital."

Mark said nothing for an instant. When he spoke, his tone was stilted. "How friendly?"

"Not as friendly as Skye." I meant it to hurt. The static

crackled between us. I could tell from his silence the barb had struck home. "I got to go."

"Yeah. I guess you do."

When I ended the call, I was alone, the guns back in the gun cabinet, the key still in the lock. I hid the key, pulled the drapes open and locked up the room. Following the sound of music up the back stairs, I found Cowboy and Auntie Maude in the twins' nursery with Marisa. She was sitting in an antique rocking chair, a baby at her breast, a blanket across her shoulder. She looked like an old photograph in the yellowed lamplight, her robe and gown spread out around her, her golden hair loose on her shoulders. Her slippers peeked out, pink and delicate against the velvety white rug.

Auntie Maude, still in dashiki and thick sweater, was changing a fussy baby, her broad back to the room. Cowboy was sitting on the small love seat, tuning an old guitar he had found somewhere, humming softly. He had discarded the duster and hat, but his worn jeans and boots still labeled him Western.

Suddenly exhausted, I sat on the floor by the love seat, yoga-style. *Nothing had happened.* The thought echoed, powerful in my mind. All that for nothing. The speed, the guns, the fear. Yet I knew how short a distance a half mile was. In five more minutes, Wayne Edward Geter and his felon friend could have been on the premises with us. No cops waiting. Just us. It could have been much worse.

The baby Auntie Maude was changing started screaming, and without warning, the older woman handed it to me. "Your namesake and godchild, I do believe."

I put the blue-clad infant up to my shoulder and tucked a pacifier into Rheaburn's mouth. He spit it out instantly. "He's hungry," I said. Marisa nodded, a sleepy smile on her lips.

Cowboy started strumming the guitar, the notes to an old

lullaby. I swiveled on the floor so Rheaburn could see him, and the crying began to diminish. Finally, Rheaburn took the pacifier and fell silent, his sleepy eyes on the guitar and the stranger's nimble fingers.

When I looked back to thank Cowboy, I found his eyes on Marisa. They were sealed on her with an intensity that closed my mouth on the words. His expression was almost a longing, a craving. The way a thirsty man might look when he saw water in the distance and didn't know how to reach it.

I glanced at my best friend in the whole word. She was returning his look.

And then I remembered Cowboy's comment when I'd asked him about dating. *"I reckon I'm too broke to date, ma'am. And maybe too old to date. For sure too tired to date. When I find Miss Right, I'll likely skip the preliminaries and just propose."*

And Marisa's words, *"I liked being married...."*

They didn't know each other. They didn't know anything about one another. But there wasn't much doubt what was happening between them as I watched. The little hairs on my arms lifted, and I nearly shivered.

I opened my mouth to stop this, and couldn't speak. My instincts were to protect Marisa, keep her safe from harm. But the words I had said to Auntie Maude were just as true at this moment as they had been earlier. Marisa was not a brain damaged vegetable; she was her own person, capable of making her own decisions. So I shut my mouth, slipped Rheaburn into a more comfortable position, leaned against the love seat and closed my eyes. Cowboy paused and changed the tune. I recognized it instantly. Elvis's "Love Me Tender," the old love ballad. When he reached the opening, he began to sing, his voice surprisingly deep and full. Without looking, I knew he was singing to Marisa.

The air in the room fairly crackled with intensity, with

longing. Cowboy sang as if his heart was breaking and only Marisa could heal him.

Great. Just freaking great. Now what? I didn't know whether to laugh or cry, cuss or throw something. What would Miss Essie think? Was Cowboy housebroke? For sure Miss Essie would blame me and Auntie Maude. Mostly me.

We left before eleven, with the words *Now what?* still echoing through my mind. Cowboy roared off on his motorcycle before I could tell him about Marisa and her injury. Before I could figure out how to take some of the steam out of the passion-charged heat in the Stowe farmhouse. The two hadn't shared three sentences, but there was no doubt that something had happened between them.

Sighing, I slid into my little car and headed home.

The phone rang. Thinking it was still part of my dream-induced fears, I picked it up and mumbled, "It isn't my fault, Miss Essie. Honest to God, it isn't."

"It probably *is* your fault, but that's not why I called. Wake up, Rhea."

"Mark?" I rolled over and pried open an eye. "It's two-fourteen in the blasted morning." Stoney was rumbling pleasantly on the pillow beside my head. "Even my cat is asleep. Call me back later."

"Nope. Wake up. Your services as coroner are needed."

I groaned. My mouth tasted like I had been chewing on old gym socks, rank and fuzzy. My back ached with the kind of pain that confirmed I had slept too long in one position. "I hate you."

Mark laughed and gave me directions. "Wear something warm. We've got a mass grave. You'll be here awhile."

"I hate you," I said again, and hung up. If I'd been awake, I would have thought of something much more piercing and adult. I was almost sure of it.

I dressed in the dark, pulling layers over my head and finding the old down coat by feel, and left the warm house, the animals still snoring, much too wise to be roused from bed at this ungodly hour. The uncertain temperatures of the last twelve hours had blown on through, depositing frost-crisp grass and ice-glazed windows in their wake. It was cold. Pulling my coat tighter, blowing clouds with my breathing, I sped down darkened roads.

I assumed that Mark was talking about an old slave or Indian or settler graveyard, something not on the maps, not marked with stone, the wooden markers long rotted away. Periodically, one was discovered in the state, and the cleanup was tedious, half archeology, half modern burial. I was almost to Stowe Farm before I put the location together with the words *mass grave*. Wayne Edward had been looking for a graveyard. Mark had a mass grave. Both were near Stowe Farm. Something was hinky. The thought woke me up just in time to turn off the state road onto an unmarked drive.

Without the police lights flashing against bare trees, I might have missed the final turn. It was a two-rut, red-dirt trail between rows of rusted barbed-wire fencing grown into the trunks of scrub trees. Branches scraped along my paint job. Behind the fencing lay an old pasture or field left to go fallow for the government subsidy money. Yellow crime scene tape cordoned off a huge area.

I pulled into a vacant slot, grabbed my folder of blank coroner reports and got out, wishing I had thought to make a pot of coffee and fill a thermos. Wishing I was still at home in bed. I stood at the periphery and watched the pandemonium.

There were so many cars, SUVs and trucks I couldn't count them, most with state and county tags. The lights were powerful enough to brighten a football field. Maybe fifty people stood around, all blowing their own clouds. The sound of motors and generators vibrated the still air, and dogs barked, their yips excited, sharpened by the metal cages that held them. County tracking dogs, state police dogs, K-9 units. Law enforcement everywhere.

In the center of the lights was an area roughly fifty feet by seventy. All through it short lengths of white string were pulled taut between stakes driven into the ground—dozens of stakes, yards of string, all resting at sharp angles like a connect-the-dots image identifiable only from high above ground. An eighteen-wheeler truck squeezed down the rutted road and stopped, cutting off all access. I had no idea what in heck I was supposed to do. All I knew was that it was cold.

Minutes passed, then a lot more. Folder under my arm, I shoved my frozen hands into pockets I hadn't used in two years and found a wadded, stiff tissue. Nasty. I couldn't even get rid of it—this was a crime scene. My used Kleenex would end up in an evidence bag.

Finally I spotted a Dawkins County ambulance. I could see two people sitting in the cab with windows rolled up against the weather. Picking my way carefully around the wide central area to the unit, I knocked on the window. The passenger door opened and warm, coffee-scented air flowed out.

"Morning, Dr. Lynch."

The voice was too cheery. I didn't even ask permission, but just climbed in and nudged a guy off the passenger seat, taking his place, shivering in my coat. "It'll be morning when someone gives me coffee."

"Looks like someone else was yanked out of bed at 2:00 a.m." It was a woman's voice. The man put a thermos cap full of brew in my frozen hands and I drank. It was hospital coffee. Thick enough to be eaten with a spoon, strong enough to make hair grow in unusual places.

"Thank you, thank you, thank you," I breathed. Five

minutes and two cups later, I looked up and focused on Gus and his partner, Carla, who must have been working a forty-eight hour shift. "And thank you for your warm seat. I think my butt was frozen. I know my hands were. I forgot a hat and gloves."

"Plenty of room in an ambulance, Doc. You gave me an excuse to stretch out in back," Gus said from the patient gurney.

"Can you tell me what we have here? Mark—Captain Stafford—said something about a mass grave. Why do you need an ambulance at a mass grave? All the people are dead."

Carla laughed. "You'd think." She looked more stout than usual in the heavy EMS coat, her blond highlights catching the bright glare. She had different-colored eyes every time I saw her. This morning she was wearing yellow contacts with striations out from the center like a stylized sun. Carla turned the key in the ignition and warm air blew out of the vents. I finally stopped shivering. "Actually, I think we're just here in case someone gets hurt on the scene. And it's not as if the county is paying us overtime or anything."

"You know we live to serve, Doc. Last night, one of the searchers chasing our fleeing felons got turned around and tripped over a skull. His radio died and his cell phone didn't work this far out in the boonies. By the time he got back to a service area, called dispatch and then figured out where he saw the skull, it was 1:00 a.m." Gus tore something with his teeth. "After that, things sped up considerably. Eat." He offered a bag of plastic-wrapped muffins, cakes and various other sinful treats.

"I hate dead bodies," I said. "I went into medicine to keep people alive, not to dig them up and chop them into little pieces afterward." I took a pack of raspberry fingers, my favorite. Delicious breakfast, made by Dolly Madison.

"What kind of grave? Please tell me it was Indian or local settlers. At least a century old."

"Nobody told us. But the Feebs and SLED are here, so it ain't something usual," Carla said.

I remembered the unmarked cars and the South Carolina State Law Enforcement car tags.

"Doc? Before you leave the scene, you need to take a look at McMurphy. He's got something going on," Carla added.

"You mean something medical?" I asked.

"Yeah. He's got these little things on his neck, like blisters," Gus mumbled through a mouthful of Cheetos.

"Like mouth sores, but worse. And he says he's fine, but he isn't. If you told him to see his medical doctor, he might listen to you," Carla said.

I yawned hugely and tucked my hands under the opposite armpits. "Yeah, okay. Bring him over. So what happens now?"

"You'll get told, I think. Come on, Gus, let's take a walk," Carla said.

"Why?" Gus and I asked simultaneously.

"I think I see a cut finger across the field." She winked at me.

Carla and Gus climbed out of the still-running unit. Mark Stafford climbed in. Ignoring him, I found another package of raspberry fingers and poured another cup of coffee. I didn't offer Mark one. Okay, I was feeling grumpy. It was after 3:00 a.m. His girlfriend was in the hospital having a baby. I was entitled.

"I used your name to request additional ambulance units for transporting bodies to Newberry, to get a forensic pathologist in from Columbia and to request the presence of the emergency preparedness director of Ford County. Hope you don't mind." Mark peeled off thick blue trauma gloves and set them in his lap, warming his hands between his thighs. ''I need paperwork on fifteen, maybe twenty bodies, all of whom need forensic postmortems and IDing. And if you don't offer me some of that coffee right now, I swear on my mother's bleached blond head I'll die of hypothermia.''

Affecting blithe unconcern, I passed the thermos top to him and said, ''This would have been considered mild weather in Chicago. Paperwork, I can do. What's going on?''

''I can't say for sure.'' Mark stared through the windshield, his green eyes on the chaos. His hands turned the thermos lid, his fingers deft, almost graceful. The way they felt when he used to touch my skin. Watching his hands made heat rise to my face. He was bent forward, nursing the coffee, his shoulders straining against the thick cloth of his winter jacket, pulling the word *POLICE* taut. The seams on his jeans were stretched as well, showing well-muscled thighs. He'd been working out. Quickly, I looked away. ''You see all those white strings, each one about six feet long, held with two stakes?''

The connect-the-dots graveyard. Dead bodies. My least favorite subject.

''Each string marks one body. Notice how the strings seem to be at odd angles? Well, they are. The girls are buried in a pattern.''

I sat up, staring into the night. ''Girls… You mean this really isn't a proper graveyard. It's like, a…mass murder or something.''

''Yeah. Or something.'' He sighed. ''Rhea, I've never seen anything like this.''

I felt instantly chastened for my selfishness, and passed him a raspberry finger. He ate it, saying nothing. When he had licked the last bit of fruit from his thumb, he said, ''It looks like they're buried at almost perfect forty-five degree angles to one another. Some are several years old. Some are…newer.''

"How new?''

"Real new. One looks fresh, possibly from today.'' He looked at me. "We called in the city cops who were on duty when the girl was kidnapped by the hit-and-run.''

"You found Melanie?'' I asked, remembering Ollie's girlfriend. The one who'd been kidnapped by the guy who'd rammed Ollie's bike and left him for dead.

"I think so. She's got on jewelry that fits her description. All the girls here fit the profile.''

"The profile?'' I asked "For the task force?''

Mark didn't even look at me. "We were trying to keep it quiet. Keep hysteria from building and keep the media from getting involved. Now this.''

I was beginning to understand.

"We've had disappearances, all girls and young women. All looked like runaways, and maybe some were. But some weren't. Finally someone put it together.''

"You figured that you had a serial kidnapper,'' I said. "So you created a task force.''

Mark nodded. "Missing for years, Rhea. Not just months. Missing for years.'' I was smelling exhaust and leaned over, turned off the ignition. The motor died. An uncomfortable silence filed the ambulance cab. Out the front window, I could see a woman waving her arms, casting weird shadows in the artificial lights. Even from here, I knew she had found another body.

"Just last month we started putting things together, and discovered that girls who fit the victim profile were disappearing from several counties.''

"So you called in the State Law Enforcement Division. Then, because you figured it could be more than just a statewide problem, you called in the Feebs.''

"But no bodies turned up. Till now," he sighed. "This is going to be a freaking circus."

"Do any of the girls look like Wayne Edward Geter's sister?"

"Not yet. Thanks for the coffee." Mark pulled a fresh pair of blue gloves from his jacket pocket and pulled them over his hands, snapping them in place. "You'll need to fill out the necessary paperwork for getting the medical examiner down here, as well as the usual bag-and-tag forms. You're not mad that I used your name to do that?"

I shrugged. "Did it give me an extra hour in bed?"

"Yep."

"Then I'm not mad. Thanks. Do I need to be doing anything right now?"

"Yeah. I think I see the M.E. across the field. You need to go talk doctor-talk. See if the two of you can find any obvious cause of death."

"I can do that."

"Rhea?"

"Yeah."

"It was two task forces. Two distinctly different types of girls who were disappearing off the streets. One group of Caucasian, blond, high school girls, or girls who look the age. They were always sent gifts of flowers and candy at least once before they disappeared. Another group of African-American or mixed-race girls, same age group. Some may have received gifts of lingerie before disappearing.

"Except for the age, there weren't many similarities between the two groups. The profiles of the crimes and the criminal minds we were dealing with were completely different. In fact, most of the black girls could have been runaways. Unlike with the white girls, the African-Americans made no contacts with family after they disappeared. Different MO."

I remembered the phone call from Wayne Edward Geter's sister after she'd vanished. I quoted what I recalled of the words she had used. "'I don't love Vance. I love Deacon.'" Mark nodded slowly. I still didn't understand why he was so spooked. "And?"

Finally his eyes settled on me, jade-green in the night, smooth and unyielding as polished stones. "And we've got both buried here." He paused, as if that were important and he was giving me time to process the information.

"Okay," I said. "I see." But I didn't, not really. I didn't want to see. But I had a feeling that I would understand soon enough, whether I wanted to or not. Cold air blasted against my skin as Mark opened the cab door and climbed out. Turning to my own door, I followed.

The medical examiner was one of two female M.E.s in the state. Dressed as she was for the weather and the terrain, I was uncertain of her build, but she was shorter than I, with close-cropped blond hair and an authoritative manner. No shrinking violet here.

"Dempsey Anne Reid," she introduced herself, not offering to shake hands. Hers were encased in thick gloves, under which I could see cotton liners. Smart. I'd have to remember to get a box of the liners for outdoor moments like this. Of course, I'd probably forget and leave them at home with the toboggan and the gloves.

"Rhea Lynch. I'm an E.R. doctor. Got conned into being an assistant coroner just this week, so I don't really know what I'm supposed to do here."

"I heard the Dawkins County coroner got shot. Someone tricked you into this?"

"Worse. She used guilt. How'd you get the name Dempsey?"

"Dad. He was a boxing fan, with only one child. Loved the sport. Named me after his favorite boxer." Dempsey opened an orange-and-white tool chest at her feet and passed me a pair of gloves and liners, which I slipped over my hands.

"Aren't you glad he didn't like Ali or Frazier best?"

Dempsey chuckled in the cold. "Yeah, I would have made a lousy Mohammed or George. Your job is to fill out paperwork, make notes for the trial and try not to step on any bodies. Okay, Stafford," she called. "I understand you're OIC here. Get me up to speed."

Mark moved out of the darkness carrying a battery-powered klieg torch bright enough to wake the dead—so to speak. *OIC* meant officer in charge in cop-speak.

"We have eighteen graves so far, and by opening four, we know we have both Caucasian and African-American victims buried here. One Caucasian female with tentative ID. Several other depressions have been identified as probable graves, but we aren't doing any more digging tonight. Here's the map showing where we found each one, in relation to the others." He passed a graph to Dempsey. I peered over her shoulder.

The handwritten map showed true south, with an inverted triangle pattern of graves above. Four across the top with eight at forty-five degree angles below them, to form triangles. Another set of three was at the downward apex of the angles, and another set was below that.

"Triangles," I said. "He's making triangles out of them. I'll bet there's a color pattern with them, too—black and white victims as part of the picture. With a large triangle as the intended result.''

''Yeah. Pointing south, if he's working upward from the base.''

Toward Stowe Farm, I thought.

Mark held up a county map, folded small to expose only a few inches of space. ''We're here. Stowe Farm is here.'' He pointed. ''And we're only two miles from where Wayne Edward Geter and his pal Graham Cornwell were caught.'' His finger moved. ''We think the guy with the broken legs knows something about this.''

''He was taking Wayne Edward here?''

''Could be. But Cornwell probably didn't put the most recent body here. He was locked up at the time.''

Dempsey said, ''How long before the Evidence Response Team is through with the first grave?''

''They're finishing up now. She's all yours, Doc.''

Dempsey bent and lifted her tool chest and an electric Coleman lantern, turning on the beam. Picking her steps carefully, she led the way into the field.

14

Hands in my pockets, considerably warmer with the layers of gloves, I placed my feet in the depressions her boots made. If there was evidence here, I didn't want to make a mistake and step on it. I also didn't want to accidentally step on any bodies. My feet sank into the disturbed earth. I'd never get my running shoes clean. I should have worn boots, but that would have meant another trip to the boxed clothes, and I had no idea which box might hold winter boots. I really needed to unpack. I was wearing new Nikes and I'd probably have to throw them away…. My mind was filled with all the mundane thoughts of someone trying not to think.

As we moved into the field, the smell hit me. The cold air had kept the stench of decaying bodies at bay until I was right on top of them.

Instantly, I was ashamed for thinking about my shoes. There were girls buried here; all had most likely died horrible deaths. As a crowd parted, Dempsey stopped, bent and set her flashlight on the ground.

Squatting next to her, keeping my knees off the red clay earth, I bent to share what she saw. The girl in the shallow depression was naked, lying on a white sheet that had been wrapped around her for burial. The sheet at her head and feet was bunched with tight wrinkles. "You get Polaroids of the grave as you opened it up?" Dempsey asked.

"Yeah. Right here, Doc."

Dempsey accepted the photographs, flipped through them and handed them to me. I didn't particularly want to look, but went through the stack quickly. It was like a fast-forward video of a grave opening. Dirt. The appearance of something beneath the dirt. The sheet-wrapped body, tied at the head and feet, clumps of red clay adhering to it. The exposed body. In the last shot, her hands lay at her sides, her feet together. Blond, delicate, she looked about eighteen. Even to my inexperienced eye, she hadn't been dead for long. There was no insect involvement, and the corneas of her opened eyes still retained enough moisture to tell they had been a fresh, bright blue in life.

While I went through the photos, Dempsey had started work. From her tool chest, she took an eighteen-inch core temperature thermometer and a scalpel. With the scalpel, she cut into the girl's right side and thrust the thermometer deeply into the body at her liver. I handed the photos to Mark. "Melanie? Ollie's girlfriend?"

"We think so. Rings on the left hand match descriptions her mother gave us."

Dempsey leaned across the grave, comparing the left and right sides. "This girl was beaten on her left side. Before death." Dempsey pointed to severe bruising from her knee up to her shoulder. Her lower left arm had an obvious deformity, as if the bones weren't in proper place. Broken.

"If she's who we think she is, her boyfriend was hit by a van. Hit-and-run," I said. "Maybe she got clipped, too. Look at the sharp line of contusions along here." I pointed to a long line of purple discoloration.

Dempsey lifted the lantern and applied the harsh light to the left side of the body. "I agree. It's awfully linear to be a beating. And look here and here.'' She pointed. ''We've got abrasions at shoulder and hip that originate at the posterior and move to the anterior. The boyfriend was hit from behind?''

I brought the memory of Ollie to the forefront of my mind. ''Yes. And he had similar abrasions and contusions. I remember someone giving that in the report.''

''No defensive wounds to the hands, but the left hand shows bruising and some broken fingers. We bagged them for evidence,'' Mark said.

I glanced at the hands. They were encased in brown paper bags, the mouths tied around each wrist. I glanced at the feet. The same process had been done there.

Dempsey moved a strand of the girl's hair. Another purplish bruise marred the left side of her face. ''Looks like she took a lick to the head, from the zygomatic bone to the squamous part of the temporal bone, maybe farther back into the parietal.'' She pressed slowly with gloved fingers.

I watched as the bones gave slightly. ''Crushed?''

''Yeah. She probably didn't live long after. Without proper medical care, she could have been dead in a few hours. I'll know better after the core temp and after we get her opened up.'' The medical examiner looked up at me. ''You got one of these?'' She indicated the special thermometer.

''No. Never needed one before.''

''Here.'' She handed me two of the long thermometers, each sealed in a plastic tube.

''Thanks,'' I said. ''But I hope I won't need them.''

Dempsey raised the girl's arm, poked and prodded at soft tissue, worked the joints at fingers, wrists and elbows. ''There isn't much rigor except in the smaller muscles. She hasn't been dead long. I hear we have to transport for PMs,'' Dempsey said, her eyes still on the pale body of the girl. ''You got it approved with Newberry yet? And why can't I do the work here? It's going to be a pain having to drive back and forth.''

"The local hospital houses the county morgue, and it has one slab and one chiller," I said. "You'd be moving bodies constantly. So you might be better off at Newberry. I can make a call, let them know what's coming their way. And at Newberry, you'll have extra hands.''

"Yeah," she said, looking around at the frigid scene, the klieg lights set up in strategic points in the pasture, hand-held flashlights moving erratically. "I know the docs at Newberry. They do good work. I may need to have more than one postmortem set up at a time. With this many bodies, I may need to do comparisons. And it would be nice to have Newberry's help. You can come along, if you want.''

"I'll pass. Thanks, anyway.''

"Think about it. You may need info for a trial.''

I managed not to groan.

"You can bag-and-tag this one. Let's see the next grave. You left it closed, right?''

"We opened four. Then stopped," Mark said. His voice was toneless. Offering nothing. Cop voice.

"If one of the opened graves is of an African-American, I'd like to see that one next. Then let me see an unopened one.''

"This way," Mark said.

I followed the group across the field, stopping when they stopped, squatting when they did. My back was already sending out warning messages. I would pay sorely for to-night.

My view of the open grave was blocked by Mark's back. I didn't bother to walk around him. I just waited. As before, photographs were put in my hands, along with a flashlight, the first shot showing a closed grave, then a depression in the earth, deepening, with something showing, a bit of sheet, this one light-colored but maybe not originally white. Finally, the filthy sheet, crusted with brown and red earth stains, tied at head and feet, following the contours of a human shape. This body had been in the ground a lot longer than the last one.

I felt my lip curl at the sight and handed back the Polaroids, fisting my gloved hands in my pockets. When I looked into the pit, it took a moment to orient myself. Where the last body had been left clean and unmarked, as if she had died quickly, this one had not. This girl had suffered. She had been beaten and stabbed, and parts of her were missing. A sexual sadist had worked her over for a long time.

The white mist of our breathing caught the light of the torches, wavering like the restless ghosts of the girls buried in the field. The cold seemed to press in from all sides.

The thick coffee and the raspberry fingers rose into my throat. I bunched my coat up, pressing my fists to my stomach. When I blinked, a negative image of the girl was impressed onto my eyelids. Because of the cold, there wasn't much active insect evidence, but insects had been at work on her at some time, especially on her abdomen from pubic bone to sternum.

"There seems to be a pattern to the insect infestation," Dempsey said, pointing. "See the shape? Vaguely triangular." She lightly pinched one of the lesions.

"It looks pockmarked," I said.

"Possibly cig-burn injury. I can tell more later. Lacerations here and here." She pointed again. The girl had been burned with cigarettes. Cut horribly. "It looks like a triangle," she said, "wide across the torso and beneath the ribs, apex at the pubis."

I stood and turned away. I had seen enough. I was going to make a terrible witness at a trial. All I wanted to do was cry. Or throw up. Or maybe kick to death the guy who had done this. Yeah. I liked the thought of that.

"Okay. Let me read the core temp on the first body, then I want to see a fresh one. I want to watch as it's opened," Dempsey said. "One African-American, one Caucasian. I want to know if the first grave is typical for the Caucasian bodies or if that was an anomaly for them. Your profiler will want to know that, too."

Then I understood what my mind hadn't wanted to know. *Them.* The cops were all thinking *them.* More than one person…

Rapists and sexual sadists rarely crossed racial lines. We had two races here, ergo, two killers. Even Ollie had said *they* when he first started talking about the van that hit him. Was Melanie an anomaly? If she'd died before they started to torture her, they may have just bundled her up and added her to their triangle grave. I hated this. I really hated this.

The small group tromped off and I looked back to find Carla on the far side of the grave. "Want to help me with the paperwork?" I asked.

"Why not," she said, her voice subdued. "This sucks. The unit is warm, there's coffee and Gus's stash of sweets is big enough to keep our blood sugar in the high four-hundreds. Hey! Stafford!" she shouted. "Doc, here, is going to need a map of the scene and a cop to tell her what's up. Why not give her McMurphy?"

"Yeah, whatever," he shouted back.

"And you better call Bobby Ray Shirley back to duty early. One coroner can't handle this many bodies."

"Yeah, yeah, yeah, okay. I'll get him in." Mark sounded disgusted.

"Very slick," I said to Carla, managing a half smile against the taste of death in my mouth. "Very slick." I was being careful not to look down into the grave. So was Carla. Concentrate on the things at hand. Think about the job.

Don't think about the awful corpse at your feet. Don't breathe too deeply. Don't step wrong. "You got us out of here and got McMurphy all at the same time."

"My mama didn't raise no dummies. The only way McMurphy will see his doctor is if you lay it on thick. Besides, I can't take any more of this. Dr. Dempsey may have a cast-iron soul, but I don't."

"You keep the coffee and the sweets coming and I can handle McMurphy. But I admit I've had enough of this to last forever." Cowardly? Who, me? Still without looking into the grave, we crossed the burial ground, avoiding white strings and stakes that marked the graves, and climbed in the warm ambulance cab, spreading out paperwork for twenty bodies. It was going to be a long night—what there was left of it. Blocking out memories of the bodies, I studied the papers.

Out in the pasture, cops and crime scene techs were putting huge white tents over the scene. The canvas caught the faint breeze and the harsh lights, undulating slowly. I thought it strange that they would cover the entire site, until I considered the possibility of rain or disturbance from low flying media helicopters. Either could ruin a delicate crime scene. And come morning, the media would turn this into a macabre party.

When McMurphy crawled into the ambulance later, I didn't have to pretend to have a strong reaction to his medical problem. The cop had a lesion on his neck that looked like a second degree burn. The blisterlike lesion overlay four thin scratches, the raised flesh filled with slightly bloody fluid. It was a vesicle, the kind made by chicken pox or herpes, but bigger than any vesicle I had ever seen, a truly nasty one. It had to hurt.

Carla took McMurphy's entrance as her cue to get some air, leaving us in privacy. I figured Carla knew what the lesion looked like as much as I did. Telling a man he had some form of herpes wasn't in her job description.

"Ralph, how long have you had that lesion on your neck?" I asked.

"Aw, Doc, it ain't nothin. Cap'n said you need a map and lingo and numbers on the graves."

"It is too something. Let me see." Without waiting for permission, I pulled at his coat collar and unbuttoned his shirt. Sgt. Ralph McMurphy was a Vietnam vet, had seen six months time in a Vietcong prison camp before escaping, and was nearing retirement from serving Dawkins County as a deputy. He was a he-man of the old order. The kind of man who never had a pain or a complaint. The kind of man who died of undiagnosed medical problems because he never saw the inside of a doctor's office until he was on death's door. I routinely pronounced such men dead.

The vesicle was about two by two-and-a-half centimeters, edematous, erythematous, with swelling in the surrounding tissues about another centimeter all around. The scratches underneath were maybe two millimeters wide, three or four millimeters apart, and about four centimeters long—altogether, slightly larger than a domino. "What scratched you?"

"Me and my pets were wrasslin'. Teacup got me a good one." McMurphy didn't look at me. No eye contact. "My wife's dog," he added.

It didn't look like a dog scratch. Unlike a typical canine one, the four scratches started on the same line. Dog toes are arranged in a curved pattern, the two center toes farther ahead and the two outer ones behind a bit. In a dog scratch, the damage at the point where the scratch originates is in a C shape. I knew the scratch wasn't made by anything canine. "Teacup?" I asked.

"Yeah. My wife has a thing for little pets. You should see the dog she got last month. One a them hairless mutts.

He's got a case of the uglies so bad it makes me think about mercy killing. Six hundred dollars for that thing and I can't stand to look at it.''

"Ralph," I said gently. "You should take that scratch seriously. It looks like herpes.''

McMurphy grew still. Then he moved away, buttoning his collar. "Thanks, Doc. I'll see Dr. Boka on Monday," he said, his voice distant. His fingers were shaking slightly, but perhaps that was from the cold. "Meanwhile, we got work to do here. Which body you want to start on?''

Dissatisfied, but with no power to pursue his condition further, I nodded and took the passenger seat. "How about the Jane Doe who looks like she died today?" I held out the copy of the site map to him. "Which one is she?''

Bobby Ray Shirley reached the site at 11:00 a.m. and took over, looking slimmer and more robust than I had ever seen him. I stumbled away, so tired I could hardly find my little car or the road to take me away from this horrible place.

I got home before noon, threw my running shoes into the big green bin that collected my garbage, stripped in the back hallway and tossed my clothes outside. I stood under a scalding shower for a long time, needing sleep. Hoping for it. Fearing it. Still feeling wired, unable to contemplate a nap for fear of the visions that might haunt me, I found a clean pair of Nikes, dressed warmly and went for a hard run, the dogs at my side.

The noon air was only slightly warmer than the night air had been, the sun shrouded behind clouds that threatened rain but probably wouldn't deliver. I ran through the fire-damaged fields, hearing the burned grass crunch beneath my shoes, smelling the sour scent of charcoal and the faint tang of far-off cows. I passed a 1940s tractor that was falling apart and the old charred building that had once housed a sharecropper family, and found myself at a pond nearly deep enough to swim in. The dogs had always liked this pond, and wanted to dive into the murky water and play, but I called them back to my side, spoiling their fun. If they noticed that I was out of sorts, they didn't act like it. They wanted a game of tag. I made them follow me back toward home and the bed that awaited me.

As I entered the yard, I took the clothes I had worn at the crime scene and tossed them over a low-hanging branch of the old oak that shaded my backyard. They could stay outdoors until laundry day. I didn't want them in the house, especially the down-filled coat. They all smelled of graveyard, but the coat seemed to have picked up the scent more than the jeans and shirts layered under it.

Still slightly sweaty, I fell across the mattress, so tired that surely I would sleep now. Stoney padded up my legs to settle on the small of my back, his purr motor at full blast, soothing, pulling me toward sleep and restful dreams. Instead, as I closed my eyes, I saw the vesicle on Sgt. McMurphy's neck, the underlying scratch mark. It looked as if it had been made by four sharp objects close together, like a human hand when the fingers are curled, almost closed. A very tiny human…

15

I sat up from the dank sheets, dislodging Stoney. Charlie Denbrow had a similar scratch in his beard. And a tiny reddish bump starting over it. Had there been more than one parallel line beneath the beard? Were Charlie and Ralph McMurphy friends, as well as co-workers? Had they gotten into something dangerous? And then a question that came out of nowhere—did their vesicles have anything to do with the triangle gravesite? The police were looking for two men. Two killers.

"Okay," I said to the darkened room. "I'm tired and probably putting too many disparate items together in one basket. The only thing the vesicles have in common with the grave is the coincidence of time. That's it." But I didn't believe in coincidence anymore. Not really.

Crawling out of bed, I dressed again, this time in jeans and a lab coat, grabbed an old, boxy, navy peacoat, and left for the hospital. I entered at the security door near the doctors' lounge and peeked in. The room was empty.

I meandered up the hall, my hands in my jeans pockets, and found a nurse sitting at the ICU desk, her head buried in paperwork. I tapped on the cabinet over Gloris's head.

She lifted her shellacked beehive hairdo and blinked. It

took a moment for her to focus. "Oh, hi, Dr. Lynch. I didn't know you were working E.R. today."

"I'm not. I came to be nosy."

"Well, you came to the right place." Gloris patted a chair. "Who and what?"

"I know I'm not supposed to ask, because he isn't my patient, but I'm curious. What ever happened to Charlie Denbrow?"

Gloris breathed out slowly and shook her head, the rolls at her middle moving with the motion. Gloris had put on a few more pounds and her scrub top was a tad tight. "He was such a pitiful thing. We shipped him this morning, as soon as he was stable enough after surgery. He had already developed a pseudomonas infection, a real resistant one. Dr. Statler saved his life, no doubt. But whether he'll make it, I just don't know."

"What about under his beard? I thought I saw something there when he was in the E.R. Before surgery."

"Doc Statler ordered him shaved so he could get a look at it. He said it was probably some herpes thing. Maybe a zoster. He cultured it and sent it off for a herpes culture. The results should be back by Monday."

Herpes zoster, or varicella-zoster, was probably the most common virus on the face of the earth. It caused, among other things, chicken pox. "Would you call the lab and ask if they have them yet, just in case the results came back this morning?"

"Anything for you, Doc."

I shook my head. I had given up telling Gloris that she didn't owe me anything for saving her life. She had contracted a life-threatening disease not too long ago, one that had killed every single person who caught it. Gloris had been the guinea pig willing to try a treatment that saved her and so many others after. She credited me with a cure, although I was only one member of the team that had come up with the treatment.

"It's not back yet," she said a moment later. "Lab says they'll call me when it gets in, but it'll most likely be Monday. Weekends are the pits for getting back results."

"Thanks." I said. "Beep me if you hear anything, will you? I saw a similar lesion on another patient last night and I'm concerned."

"Will do."

I left the hospital, feeling twitchy from lack of sleep, but I still didn't want to go home. The two cops had one thing in common: vesicles over healing scratches. There was no evidence to connect them as killers and sexual sadists, even if the herpes was a sexually transmitted disease. The connection in my mind was the result of a sleep-deprived brain. Just stupid.

Shucking off the lab coat, I climbed into my car and drove slowly out to the Stowe farm to see Marisa. A spatter of welcome rain hit the windshield as I drove, as if the sky were spitting at me. The day was cold and growing colder. And it got a lot colder still when I saw the motorcycle parked next to Marisa's back deck.

A Honda Valkyrie in slick black. A leather duster tied to the seat. Cowboy. I parked, turned off the engine and sat in the car, considering.

I had spoken the truth to Auntie Maude when I claimed that Marisa wasn't in some brain-damaged vegetative state where others needed to make decisions for her. But at the same time, she was vulnerable. She was rich, lonely and the mother of two, without the communication skills to make it in a modern world. Taking my coat with me, I climbed out of the car and up the back steps.

The sound of guitar music and the smell of stew hit me as I entered. I waved at Auntie Maude, who was stirring a pot at the stove, and followed the chords to the snug nook under the back stairs where Marisa played with the children. The nook was part of a larger room, with a fireplace, hooked rugs, two ancient and cracked leather sofas, a desk and side tables. A pleasant room, with the gas-log flames leaping and lamps lit against the cloudy day. There had always been a sense of safety here.

I stood in the doorway and stared at the cozy scene. A Christmas tree, twinkling with lights and decorated with stuffed animals and a teddy-bear angel on top, stood in a corner, wrapped gifts beneath. Marisa was half-visible in the rocker, nursing, her back to the door. Toys were scattered all over—a plastic train, a plastic telephone, a windup swing, stuffed animals, a set of Raggedy Ann and Andy dolls, and a twisted Gumby. Cracker crumbs were ground into the rug, a pacifier lay beneath a chair, a diaper bag covered with miniature clowns hung on the sofa arm.

Beside the diaper bag sat Cowboy, dressed in a plaid flannel shirt, jeans and boots, a baby over one shoulder, a guitar gripped in the other hand. He set the instrument down as he met my eyes, and began to pat the baby's back, burping him. My breathing sped up and my stomach tightened. Cowboy was burping Rheaburn as if he knew what he was doing. Something about his ease with my godchild bothered me. A lot. And I let him know it with my eyes.

Cowboy watched me. I didn't speak. I didn't blink. His patting stuttered and paused before resuming its original rhythm. He looked slowly around the room, over the stuffed animals and toys, his gaze alighting on Marisa for a long moment. He tightened his lips, nodded once as if to himself, and made eye contact with me again. His head jerked toward the outside wall, and I understood that we were leaving the house. I nodded and went back to the kitchen without speaking to Marisa.

Auntie Maude was no longer standing over the pot on the stove, and there was no coffee, as there would have been if Miss Essie were nanny, or Miz Auberta was work-ing. But there was a pot of tea on the tea warmer and I poured myself a cup, tasting it. A strong, rich, black tea, aromatic, with a slightly nutty flavor. Feeling decidedly British, I added a cube of sugar to the cup and slid into my peacoat and out the door.

Settling on the steps overlooking the barn and the hills that rolled toward the woods, I sipped at the tea, weariness blanketing me like a heavy cloak. The raindrops had stopped, leaving the wood damp and icy against my back-side. After a few minutes, the door closed behind me and Cowboy sat on the vacant step just above me, his booted feet spread, arms on his knees with hands dangling be-tween. No coat in the chill air. For a long moment, neither of us said anything. Finally, I broke the silence.

"You're in love with her, aren't you."

I heard him take a slow breath. "Seems that way," he said. His voice was quiet, thoughtful, maybe a bit wistful. "I didn't plan on it."

"You know about the injury to her brain?"

"Not much. Enough to know she can sing any song she ever knew, but verbal communication is a problem for her. Enough to know I can teach her new songs, but it takes a while for her to learn. Enough to know she's a caring, lov-ing, tender woman with a smile that lights up my whole soul." His voice grew hard. "Enough to know she's been abused and that some fool idiot left her for another woman. His loss. My gain." After a moment he asked, "Are you planning on trying to stop me from seeing her?"

I almost laughed. "I've never been able to stop Marisa from doing anything. Not before her injury, not after. But she's vulnerable. And I won't see her hurt." Without a change in tone, I told him about the injury to Marisa. I turned slightly and met his eyes. "You hurt her, and I'll come after you with that shotgun inside and put more holes in you than any surgeon could ever hope to close."

Cowboy's lips twitched. "Long as we understand one another." He shivered slightly in his flannel shirt.

I turned back to the view of the low, rolling hills and sipped at the tea. "What prospects do you have financially?"

He laughed through his nostrils, a half-disbelieving sound. "That's mighty bold of you, Dr. Lynch."

"Marisa's rich. You after her money?"

"From bold to insulting." When I didn't reply, except to stiffen my mouth, Cowboy said, "Money for money's sake never meant that much to me, ma'am." He looked around. "Risa showed me around while the twins were asleep. I admit that the cattleman in me appreciates the richness and the value of this land. Appreciates the water resources on it, especially the horses that wintered here for generations between horse racing seasons. I itch at the sight of some of the breeding stock that's still here. I haven't been on a horse since last Christmas.

"But this farm is old and worn. The land needs attention it hasn't had for years. Some pasture needs to be plowed up and reseeded with a different kind of grass. The fencing is down in places, leaving some pasture unusable. The barn has rot at the beams in the back.

"I'm not rich in money, but I am in skills and I know what this place needs. I also think I know what Marisa needs. And I'm not without prospects. Ma'am." He sounded half-amused, more at the nature of the conversation than at me, as if he realized that I was acting in the place of Marisa's father. We were having the "What are your intentions toward my daughter" talk of generations past. I should have been embarrassed, but I wasn't.

Cowboy looked up into the sky as if to decide whether to continue or not. Finally he said, "The government will pay my medical school loans if I do service in a place like Dawkins County. I intend to apply to do my two years here, where I can be close to Marisa. I could work at Dawkins E.R. afterward.

"As a doctor, I can make enough to help keep this place up. I can turn over my land and stock back home to my baby brother. He's been running things for a few years anyway, with me in school. I'd be happy at Stowe Farm for the rest of my life, making this place a showcase, if that's what Marisa wants. Or just keeping the land up for the twins' inheritance if she'd rather."

"Sounds to me like you'd be giving up quite a bit to stay here. A life and lifestyle. Land. Family."

"Some things are more important than land." I could hear the smile and the heat in his voice. "And as for family, I have a younger sister who is someone to love and be loved, I have the memories of two good people who raised me and died young. As a man, with nothing else much to give, I can offer Marisa and her two babies my whole heart and my whole soul." Cowboy leaned down and looked at me hard. "I'm good with my hands and free with my heart because I've never given it before."

Something inside me turned over at the honesty and longing in his voice. His words sounded too good to be true, as if love at first sight really did exist in this world. But Cowboy needed to know what he was facing with Marisa. And I needed to know that he knew.

"This farm is worth about three million," I said baldly. "Marisa herself is worth about that much again in stocks and bonds. And when the market recovers it'll double."

Cowboy sat back quickly. I could feel him studying the side of my face to see if I was serious. "Holy moley."

I laughed a bit ruefully and glanced back at him from the corner of my eye. "Land is valuable here, and while land prices in Dawkins County aren't as spectacular as, say, close to Atlanta, they are still pretty dear. Marisa is a rich woman. I don't want anyone to come along and make her fall in love and take her money. She's got friends who would make life very painful for someone who tried.''

''You may consider your warning delivered, Dr. Lynch, ma'am. But I still intend to court Marisa, and I'd be appreciative if her friends were for me instead of against me. And if the shotgun remained unloaded and locked up.''

''I do suppose that might make things more pleasant all around. Less messy, too. Tell me about the land back home you mentioned.''

''My great-grandfather settled in West Texas before there was a town for a hundred miles. He bought, stole or card-sharked a two-thousand-acre ranch from a Spaniard named Corazon. When the man shot himself over the loss, my great-granddaddy married the widow and took on her orphaned daughters. When they passed away, their only son stayed on, inherited the land, married an Indian woman and had six kids.

''My brother and sister and I are fourth generation on that ranch. Though we've sold off a good bit over the years, we still have about twelve hundred acres, with water and pasture rights to a good bit more. We still live in the original house, though it's been upgraded a few times. I run cattle for the beef industry, with a project to bring back the longhorns on the side.'' I could hear the pride in his voice. The sense of history.

''My baby brother took over the ranch while I'm in school. Peter is a whiz, a major in agriculture and dual minors in Spanish and art history, if you can believe it. Peter wants the ranch. It's half-mine. I thought once upon a time I would go back, practice in the E.R. of the local hospital, work the ranch on the side. But now...'' His voice fell silent.

''And the sister?''

He was quiet for a long moment. "Emiline was a real gift. A late baby to Mama and Daddy. She can't decide if she wants to be a rodeo star or a country-and-western singer in Nashville. Prettiest thing on God's earth, so talented it scares me, and she's so full of love it breaks your heart just to be around her. One of God's good people."

Cowboy popped his knuckles hard, first one hand, then the other, the pops sounding like gunshots. "I brought her with me when I came East. She's in a private school in Ford County, staying in a dorm with a few other kids her age. She likes it okay, but she misses the ranch. She'd like it here.

"And now I have a question." Cowboy's eyes went cold as a frozen lake beneath cloud-filled skies. "Her husband. He leave her before the injury or after? Before he knew about the pregnancy or after?"

"Why? What difference would it make?"

"So I'll know just how hard to hit him when I see him."

In spite of myself, I grinned. "He was fooling around with Sarah Gibbons before the injury. He left Marisa after. Far as I know, he didn't know about the pregnancy before his affair or before Marisa was injured."

Cowboy nodded, the fingers of one hand caressing the knuckles of the other. "Her divorce final?"

"Yeah. It is. Do me a favor. Don't kill him and don't get arrested or sued. Any other injuries I'd be really happy to hear about over coffee. My treat."

Cowboy gave that little laugh again, his eyes tight, as if he was focused on something in the future only he could see, and it was a real pleasure.

I turned back to the far horizon, my amusement fading. Long minutes went by with us watching the trees move in the distant breeze, watching horses in a far pasture romp in the cold air. I said, "You're going to propose, aren't you?"

"Reckon I am. I was thinking of waiting a bit, though. Like a week. Maybe."

I almost laughed. "That's waiting a bit? Marisa is lonely. She liked being married. Don't hurt her."

"Thank you, ma'am," he said softly, and stood to go back inside.

"Todd?" He paused on the top step at my use of his given name. "She's not on birth control."

He laughed that little nostril laugh. "I'm not planning on ravishing her tonight, Rhea."

I nodded. "Maybe not. But I can't say the same thing for Marisa."

When he laughed this time it was a full laugh, belly deep, with wonder in his tone. "I do thank you for the warning, Dr. Lynch. I do thank you."

16

WILLFUL OLD BAT

Staying over for supper with the Braswell household, I ate venison stew made by Auntie Maude and cheese bread baked by Miss Essie. It was a perfect combination, the chunks of tender venison, tomatoes, potatoes, summer okra grown by Miz A, mushrooms and celery, seasoned with leeks, chives and rosemary, all sopped up with the bread and its swirls of cheese. Auntie Maude served dark beer with the meal and I had one, finding it peaty and thick and almost smoky. As a rule I didn't like beer, but the Guinness extra stout was wonderful, a compliment to food rather than a teenager's excuse to get drunk.

Of course, with the eye contact between Marisa and Cowboy, alcohol wasn't a necessary adjunct to a state of inebriation. They were almost giddy with the chemistry between them. It fell about the room like sparkles from fireworks. You'd have to be blind, deaf and dumb to miss it. Auntie Maude wasn't any of those.

After the meal, she followed me to my car and stared down at me from the deck with a fierce scowl on her face. "What did you tell that young man when you had him out here? I will not see that splendid young woman hurt further. Not while I am in this household."

It was amazing. Auntie Maude had been at Stowe Farm for only a few weeks, yet already Marisa had won her devotion. But then, Marisa had that effect on everyone she met. We all wanted to protect her.

I opened the car door and looked up at Auntie Maude. "I told him if he hurt her I'd take the shotgun and fill him with holes. I told him she wasn't on birth control. I explained about the injury. And about Marisa's money. To his credit, he didn't know what she was worth, and he wants to rearrange Steven Braswell's face for her. And he's got land and holdings back west, so he's not exactly penniless." That about summed it up. And I had cleverly slipped the part about birth control into the middle where it might go unnoticed.

Auntie Maude stared at me a moment, her brows lifted almost to her hairline. Her only comment was, "Birth control? Hmm. Perhaps that was wise." She turned and left me without a word. I was dismissed.

When I got home, fatigue clinging to me like a second skin, the light on my message machine was blinking red. I threw myself across the bed and punched Play. The first message was an invitation from Eli for lunch, my first indication that he ate anything other than eggs and bacon. The second message was also from Eli, his voice softly growling an invitation for dinner into the phone, a powerful burr of sound that made my skin feel warm. Some men knew how to do that, cause a woman—any woman—to react to their presence, even a recorded one. For just that reason, and because he had somehow procured and used my unlisted number, a fact I didn't much like, I had no intention of calling Eli back. He could be one of those men who got fixated on a woman and pestered her to death.

The third message was from Miss DeeDee, sounding like a sweet Southern belle, not like the dangerous psychotic homicidal maniac she really was. Some people had a slight edge when it came to hiding their true natures. Miss DeeDee had that commodity in spades.

I wasn't returning the call to Silver Lakes Psychiatric Hospital either, but the phone rang while I was erasing the messages and I made the mistake of picking it up. Miss DeeDee's dulcet tones greeted me. I think I groaned.

"Rhea, dear. So delightful to catch you at home. I called earlier, but my message must have been lost somehow. Are you well? I do worry about the long hours you work."

I sighed softly and rolled across the mattress, ignoring my back pinging with distant pain. It was Saturday night, I was exhausted, I wanted to sleep, and now I had Miss DeeDee applying a guilt trip. Lovely. I might be tired, but I wasn't about to let her control the conversation without a fight. Sounding as sweet as she, I said, "Miss DeeDee, I'm doing fine. How are things at the loony-bin? Is your medication helping?"

Miss DeeDee ignored my deliberate social gaffe and got in a gentle parry of her own. "Dear, do you remember the spring just after Marisa's parents were killed? We three took a picnic down near Landsford Canal landing, when the spider lilies were blooming. The summer I taught you both to shoot and play poker," she added.

I remembered both the picnic and the entire summer. Marisa had been inconsolable. I had never left her side and Miss DeeDee had outdone herself to keep Marisa occupied and busy. Yet she also provided opportunities to visit the cemetery. It had been a dance of healing and grief for months.

Miss DeeDee had been the perfect chaperon and protector, always knowing what Marisa needed, and furnishing it. By necessity, perhaps, that attention and concern had extended to me. I had been included in the warmth of Miss DeeDee's gentle affection, and Miss DeeDee had to know what the mention of that summer would do to me. It slipped

through holes in my defenses I didn't know I had. Made
me want to swear and hang up. Instead, I said, "Yes, Miss
DeeDee. I remember." Point to the old bat.

"Do you remember when we first came upon the spider
lilies, like a glistening carpet across the Catawba River? Do
you remember what Marisa said?"

Unwillingly I quoted, "'Heaven couldn't be more beautiful. Mama and Daddy must be having a wonderful time
up there.'"

"It was the start to her emotional healing, the first time
her grief gave way to joy."

"I remember." I also remembered being grateful to Miss
DeeDee for bringing us to the landing so Marisa could have
the experience. That gratitude was what Miss DeeDee
wanted me to remember. The witch.

"Miss DeeDee, what do you... What can I help you
with?"

"Well, dear, it's likely nothing, but I heard a little rumor.
Well, several actually. Normally, as you know, I never listen to rumors."

Miss DeeDee knew everything before it happened. She
was a regular rumor distribution center. But I didn't say
that. The guilt complex that thrived deep in the soul of
every Southern woman was suddenly working overtime in
me. Had to be the lack of sleep.

"The most unusual thing I heard is that there is a graveyard on Stowe Farm, with a serial killer running around
kidnapping young girls off the street and doing unspeakable
things to them. Please tell me this isn't so."

While sleep pulled at my mind, I explained about the
graveyard, the murders, the girls, the task force, and about
how I was made into an assistant coroner. And how I hated
it. I stopped midcomplaint when I realized that I was un-
burdening myself on the woman who had hurt Marisa.

"Miss DeeDee, I'm dead on my feet. I have to get some sleep."

"Of course, dear child. Forgive an old worried woman her fears and concern for the town she's left behind. Just one more thing. I understand that Marisa has a new…beau? A cowboy?" The last was dripping with distaste. With one word, she made it clear that a man in such an occupation was unsuitable for a woman in Marisa's position. The fact that I had thought that very same thing nagged at a corner of my mind.

"Miss DeeDee, Todd Sinclair is from an old established Texas family, with ties to the state government and to Washington," I said. Well, the man had a ranch. Ranches were under the control of the agricultural department, weren't they? That was government, wasn't it? Sort of?

"He's a fine family man, never married, in his E.R. residency, with the care of a young sister to his credit." Okay, I was defending the man I had just threatened to fill full of buckshot. I'm not particularly consistent. But I remembered Marisa's love-lust-heat in the kitchen over venison stew and cheese bread. Stopping that relationship might be like trying to stop a fully loaded locomotive.

I had never loved like that before, nor been loved like that—that sort of instant passion, till-death-do-us-part kind of love. John came close; we had seemed perfect for one another. My eyes closed. I think I drifted off in some kind of romantic vision. Or sleep.

"Rhea? Are you still there?"

I sighed, this time not caring if Miss DeeDee heard or not. "Miss DeeDee, I'm crashing. I have to go. We'll talk some other time."

"Of course, dear, but I'll be wiring you some funds to hire a private investigator to look into this Todd Sinclair person. See that you obtain the services of a suitable firm."

I started to object. It wasn't necessary to hire a P.I. I liked Cowboy. Even if he was in Marisa's bed at this very minute. And if I hired a P.I., my lies about his background would be exposed. But I was too tired to fight the good fight. "Fine, Miss DeeDee. I'll handle it for you." I think we said polite goodbyes. I don't think I called her a willful old bat locked up in a padded cell. But I thought it.

I woke at midnight, when the alarm shrilled, and dressed warmly, this time digging through boxed clothes in the unused guest room to find smooth rubber boots. The house was being decorated one room at a time, but with nursing school and feng shui-ing Miss Essie's house, Arlana hadn't had time to finish mine.

My back gave a single mighty twinge as I was changing clothes, reminding me to gather the X rays and medical records from my stabbing. I'd drop them off at the horse-and-human chiropractor on the way to the hospital with a note requesting an appointment for a little miracle.

There were messages on the machine, phone calls I had slept through, but I didn't bother to listen. I couldn't care less what might be happening in the world. I had to go back to the graveyard for the night shift. Nothing else seemed to have much importance after that.

The night wasn't as cold as yesterday, my breath only a light mist when I exhaled. I had been away from the triangle graveyard for twelve hours and had managed to sleep just enough to make me feel worse. Yawning, I left my records off in the chiropractor's mail slot, then drove the distance to the crime scene. The media had figured out what was going on. There were news vans from all over, cars with rental plates, SUVs with TV and radio station parking stickers. I drove on past, calling Mark on my cell phone and telling him I was unable to get to the site. He sent me around another way, one guarded by an officer and cordoned against parking. It was to heck and gone from the main entrance, but more open. My car didn't get scratched this time as I drove in.

Bobby Ray Shirley met me with the forms and the paperwork completed for ten bodies, which brought to fifteen the ones that had been bagged-and-tagged. He bent into my open window, looking haggard and far less energetic than he had at noon. Shell-shocked. A thousand-yard stare and sallow cheeks. With his heart, this investigation might be too much for Bobby Ray.

"I called, left a message. Coulda saved you a trip if you'd called me back. We discovered more graves, for a total of twenty-four bodies to be exhumed. But we're calling it a night," Bobby Ray said, tossing the forms across me to the passenger seat. "There's no one left alive and no reason to kill ourselves. Sheriff is putting a guard on the site and one at the road. Feebs put up a chain-link fence."

"Around the whole place?"

"Yep. To keep the souvenir hunters and media hounds out. I'm outta here."

"I guess I can go, too, then."

"Less you feel like sticking around for some sick kinda reason."

"Not me," I said. "I'll take the morning shift, though."

"Good, 'cause I'm beat," he said, and I wheeled my toy-size car around and back down the road to my bed. I didn't remember making it inside or back to the mattress. When I woke on Sunday morning after a night of unsettling dreams about desecrated bodies, blood and entrails, I was still fully dressed, down to the smooth rubber boots. I brushed my teeth, ran a comb though my black locks, changed undies and boots and this time listened to my messages before I took off again.

There was only one new one. Mark. "Breakfast briefing at the bus station at 7:30 a.m. Be there." Succinct. Rude, but succinct.

Like all small towns in the rural South, nothing was open at 7:30 a.m. in DorCity. On this Sunday, the only things moving were the cars of shift workers leaving the few mills still in operation, the last stragglers of the Saturday night partygoers dragging in from Charlotte where the laws on alcohol purchase and consumption were much less strict, and the first of the early-bird churchgoers on their way to whatever churchgoers did at the crack of dawn.

The bus station wasn't a restaurant by that name, it was the actual Greyhound Bus Station, run by Darnel and Doris Shirley, a decrepit couple who worked six days a week selling bus tickets and running the little mom-and-pop café inside. Normally, Sunday morning was the day they slept in, but this Sunday was obviously an exception. There were something like fifty cars in the lot and lining the street, most unmarked Crown Vics—the favorite vehicle of law enforcement—and others with official tags. My little BMW stuck out like a high-priced extra thumb.

I crawled out of my car, pulling the peacoat around me, and stumbled into the café feeling better instantly as the smells of coffee, bacon grease and biscuits hit me. I found an empty place and signaled to Doris for coffee. Trellie, their midlife surprise who grew up to become a local beauty queen, brought me a pot and a mug, extra sugar and cream.

"Your usual, Dr. Lynch?"

"Sounds good," I said as I added two sugars and two creams and drank. "Can I have a stack of pancakes, too? Buckwheat?"

"Coming right up. I'd be big as a house if I ate like you, Dr. Lynch. You must have a fast metabolism."

Running five miles a day helped, but I didn't bother to say that. Exercise wasn't a regular part of most locals lives.

Even the mention of it made their eyes glaze over, and I wanted my breakfast pronto.

The morning meeting started during my first bite. I listened with half an ear while I shoveled in scrambled eggs, crisp bacon, grits and pancakes smothered in butter and honey. And half a pot of coffee to wake me up. After a few words by the sheriff, Mark propped up a county map and a dry-eraser board near a podium I hadn't noted in my half-asleep state. He welcomed everyone, then brought us up to date on the location of the gravesite, the number of bodies now established, the confirmed and suspected IDs, the interest of the media and the fact that a press conference had been scheduled by the sheriff for 2:00 p.m.

He explained that a special ERT—whatever that was— had been formed as part of the CIRT. Cop-speak was worse than med-speak. At least with doctors, I understood what was being said. Here I was lost.

Mark then spelled out the organization of the task force, according to who was top dog and who got pecked on, though he was much too polite to call it like it was. He couched it in terms like, "The SAC on the Violent Crime Squad from Columbia, Jim Ramsey, was brought in by local law enforcement and has since brought in an additional thirty agents to assist…blah, blah, blah." I attended to my grits, too sleepy to care whose gun was bigger. Far as I was concerned, if there was a living body, I outranked them all and they'd better get out of my way. If it was dead, the winner didn't matter to me.

Mark told us that two investigators from the Criminal Investigative Analyst Unit, courtesy of the National Center for the Analysis of Violent Crime in Quantico, had been called in by Special Agent in Charge Jim Ramsey, and had arrived by United Express Dulles to Columbia two hours past. Their job was to give psychological and sociological analyses of the perpetrators. A stranger in a suit took pity on me and penned the word *profilers* on his napkin.

I nodded my thanks. Serial killers in town, chased by the profilers. Gotcha. Then my breakfast companion added, "Special Agent in Charge—SAC." I grinned my appreciation. Borrowing his pen, I wrote ERT and CIRT, and he wrote "Evidence Response Team" and "Critical Incident Response Team." I was catching on.

Turning his back on the room, Mark taped a diagram to the wall. It was an upside-down computer simulation of the hand-drawn diagram I had seen—the triangle made of triangles. This one was composed of blue, red and black bars, with red for Caucasian, blue for African-American and black for graves that hadn't been opened yet. There were twenty-four bodies in all.

"The forensic pathologist has determined that the base of the large triangle, and several of the A level triangle arms are over ten years old," Mark stated.

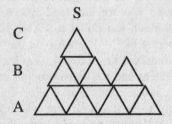

"Somewhere in the middle of the small triangle sides of A level, the perpetrator took a five-year break from burials, to start again around the year 2000. As the triangle rises, the graves become younger, or fresher. The most recent burial is at the inner arm of the highest triangle, at site C3, the victim Melanie Varnadore."

I tuned Mark out and went to the bus station counter for a fresh coffeepot. Darnel, Doris and Trellie were nowhere to be seen. It looked as if they had vacated the premises, leaving the station for the cops. Taking my seat again, I nodded to the helpful cop at my left and refilled the cups at my end of the table before passing the pot around.

Dr. Dempsey Anne Reid took the podium next, telling us what she had discovered on the first postmortems, particularly Melanie Varnadore, age sixteen. I watched Dempsey as she talked, her voice sharp and brittle. The forensic pathologist looked like death warmed over. Okay, that was a bad analogy for the situation. She looked like she was running on caffeine and nerves. There were large, dark circles beneath her eyes, and I got a sense of disconnection from her, as if she had gone on autopilot at some point and hadn't found her way back. I wondered if this was her first serial murder investigation.

"I'm not going to bore you with postmortem facts that don't pertain to your investigation. My preliminary findings are in the report being handed out now, and indicate Melanie Varnadore died within two hours following a blow to the left side of the head that crushed her skull and caused massive bleeding. These and her other injuries are consistent with trauma from a vehicle-versus-pedestrian incident. My best estimate is that she never regained consciousness."

A young plainclothes cop—likely a Feeb, going by the quality of his suit—set a thick folder in front of me. I opened it up and closed it almost instantly. Color photos of bodies in various stages of decomposition and postmortem slicing-and-dicing didn't go well with the eggs and bacon. I'd just listen.

"Unlike the other victims we have uncovered, there was no indication of sado-sexual trauma." She looked up. "We'll get to that in a moment. But please note that while Melanie Varnadore was the victim of sexual assault, it occurred postmortem.

"Because Melanie was the most recently deceased, and because she was the only victim discovered so far who did not sustain injuries consistent with other types of trauma, her case is noteworthy more for the discrepancies, for what was *not* done to her, than for what was.

"The two consistent aspects in all the PMs, both Melanie's and the victims' who preceded, were the postmortem sexual assault and the chemical analysis," she said. "Testing showed fatal concentrations in both blood and urine of GHB—gamma-hydroxybutyrate—and its precursors, GBL—gamma-butrolactone—and BDL—1,4-butanediol. She lived long enough to be dosed with massive amounts of what is most commonly a homemade drug, easy to make on a household stove. For the purposes of this discussion I will simply refer to this sexual amnesiac sedative and its precursors as GHB.

"Because of the presence of GHB in Melanie's system, I ran preliminary testing on three of the Jane Does." She looked around the room. "They all showed some traces of the drug. Melanie Varnadore, the most recently deceased victim, had the highest concentration of GHB, perhaps because she died unexpectedly, before the drug was out of her system. This is what you were looking for, gentlemen, ladies. This is your key. GHB."

I wasn't sure what Dempsey meant by *this is your key.* But I knew GHB. It was one of the date rape drugs. It could be cooked up on a stove with over-the-counter drugs and common kitchen and household substances. In other words, go to the neighborhood drugstore, buy a few things off the cold and allergy aisle, take them home and raid the pantry. A few hours later you have GHB. Any high-schooler could cook it up.

Then, a trip to the burger joint or nearby bar, and it didn't matter how dull, ugly, pimple-faced, uneducated, gangly, geeky, fat, unwashed, disgusting or unsophisticated you were, you had your pick of the ladies. And they couldn't say no.

During my residency in Chicago, I saw two young girls in the E.R., brought in by one girl's mother. She had been irate that a "friend" had bought them liquor and gotten them drunk. She wanted proof so she could have the guy arrested. At first I agreed that they were both drunk or stoned. But all the tox screens came back negative. Then one of the girls noticed that she was bleeding and sore.

A few hours later, I had proof that the girls had been dosed with GHB and raped by multiple assailants. Fortunately, a cook at the local fast-food joint had seen them talking to a member of the high school basketball team. Even more fortunately, the idiot and his pals had video-taped the incident. They were tried as adults and went away for a long time. Another example of people who deserved cruel and unusually appropriate punishment.

I had been pretty liberal when I started college. But after only a few years working in the public sector, I was ready to pull the switch myself on some of the not-so-good citizens it was my displeasure and obligation to treat.

"Now, if you will please turn to the next report, you see before you the preliminary findings on Jane Doe from section C, site two, an African-American female," Dempsey said. I wondered if I had missed anything important. "She was buried at a forty-five degree angle from C3, her head nearly touching Melanie's, and appears to be the second most current burial. Note the estimate of age, body weight, general health, location of scars and tattoos, and other data that may assist in determining an ID from your files. Skip to page three for photographs of the body, and we'll start at the head and work our way down."

I flipped to the proper page and again closed the folder. I had seen this girl up close and personal. I had no need to go through her extensive list of injuries one at a time. No need to understand and emphasize how awful her last days and hours of life had been. I didn't want to know. Instead, I sipped coffee and watched the men in the room with me.

Cops everywhere had the same look—closed, hard, just a bit mean, an expression that molded their features over the years into an unreadable mask. A look that said they were here to do a job and they knew they might die while doing it, and die violently. Beneath the mask, most were idealistic, caring men and women who wanted to make the world a better place. A few wore that mask as a thin veneer over a reality of cruelty, anger and personal viciousness that might rival any of the felons they brought to justice. Others wore it because they had seen it all and their vision of the world and its people was forever tarnished. But they believed, one and all, in what they were doing. Keeping the public safe. And right now, the public was in danger from sadists who took pleasure in torturing and mutilating their young female victims.

Scattered throughout the group were the Feebs, sitting so straight they looked as if they had two-by-fours up the back of their suit coats, the county deputies slouched in combat black, city cops in navy, plainclothes investigators in khakis or jeans, dark windbreakers with the word *POLICE* silk-screened in white tossed over their chair backs.

There were county emergency personnel, the crime scene team, and the Ford County Emergency Preparedness director dressed much like the investigators. I'd have to learn his name eventually. All of them looked tired, faces stiff with an undertone of weariness and grief, as if they had seen too much evil in the last thirty-six hours. Way too much.

17

I DON'T SLICE-AND-DICE

When Dempsey stopped speaking, a tall, slim federal agent stood and took her place. It was Jim Ramsey. I'd first met Jim a few months past, when he had been number three man in a group of three, the one making the calls, taking the faxes and keeping the notes. Low man on the totem pole. He had proved himself and moved up fast in the FBI office based in Columbia, the state capitol, but I hadn't known he had been promoted to special agent in charge of something. Of course, I still didn't know what he was in charge of, but it sounded impressive.

He was now dating my favorite nurse, Ashlee Davenport. Lately, she had been wearing that glow a woman gets when the relationship meets all her romantic, physical and libidinous needs. She was routinely being teased about her sex life, but so far had neither confirmed nor denied the speculation that she was getting lucky on a routine basis. Jim nodded and introduced himself, leaving out the part about dating Ashlee.

"To bring you all up to date, we have a primary suspect in the kidnappings. Dim the lights, if you will," he said to someone in the back of the room. A slide projector was whirring and, with a click, a photo appeared on the wall.

It was a police file photo of a twentyish white male with luminous blue eyes and a receding hairline. He had the puffy face of a man accustomed to a daily regimen of fast foods, beer, salt, caffeine and the remote control.

"This is Herbert Reginald Gaston when he was arrested in Columbia in 1992 for the death of Rochelle Schwartz. His most recent AKA is Deacon." The man wore a sullen expression, his hair thin and greasy. Not the kind of man who was likely to find attracting girls an easy task.

With another click, the photo was replaced. This slide showed a blond teenager supine on a striped mattress. Her face and body were covered with welts and bruises. "Rochelle Schwartz. She died during rough sex while heavily dosed with GHB. The crime was called in to 9-1-1 by a friend of the victim who happened to arrive at the scene. Deacon pleaded out to manslaughter and served five years. The sentence would have been longer, but Rochelle had a prior for prostitution and possession, and word on the streets was that she was a willing participant in sadomasochistic activities, making it difficult to prove the death was intentional.

"Herbert Gaston—" his mug shot reappeared on the screen "—who now goes exclusively by the name Deacon, served his parole and disappeared. Because his crime didn't fit with the profile being used at the time, he was never listed in the sexual offender database. Call it a snafu, call us screwups. The press certainly will." The audience laughed uneasily. Human error wasn't allowed in law enforcement or in medicine. I could sympathize.

"According to friends and family interviewed so far, Deacon has not been seen or heard from in two years. It's now believed that Rochelle Schwartz was not Deacon's first victim, but rather, a murder that went wrong. From the age and decomposition of the graves at the base of the large triangle, we think she may have been the seventh in a killing spree that took a hiatus for the five years of his incarceration."

In other words, he was a sneaky SOB who got away with something six times and returned to the same activity after he was free again. I freshened my coffee and tucked my hands in my armpits for warmth. The room wasn't cold, but my hands were icy.

"In the state of South Carolina, we have been working two strings of disappearances for almost twelve weeks. The first involved a group of young, blond, Caucasian females, the second a group of African-American females. We got our initial break when the witness to Melanie Varnadore's kidnapping got a good look at the man who rammed her with his van and took her. The man was later identified as Herbert Reginald Gaston. The waitress was also able to confirm that a second man, an African-American, was driving the van that hit him. That was the first concrete indication we had that Deacon was not working alone.

"The suggestion was made at the time that two kidnappers were tag-teaming for victims. That scenario was dismissed as unlikely, but following the discovery of the gravesite we have now confirmed that the two men *are* working together and have been for an estimated two years, using two somewhat different MOs in choosing and taking their victims.

"Young, light-skinned African-American girls and women have been taken off the street after receiving lingerie-type gifts from an anonymous donor. Young, petite, blond, blue or gray-eyed Caucasian teens are lured away in a similar manner, but the gifts appear to be flowers or candy. Then hours or days later, the Caucasian girls make a phone call home, a device—call it a psychological quirk—that set this perpetrator apart. The African-American girls were never allowed to call home.

"And of course, making the job of the task forces harder,

there are girls who physically matched one of the perpetrator's preferences, but who left home for reasons of their own. These had to be separated out from the profiles.

"We know that both sets of young women, after being picked up by one or both perpetrators, were taken to an unknown location and tortured and killed, then buried in a geometrically patterned common grave that may have meaning only to Deacon. Let me say again, the gravesite was the first concrete indication that the two task forces were working the same case." He paused and took a breath that looked as if it might hurt. I wondered if it had been his decision to keep the two task forces from joining sooner.

I suddenly flashed on the vision of the graves and the victims in each. The sheets were wrapped and tied in just the way a hospital worker might wrap and tie a patient who had expired. I sipped my coffee. Did Deacon have hospital or morgue or EMS experience? I'd have to pass that question along to Dempsey.

"We are combing records of Deacon's friends in and out of prison, for all known African-American criminal associates now released, and will narrow that search to someone who matches the profile to be provided by the analysts from Quantico."

Jim motioned for the lights to be brought back up. "As you know, sexual predators seldom cross racial barriers for their victims. It is usually a black-on-black and white-on-white crime, a single perpetrator with his own unique methods of finding, taking, torturing, killing and disposing of the bodies of his victims, based on his own particular psychological profile. When our two bad guys joined forces, more than just their methods of procuring victims may have changed. The M.E. has warned that as they blended their individual brands of depredation, their MOs of torture may have been evolving as well. Nothing about this gravesite or its victimology may be static, but rather, mutable. All that said, with the identification of Deacon, the jobs of the task forces just got a lot easier.''

I looked back up at the photograph of Deacon. A socially undeveloped, dissatisfied man. Petulant. Out to get back at the women who had rejected him. But why bury the girls in a triangle? Something to do with religion, like the name Deacon? The Trinity, maybe?

The sheriff stood up to talk again, giving the short list of speakers needed for the press conference. My name wasn't on the list, but Anita's was. I didn't raise my hand, wave wildly for attention and explain that the coroner was still hospitalized and couldn't attend. Call me lazy or camera-shy, but I had no intention of showing up for a press conference unless handcuffed to a podium.

Three other suited-types spoke while breakfast headed for my hips and thighs and I allowed my backside to slide down the seat into a slump. Admittedly, I dozed. Hopefully, I didn't snore. But I woke fully when Mark stood and introduced the lead analyst from Quantico, which I knew was where the FBI had its headquarters and training center, and where Mulder and Scully worked on TV.

Most of my involvement with the FBI had been via the TV screen, and the real agents never fit the image. The men weren't tall, young, good-looking and brooding, dressed in Armani suits and watching the sky for aliens. This analyst was bald, short, middle-aged, soft around the middle. He was dressed in an off-the-rack suit, spoke with a slight speech impediment that affected his *s*'s, and looked like a scruffy physics teacher, rather than someone who made his living peeking into the darker recesses of abnormal psychology. I couldn't wait to see his partner, the anti-Scully. Maybe she would be tall, muscular, masculine, dressed in combat boots—and would believe in the paranormal.

"My name is Haden Fairweather. I have a Ph.D. in behavioral sciences, a Master's in criminal justice, and have worked with the Federal Bureau of Investigation for fifteen years. The last seven have been as a supervisory special agent, field office program manager and violent crime assessor with the National Center for the Analysis of Violent Crime.''

As he spoke, the men and women in the room shifted in their seats like iron filings turning toward a magnet, almost mesmerized. The man at the podium wasn't particularly charismatic. Wasn't good-looking by any denotation of the word. Wasn't an exceptionally good speaker. But he had all the cops riveted. My pen pal to the left wrote, ''violent crime expert *and* profiler'' on his napkin. I nodded. Fairweather was a man who regularly waded through bloody hells and back, looking into dark and tormented and vicious psyches, and still somehow kept his sanity. The cops were impressed en masse. Not an easy feat.

''On the flight down, my partner and I studied all the information faxed to us, all the crime scene photographs you had time to upload, the preliminary postmortem autopsies, all the data on the known perpetrator, Herbert Reginald Gaston, and his standard operating procedure for choosing and acquiring his victims, and as much physical evidence as was available in the law enforcement center when our flight took off. I will be meeting with the team leaders of the ERT, the medical examiner and various others of you to garner information as needed. We will also be studying the gravesite, and we appreciate you keeping it as pristine as possible for us.''

Haden touched a forefinger to the bridge of his nose as if to push up missing glasses, his gaze taking in the entire room as he introduced himself and made opening remarks. Perhaps he was wondering how many of the assembled had stomped on his pristine gravesite. I saw several agents shrink visibly under the gaze.

"However, from the evidence reviewed thus far, we have drafted a preliminary victimology profile. A very hasty, inadequate, preliminary report. Please remember that. A detailed report takes time, and while I know you all are eagerly wanting the final, full report, I am loathe to give you much this morning that you don't already know." Haden blinked several times as if contact lenses were bothering him. I could hear myself swallow and quietly put down my coffee cup so as not to disturb the ambience of awe in the room. These people acted as they were in the presence of something almost holy.

"Our perpetrators are as follows. First, a white male, age twenty-nine, with a very organized mind and very specific preferences in his criminal methodology. His is a note-taker mentality."

Haden smiled as if that was amusing. Around me, the cops were all taking notes, so maybe the quip was funny.

"We know from a previous psychological evaluation and court records that Herbert Reginald Gaston, aka Deacon, was a victim of ritual sexual, psychological and physical abuse in his youth, perpetrated by his mother and allegedly by other members of an extreme religious cult, with which they lived for a number of years. This cult is now disbanded, its members scattered.

"His mother was a young single woman unable to deal with her own abnormal upbringing or with the frustration of raising an intelligent, energetic son. And as is common with such psychological profiles, Herbert Reginald Gaston grew up to become a socially maladjusted loner.

"His preference for blond young women is very likely a reflection of his unresolved relationship with his mother, however much that psychological projection has been overused and overdiagnosed. His use of the sobriquet Deacon is believed to be indicative of the extreme cultlike religious lifestyle espoused by that mother and foisted upon her son.''

I drank again, swallowing quietly. I had figured that he was called Deacon because of religion forced down his throat as a kid. Or because the deacon was in charge, the deacon ran things, the big man on church campus. I hadn't considered that the religion could have included ritual child abuse.

"The escalating violence perpetrated on his victims, and the fact that he is taking more victims more often, in increasingly violent and public methods, is indicative of his decompensating mental state. The violence that has thus far satisfied his aberrant psychological cravings is no longer sufficient to feed his emotional needs, and the addiction to that violence is growing. He has begun to make mistakes.''

A hand went up near the front of the room. Haden shoved at his not-there glasses. "Yes?" he asked.

"What about the triangles? Religion, too?" a voice asked.

"Absolutely. Though my partner suggested that there is a third party to the killings—hence the triangle—I think that highly unlikely, simply because the triangle was used even before the second party joined Deacon. So, I believe we are dealing with a cultic religious aberration. However, as I said before, the psychological profiles will expand as we obtain and add more information into the mix.''

Haden shuffled two papers and centered a third on the podium. "Both from witness accounts and the physical evidence recovered at the gravesite, we know the second man is an African-American male. He is likely violent in many of his past relationships, but with no particular aberrant psychological tendencies of his own beyond a preference for young, light-skinned African-American females. Rather, he appears to be a man who may have been caught up in the vision of his partner. His is perhaps a malleable interpretation of violence.''

The phrase seemed to ring inside my skull. *A malleable interpretation of violence.* It made my hands colder to hear the horrors I had witnessed translated into the sterile context of this man's vocabulary and profession.

''From evidence the medical examiner was able to recover, we deduce that the damage on his early victims was exploratory. It is clear that he was researching, experimenting, defining his own methods and techniques. While he has adopted many of his methods of injury and torture from Deacon, his victims indicate that he has recently begun to refine these methods, centering on the triangle of physical damage learned from Deacon, using different instruments to achieve his own pattern and signature. Beyond that, the one thing the two men have in common is postmortem intercourse with the victims.''

I shook my head and drank down my coffee, freshened it yet again from the pot on the table. There were some things I just didn't need to know and that was one of them. I worked on live bodies, I reminded myself. I didn't slice-and-dice afterward, looking for reasons why. My new mantra—*I don't slice-and-dice.*

''From the evolving victimology alone, we believe that we can eliminate three of the five possible African-Americans on your short list as the second Triangle Killer. Snappy name, by the way.'' He smiled, and a ripple of wry laughter ran through the audience.

''At this time, we believe you can remove both of the men with a high school education, and the man with two years of college. The most likely candidate for Herbert Reginald Gaston's partner would be an individual with a lower-than-average IQ, perhaps as low as eighty-five. The two men who fit the existing preliminary profile, both of whom served in prison at the same time as Deacon, are Antony Tabor Stroud and Di'Juan Michael Crank.''

There was a rush of motion as the assembled law enforcement officers dived into their papers and began separating out profiles of men no longer considered potential Triangle Killers. The excitement level in the room went up a few dozen degrees. The cop look that had frozen most faces was gone, replaced with an almost uniform childish exuberance and an underlying hint of triumph. Now they knew where to look.

I stood and went to make fresh coffee. Behind me, the profiler continued to speak.

''Whichever has the familial or criminal connection to Deacon would be your most likely suspect.''

I poured grounds, measured water. My icy hands were shaking. Too much coffee or too much horror? I clenched my fingers and opened them, tried to force them to stillness. They didn't consent. I'd get Mark Stafford for making me part of this mess. Somehow I'd get him.

After the meeting, Dempsey stopped me and let me know that I didn't have to stay at the mass gravesite full-time. Enough work had been done at the crime scene for the coroner to visit and do paperwork as needed, once or twice a day. That was a relief. I had already been thinking about how to get out of hanging around for twelve hours a day. Proof of my laziness. I shared with her my impression about the way the sheets were tied, at head and foot in a typically medical manner. Dempsey agreed that was worth looking into. Just small talk between the girls, when the girls were surrounded by mayhem and murder. I didn't know how the M.E. stood it day-in and day-out.

When Dempsey left, I propped my backside against my car door, crossed my ankles and waited in the ineffective sunlight for Mark to appear. I said nothing as he left the bus station café, but his eyes found me across the lot, and he nodded once in acknowledgement. I was patient as he spoke with several groups and individuals, making his way slowly toward where I stood. He paused and tossed his briefcase into his SUV and shrugged out of his wind-breaker.

When the lot was almost empty, he stopped in front of me, his booted feet wide, my crossed ankles between them. Clasping his hands together behind his back, he said, "So."

Some conversationalist. I inclined my head and got straight to the point. "Maybe I slept through it, but I think you left out the possible connection between the killers and Wayne Edward Geter and his new pal who escaped from the jail."

"You noticed that little omission?" A half smile tugged at his lips. Mark had lips that turned up a hint at the corners anyway, as if a smile were perpetually hiding there, waiting to be exposed. The facial hair helped hide the little smile, but it was there now.

"I noticed."

"And?" he asked.

"And Graham Cornwell was taking Wayne Edward to the gravesite to look for his sister, wasn't he?"

"We think so. But Graham clammed up when he was caught. Called for his lawyer. And he had broken legs."

I understood where Mark was going. "Which means that he's on narcotics."

"Bingo. His lawyer won't let us talk to him while he's on morphine for fear he might accidentally perjure or im-plicate himself."

"But you think this Graham knew about the mass grave."

"We think he'd been there. We think he was taking Wayne Edward directly there. In the dark. Without a map."

"He was in jail when Melanie was kidnapped?"

"Nope. But he has an ironclad alibi. He was in a pool hall. One of the sheriff deputies saw him there. Took note."

"So?"

Mark's smile tugged wider. His left foot moved in, trapping my ankles between his. It was a curiously intimate action, as if he had touched my face. "We think Graham knows the other suspect. We think he's been to the grave. We think he was brought there by Di'Juan Michael Crank, his older half-brother. Who happened to serve time in the same institution as Deacon."

"You figured out that Crank's the other killer, and you didn't want to tell anyone? I don't believe that."

"Well, we actually put the relationships together about an hour before today's meeting. But it was nice to have Fairweather confirm it with a psych profile." Teeth flashed beneath the mustache. "Didn't believe me, huh? I always did love a smart woman."

I managed to keep my mouth shut against any Skye comments, but it was a near thing. I pulled my feet from between his and walked around my car, beeping the door lock open as I moved. I got in and started it up, pulling away from the bus station. Mark was left in the empty lot, his booted feet planted in the dust.

It was Sunday morning but I drove by the chiropractor's office, the one who had worked on the horse and made it all better, just in case. Surprisingly, there was a car in the lot, so I pulled in and parked. The house was old, maybe as much as seventy-five years old, with ancient oak trees in front and back, a climbing rose empty of blooms ascending an arbor, azaleas draped in the decade-softened shape they acquire with judicious pruning and little sunlight. I climbed the three steps to the generous porch and knocked on the door, leaning close to the sidelight window so I could see inside.

A tall, cadaverous man wearing a dress shirt, tie and suit pants, but in his sock feet, came to the door and peered through the uncurtained sidelight. His brows were raised, his forehead wrinkled as if there was no tissue between skin and skull and the flesh just rolled up over bone.

"I'm Rhea Lynch," I said, knowing that my voice would carry through the old glass in the windows. "I dropped off my records?"

The door opened and the thin face was wreathed in a smile. "Come on in. I'm just doing some paperwork after church." The door opened as he spoke and the scent of fresh coffee wafted out. "I looked over your reports. Nasty repercussions from a wound that didn't appear to be very deep. I'm Dr. Marston. Call me Martin."

Over his shoulder, a photocopy of a photograph caught my eyes. It was a missing person's notice for Holly Aimes, tacked to the corkboard over a computer terminal. The teen-aged girl in the photo was blond, blue-eyed, petite, athletic. I shuddered. Missing since September last year. Was she missing, off with a boyfriend? Or missing like Zack's daughter, off partying? Or missing, as in abducted and dead? How had so many of three counties' young women gone missing without anyone really noticing? Did so many disappear every year that an additional one or five was no big deal?

"Dr. Lynch?"

I turned at the voice and lifted my eyes up to the thin face of the chiropractor. He stood well over six feet, an Ichabod Crane look-alike in dress socks. "I'm Rhea. They haven't found Holly?"

"No. She's a patient's daughter. The police thought she was a runaway at first, because of the phone call she made home. It seemed that she had left with a boy from school. But then they started taking it seriously, thinking that some-one took her. We were hoping for a ransom demand."

I looked back at the photo of the girl. She was pretty and so very young. I saw, as if burned into my eyelids, the visions of the exhumed bodies out at the triangle graveyard. Tortured and abused. Aching cold, dark, steeped in the smell of death. The skin of my hands burned with the memory of cold. I blinked to dislodge the sight, but the smell stayed with me, trapped in my thoughts and writhing. "And now?"

He sighed. "Now they think she's one of the ones they found buried on that farm. I've known Holly since she was in grade school. She's a good kid. Or maybe *was* a good kid," he amended.

I dragged my eyes away from the missing-person poster, desperate to do, think about something else. "I saw you cure the horse out at Stowe Farm. That's why I'm here. I have pain no one can seem to fix, Dr. Marston."

"I've got an hour. My wife's at her mother's. Let's do a thorough examination and see if I can help. I've studied the X rays you left, but I want to see what we have pressurewise on you. And call me Martin." He smiled kindly, much like an old-world doctor might have, or even a doctor from fifty years ago, though he had to be in his early to mid-thirties. I got the impression that he might listen to what a patient had to say. "Come with me?"

I followed the tall doctor back to his examining room, down a wide hardwood-floored hallway, plaster and trim painted a pale cream, an attic fan overhead, the kind of interior old houses in the South were famous for. The house was aligned to allow for the prevailing westerly winds to cool it in summer, the hallway like a tunnel to funnel the breeze. He stood aside to allow me into the brightly painted examining room, once a bedroom in the old house, now fitted with an adjustable motorized table, cabinets around the yellow walls and a plastic skeleton hanging near the window, this one with rubber nerves and tendons protruding from the spine.

"Have a seat." He indicated a tall stool, one high enough for him to work on me without straining his back. I thought that seemed appropriate for a chiropractor.

I felt myself relaxing as he did the usual blood pressure and temp checks, pulse and respiration, then thumped and twisted me in a very thorough neuro-check. He even examined my ears and pupillary response. As he worked, the memories of the girls and the graves began to soften and fade, the smell of death began to wane, leaving only this place, this moment.

"So, how were you injured?" he asked as he worked. As I told him the story, he continued his exam, pausing only once to question me when I told him about the scalpel I was cut and stabbed with, and the subsequent rehab, then the reinjury lifting my dog across my shoulders. I hadn't even felt that one until the next day.

Martin put me on the exam table and had me move my arms and head, shoulders and hips in various positions, hold them an instant and move again as he lifted my feet, bending my legs at the knees, touching my back. When he sat me up, his long face was thoughtful.

"Well, I think I can help you," he said slowly, musing, "but it's going to take some time. You've healed out of alignment, and it'll take me some sessions to get you realigned and make it hold."

"You found a reason for my pain? *Already?*" I was surprised, and not completely convinced. No one else had been able to explain it.

"Yes. I believe you have right flank pain, beyond the normal time of healing, because of altered afferent sensory input from an overstimulated nociception mechanoreceptor."

More med-speak.

"This area of the spine—" he touched my back "—is a weak link from the changes in anatomical vertebral alterations, particularly in the joint facet capsules from thoracic number twelve. When you move like this—" he tilted my body, raised my right arm over my head "—you get a spasm."

"No kidding," I gasped as pain lanced around my chest and up to my head.

He dropped my arm and massaged the muscle with his thumb until it started to relax. "All of your pain is coming from a misalignment of the thoracic number twelve over the lumbar number one vertebra—" he twisted the vertebrae on the skeleton as he talked, to demonstrate "—with the overstimulation of type three mechanoreceptors in the ligaments along with the nonconforming nociceptors."

"You say the sweetest things." I cut my eyes at him as I said it, and Martin laughed.

"I usually just say that the vertebra are almost overlapped, pressing nerves and compressing ligaments, giving you a muscle spasm. It's pain that no pill or muscle relaxer will correct, because the meds don't correct the underlying problem. Look at your X rays."

He stepped to a viewing screen, flipped a switch, and my X rays appeared. I could see the twisted spinal processes, but had never thought the slight irregularities of placement were that important. Martin thought otherwise. "Here is the damage causing your problems," he said, pointing. "And I can get them back into place."

"Like you did the horse." I grinned.

"Like that," he said seriously, "but it'll take twelve adjustments, maybe eighteen, to make it hold, and you may experience some burning sensations for a few days, as the nerves react to the decrease in pressure."

"Let's do it."

When I left Martin's exam room, I felt better than I had

in months, ready for almost anything. Until I passed the picture of Holly, and the memories and that smell came crashing down on me. How many more victims would die before Deacon was stopped?

18

DRUNK DRIVERS, HIGH-SPEED PURSUIT AND
FREEZER-BURNED WAFFLES

Though my stomach was still pleasantly full, I stopped by
Miss Essie's. I didn't know if I'd ever visited when I wasn't
hoping to cadge a meal. There's a first time for everything.
When I knocked, Miss Essie peered out, looked me over
and opened the door. She sniffed. "You done eat. I can
smell the maple syrup on you. Want coffee?" She was
dressed in a navy house dress with two T-shirts beneath—
one purple, one light blue—thick purple socks and fuzzy
pink slippers.

"Please."

"Well, hurry up and get inside. It cold out there."

I sat at the table in the corner of the kitchen and accepted
a steaming mug as Miss Essie settled across from me, her
heavy purple winter shawl wrapped around her shoulders.
We sipped in silence, the kind of companionable silence
achieved after years of friendship—or family.

"That man a yours. He in a peck of trouble."

I looked over the lip of the mug, surprised. This was the
first time Miss Essie had mentioned Mark and his paternity
suit. I said nothing, but took another sip.

"He a fine man, that Mark Stafford. Come from good

peoples. But he let hisself get caught in the snare of a woman who took him into her bed—''

''Mark could have said no,'' I said flatly. ''She didn't hold a gun to his head.''

Miss Essie raised her brows. ''That true. But he a man. Most got the strength of character of a he-goat when a woman wiggle herself at him. Ain't worth two cents.''

Morose, I stared at my coffee. ''Mark is better than that. Well, most of the time.''

''No, he ain't. 'Specially when the woman he love is breaking trust with him.''

I looked up, shock freezing in my chest. I put down my mug, tucked my cold hands between my thighs. ''He talked to you, didn't he? About the fact that he had to kill Taylor Reeves because I didn't tell him…certain things.''

''Ain't like he could talk to that empty-headed thing what give birth to him. Clarissa Stafford got plenty thoughts in her mind, but they all about what circle groups she got today, when the garden club meeting and when her hair appointment be. Sometimes a man need to talk to a woman what got a brain in her head.'' Miss Essie shrugged and sipped. ''He couldn't talk to you, so he pick me.''

''And?''

''Some things said in confidence. But I can tell you this. That man love you. He shamed of the mistake he make with that little girl. He want everything to be right and good with you again. You gone be forgiving of him? Take him back?''

''Will he cheat again?''

Miss Essie shrugged by tilting her head and raising and dropping her brows. ''He a man. He didn't say no that one time. I like to think he learn his mind, learn his lesson. I don't know. Can't no one promise. Life ain't that sure.''

''I want a one-woman man, Miss Essie.''

She snorted, a faint *harumph* sound in the back of her

throat. "You had that with John Micheaux. He a one-woman man. You drop him when he push you too hard and tell you how you got to live like he say, 'stead of how you plan. You want more than just a one-woman man. You want one who respect you, respect who you is and who you can be. Look up to you, like you want to look up to him. But you missing something. Something important. What you missing is passion."

I grinned at Miss Essie and picked up my mug.

Her eyes flashed purple fire. "Don't you grin at me, all smug like. Like I a old woman and you seen it all. I seen more than you have." She thunked down her mug. "I asking you, you ever had passion with a man? That kind of fire in the belly that make you do something you never do before? Be something you never was before?"

I looked away, focusing on the morning sunlight streaming across the lawn. That kind of passion wasn't for me. I avoided any strong emotion, whether it was anger, joy or even sexual tension. I liked my life ordered and planned and steady, and I liked my men the same way. If I was honest, I'd admit I didn't like surprises except in my work, and sometimes not even then. Did that make me a coward? I was uneasy with this conversation. It was so *not* Miss Essie.

I remembered the gravesite. Deacon and his partner had passion, lots of it and none of it good.

"I talking to you like a woman growed, now, not like a child. Mark Stafford a good man. I think you belong with him. But if you don't have passion with him that sweep away everything else, then maybe I wrong. Maybe you need to find a man who stirs you blood with that fire in the belly. To my way a seeing things, only after you feel that kind a passion and decide how you gone deal with it, do you find love with a man, love that stay strong and sure. And it ain't always that same man what stir the blood."

Her advice could be interpreted to advocate a wild fling before marriage, but I understood her assessment. She was talking about my mind, my choices when faced with passion that swept away everything else in life. Wild passionate abandon was something that most women found in their twenties. I was thirty years old and alone. My biological clock was ticking—if I wanted children. Which I might. Maybe.

I had made intelligent choices when it came to the men in my life. And yet both men I thought might make good husbands went off and slept with other women, John with a natural blonde with massive boobs and a body made for childbearing, and Mark with a frosted blonde, twenty-something with perky boobs. What was it with men and blondes and boobs? And now Miss Essie wanted me to go find a grand passion, when I didn't want that kind of passion at all, grand or small. Life wasn't fair.

And then I thought of Eli Cordell, the way he looked as he leaned against my car, all muscle and toned strength. No gentleness at all. There would be plenty of passion there, but I didn't think there would be anything else. Would there be trust? Would there be safety? Monogamy? I couldn't see that kind of man providing me with the children I might—maybe—want someday, playing ball, and catch, and hide and seek. I could see Mark doing all that. I could see Mark making a good father, if that was the kind of life I wanted. And while there wasn't soul-stirring passion like Miss Essie spoke of, there was certainly heat of a kind. Maybe there would have been passion, if I had let myself get close enough.

So why did thoughts of Eli keep coming back, if Mark was the man for me? Was that revenge on my part? Letting myself react to Eli to spite Mark? Was I that shallow? Or was it real chemistry, pheromones, and what might prove to be earth-shaking passion?

While I debated telling Miss Essie about Eli, a noise came from the back of the house and Arlana shuffled down the hall into the kitchen, eyes closed. She wore one blue slipper and one green one, a huge oversize T-shirt with a rip at the shoulder and a silk-screened bunny eating a carrot on the front, and red-and-blue-plaid flannel bottoms that dragged on the floor. Her hair was in a floral green, silky net, like a shower cap made out of shiny nylon, one ear exposed, one covered, and a mark on her cheek made by the elastic band and crumpled sheets. Sleep sand was crusted in the corners of her eyes.

She slumped at the table, one arm outstretched across the top, her head resting on it. Miss Essie got up and poured a glass of orange juice for her. Roused by the scent of the OJ, she pried open one eye and found the glass, put it to her lips and drank it down in one long swallow. She focused then on me.

"Oh. It's you." She licked her lips to get the last drop of juice. "Thought I heard voices."

"Morning." I had seen Arlana before this early in the morning, but the older she got, the worse she looked upon waking. Today was pretty awful. Reminded me of me.

"I need Christmas shopping money. How dirty is your house?"

I winced.

"Good enough." She closed the eye and slumped back to the tabletop. "I'm cleaning your pigsty Monday. Take your dirty clothes to the laundry so I don't get lost in the heaps and have to call 9-1-1 to come dig me out."

I laughed.

"Go ahead and laugh, white woman. Don't mean you won't get a tongue-lashing for letting it get nasty again. Every time I clean it, it worse than the last time. Filthy place. You still got that nasty cat?"

"He has me."

She made a sound close to what Miss Essie made when she was disgusted. "You coming to church with us? We got church all day, starting at two, and singing tonight."

"You want me to sing?"

The other eye opened this time. "Come to think of it, no. You sing like something dying. Bet you got an excuse for today, too."

"I have to work. I'm the new assistant to the coroner." Miss Essie had been trying to get me to a church—any church—for years. It looked as if her great-granddaughter was taking up the quest.

"We'll pray for you, child. That a hard business," Miss Essie said. "You help the police, and your man Mark, to find the evil men who taking and killing them girls, 'fore another one gets took. And you find out if two of them poor girls is Elorie and Natasha. I hear they mama's suffering right now, full of fear that her girls is buried out in the field. She need to know so she can grieve if it be so."

I sipped my cool coffee. "I'll do my best."

True to my word, after gathering up my dirty clothes from the floor and hamper and stuffing them into the drawstring bags I used when toting them to the laundry, I headed out. I spent all day at the mass grave. It wasn't required, and I had thought I might doze the day away in bed, but after the talk with Miss Essie, I didn't want to stay home. I was feeling itchy and wanted someplace quiet to think. A graveyard was kind of a weird place, but it offered something I needed—an illusion of doing something important for the missing girls.

I stopped in at Marisa's about midday, safely after church, hoping to procure a meal. She and Cowboy were making goo-goo eyes at each other, the sexual tension so thick I could almost feel it in the air. Disgusting. So I went back to the grave, napped in my car, filled out paperwork when needed, and neatly managed to avoid the press conference, participation in Sunday sermons, and any calls wanting me to come in to work early.

Napping in my car, heated by winter sun on the windshield, I caught up on some of my missed sleep, which I needed pretty badly. The only useful part of my day was when Gloris beeped me. I curled into the seat and dialed the number to the Intensive Care Unit.

"Dr. Lynch here," I said, yawning when she answered.

"Oh, Dr. Rhea-Rhea. Thank you for calling. I just wanted to let you know about that herpes report." When I didn't respond, she said, "On Charlie Denbrow?"

"Oh, right. Sorry, Gloris. My brain's asleep. What's up?"

"Dr. Statler told me to tell you it was negative. The vesicles are something else."

"Really?" I was surprised. It had looked like herpes to me. "Well, thanks, Gloris. I appreciate it." A moment later I clicked off. So what were the scratches and vesicles? Weird. But not weird enough to keep me awake. With the memory of the strange scratches and the blisterlike welts on my mind, and the sound of shovels and equipment working in the background, I fell asleep.

When I awoke, it was 6:00 p.m., fully dark, and the cops were through. All the bodies had been exhumed, catalogued, classified, bagged-and-tagged for PMs in Newberry and shipped. My paperwork was finished.

I drove away while the Feebs were still arguing about when to take down the fencing, and the state boys were pulling up tent poles. It was over.

Sunday night in the E.R. of Dawkins County Hospital meant baby night. I had seen three toddlers who had attended the same church nursery that morning, two fussy babies with temps and frazzled first-time mothers, the usual

MVAs DFOs, OFWs, PIDs and FOSs—med-speak for moving vehicular accidents, done fell outs, old folk work-ups, pelvic inflammatory disease, and people with impacted bowels. I was finishing my first cup of coffee of the evening, made fresh by Ashlee Davenport, who made really great coffee, when the police scanner went crazy.

"Attention all units. Attention all units! Proceed code three to the Church of the Holy Spirit and Tongues of Flame on Appletree Road. Code ten eighty-eight! Repeat! Code ten eighty-eight! All units be advised that a female has been taken from the road in front of the Church of the Holy Spirit and Tongues of Flame. She was last seen being pulled into a dark colored panel van. Be advised that church members are in pursuit east down Appletree Road toward Five Points! All units check in!"

I grabbed the police code sheet off the wall. I had never heard a code ten eighty-eight. It was a kidnapping.

"Unit 135 checking in. I am approximately ten miles away from Five Points, down West Appletree."

"Dispatch, unit 182. I'm four minutes from Five Points. Coming in on Frostybridge Road."

"Dispatch, unit 214 checking in. All units are to proceed toward Five Points. I want a cordon on Five Points at two locations on each road. One near the intersection, and another approximately a half mile out. Stop all vehicles outbound until further notice. Give me your twenties," Mark said, asking for the locations of all the county deputy and city police cars. "And dispatch, get me more vehicles. Call out the state boys and the Feebs. I want cars and bodies."

Other units began checking in, Mark placing them where he wanted them down the five roads that comprised the fender-bender intersection of Five Points.

"Unit 214," dispatch said, "please be advised that I have contact with the civilian pursuers via cell phone. They are in pursuit of a dark colored utility van moving at a high rate of speed. No tags on the van.''

"Can they state their ten-twenty?" Mark asked, sounding wry, wanting to know if the chase cars knew where they were. One of their own had been taken. Church members, full of the Spirit and possibly some spirits, had taken off in pursuit. And then the name of the church hit me.

The Church of the Holy Spirit and Tongues of Flame was where Arlana and Miss Essie attended. Melanie Varnadore had been stolen off the street, taken away in a dark green utility van. The coffee burbled uneasily in my stomach.

"Ash," I shouted, "come listen to this!"

I dialed Miss Essie's house while the short, mostly blond nurse came into the break room and freshened our coffee cups. No answer. I dialed again and checked the LED readout to make sure I had hit the right numbers. Still no answer. They were at the church. Singing. Where else would they be on a Sunday night? Was the young girl Arlana? Was the van the same one used to take Melanie? Was this Deacon? Had he lost all restraint when his graveyard was taken over and desecrated by police?

The dispatcher buzzed, "All units, be advised that the victim of the code ten eighty-eight is a light-skinned African-American female, with dark brown hair, wearing a greenish-blue dress and carrying a navy handbag. She is five feet four and one hundred twenty-five pounds with green eyes."

It sounded like Arlana. I dialed Miss Essie's house again. Still no answer. And I suddenly couldn't remember Miss Essie's cell number. Feeling sick, the caffeine zooming through my system, I turned up the scanner volume, opened the freezer and found a package of freezer-burned waffles. I toasted them while the chase went on around me and the break room filled up with employees.

"Dispatch, 214." It was Mark's voice, tense, volume just a bit high as he shouted over the sound of his siren. "We got Highway 9 and Rollins Creek Road barricaded at a half mile out. Nobody in or out unless they stop. I'm on my way back toward Five Points. What about Appletree and Frostybridge Road?"

"Unit 135, on my way, Cap'n. I'll close off Appletree at the old Esso station."

"This is 315 and 182," the sheriff's voice said. "We'll take Frostybridge Road at one half mile and near the intersection. No traffic so far, and we'll be in position in three."

"Dispatch, where are the civilian pursuers and how many are there?" Mark asked. "Can you patch them through?"

"Negative, 214. The connection is staticky, and they keep drifting in and out. Must be between towers. Shall I have them call your cell directly?"

"Negative. What's their status and number?" he repeated.

"We have six civilian vehicles in pursuit. Stand by for status." The dispatcher's voice came back on a moment later. "They lost sight of the van at Five Points. Civilian vehicles have separated. Three of the five roads that converge at Five Points are covered by law enforcement, leaving only Slocum Magpie Road and Frostybridge not yet secured.

"Three civilians are taking Slocum Magpie and two cars are taking Frostybridge. One civilian vehicle is remaining at the intersection. Unit 214, please be advised that there appears to be Signal 045 on some of the civilian pursuers."

Signal 045—alcohol. A pint or two had made the rounds during the church session. Drunk drivers in high speed pursuit. This could get dicey. I glanced at Ashlee. She sighed and shook her head. "Typical."

Setting the waffles on a plate, I added butter from a condiment package and syrup from another. I cut the waffle with a plastic knife and ate with a plastic spoon. My hands were shaking.

"Unit 214, this is dispatch. I've lost communication with the civilian chase cars."

I could hear the sound of tires squealing and a siren going. "Dispatch, this is 214, I'm on Slocum. I see…aw, man. Dispatch, notify 9-1-1 we need a wrecker and ambulance on Slocum Magpie Road at the check cashing place. They slid down the hill. Stand by." A moment later he came back and said, "Dispatch, we may have a couple injuries. Two of the civilian pursuit cars locked bumpers and went off the road and down a ten-foot gully. Get a patrol vehicle out here. I am leaving the scene to continue pursuit. Can you raise the cell phone of the civilian pursuers?"

"Negative. I've lost them."

"Ten-four." I could hear the disquiet in Mark's tone. Had the van gotten away? Minutes passed.

"Dispatch, this is unit 214. I have the last civilian pursuit vehicle in sight. It's pulled over to the side of the road, emergency lights flashing. Stand by."

"Unit 214, unit 135 is en route to back you up, with an ETA of one minute."

"Ten-four, dispatch. I hear his unit siren now."

I finished off the waffle. Wished for something else. Maybe a steak. I probably needed protein. Or Maalox. Or a steak with a Maalox chaser.

"Dispatch, this is unit 214, see that another wrecker is sent to Slocum Magpie Road at the creek bridge to assist civilians. We have a deer-verses-auto. Unit 135 and I will continue on down Slocum Magpie."

From his tone, I could tell that Mark had lost the van. I tried to remember what Slocum Magpie Road was like. All

I could recall was a two-lane blacktop with numerous one-lane turnoffs leading to mobile home parks, farms, a hunting preserve, junkyards, a beer joint or two and a new housing subdivision on an old farm. Tough locale to search house to house. I moved from the break room to the county map and found Five Points, out in the middle of godforsaken nowhere. It was miles from Stowe Farm.

"This is 315. Two-one-four, I see no reason to continue the barricades."

"Ten-four, 315. Suggest that all units move in toward Five Points. Two units to remain and stop all incoming traffic, all other units to proceed to my twenty for further instructions."

I waited in an agony of worry, dialing Miss Essie every few minutes, leaving numerous messages. Wanting to call Mark and ask him the name of the girl. Being forced to leave the scanner twice to care for patients. Feeling the strain of not knowing.

The messages on the scanner decreased in number and became more terse. Codes instead of messages, clicks instead of codes. Pressing the Transmit button on the side of a police radio created a click, audible to anyone listening. Officers who knew what the number of clicks meant could communicate without actual words that might give something away to bad guys listening in. It was necessary in an emergency. But it was downright painful when the family of the victim was hoping to hear good news.

Half an hour after the chase started, a knock came at the break-room door. I looked up to see Cowboy, his duster swirling about his calves. "Marisa said to come. Any news?"

Tears pooled in my eyes and I stood quickly, going to the coffeemaker, busying my hands with making a fresh pot. "Nothing. I don't even know if it was Arlana. No one will answer at the house."

"I rode by. No lights, no car in the garage." He slipped off the duster and tossed it over the back of a chair, taking the seat. Air whooshed out as he sat. "What can I do?"

"Nothing. We can't do anything."

"That's the pits, ain't it?"

I laughed and wiped the tears from my eyes. I had no idea how many scoops of coffee grounds I had measured out but it looked like a lot. I was making cheap espresso.

"I can see patients if you need, so you can sit."

"Thanks. We may need the help, if the accident victims are hurt." I finally turned around and looked at him. His blue eyes were watching me, concerned. We were alone in the room. "Well?"

He grinned slowly. "Well, what?"

I scowled at him. "You know what. What's going on with Marisa?"

"How does a spring wedding sound?" His eyes grinned up at me, crinkling heavily at the corners. "You get to be maid of honor."

"You were going to wait a week or so."

"I was. I couldn't."

"You Texans move fast. I'm not wearing a peach satin dress with big puffy sleeves."

"Marisa won't talk about the wedding yet." When I raised my brows in question, he sighed. "Okay. She hasn't said yes. Yet. Risa says I have to pass muster with Miss Essie first. Any tips?"

I knew he was trying to distract me, and I was grateful. "Don't chew on the furniture or pee on the carpet."

He laughed, the sound carefree and happy, the tone drawing a stiff smile from me. "That much I can manage," he said.

"Dr. Lynch?" Ash called from the nurses' desk, uncertainty in her voice.

I went to the door.

"Skye McNeely just had her baby."

My smile fell away. From Ash's expression, I knew there was more. I waited.

"He's got a Mongolian Spot on his back."

A Mongolian Spot was a brown spot located low on an infant's back, at the base of the spine. It was indicative of African-American heritage. To my knowledge, Skye McNeely was Caucasian. I knew Mark was, as I had seen generations of photographs on the walls of the house at his family farm.

Skye had accused Mark of paternity. An African-American man had fathered her child. Hence, the father of her child wasn't Mark. Simple deduction.

I was surprised that I didn't feel some amount of elation or relief. I felt nothing. Mark had not fathered Skye's child, but that didn't mean he hadn't tried. He'd slept with her while I was recuperating from a stab wound. I still didn't know what that meant about the kind of man I had thought I loved. I was still hurt and angry. But then, there was that curious reaction I'd had when Charlie Denbrow was shot and I thought it might be Mark.

"Thank you, Ash."

She nodded and added, "The baby's only one pound four ounces. They are shipping him to Spartanburg tonight." Eyes downcast, she slipped back to the desk.

"You want to tell me the significance of that comment?" Cowboy asked.

"No." I smiled to lessen the impact of the word. "Maybe later."

The ambulance radio came on, alerting us to multiple incoming injuries. Cowboy didn't have final privileges yet. I had paperwork to complete, phone calls to make and orders to give. Putting the problems of Mark away in some deep place I hadn't looked at recently, I went to work. Hot time in the old town tonight, I thought, the unspoken words tinged with an underlying sadness.

19

At 2:00 a.m., the E.R. phone rang the distinctive double ring of the outside line, and I grabbed it. Miss Essie was crying on the other end. Neither of us spoke. A cold fist gripped me. My breathing sped up, coming in little puffs of pain. "Miss Essie? Are you all right?" I finally asked. "Miss Essie? Was…was it Arlana?"

"Oh, that poor child. That poor child. Her mama jist dying with worry. Jist dying. We stayed and we prayed. And we prayed and prayed. And God don't seem to be hearing us. He don't. And Lord, you jist got to hear us. The policemen don't tell us nothing. Those evil men, those evil, evil men. They took her away. They—"

"Miss Essie!" I said loudly, to yank her from the incoherent misery. "Who was it? Who did they take?" My hand fisted on the chair arm before she stopped sobbing and answered.

"Shaniqua Reynolds. They took her right in front of the church, they did. I was right there, right there, and I didn't see. Didn't see them take her."

I fell back in my chair, one hand covering my face. It wasn't Arlana. Arlana was safe. I inhaled, aware that I hadn't done so in a long while. "Where is Arlana? Is she all right?"

"Arlana asleep in her bed. I look in on her jist now, to ease my worried soul. She a beautiful child. And I so shamed when I touch her face and know she safe, when little Shaniqua been took by them men. So shamed."

I comforted Miss Essie as best I could. I wasn't very good at the comfort stuff. Never had been. But I made appropriate noises and promised to call her if I heard anything, no matter how late it might be. "I'll sit here by the phone and by the scanner and I'll let you know. I promise, Miss Essie."

"You my good girl, Miss Rhea. My good girl to keep watch through the darks of night. I depend on you so." She sounded exhausted, her words slurred with tears and worry.

"Get some sleep. I'll keep watch for you." I echoed the antiquated phrase and moments later hung up. But there had been no news so far, and I didn't think there would be anytime soon. I'm a natural born-and-raised pessimist. I shuddered hard, the fear racking through me like electricity.

It hadn't been Arlana. And earlier, it hadn't been Mark. I'd dodged a bullet twice now. How long before it hit home and someone I loved was hurt? Selfish thought. But then, I'm selfish, too. A pessimistic, selfish woman.

The scanner crackled all night, the comments becoming fewer and further between, until 3:23 a.m., when Mark's voice said, "Dispatch, this is unit 214. I'm 10-7 at the hospital for half an hour."

Mark was here. Hearing the familiar cadence of booted feet, I closed a boring article in the *Journal of the American Medical Association* about the latest on the West Nile Virus. I waited, my gaze on my hands.

A red rosebud dropped into my lap. It was a beauty, just about to open. The color of old blood. I lifted my head.

He stood in the doorway, his hands gripping the door-jamb over his head, black police jacket unzipped and pulled to the sides, his torso stretched taut, belly concave beneath an olive-toned T-shirt. Mark was in black combat pants and black steel-toed boots, his 9 mm at his side.

I picked up the rose and set it on the table, careful of the thorns on its long stem. I had a feeling that Shaniqua would never receive roses again, except on her coffin.

He met my eyes, his green ones solemn, searching my face. "You heard?"

"I heard. What's the latest about her?"

"Her family disowned her." When I looked confused, he said, "Skye. Her father's a born-in-the-wool racist. He disowned her when her baby was born black."

"I was talking about the kidnapped girl," I said distinctly.

Mark's eyes glinted. After a moment, he dropped his arms and moved across to the coffeepot. I heard him pouring a cup, identified the sound of two sugars being torn open and two creams. He settled beside me. "I guess we need to talk."

I almost laughed. "Now you want to talk?" I felt the stress and anger of four months rise into my throat, my hands rolling the magazine into a tight spool, crushing the slick paper. When I spoke again my words were strained, a hoarse whisper. "It's been four months, Mark. The time to talk was the night you found out about the pregnancy. You left me hanging for four months. Not knowing what you were feeling or thinking."

"I was trying to protect you."

"Protect the little woman." I held his eyes, the words soft, scathing. "Make all the decisions so she doesn't have to worry her little head about them. My oh my, how kind of you, you big strong manly man." Sarcasm dripped off my tongue. "This is my life." I tapped my chest hard with the magazine. "Mine, not yours. I have the right to deal with problems the way I see fit."

"And if dealing with it meant dumping me?"

"Then you would have been sleeping in the bed you made."

"I'd rather sleep with you."

I blinked.

His voice dropped, eyes so intense they were hot green flame. "I'd rather be with you every minute of every day. I'd rather buy groceries with you, cook dinner with you, clean house with you. I'd rather run with you, laugh with you and watch movies with you. I'd rather be your husband. And I still intend to be. Whether you like it or not."

My magazine unrolled with a slap.

"I knew it wasn't my baby. I *knew* it, but I had no proof. And what if I was wrong? What if that kid had been born full-term and white? What if there had been that one in a million chance of a baby from the one time I screwed up and slept with her? What then? What if I had told you and we had fought this together?"

"But you did sleep with her." The words were so soft I didn't know if I said them.

The silence stretched out, rigid and brittle. "Yes. I slept with Skye. I admitted that when I tackled you in a ditch." A pained smile died stillborn. "I slept with her after I killed a man because you didn't trust me enough to tell me what you knew. I killed a man, Rhea. I killed him to save you. And I'd do it again in a heartbeat. But I didn't *have* to kill him. And he'd still be alive if you had trusted me even a little. And knowing that—*knowing* it body and soul—almost destroyed me, Rhea."

I knew it was true, but even so, anger roiled in me at his words. I agreed it was my fault Mark had killed Taylor Reeves. But it wasn't my fault he'd slept with Skye. I looked away, down at the curled journal in my lap. I didn't know what to say, how to explain what I was feeling. My throat was so tight I thought it might squeeze shut and strangle me.

"I've had four months to think. And I know what I want out of this, Rhea. I want you. I want to start over. A fresh start."

"Fresh start? There's no such thing. There's only what is now." And what could be if I chose it. What did I want with Mark? I didn't know. "And if I disappoint you again?" The words dragged out of my mouth. "If I have a reason not to tell you something you might consider vital, a reason based on the ethics of my job, and you have to shoot someone or a cop gets hurt or you get put in a precarious position? What then? You go and sleep with someone else again?"

Mark jerked as if I had slapped him, the tic in his cheek jumping erratically.

In a single fluid motion, he stood and pulled me to my feet, his hands fierce on my arms. His face bent, eyes flinty, staring into mine. Then his lips crushed against mine. His tongue pushed through my mouth, touched once. An electric heat shot through me, pooling like velvet, a curling need that shocked me. His mouth gentled, and my hands touched his sides, hesitantly.

He pulled away. Shook me slightly. "I'm not giving you up," he whispered.

"I'll think about it," I said breathlessly.

Mark was gone, dropping me so suddenly that I fell into the chair behind me. Ash poked her head into the room. "You okay, Dr. Rhea?"

"I'm fine," I said, not sure I was telling the truth. I looked over at the rose and wondered where he had gotten it at this time of night. It had one of those little water container things around the cut stem.

Mark's voice crackled on the radio, telling dispatch that he was back on the road. Instead of acknowledging, the dispatcher said, "All units, all units, code ten seventy-eight and code ten thirty-three. Repeat, code ten seventy-eight and code ten thirty-three at the site of the mass grave. Code ten-forty-three. All units give me your ten-twenty and ETA."

I grabbed the police code sheet off the wall and looked up the numbers. Seldom did the Dawkins County 9-1-1 dispatcher solely use codes to inform officers what was needed. This time she was asking for help at all possible speed, telling all officers on duty that an officer at the mass gravesite needed help. Weird. The place had been closing down when I'd left less than twelve hours earlier.

"Ash, you hear this?" I called.

"I hear it. Wonder what's up." She appeared in the doorway again, her eyes on the scanner as if willing it to speak.

A strange voice said, "Dispatch, this is unit 527. Code 10-52 and code 10-60 requested at the mass grave. Repeat, code 10-52 and code 10-60 requested at the same 20."

I looked up the numbers; the strange voice and code number were asking for the coroner and an ambulance. At the empty gravesite. My fingertips were itching. I looked at the red rosebud. Water was leaking out of the little plastic container at the end of the long stem, pooling on the table. It was bound to wilt.

"That's you, Dr. Rhea. They want the coroner."

"I can't leave this place uncovered. That's abandonment."

"Michelle Geiger is still upstairs in OB with Skye

McNeely. She lost a lot of blood and the doctor was sticking around. Maybe she can cover for you?"

"Call up there and see." Cowboy had left when things quieted down. I needed him now, but he was likely back in Charlotte. Or in Marisa's bed.

Michelle Geiger was in the E.R. in three minutes. "More trouble in the streets?" she asked, a smile lighting her long face.

"More like more trouble in the boonies. Can you cover?"

"I'll be here at least an hour. If I have to leave I'll call Wallace."

"You'll make his day. I'll try to be back by then." I grabbed my lab coat and raced for the E.R. air-lock doors. "Ash, call dispatch and tell them I'll meet at the gravesite in fifteen. Ten, if they don't stop me for speeding." I had my rubber boots in the trunk, along with PPEs. At least it was warmer outside this time and I wouldn't freeze without the down coat that was still hanging from a limb in the backyard. I gunned the motor and squealed out of the lot, heading toward the mass grave.

I made it in twelve minutes, leaving rubber skid marks at three intersections. A news van from a Charlotte NBC network tried to keep up with me for several minutes, but got left at the first intersection. Not as nimble as my little car.

I cornered neatly at the final turn, the one that had been chained after the discovery of the bodies. Moving easily among trees whose branches had been pruned back to allow access, I approached the field. Klieg lights had been set up in two places, throwing the area into harsh shadows and glaring brightness. A cop wearing an orange vest saluted me and gestured me to a parking spot with his flashlight. I was pulling on the ugly boots and PPEs almost before my key was out of the ignition. Cops were talking loudly; blurred forms strode back and forth across the field. More cars were pulling up all around me as I dressed, but no ambulance was here yet. I shivered and wished for the peacoat I had left at home.

Outfitted in PPEs and boots, I grabbed my black doctor bag, tucked in my cell phone and moved into the congested area. A cop was sitting on a stump, surrounded by uniformed bodies, a bloody rag to his head. "Let me in, I'm a doctor," I said, recognizing the big, burly deputy. "Hi, Malcom. How you doing?"

"Not so good, Doc. I got cold-cocked." Malcom Haskins's face was ashen in the too-bright lights. Using my handy-dandy little Maglite, I checked his pupillary reflexes. They were at two and six, a difference I didn't like.

"Your pupils are normally the same size, right?"

"Yeah. I guess so. Why?"

"Well, they're a little different right now. Not quite equal. The right is a little sluggish." I pulled gently at the rag he held to his head. "Let me see that wound."

The laceration was about three inches long, and deep enough to show skull beneath the kinky black hair and tissue. I got a good look before blood spurted at me. I reapplied pressure, careful to employ just enough to stop the arterial bleeding and not enough to worsen any possible skull fracture. "So what, then? I got a concussion?" Malcom asked.

"Maybe. Open my bag?" I asked an officer standing near. "Did you lose consciousness?"

"Yeah. I guess so. I woke up maybe fifteen minutes ago? SOB got me and buried another one before he left. Don't you go telling my Arlana I got hurt. She'll have a fit."

I had forgotten Malcom Haskins had dated Arlana. She'd give him a tongue-lashing from here to next Tuesday if she found out. "It'll be our little secret. How long were you out, do you think?" One-handed, I searched for packets of sterile 4X4 gauze and tape, a bottle of irrigation water.

"Maybe twenty minutes? They tell me I was talking to 135 on the radio when I heard something. And then nothing. I thought I saw lights pulling by me when I woke up. Seems like I heard yelling. I tried to find my radio, but it was gone. And so I found this rag to stop the bleeding. Doc, I'm feeling a little woozy." Malcom's knees began to draw up slightly. "Like...maybe I'm gonna puke."

And he did. All over my nice clean smooth rubber boots. At least he missed the open medical bag. I held his head, and another cop held his shoulder to keep him on the stump as Malcom emptied his stomach contents. I smelled sour pizza.

"Doc, my head's really starting to hurt. Oh, man." He grabbed his skull, rocking with the pain. Gagging with the motion. Whoever hit him had intended him to be out for a long time. Or had left him for dead.

"Where's the ambulance?" I said. It sounded like an order, and the cop beside me pulled his radio instantly and keyed for the information.

"Dispatch, this is— It's here, now, Doc." He pointed with the radio. "Looks like two of them. Must be a boring night, for two to come out."

"Like it had nothing to do with the panic in the dispatcher's voice," I said dryly. "Hold this," I instructed him, indicating the rag on Malcom's head. "Not quite that much pressure. Yeah, good." Pulling out my cell phone, I called the E.R. When I got Michelle on the line, I said, "Call and see if Medic is available and what an ETA would be to Carolina's Medical. If it's too long, get whoever's on call for radiology up stat. I'm sending you a patient. He needs a head CT, presumptive concussion, rule out dural or subdural hematoma.'' I gave her the little information I knew and signed off, wondering if I should call for the Medic chopper and fly Haskins out directly from the field.

But it was safer for Medic to land in the well-marked landing site on the hospital grounds. And safer for Medic meant safer for Malcom.

The EMTs took over for me in less than a minute. I gave a fast report and stepped aside, holding my black bag, feeling a bit weird doing things backward. I usually took report and patients from them. When Malcom was well in hand, I turned and stomped the residue of vomit off of my boots. The stench was particularly vile. Yuck. Double yuck. With a grin that said he'd been there, a paramedic passed me a liter of sterile water and nodded to my feet. ''You stink, Doc. Help yourself.''

''Thanks,'' I said, and upended the water all over my boots. I still smelled of vomit, but now it was not a primary scent.

''If you've finished playing, there's work to do,'' a voice said.

I looked up and saw Mark, narrowed my eyes at him. ''You want to rephrase that statement, Captain Stafford?'' I said. And maybe apologize for being an idiot? But I didn't say that part.

He looked away and back. ''I have a body for bagging-and-tagging.''

''I thought all the bodies were taken out of here.''

''The guys who hit Malcolm buried a fresh one.''

I remembered the cop saying something about a new body. ''And?''

''It looks like the girl who was taken from the church tonight.''

I glanced up quickly, meeting his eyes, understanding the anger in Mark's voice.

"They butchered her. Fast and dirty." His jaw ground in the harsh light.

I knew what he was thinking. He had failed her. He hadn't found her in time. She had gotten killed on his shift. I wanted to tell him it wasn't his fault, he had done the best he could. But I knew from my own experience that was never enough. Not nearly.

"You're telling me the same guys came back—to the same graveyard where the bodies have been removed—hit a cop without killing him and buried another body?"

"That's what I'm telling you."

"That's insane," I said.

"That's the point, Doctor."

I made a sound that reminded me of one of Miss Essie's snorts of disbelief. "Let's see her."

While changing gloves for a fresh pair of thick blue latex ones, I followed him around the field, around the oldest graves in the A line, past the B graves, and south into the C graves, near the top of the pyramid. Where the freshly dead had come from.

The grave was open. The sheet blood-soaked. I forced myself to bend over the girl and check for signs of life. There were none. Shaniqua Reynolds was gone.

Mark was right. It had been fast and dirty. They hadn't lingered over her. Hadn't taken their time. "She expired," I said softly, pronouncing her officially for the record. I set my bag down and found one of the core-temp thermometers Dempsey had left me, and a sterile scalpel. "I have the paperwork in my car. We could request a transport for now. Dempsey might need to see this one quickly."

Opening both scalpel and thermometer, I palpated the location of the liver and sliced deeply with the scalpel, hating the feel of carving flesh beneath my blade. With a quick lunge, the thermometer followed. I felt slightly sick at the sensation of piercing tissue. Mark stood over me, saying nothing. I put a hand on her flesh. It was cold. The cold of death.

After the requisite time, I read the thermometer and recorded the results of the core temperature: 95.6. This girl had been dead only a little while. I dropped my head. Above me, Mark read the number and cursed vilely. I nodded to show I understood.

Then a soft sound came from the darkness. Mewling.

20

"You hear that?" I asked.

"Cat?"

"I don't think so. I think…" I stood, grabbed my bag and moved into the darkness. Mark walked beside me, placing his flashlight in my hand. I shined it over the brush, moving slowly left and right.

"Stop," Mark ordered. "Back up."

I returned the beam to the right. It focused on something in the night. Slowly the thing took shape. Developed form. It moved. "Oh, my God," I said softly.

"Get an ambulance over here! Medic!" Mark shouted. "Get us some lights!"

People came at a dead run, charging through the field around which Mark and I had walked carefully, hoping to preserve any evidence that might have been missed. The ambulance roared and bounced across the ruts of the opened graves. I crashed through the brush, approaching the thing in the weeds. Shouting, others followed.

She was lying in the brush, nude, curled in a fetal position. Ropes bound her legs together at the ankles, and her wrists. There wasn't much flesh left on her torso, wrists and ankles, or inner thighs. Red dirt, twigs, leaves were ground into her skin and the wounded tissue, as if she had rolled through the graveyard. Her face was bruised and torn, beaten.

There was so much damage on the girl that I didn't know where to start. She was breathing, sucking in soft little gasps of air through blistered lips. Her eyes were closed. Her flesh had been cut and burned so badly there was almost no safe place to touch her.

I knelt in the grass at her side. There was no sign of arterial bleeding, no spurts of blood, only slow leaks of thin blood and serous fluid from wounds fresh and several days old. I put a hand on uninjured skin at her upper arm. She was icy, almost as cold as the body I had just pronounced, skin pulled into tight pimples of chill-bumps like chicken skin. I checked her pulse at her carotid. It was fast and irregular, missing beats.

"Burn victim," I said to myself. "We'll treat her like a burn victim. Worry about the lacerations later." I would need a burn pack, sterile water, clean sheets. "Hypothermia and dehydration first, along with tissue protection," I murmured. We didn't have access to vast amounts of warmed irrigation fluid. In this weather, with the risk of hypothermia, I didn't dare consider washing her down too thoroughly. I'd have to do what I could and hope for the best.

"Preserve the trace evidence, for God's sake," Mark said. "Can we bag her hands?"

I stood so fast the blood rushed from my head and the world blackened in front of me. Blindly, I grabbed Mark's shirt in one fist and twisted. "This is my patient and I don't give a good blasted damn about your evidence," I hissed, a red haze growing over my vision. "My patient first. Your evidence after. Long after!"

"I didn't mean—"

"Like hell, you didn't."

He shut his mouth and stepped away. I dropped back to

my knees. "Get these ropes off her," I demanded. Mark pulled a knife from his utility belt and went to work on her wrists by the light of the single flashlight.

The ambulance bounced to a stop beside me and Gus ran to the back. Hybernia ran toward me, the huge EMS pack in her hands. She stopped, her breath making a harsh sucking sound as she dropped to her knees. She was whispering under her breath. I didn't want to know what she was saying.

She ripped open a burn pack. Gus landed beside her and then jumped up and ran back to the unit, returning with warmed saline. He opened fluid and carefully poured it over the girl, two bottles, 4,000 milliliters, rinsing away the detritus stuck to her skin. Hybernia layered on sterile gauze. I didn't have to say anything, just offered a hand where needed to hold the gauze in place. Mark finished cutting through the ropes on her ankles, saving them in an evidence bag.

Hybernia unwrapped one sterile paper burn sheet and covered the girl in it, then unwrapped others, the crackling loud in the silence of the graveyard as she and Gus layered the girl in them.

Carefully, we rolled the thin form onto a regular sheet and wrapped her in other sheets, followed by heated blankets.

"Okay, guys, we want her on the stretcher and into the unit where it's warm," I said. "Then we want IVs times two at the AC and warm fluid. She's had blood loss so we're going for LR if it's hot," I said, referring to Lactated Ringers, an IV fluid that would do the same work as saline and also act as a blood volume expander, protecting against shock.

As I talked, Gus had maneuvered the ambulance gurney into position and dropped it to the ground. "On three," he said, and he and Hybernia and about seven cops gripped the corners and sides of the bottom sheet, and lifted the girl to the gurney. They settled her gently and covered her in more warm blankets. In seconds we were all in the unit— Gus, Hybernia, the girl and me, my black bag in hand.

"How far are we to the hospital?" I asked.

"'Bout six, seven miles," Gus said, without his customary smile. "Why?"

"We can't really help her at Dawkins," I said, thinking out loud. "She needs burn-type care." Remembering Mark's comment, I added, "She also needs a forensic nursing team to work on her, which Dawkins can't even begin to provide. But…she needs other things more, so we're going to Dawkins," I decided.

"You're the boss," Gus said. "But I'm driving." He took his seat as Hybernia and I began the gruesome procedure of taking vital signs and finding IV sites in the girl's wasted body. As we bounced over the ruts in the graveyard, Hybernia swathed the girl's right upper arm in soft cloth and wrapped a blood pressure cuff on her. After a moment, she said, "Blood pressure is 80 palp. Pulse is pretty irregular, but I'd say maybe 125. Respiration at 22, give or take." *Palp* was short for palpate, and meant Hybernia couldn't hear the pulse through the stethoscope, but could only feel it. A dangerous sign of shock and blood loss. She slipped green tubing over the girl's nose and turned on oxygen at three liters. Took her temperature with a little digital device that measured the air temp in the girl's ear canal. "Too low to read."

"What're its limits?" I asked.

"I don't know. I never had one so low I couldn't read it."

The ambulance paused and I heard a window go down, followed by Gus's part of a conversation. "Thanks. I'll tell her. No, we're heading to Dawkins. Sure. Whatever floats your boat."

Heat blasted from the vents as I cradled the patient's arm in the warm blankets and the burn wrappings and tied on a tourniquet. I was hot in the PPEs, and trickles of sweat started under my arms. The patient had one thin line of blue beneath the pale flesh at the elbow. I reached past Hybernia for the IV equipment, as she began assembling the IV bag of warmed Ringer's and the device that kept it at body temperature.

I cleaned the girl's arm below the blood pressure cuff with alcohol and inserted the 14 Jelco. I was lucky. Instantly I had blood backflow that let me know I was in the vein and not under the skin beside it. I held out my hand for the IV line and Hybernia placed it in my gloved palm. I withdrew the needle, leaving the plastic sheath in the patient's arm, attached the sheath to the IV line. Hybernia opened up the fluid as I popped the tourniquet off.

The patient started shivering instantly as the heated fluid hit her system.

"Good," Hybernia said. She moved to the head of the gurney, not an easy feat in the ambulance, and found the other arm. In moments she had a second IV. She was sweating, too, beads forming on her forehead and across the bridge of her nose. Hybernia's muscles bunched and glistened as she moved, her hours in the gym paying off in the field.

In the cab, Gus was giving a report to the hospital. He had been listening to our conversation and results, and asked me for orders even before I thought to give any. I relayed what I wanted waiting when we arrived at the E.R., but kept my attention on the girl. I thought her skin looked a bit warmer, a fraction less blue.

When we had done everything we could, I sat back and pulled off the paper coat and filthy latex gloves. My hands were sweat-slick inside and I wiped them on my scrub pants, which were mud-caked from knees to hem. My boots still smelled of vomit. Or maybe the stench was now from the patient.

I took my first good look at the girl. She had lost a lot of weight recently, and mottled skin hung at arms and thighs, along her back and sides. She was blond-haired and young, and I wanted to cry for what had been done to her. The protective instincts that caused me to snap at Mark blossomed. If she lived, this girl would need huge amounts of care, not just nursing, but emotional, psychological and physical rehabilitation. She was a mess. They had kept her a long time.

Her shivering worsened. But she opened her eyes. Blinked. Searched for the voice near her.

Hybernia was still muttering under her breath, but I could hear her now. She was soothing the patient. "It's all right, honey. We got you now. They can't hurt you no more. You're just finer than frog's fur, yes you are, and we'll fix you right up. Protect you from the bad guys from now on. You're safe now. You're safe."

I smiled. Hybernia was gruff, sometimes a bit profane, but she was good-hearted, gentle with her patients.

Softly, the girl mewled, the tone of a kitten abandoned by its mother. Hurt. Lost. I checked her pupils. Dilated fully.

"I'm here for you, sweetie. I'm here. You hang on and we'll get you something for the pain in a minute. Doc, can I administer some painkiller?"

"Go for it," I said. "I should have thought of it myself. Two milligrams morphine IV? And two more if there's no relief, for a total of four milligrams."

I pulled on a clean pair of gloves and smoothed the girl's hair back. "What's your name?" I asked softly.

Finding me with her eyes, she struggled to focus. She licked her lips with a parched tongue. Tried twice to speak. "Beata. Beata Geter," she croaked.

I paused, my hand in her hair. Wayne Edward Geter's sister. I smiled gently and bent to her ear. "Wayne Edward is okay. He's been looking for you. He never stopped. He never gave up. He loves you."

The mewling coarsened into a sob, as dry-eyed, she cried. The tone was relief. The beginnings of surprise. She was safe. It wasn't a dream.

We pulled up on the ambulance ramp and Ashlee ran to help us, easing the stretcher legs to the ground and kicking the support struts to a locked position. Working as a single unit, we rushed into the emergency room. I felt an instant sense of relief as the doors closed behind me. I was back in my element, where I belonged.

For a moment I stood in the back corner of the room, watching my team work on my patient, my black doctor bag crushed to my chest.

After twenty minutes the X rays were ready to be taken, another IV had been started delivering ancef and saline, and blood work had been drawn to check for electrolyte balance, blood loss and a CPK to rule out rhabdomyolysis, a condition of muscle breakdown not uncommon in patients who had been restrained and unmoving for long periods of time. Beata's temperature had risen to 94.6, and my own quivers had stopped. When I looked away from the patient and met Mark's eyes across the room, his face was expressionless, eyes deadened. I headed to the doorway and he turned, waited for me in the hall, hands shoved deep in his pockets.

"I know you didn't mean to treat my patient like a piece of evidence, a corpse heading for a forensic postmortem," I said. "I took it wrong. I'm sorry. And I'm sorry I grabbed your shirt. It was unprofessional. It was rude."

There was little in his eyes, but I thought he might be considering my words. "Thanks. She gonna be okay?"

"Probably not. But she'll live, barring complications like infection and shock. She told me her name."

Mark's eyes showed a spark of life. "And?"

"She's Wayne Edward's sister, Beata Geter."

"When can I talk to her?"

I opened my mouth to say never, but Dr. Haynes, the pediatric specialist on call, was walking into the trauma room. Beata was no longer my patient, so it wasn't my decision.

"Come on, Rhea. You know I need to talk to her," Mark said with a half smile that showed his words weren't a complaint, "and the Feebs will be here shortly. They'll want to talk to her, too. And there'll be others, most likely."

I nodded into the room. "You'll have to ask Haynes," I said. "I'll put in a good word for you."

"Thanks. Here. I thought you might want these." He held out my running shoes, and I was oddly touched that he had thought about my comfort in the midst of the crisis. "I got them out of your BMW and asked one of the smokies to drive it here. It'll be here in an hour or so."

I smiled and took the shoes and tucked them under an arm. "Thanks. I'm going to shower. Change clothes." I looked down. "My boots still stink from when Malcom got sick on them."

"They flew him to Charlotte Medical Center. He's getting a Cat scan now."

"Was he still conscious?" I asked.

"Last I heard. But he's having trouble staying awake. That's a bad sign, isn't it?"

"Yes," I said softly. "It is."

Mark took a deep breath. It sounded shaky. "You need a ride home?"

"Not right now. I think I'll hang around here for a while. See how she does in an hour or two."

Mark lifted a hand and slipped his thumb along my jaw, the action gentle. Along my bottom lip, featherlight. The touch tightened things deep in my belly, where they didn't show. And I suddenly remembered my fear when I'd thought he had been shot. If we made up, if things worked out between us, how many times in the future would I experience the same fear? How many times over the years would my belly clench when the emergency scanner went off? Could I take that constant fear? Did I want to?

"I meant what I said." His voice dropped. "And if you need a ride home sooner than when your car gets delivered, I'll be here awhile. Or I'll come back, pick you up." He almost smiled. "We can argue on the way home."

I was tired of arguing. Tired of the constant competition between us. That wasn't exactly a healthy relationship. "I don't want to argue anymore, Mark. But thanks for the offer of a ride. I may take you up on it."

"Good. Let me know."

21

SOUNDS LIKE THERE'S A "BUT" IN THERE SOMEWHERE

After I conferred with Haynes about Beata Geter, I headed toward my call room, fishing in my pocket for the key to the lock as I walked. It clicked open, letting me into the quiet sanctum. I latched the door, opened my canvas bag and pulled out the small case of toiletries and the extra scrub suit I kept stuffed there for emergencies.

Exhausted, numb from the long night and knowing I would soon be needed back at the mass grave for my coroner's skills—or lack thereof—I headed for the shower. Putting the stinky boots in the corner of the stall to rinse, I washed my short black hair, actually bothered to shave my legs, and smoothed on almond-scented jojoba oil as the boots got a long soaking.

When we three smelled better, I dressed in the clean scrubs, lab coat and running shoes, ran a comb through my hair and looked at myself in the steamy mirror. I no longer looked quite so whiny as I had only a few days past. But I didn't look quite like myself yet, either. I was tired. More tired than I could remember since medical school and residency.

Smiling at my reflection, I left the shower, put my dirty and used stuff in the bag and walked back through the E.R.

It was pretty quiet—only three patients, and Haynes in the back, chatting with Dan Hoffman, who was pulling E.R. day-shift duty. I saw the patients and wrote orders before going to the phone.

Using the hospital line, I called Miss Essie to tell her about Shaniqua, and instead listened as she cried. Word was already out about the fate of the girl taken from the church, right in front of the congregation's eyes. I didn't ask how she knew, but I was glad I hadn't been the one who had to tell her that Shaniqua was dead.

Not knowing I had been at the graveyard, Miss Essie told me what she had heard. I sat at the desk, listening to a garbled version of the discovery of Shaniqua, and didn't give the correct version. Miss Essie's was less awful than the truth. And then she told me that two other girls from the community were dead as well, their bodies identified from the triangle graveyard. Elorie and Natasha Curtis. Sisters. Gone. Miss Essie was inconsolable. I listened to her misery and knew I should be at her house instead of on the job.

"I'll be there in half an hour, Miss Essie," I said, feeling desperate.

She took a deep breath. I could hear the tissue at the back of her throat move with the painful effort. "I won't be here, chile, though you a sweet thing to offer. I be at the church with the families there. Word come we to gather and pray and grieve today, and help them poor families make plans. Thelma Curtis got no money to bury them girls and we got to put some together, do them right with they funeral."

"I'll give a thousand dollars toward the Curtis funerals. Each," I said, before my good sense stopped my mouth and compassion and guilt.

"You jist the finest child," Miss Essie said, crying again. "Jist the finest God made."

I knew I wasn't, but I didn't argue, I just listened. After twenty minutes, I hung up.

Beata was still in the trauma room and Mark was with her, smiling gently down into her face. I stood on the outside, watching through the wide glass doors. I could see from the monitor that her temp was 96 and her blood pressure was stabilized. We'd be flying her out soon.

One-handed, Mark stroked Beata's face, pushed her greasy blond hair back from her eyes. Not at all coplike. A nurse I didn't know watched the scene with tears in her eyes. I saw Beata reach up and take Mark's wrist in her fingers. She was trying to tell him something, her throat working as if speech was painful. He tensed, his feet about to take off at a run. Instead, he smiled again and said something else. Then he disentangled her fingers and backed away toward me, so that I heard his last words.

"I'll call you tonight. I promise. And I'll try to bring word from Wayne Edward. You try and rest. Okay?" Stepping from the room, he turned, his eyes alight with excitement.

"She told you something, didn't she?"

"Two things. The name of the other guy. She verified it was who we thought, one of the cons Deacon met in jail— Di'Juan Michael Crank. And she said she was kept in a small house with trees visible through the windows. Windows not sealed, just ordinary glass windows."

"She was kept in a remote place. Where no one would come upon them, and no one would hear her screaming," I said.

"Very good. In the country, because of the trees. And twice she heard a train. Twice in all the time they had her. So the train is one of the ones that runs only a few times a week."

I asked a question that had been burning in the back of

my mind for hours. "Why was Beata in the graveyard? Did they dump her? Bury her and she crawled out?"

"Nah. That girl's something else." He shook his head in admiration, as proud of Beata as if she had been his own kid. "She was tied up in the back seat of the car they were using. When the guys were digging the grave, she managed to open a door on the other side of the car and roll out. And she kept on rolling till she was far enough away that they couldn't find her in the dark."

I didn't know what to say to that. I settled on "Wow," knowing it was totally inadequate.

"Yeah. She's gonna break this case for us. Beata's innate sense of observation and Deacon's own stupidity. I'm outta here. I gotta see some county maps." Mark chucked me on my chin, turned on the toes of his black combat boots and took off for the outer doors.

"Good luck," I said. But he was gone.

I spoke with Ashlee and looked in on Beata. Dr. Haynes had already called in Medic to fly the girl to a burn center, and he was staying with her until the chopper came, even if it took a long while. It was unspoken but a very real fact—this child would not be left alone. Someone would stay with her every moment she was in the Dawkins County E.R.

My eyes were so heavy I thought I might trip over my lids, so I returned to my call room, wrapped up in a scratchy blanket and fell on the bed. Within minutes, I was asleep.

I woke with my heart slamming in my chest, lids glued closed with sleep. I couldn't have said how, but I knew I wasn't alone. Breathless, I forced open my eyes. And focused on Eli Cordell.

He was sitting across from me on the only chair, stretched out, resting on his tailbone, neck at the chair back, an odd stillness gathered about him like a shield. His black-denim-clad legs were outstretched, booted feet on the tile between us, white long-sleeved dress shirt folded up at the cuffs, black T-shirt beneath. A brown leather bomber jacket rested across the rolling, adjustable table to his left. His brown eyes were focused intently on me.

I met his gaze, waiting. Not entirely sure I was safe at the moment. My heart thudded in fight-or-flight readiness. He had left the door to my room wide open. If I screamed, I might be heard.

"You did good, saving that girl." When I said nothing, he continued. "They're all talking about it at the desk. How you went out in the dark, found her in the woods. You treated her and brought her here." I shrugged. His lips curved at the corners for just a moment. "Superwoman."

With an indelicate snort, I sat up on the bed, feeling the pull of my injured back muscles. My heart rate lowered fractionally, steadied into a normal beat. He hadn't rushed across the space between us and ravaged me. He was a security expert, not a criminal, for heaven's sake.

Scrubbing my eyes fully open, I said, "Not superwoman. Just a tired doctor conned into being the acting coroner for a while." I stretched, pulling at muscles stiffened by sleep, the cotton blanket bundled about me. I had kicked off my shoes while I slept; they were on the floor in a two-shoe pile, and my toes were cold in my cotton socks. "I admit that I was pretty happy to be doing something on a live patient. I'm not cut out to be a pathologist."

"Punny," he said, straight-faced.

I laughed. My stomach grumbled. "How'd you get in here? I know for a fact I latched the door."

"Cheap latch. Took about three seconds. Someone called the media," he said, his face still giving away nothing. "Reporters are staking out the different entrances, waiting for you. The doctor, coroner, heroine. Your name made the news.''

I grimaced. ''Well, that's just fine and dandy.''

''Your boyfriend left a message at the desk.'' Eli passed a crumpled piece of paper with Mark's handwriting on it across to me. ''Says he got called away and can't take you home. That's the bad news. The good news is that a guy named Jacobson can do the bag-and-tag. You don't have to go back to the graveyard. Says to have one of the EMTs get you out of here unnoticed, if you want. Media staked out your car after a highway patrol officer delivered it to the doctors' parking lot.'' His chocolate eyes were locked on mine. There was something coiled there, behind the motionless facade, in the dark depths of his eyes. I couldn't read it.

''You read my note?''

''Yes. And tracked you down to offer a counterproposal. Unless you want to talk with reporters.''

I considered his statement as I watched his face. ''I'm not interested in talking to the media.'' I pulled my legs back under the comforter and sat cross-legged, warming my toes. ''He's not my boyfriend,'' I said finally, hearing, almost tasting, the words and the sadness that laced them. ''Not really.''

''He seems to think he is.''

I looked at the note, which was signed *Love, Mark*. ''Yeah.'' For a moment, I considered both Mark and my ex-fiancé, John. ''I seem to attract the kind of man who makes up his mind without input from me about everything—how we're going to handle unpleasant situations, problems, lifestyles, and our relationship. All by himself.'' I was surprised to hear the words come out of my mouth. I wasn't usually so forthcoming about personal things with strangers. I wasn't usually forthcoming about personal stuff with anyone. And I didn't usually sound so bitter.

My stomach grumbled again. I couldn't remember the last time I'd eaten a meal. Maybe breakfast with the cops on Sunday morning. "What's your counterproposal?"

"I can get you out of here without the media knowing." A half smile was hovering on his lips.

"Sounds like there's a 'but' in there somewhere."

"There is. You have to have breakfast with me." The smile on his face warmed.

"You have this breakfast fetish." I narrowed my eyes. "You're not one of those guys who eats tofu and protein shakes with seaweed in it, are you?"

The grin widened a fraction. "Not unless you *want* tofu and protein shakes with seaweed in it. I can probably find a place that offers that kind of slime."

"I'm more in the mood for bacon, eggs, a stack of pancakes and then a good five mile run." I watched his eyes as I spoke.

His head inclined a fraction. "I could use a good run. I know a track not far away."

I considered his offer. "The bus station?"

"Media will likely be there."

I grimaced. "International House of Pancakes? Closest one is in Ford County."

He showed teeth in his grin, amusement obvious, and the expression transformed his face. He looked younger, less dangerous. I had the feeling he didn't smile often. "I have a private booth there."

"I'll need running clothes."

"My sweats will be a little baggy on you, but they'll do in a pinch."

"I need to drop by a chiropractor's office first."

"We can do that."

"Then you'll take me home?"

"Safe as a newborn baby in its mother's arms." But

there was something else in his eyes, something deeper that I didn't trust completely.

"Yeah. Breakfast and a run are fine," I heard myself say.

He smiled at me, the movement of his lips long and slow. "No tofu."

After giving me a cardboard box to hide my boots, filthy clothes and black doctor's bag, Eli guided me through the hospital to the rear door used by maintenance workers when bringing in replacement light fixtures, plumbing tools, ladders, stuff they wouldn't want visitors to notice. I wondered how he had learned the layout so thoroughly in such a short time.

Eli looked out, his eyes flicking around, noting every shadow, every cranny where problems might lie. The place was half-lit and deserted. It was also cold. I shivered in my scrubs and lab coat.

"Wait here. I'll pull up in a black Land Rover and angle it so you can get to the door in three strides. When the door opens, you come out." His eyes studied me. "Take off your lab coat. You'll look less like a doctor." He turned and left, his feet silent on the tile floors, his body padding like a cat's down the hallway. He moved with dangerous smoothness, as if he knew where each foot should land, as if the air currents told him what was coming next.

He also had a remarkably tight butt. I shook my head and faced the outer door. I had no business noticing a man's backside. I had missing and dead girls to deal with. A lot of them. I had Mark to deal with. Or not. I didn't know what I wanted with Mark. I remembered the heat when he kissed me, that curling, drowning need waiting to be explored. How was I supposed to know what to do about that? How did normal women figure it out?

I wasn't a normal woman where men were concerned.

When most girls were learning the ways to read sexual tension and manipulate men, I had been trying to survive. When other girls were learning how to French kiss, I had been working part-time in a car wash after school to put food on the table while watching my mother die of cirrhosis and dissipation. Boys had been the furthest thing from my mind. When my mother died, I had managed to graduate high school, get through college and get accepted in medical school. I was still paying on the medical school loans, though if I worked in Dawkins, a depressed part of the country, for two years, the government would pay them off for me.

And then in the last half of medical school had come John.... We had been perfect together. Just not perfect enough to last beyond E.R. residency in Chicago.

A black SUV the size of Montana pulled up and angled to the door. Shaking away the dumb memories, I yanked off my lab coat, stuffed it into the box with my medical bag and moved out of the relative warmth of the hallway into the frigid cold. The Land Rover wasn't warm yet, but its windows were tinted and that had advantages, as a news van pulled around the corner, a camera held out the door window taking footage the station might need someday. I pulled the door shut before I became part of the shot.

The SUV was fantastic—rich, dark gray leather upholstery; its dash filled with all sorts of equipment I didn't recognize except for the radio, the CD player, the GPS thingy and the compass. What kind of man needed both global positioning satellite equipment and an ordinary compass on his car? Eyes still glancing edgily, Eli whirled the wheel and moved slowly out of the area as I buckled in. The news vehicle didn't follow.

The seat beneath me began to warm with an electronic heat, but it wasn't enough and I shivered again. Eli glanced at me. One-handed, he tossed me his jacket. "Here. It's nipply out."

I looked down and sighed. Miss Essie would have a fit. I hadn't worn a bra and it showed. And it appeared that Eli wasn't the kind of man who would either miss the obvious or neglect to say something about it. *Nipply*. Mark would have said nothing, or simply have offered me his coat. Which was better, the polite blindness or the amused commentary?

I pulled on the warm jacket, which smelled like old leather and Eli, slightly musky, and my body reacted to the scent in ways that left me uncomfortable. I should be grieving for the dead girls or still seeing nightmares from the triangle graveyard of horrors, not noticing things about strange men. Besides, I wasn't entirely certain that Eli wanted me for the reasons my instinct said. While I was honest enough to sense his attraction, there was something else beneath it all. Something else he was after. And my reactions to him were likely based on the fact that Mark had been gone for months and John for months longer. I had been alone a long time. Shallow comfort.

No matter the reason, I didn't like women like me, the kind of woman who got turned on by a man for his scent and his butt and his neat car. I laughed under my breath, the sound wry and a little harsh.

"What?"

"Nothing I want to say out loud."

"Thanks." That half smile was in place again. A little quirky now.

"For what?"

"For whatever you don't want to say out loud."

I laughed aloud this time. "You have a bit of an ego problem, don't you, Eli?"

"Got an ego. Never been a problem."

Snuggling into the leather jacket, I felt my shivers ease.

We arrived at the chiropractor's office and Martin hurried me in, did a quick exam and an adjustment. My back was feeling better and better.

But Martin had dark circles beneath his eyes. A black ribbon had been taped to the photo of Holly at the desk. He saw me looking and volunteered the information.

"She's dead. They identified her this morning as one of the Triangle Killer victims."

I just nodded and turned away, not wanting to see the tears that gathered in his eyes. Three counties would be grieving soon. Acres of land draped in mourning black.

Later, Eli headed toward I-77 and the fifteen-minute drive to Ford County, the sun hidden behind golden clouds on the horizon. Twenty minutes after my appointment with Martin, we were sitting in a booth at International House of Pancakes, the waitress having greeted him by name and taken us to a table in the back, while Eli rattled off our orders without asking me what I wanted. He faced both the windows and the front entrance, at an angle to the kitchen doors. It was the only place in the joint where he could see everything at once. "Nice booth," I said.

His lips twitched. "Glad you like it."

"They really saved it for you, didn't they?"

"I'm a little early. I usually run first, then eat."

I nodded, easing the tightness of the jacket a bit as heat flowed through me. "It's going to be hard to do five miles with three pounds of fat, carbs and protein in my stomach."

"We could stop off for a nap at my place first."

"I have a feeling that this conversation is one most women have in college with steroid-jacked jocks." If he caught the "most women" comment he gave no indication. "Do men ever grow out of talking about anything but wild sex?"

His grin took on a lazy softness. "I was talking about a nap. You made it sex."

Yeah, I did. Something about him made me think about taboo things, and then brought my mind back to Mark with this odd little rush. I thought it, but didn't say it. Instead I said, "So what do you want that has nothing to do with wild sex?"

His eyes sparked as I spoke. Okay, that was almost as bad, and not quite what I meant to say. But the waitress brought coffee, biscuits and butter, and I was suddenly too hungry to care what had just come out of my mouth. I poured us coffee from the little blue plastic urn and satisfied my hunger. Well, the only one I was willing to admit to.

22

COLD SHOWERS OR A HARD RUN?

Eli ate like he moved, with an economical grace that was somehow predatory, but at least he didn't seem to expect me to say anything after I put my foot in my mouth and danced on my tongue. After breakfast, wordless, he tossed a ten and a five at the waitress and led the way to his vehicle. Still not speaking, he drove to the outskirts of the town and down a winding dirt road. We were only three or four miles from the bustle of early morning traffic in Ford City and yet the location was remote. I couldn't even hear traffic.

The building—a blue, nondescript, steel warehouse-type construction—was tucked into the edge of a small copse of trees, bordered by a cow pasture with brown-and-white cows and a small stream where huge boulders were clumped, as if dropped by the hand of a glacier on its way south. On the building's side were painted the letters SSS in dark burgundy. Three other cars were parked there, the building had no windows and Eli didn't fit the profile of the Triangle Killers, and only after reminding myself of that did I get out of the SUV.

"See, you're safe." He opened the building's door with

a key and a complicated routine of button pushing. "Not an apartment."

"Cute. Frankly, I'm not sure anyone is safe anywhere with you. You are a very dangerous man."

The lazy grin came back and this time my blush got its way. "My brother's inside. Safe enough?"

"Better," I acknowledged.

The building was divided up with two regular offices in the front, tiled and carpeted, white walls, white woodwork, a dropped ceiling and standard office furniture, though more standard to the average CEO than the average office manager. Modern cherry pieces, all matching. Yards of desks in each office, acres of shelves behind raised paneled doors, some hanging open, and a multitude of computer paraphernalia. The back of the building was accessed through a door between the offices.

Even more lanky sitting up than he had appeared lying on a stretcher, Levi Cordell wore jeans, a loose T-shirt and a bulky sling securing his injured arm close to his side. He was in the office to the right. Three color televisions were on, but muted in the corners of the room. Mozart played on the overhead quad speakers, and three computers sat on the desk, screens lit. Levi looked up as we entered, the fingers of his good hand dancing over one keyboard without his looking. Multitasking didn't describe his actions. Not at all. More like multitasking times ten. He kept working as he focused on us.

"Levi? Rhea. Rhea, Levi," Eli said. "I believe you know one another."

"My hero doctor," Levi said. "Saves shot computer specialists and tortured teenaged girls. You got her out."

Eli nodded. "We're going to work out, then run."

Levi grunted and turned back to the computers.

"Eli and Levi," I said as the names came together in my mind. "Jewish?"

"Christian fundamentalist."

"Didn't take with you, did it?" My mouth was on a rampage. I bit my tongue to deaden it.

He laughed and opened the door into the rest of the building. The rear three-quarters of the steel structure was far larger than it seemed from the outside.

Part of the area was a storage cavern, filled with boxes and tables and shelves, all full of computer and weapon hardware. The rest held an exercise room, kitchen, living room with leather sofas and two wide-screen TVs. There were two bedrooms and a bath at the back. Fans circled lazily overhead. A running track wound around the outer perimeter of the central open area. I nodded thoughtfully and couldn't keep a trace of sarcasm out of my voice when I mimicked him. "You know a track."

"It's home."

I followed him to the bedroom on the left, windows high on the outer wall letting in light, skylight at an angle throwing shadows on the near wall. The bedroom was done in shades of dark green and taupe, with a solid green comforter on the bed and an Oriental rug on the floor. The place was clean but the bed wasn't made, clothes were piled in a chair. He didn't seem to notice the clutter. I liked that in a man.

Eli tossed a pair of black sweats onto the bed and took a second pair in hand. "Change in bedroom or bath?" Not much for words, was Eli.

Maybe that was why I was suddenly running away with diarrhea of the tongue. I was used to being the silent party in most relationships. That made me pause. This was not a relationship.

"Bath, please." I took the black sweats from his hand and gave him his jacket. It was like sliding out of a warm embrace into the cold reality of the world, but I gave it back. I had to get me one.

A workout was what Eli had said to his brother, and a workout was what I got. He started off with stretching that replicated what I did every day before a run, but worked harder on the upper body. I knew I needed some upper body work, so I studied what he did and copied it. I had a feeling he didn't care if I joined him in everything or not, but it looked strenuous, remarkably intense, and I needed to move. Unfortunately, halfway through some utterly complicated stretch, my back went into spasm. I lost my breath and made an almost silent whistle in my nasopharynx. My knees buckled.

Eli's arms were around me instantly. His hands guided me upright into normal posture, slipped up under the sweatshirt and found the muscle that was screaming with pain as it wrapped around my chest wall and squeezed.

"Here, on the couch."

Unable to breathe without squeaking, I let him guide me to the couch and lower me facedown. Throwing one leg over my body, he pushed up my sweatshirt exposing my back, and went to work on the muscle, kneading it out of a charley horse into complaisance, moving up and down along the spine for long minutes until the muscle was almost smooth again. His hands and the scent of leather calmed me. The pain began to ease. I recalled how to breathe again. Finally his hands stilled. A light came on behind the couch. "What's this?"

How do you tell a man you'd gotten stabbed? When I didn't answer, Eli said, "This wasn't an accident. The edges of the wound are too crisp and clean. You were stabbed, cut deliberately." His voice was hard.

"Um-hmm," I mumbled finally. "Not that long ago," I said into the supple leather. "Sometimes it spasms."

"Did he get the kidney?"

"Not quite. Just some muscle and nerves and a nice juicy vein."

"What'd he use?"

"Scalpel. I made it bleed so help could find me. That's why the scar seems to go off in three or four different directions." I had no idea why I was telling him so much about me. Things just kept sliding out of my mouth of their own volition.

Eli's hands went back to work on my bare skin, warmth in his palms, gentle pressure in his fingers, fierce anger in his words. "The guy who did it?"

"Dead," I murmured, and sighed with pleasure.

"Good." His tone was implacable. If I hadn't been so comfortable, I'd have shivered. "Who got him?"

"Mark." And then he'd gone to bed with Skye.

The hands began to work lower, on the base of my spine. I should have said stop. I should have, but I didn't. Not when his hands moved leisurely up my sides. Not even when I was shivering from something besides the cool air from the fans blowing across my skin, and the heat of his palms. His hands gripped me, turned my entire body face-up and settled me back into the leather cushion.

He was straddling me. His eyes were dark, one hand on my ribs beneath my shirt, palm warm. Slowly, he lowered his face and kissed my lips. A brush of silk. Lips to my cheek, my eyelids. Back to my mouth.

The sensation was electric. I pulled away from him, shoved against his chest. Stunned, I opened my eyes wide.

Slowly, he eased back onto his elbows and stared at me. His lips dropped once more and touched mine. So gentle. Warm.

"I want you, Rhea." His voice was a soft rumble. His smile was full, not that half quirk that hid more than it revealed. "Guess you can tell that."

I nodded, unable to speak.

"But I won't take you. Not until you make up your mind

about the boyfriend." He kissed me again, once. "If we do this, we do it right. Just you and me. No baggage."

Something inside me protested, but I nodded again. "I didn't—" I stopped and licked my suddenly dry lips. "I didn't plan on this." I wanted to blame my reactions to him on Mark's betrayal, but I couldn't, not entirely.

"Neither did I. I had other things…" He stopped, as if he'd almost said more than he intended. "And right now, wanting you doesn't fit in with my plans."

I didn't know if I should be insulted or not. "What plans? What do you want from me?"

The half smile was back, his eyes shuttered. "Originally? Other than the fact that I'm attracted to you? I'm a selfish bastard. I wanted free medical help with Levi. Now I want in on the investigation about the triangle grave. I wanted you to use your womanly charms to get the boyfriend to ask me in."

"And now that you know there's this not-quite-boyfriend thing going on with Mark and me?"

"I still want an intro. That's all."

"Why should he ask you in? And why do you want in, anyway? You're not a cop. Not a reporter."

"I have lots of neat toys that might be useful in the investigation. Government surplus stuff. I hear Mark likes toys."

I noted that Eli didn't reply to both questions, but I didn't push it. His eyes roamed over my face when I said nothing. One corner of his mouth lifted in a wry smile. "I can't see you as a quick fling, Rhea. Which is what I want from most women." His eyes held mine, searching for something. I couldn't tell if he found what he was looking for. "When you make up your mind about the boyfriend, call me."

This wasn't me. Not me on this couch with a man I had only recently met. I was the sensible one, always had been. And this man was not a sensible choice. Not at all. Slowly

I dropped my arms. I wanted a one-woman man. Once I had wanted it to be Mark, but he had kinda screwed that one up. I blinked away the thoughts. They were too weird. "Cold showers or a hard run?" I asked.

He laughed. "Run." He levered himself off of me and swatted my hip. "Move. I'll catch up."

After the run, Eli suggested I work on upper body strength training. I needed that, and didn't bother with it at home. I was a runner, not a lifter, but I was in a complacent mood and did what he told me, three reps of this, three of that, increasing weights each time. If it had been Mark telling me what to do, I'd have been trying to outdo him or ignore him. Comparisons. Did other women really do this?

Following the workout, Eli changed back into street clothes, telling me he'd shower later, and to keep the sweats. "Only a woman could still be cold after a workout," he said. I looked down. Yep. Still cold. He tossed me his jacket and led the way to the SUV. It was an older Land Rover, the kind built before they were suburban status symbols, when they were workhorses. It was fully restored, a special edition, hence all the bells and whistles on the dash, most of which he had retrofitted. I had a feeling that the vehicle hid away other tricks I couldn't see. I thought I spotted the grip of a gun in a side pocket, before he closed his door.

As he drove, black shades hiding his eyes, Eli told me about himself. I was sure it was an edited version, especially the abbreviated account of twenty years in the armed forces. He simply said he was part of the army's Delta Force. When I pointed out a jagged scar on his forearm, he shrugged and stated "Shrapnel," as if that said it all. And maybe it did. But I was never one to leave well enough alone.

"Shrapnel from what?"

"Probably a brick-and-cement wall I got pinned down behind. Just a flesh wound."

"Delta Force guys are usually pretty skilled, lots of multispecialty stuff, right?"

He shrugged again, eyes on the road, zipping through traffic. He didn't answer.

"Languages, weapons, explosives, communications, all that stuff."

"Pretty much," he grunted.

"You always open up this much to the girls you want favors from?"

His eyes slit in my direction. "I'm thinking I want more than that from you."

"So?"

He sighed. "I'm fluent in two dialects of Spanish, plus Arabic and Farsi, and can muddle around in French, Basque and Italian. I can fire any weapon that can be fired, hit most anything I aim at, explode anything that needs to be exploded and some things that can't, and I have special training in security systems. Satisfied with the sharing?"

"You made an F on the communication lessons, huh?"

Eli grinned, shook his head and said nothing. Satisfied, I snuggled back into his jacket and fell promptly asleep.

"This the place?"

When he spoke again, I checked to see if I had drooled on his leather collar, wiped my mouth on the back of my wrist and sat up before I answered. I really needed a full night's sleep, say twelve hours of uninterrupted slumber. When I saw what was waiting for me in the yard, I figured I wouldn't be getting that anytime soon. I groaned and sighed. "Yes."

My house was brightly lit by midmorning sun; the back of my Z3 gleamed where it peeked around the corner. And a news van was parked out front. A woman in dress slacks and a wool jacket was pacing on my front lawn, a cell phone to her ear. "Anne Evans. She's with the Charlotte newspaper. She tried to interview me once before."

"And?"

"I wasn't interested. I'm still not interested." I remembered Shaniqua's broken body and Beata's soft mewling. I did *not* want to talk to the press.

Eli cruised on past my house and Anne didn't look up. I watched as she climbed the steps to the front door and pushed the bell several times. It looked as if she had been at the process awhile, long enough for her to get frustrated, long enough that my dogs were sitting on the porch watching her, tongues hanging out the sides of their mouths. I laughed.

"What?"

"Bell's broken."

I watched Anne bang on the wood door. "Now that might have gotten me out of bed, but it wouldn't have made me talk to her." I dug into my bag and found my cell phone, speed-dialed Mark's cell. He lived across the street, sort of catercornered from me, and that was part of the reason I had found myself sitting in my front window watching the street. One quick kiss on a leather couch with Eli and I had a feeling those days were over. Go figure.

"What?" Mark growled, genial as ever.

"You mind sending a car to my house to run off a reporter so I can get in without a game of twenty questions?" I asked. I could be genial, too.

"I'm at the house. I'll be there in two." He hung up. I glanced back and saw the dark green Jeep Cherokee in front of his house. I hadn't looked that way when we drove past. Yep, I wasn't grieving for Mark anymore. Now what? On to another man? Or back to Mark, this time with eyes wide open? Woman stuff. Dull. Boring.

Eli turned around up the street and parked in front of the

house with the yellow crime scene tape. The house where Wayne Edward had shot and killed his foster father. We had a pretty good view of my house and yard.

Mark pulled out of the drive in front of his house and into mine, hauled himself out of the Jeep and strode over to Anne. Her pageboy haircut, usually tousled into untidy waves as if by nervous raking, ruffled in the breeze. Two minutes later she got in her van and drove off. Mark pulled out his cell, and mine rang. "It's clear," he said, as Eli cranked up the massive Land Rover and coasted down the street to my house. He parked in front and killed the engine. We both got out, and I grabbed the cardboard box holding my bag, boots, scrubs and lab coat.

Mark watched us cross the lawn toward him, his eyes hidden behind dark, wraparound shades. He was dressed like a typical plainclothes cop, T-shirt under white button-down, jeans, police windbreaker, black lace-up boots. He stroked his mustache once. He had shaved his beard.

Now that he's proved innocent of the paternity suit, he shows the world his face again? A nasty little voice spoke in the back of my mind. My dogs ran across the lawn and jumped up on me, whining and woofing. I scrubbed their ears and backs and bellies as I walked, and accepted my daily chin laving.

Eli and I stopped in front of Mark. "Thanks," I said. The two men, both in shades, glanced at me and then looked one another over. Great. Two alpha males deciding how they wanted to play this game, and one of the prizes was me. Well, they could decide anything they wanted. I didn't feel like participating in their stupid male contests.

"Mark, meet Eli. Eli, meet Mark. You both like toys." And me, but I didn't say that. I snapped my fingers at the dogs, whistled in that breathy way I had and headed for the back of the house.

"You can keep the clothes and jacket. I'll get them next time," Eli called.

I paused, my back to them. "I'll leave your stuff at the hospital E.R. desk when I work next," I called over my shoulder. "You can make a special trip to pick them up. Men," I added under my breath. Without another word, I left them and entered my house, picking up my ringing phone as I entered.

"Girls day out?" the plaintive voice asked.

I sighed. It was Monday. And I had forgotten Marisa.

23

When I next looked out my window, the SUVs had disappeared. There wasn't even the tingle of male testosterone left hanging in the air. Having them both gone was a relief. I somehow felt that doctors weren't supposed to be attracted to strange men, as if we were better than that, and I was uncomfortable with my own reactions. Maybe wading around in dead bodies had caused chemical changes in my brain.

Smiling at my whimsy, I called Shirl, who planned to meet us in Pineville, then called Marisa and told her I'd pick her up in an hour. I put together a quick Christmas shopping list, omitting both Mark and Eli, who were either duking it out right now or bonding over guns, knives and toys that go bang in the night at Puckey's Guns and Things. Trying not to think about it too much, I added Miss DeeDee back to the list.

It was true that Miss DeeDee had access to the phone, the Internet and her credit cards, she was rich, and she could order and have shipped most anything she wanted. But six months worth of Marisa's comments about family and forgiveness were tiptoeing through my gray matter and I decided that while Mark was not yet deserving of forgiveness, I might make a token gesture in the direction of Miss DeeDee. After all, she was locked up in the padded loony bin where she couldn't hurt anyone else. And even though she was the devil's handmaiden, Marisa still loved her. The old bat didn't deserve it, but Marisa had forgiven her. Maybe I could think about her in a less malevolent way myself.

As I was gathering the last of the dirty clothes and sheets into a ball, I found Eli Cordell's business card, stiff in a scrub shirt pocket. Slowly I sat on the edge of the stripped bed and dialed the number at the bottom.

Levi answered. "Symtech Security."

"This is Rhea Lynch. Your brother just dropped me off, and I forgot to ask him if you took small cases."

"Some, Dr. Lynch. I have a feeling Eli would take anything you tossed his way."

The statement threw me. "I beg your pardon?"

I could hear the amusement in his voice and Bach in the background. "My brother's never brought a woman home before. Sure never introduced one to me before. And he's never ever taken off a day of work to run with a woman and drive her home, not unless there was money in it. And I didn't get the feeling you were a paying job."

"Uh, no." I picked at the mattress cover.

"So, yes, I think Eli would take any job you tossed his way."

I would think about that later. Much later. At about the same time as I thought about the kiss on his couch. "Would you run a security check on a man who is dating a friend of mine? A very special friend. The man's name is Todd Sinclair." I told Levi all I knew about Todd, gave him Miss DeeDee's credit card number, her contact numbers at the mental facility, e-mail address, and my own numbers. After the conversation ended, I reconsidered what I had just done. It was possible that if Marisa discovered I'd run a security check on Cowboy, she'd never speak to me again. Well, it would at least put a strain on our relationship. I had to confess first thing.

"First thing we'll do is pootle round the mall and do the Christmas shopping. Nothing too expensive, though," Shirl warned after we met her in Pineville. "I'm broke. Then we'll have a cuppa. But no porking-out—I'm watching my figure. Cam's no chubby-chaser and I tend to be a bit of a tubby if I'm not careful. Lastly, we'll go to the spa and have them pamper us to within an inch of our lives." Sitting atop the seat back in her convertible, she unbraided her long red hair and wound it atop her head in a messy bun. When she was done, she raised the car's top against possible rain and hopped to the ground at the Carolina Place Mall parking lot, locking the Porsche and setting the alarm.

Dr. Shirley Adkins was a short, very British woman who dated the most gorgeous man on the face of the earth. And kept him in line by acting as if she might dump him at any moment. If he knew how she agonized over every word, thought and deed, she'd lose her allure and he'd likely dump her. Sad but true. So much for a grand passion.

I propped myself against her red sports car, crossed my arms over my chest and said. "Before we go inside, I have a confession to make."

"Oh, ace!" Shirl squealed. "Are you getting laid by some divinely handsome man? The one who loaned you this leather jacket? I do love a nice leather jacket, especially one with bullet holes in the sleeve." She fingered a hole I hadn't noticed, her face avid with curiosity. *Bullet hole?*

"No." I shifted uncomfortably. I hadn't expected anyone to notice that I was wearing a man's bomber jacket. "I have to confess that Miss DeeDee is doing a background security check on Cowboy."

"What?" Marisa said, her mouth dropping open.

"And I helped her set it up."

"Well, of course you did." Shirl patted my arm. "It's a perfectly sensible decision. Far more sensible thinking than that barmy old boot would come up with normally. Stop making that face, Risa, I have it on good authority it'll freeze that way. Of course you run a security check on a man who dates Marisa. She's positively filthy."

"Filthy?" I asked. I hadn't expected an ally. I had expected Shirl would side with Marisa and scream at me. Which was why I confessed in the parking lot and not inside, where shoppers might be offended by the words Shirl would hurl my way. She had been raised rich, but garnered most of her slang off the streets of London. Shirl was often, um, indelicate, in a street-smart, borderline obscene, wisecracking kind of way.

"Rich. Filthy rich. Rich as Croesus. It's up to us to protect her, even if she doesn't see it that way. You did the right thing. And you must share all the details with Marisa so she never has to worry if her Cowboy loves her for her money or her sweet self. Close your mouth, Marisa. You look a right barmpot with it hanging open like that."

Marisa closed her mouth, her expression still incredulous. "But—"

"But nothing. Now, let's go spend lots of money. Yes, I know I said I was broke, but I have plastic." She waved her platinum card and sang off-key, "And girls just want to have fun!" Tucking the card in her bra, Shirl took us each by a hand and tugged us toward the door.

We spent the day just as Shirl had said. First there was shopping—where I found something for everyone on my list by simply handing it to the shopping queens and letting them take over. They spent a small fortune and even picked out gifts for each other, from me, and had them wrapped to maintain the surprise. Afterward we dined. Shirl chose a sushi joint and I ate way too much, especially after the big breakfast I had eaten. And then we drove to Ford City, where we were slathered and polished and wrapped and filed and painted and massaged at a salon on Main Street, and I fell asleep to the sound of new age music while a brutal woman with extremely strong hands kneaded my muscles into slag—Shirl's term, not mine.

We talked endlessly about the twins and how simply precious they were. Asked to watch as Marisa retired to a private place to pump her breasts for their supper. Got kicked out. We gossiped about Cowboy and teased Marisa about her healthy complexion. Discussed what kind of fast little sports car Shirl would buy next fall. Gossiped about Cam, and teased Shirl about *her* healthy complexion. And after several hours of that, they both stared hard at me and decided that someone had added a little color to my face, too. And the grilling started.

For the first time in my life, I confessed everything and half bragged, half complained about a man. Two men, actually. It was wonderfully liberating. It also felt pretty good to have two men to discuss when my friends had only one each. That had certainly never happened before. And if I implied a bit more to the kiss on Eli's leather couch, well, a little hyperbole seemed both expected and forgiven.

Of course, I then had to listen to their twittering about how I had been alone too long and how I needed a man. Needed sex. How I would dry up and blow away if I waited too long. "Use it or lose it, luv," was the way Shirl phrased it. Which made us all laugh like demented and drunken farmhands. "Or take them both," she suggested. "Together." Which made Marisa hoot with laughter. Silly stuff. The kind of things girls say to one another when no men are around.

As the hours passed, I carefully did not think about dead

bodies or mass graves or serial killers. Very carefully. Very deliberately. I though only about this moment, these friends and being alive.

In spite of the thoughts that tried to intrude and spoil my day, the jaunt got mixed up in my mind into one big gig-gle—again, Shirl's word—and for the first time in my life I found myself not minding Girls Day Out.

I told them all about Miss Essie's interrupted lecture on passion and they both squealed with delight, bringing the hairstylist at a run. Okay, we were a tad noisy. Miss Essie had said, "But he a man. Most got the strength of character of a he-goat when a woman wiggle herself at him. Ain't worth two cents." We all tried wiggling, up the aisle and out onto the Main Street sidewalk, to see if it sent every man who saw us into a mating frenzy. It didn't. Maybe we didn't wiggle the right way.

But we did have a wonderful time. And we tipped the poor spa people extremely well for their panic attacks and trouble, especially the makeup artist who gave us all make-overs.

"Poor little batty–boy–poofter, we'll tip him well and he'll remember us fondly," was Shirl's way of thinking. I didn't know exactly where the terms poofter and batty–boy came from, and didn't ask. It didn't take a genius to tell they were slightly insulting, but Shirl was on an East Lon-don slang rampage, words she'd picked up from a forbid-den friend when she was a teen. And we were having fun. Scads of fun.

And not once did I notice the old gray hatchback Honda that followed us from place to place. Not once.

It was nearly dark when Risa and I stopped at Stowe Farm, and Malachi and I unloaded the small car, separating the packages that were hers from mine. The Z3 was packed to the ragtop with trinkets and the trunk held bigger purchases, some rather the worse for wear, having been squished down by the trunk lid. Just as I closed the trunk, Miz Auberta ran from the house, waving her arms in the air. "Miss Rhea, Miss Marisa, come in right now! Right now. Hurry!"

Marisa jerked. "Twins?" she shouted.

"They're fine, right as rain. It's Miss Rhea's man. There's a gun battle!"

I dropped the package I was holding and abandoned Risa, racing for the back door. The scanner was screaming.

"Backup! Where's the backup?"

"Medic! Haskins. I'm hit."

"Chambers, can you get to him?" Mark shouted. Gunshots exploded in the background. Handguns. Shotguns.

"Ten-four."

"What do we got?" the sheriff asked, pomposity missing from his voice.

"Two shooters with—Jesus, you hear that?" A gun blast that sounded like a small cannon. Another. And something else in the background.

"What is it?"

"Chambers, look out!"

The sound resolved into a motor racing, a high-pitched squeal that was abruptly loud and then fading. The sound of a man screaming in the background. Dozens of gunshots.

"Cap'n, where's medic? Haskins took one in the thigh!" No answer. A long moment of silence passed. Too long. I gripped the kitchen counter. "Captain Stafford?" Another silence. "Anybody seen 214?"

"Negative." "Negative." Two cops answered.

"Ambulance is two minutes out. On my way. Just getting the first-aid kit from my car." Mark's voice, calm and controlled.

And something icy inside me shattered. Mark was alive. Not hurt. Shivers gripped me. I wavered on my feet, pulled

Eli's jacket around me. Accepted the drink Miz Auberta put in my hand. Drank it, scarcely noticing the fiery path it traced down my throat.

"We got somp'un in here, Cap'n. You better take a look."

Moments later I heard, "Dispatch, this is 214. Ten-sixty. I'll be sending a car to pick her up."

Marisa put her arm around me, led me to the table and sat me down. I drank again, this time tasting Miz A's spiced rum. Wordless, Risa stroked my face, massaged my neck as she might have petted a puppy, her blue eyes wide and tender. Waiting with me.

Over the scanner, we heard the ambulance pull up. Heard the tension lessen from the men's voices. Heard them co-ordinate with the state boys and a helicopter with night vision equipment that was letting them track two men on dirt bikes.

"Mark's okay," Marisa said.

"I know. This time."

She pursed her lips, looking like and yet unlike the prim Marisa I knew. She was luminous with some kind of shiny stuff on cheeks and brow bones, her natural peaches-and-cream skin brightened in some indefinable way with peach blush, and her bluer-than-blue eyes were almost startling with the lapis eyeliner and mascara. "You love him."

I looked away. Did I? This didn't feel like love. It felt like pain and fury mixed. Mark wanted to marry me. Did I want to marry a cop? Overall, this was a peaceful county. But when there was trouble of any kind, Mark would be there. Always. How many years would I spend nights like this before he was shot and killed on duty? I shivered, Eli's coat no help. "I don't know what I feel, Risa. And if I do love him, I don't know if I can trust him. And that's what this is all about. Trust."

She grinned evilly and stumbled over the phrase. "Run a…security check."

I smiled. "I already know he cheated once. But we weren't going together then, so that makes it not cheating. I think."

"So wiggle at him." She shimmied her shoulders.

I laughed. "Thanks, but I'll pass." I had no desire to look like a fool. Wiggling fell under the category of "some women have it and some don't." I didn't. We chatted quietly for an hour, put gifts beneath the tree, played with the twins, while all the time a refrain was playing in my mind. *Mark wasn't dead. Again.*

A knock came at the door. Moving from the playroom, I opened it and found myself staring into Eli's eyes. And my beeper went off.

Without looking, I thumbed off the beeper and stepped back to let him enter. He was dressed in ratty jeans that molded to his form like a second skin, western boots, a long-sleeved T-shirt and a leather jacket vaguely similar to the one I wore, but newer. I bet it didn't have a bullet hole in it. But there was something else new about Eli. He was wearing a shoulder holster he didn't bother to conceal, and a big gun was in it. I guessed a .40 caliber, or maybe a .44, something Dirty Harry might covet. Eli's eyes never left my face as he entered, but I saw him check out the room in his peripheral vision, counting the people in it, noting what they were doing.

Turning away from his gaze, I checked my beeper. Dispatch. I realized that the police code ten-sixty had been for me. They had a body at the scene where the gun battle had taken place. As Eli introduced himself to the women, looking into Marisa's eyes for a long moment, I dialed the dispatcher and was given the message.

"I have to go," I said.

Eli was beside me. "I'm your ride."

"Why?"

"Because I said so. Because your boyfriend said so. He called me. And because you were tailed all day by one of the Triangle Killers." The words fell into the room like a thunderclap, their energy a discharge of shock.

"Rhea?"

"It's okay, Marisa." I had to uncurl my fingers. They had made claws. "How do you know that?"

"When your name went out over the airwaves as the person who saved Beata Geter, the profiler suggested that the killers might take revenge. She's gone into victim protection and they couldn't get to her, but they could get to you."

"Revenge?" Marisa wrapped her arms around me from behind and I gripped her hand. "Rhea, don't go home tonight. Don't go anywhere. You stay here!"

Eli's eyes were piercing, boring into mine, his mouth hard. "Stafford wanted to keep you under wraps, but he was overruled by a special agent who said he knew you well enough to say you would want to act as lure. I agreed, but there was the problem of possible collateral damage."

"What did you have to do with it? And what collateral damage?"

"I was with Stafford when the profiler showed up. Marisa was the possible collateral damage."

I pulled Marisa around beneath my arm and looked her over. He was right. Though she was older, with her blond hair and vivid blue eyes, she fit the profile. And if someone had hurt Marisa, I'd have ripped him up with my bare hands.

I wrapped my arm tighter around her shoulders. "Someone put Marisa in danger without asking me. Who?"

Eli's lips twitched fractionally. "I figured you'd say that. Which is why I made sure you were followed all day. Special Agent Ramsey wanted me out of the way, but I'm kinda hard to unload."

Jim Ramsey was dog food. "And?"

"And I've been out of the loop, so I don't know how he got permission to use an uninformed civilian as bait, but he did. An old gray Honda picked you up at your house and followed you to Marisa's, then to Pineville, and back to Ford City. Then he left. I was watching as a plainclothes cop put a tracking device on his car. They were able to follow him back to one of his hideaways."

"He followed us shopping?" Marisa asked.

Eli smiled fully, turning on the charm to my friend. "No, ma'am. He waited at Rhea's car, watching it, while an agent watched him. I followed you shopping. I liked the outfit you got for your daughter." His eyes glanced at me. "The dance on Main Street was a little odd, though."

Marisa laughed nervously, her elegant little twitter, but she pulled away and moved to where she could view Eli better. "We wiggled. It didn't work."

"How so?"

"No men went wild."

Eli's grin spread wider and he turned his eyes to me. "One did. But he was working."

I blushed, and Marisa saw it. "You got red! You never b...blush."

"Eli has an ability to make me blush that makes no sense at all," I said before I thought. When would I stop speaking before I think?

Marisa's eyes opened wide and her mouth pursed. "Make sense to me." She walked around Eli. "He's hot! I like him."

Eli laughed and I shook my head. Marisa was still in Girls Day Out mode. "I'm not leaving until I get Marisa protected. They know where she lives. She fits the profile enough to make her attractive to them."

"I'll call Stafford. He can put a county car in the yard."

"Before I leave. And then I'm dropping by my house to feed my dogs and get my boots. Then you can take me to…wherever."

Eli pulled out his cell phone and made a quick call, his voice pitched low. After the call, he slipped the phone into a pocket. "Question. You would have been agreeable to being bait?"

"Yes. I'm no longer a civilian. As special assistant to the coroner, I'm part of law enforcement. Acceptable bait, as long as Marisa wasn't involved. Jim Ramsey had no right to risk her."

Eli smiled, his eyes intense. "Time to go."

"The cop?"

"There's a deputy four minutes out."

"Follow me to my house."

Eli sighed. "Fine. But I'm hungry. We eat on the way to the site. You ladies got sushi. I got a cold chicken salad sandwich."

"And I'm going to see the twins to bed first," I said, feeling stubborn, knowing my life was going to change rapidly in the next few days. Without waiting for his reply, I put a baby in Marisa's arms, grabbed the other one and pulled Marisa up the back stairs.

Minutes later, lights pulled up in the yard and a deputy knocked at the door. "Now," Eli said, sticking his head in the nursery. I said hello to Dickey Lambert on the way past, my upper arm in Eli's inflexible grip. He saw me to my car, his eyes darting about the darkness, and he followed me home in the huge Land Rover.

When we got to my house, I looked the small bungalow over to make sure everything was the same as when I'd left it. With killers on the loose, I was worried about unexpected and unwelcome visitors. A girl can't be too careful.

The dogs didn't take to Eli now that he was inside, greeting him with heads down, ears back, ruffs at full alert, sniffing his boots and crotch, standing between Eli and me for my protection. Unmoving, Eli stared down at the dogs until, surprisingly, they finally both sat, lay down and rolled over, exposing their bellies to him. Pup first, then Belle. Pup even whined in submission. Weird. I had never seen the dogs act quite that way. As if they didn't like him, but knew he was a bigger, meaner dog than they. And they didn't woof down their food when I poured it; rather, they sat and watched Eli, positioned between their bowls and the stranger.

My house—cleaner than it had been in months, since the last time Arlana had shoveled me out and scraped off the mold—smelled like vanilla from the candle jars she had left lit, and which I blew out as I passed by. Ignoring my invitation for him to wait in the kitchen or the living room, Eli slumped in the small upholstered chair in my bedroom and watched me as I dumped gaily wrapped packages on the bed and hunted around for my rubber boots. Stoney jumped to his lap and curled up into a ball, purring his V8-motor purr of total happiness. As if unaware of his hand, Eli stroked the cat the length of his body. No wonder the dogs didn't take to him. Eli was a cat man.

"You haven't taken off my jacket." His voice was a burr of sound, not unlike the cat.

I had noticed that, too. And unless he took the jacket off of me, I wasn't giving it back tonight, either. "I looked for one like it today. Couldn't find one." Stepping into the bathroom, I glanced at myself and did a double take. I looked fabulous. I never wore makeup, never shaped my brows and usually trimmed my hair with surgical scissors, but the makeover and haircut were a special at the day spa.

Marisa and Shirl both had one and insisted I did, too. Now my eyes were huge, outlined in kohl that smudged into the lids, my brows plucked and shaped, which had hurt like heck but was clearly worth it. The lipstick was a dark wine. All dressed up, and a corpse to go to.

"The coat is Italian. It was purchased in a market in Basra. The market got bombed the next day. You won't find one like it. It's not replaceable." I could hear the amusement in his voice.

Slipping off the topic of conversation and dropping it on the bed out of his reach, I pulled a flannel shirt over my tee, buttoned it halfway and tucked it into my jeans. Eli's eyes followed my hands as they slid into my jeans and out. I bent and took the bomber jacket, pulling it on.

I didn't hear him move, but Eli was beside me, his hands on my waist under the jacket, rotating me. His mouth found mine. He backed me to the wall, lifted me to my toes and held me there. His lips pulled away from my mouth, touched my neck, my ear. His breath was hot, fast. "I've never been a patient man. So don't keep me waiting too long. I might take matters into my own hands."

My head rolled back hard against the wall, so I could see him. "And then?" I asked, not recognizing my own voice, deep and husky.

"And then Mark Stafford will be a thing of the past and the decision will be taken out of your hands." One hand moved up and cupped a breast through my clothes, resting. Not moving.

Carefully, I lifted his hand away, back to my waist. "I may have said this before, but you have an ego, Eli Cordell."

"Not the only thing I've got."

His cell phone rang. Eli cursed and lowered me to the floor. I stepped away. Thank God for cell phones.

"She had to feed her dogs. Get warmer clothes, her legal

papers. Yeah. We're on the way." He hung up. "Stafford. You ready?"

I ran a hand through my newly shaped hair and felt each strand fall into place. I still had a corpse to go visit. I zipped up the jacket as if to belatedly protect myself from a mauling. I wasn't a sixteen-year-old girl, all hormones and no idea of who I was. I took a breath, the sound shaky. Maybe if I had experienced this at sixteen, I could handle it now.

I picked up the coroner folder and turned back. Eli stepped close and kissed me again, his lips softer than silk velvet. "Don't make me wait too long, Rhea." For the first time, it was more a request than a command.

I nodded. "I'm…I'm working on it."

Silently, he led the way from my house.

24

HUNG UP BY MY THUMBS AND ELECTROSHOCK THERAPY

We didn't speak as Eli drove through Mickie Ds, ordered for us both and then motored deep into the middle of godforsaken-nowhere, eating quarter-pounders and fries and vanilla shakes, each concerned with our separate thoughts. My mind was a two-way track, half memories about the graveyard, half consideration about Eli's mouth against mine. The graveyard was harder to put aside, which may say something about my less-than-romantic nature. To change the direction of my thoughts, I asked, "How do you know this area so well?"

His eyes flicked at me in the darkness, that half smile in place. "I feel the same way."

"Beg your pardon?"

"Edgy. Like I'd rather toss you to the back seat and make love to you than go off into the woods to look at dead people." When my mouth dropped open, he added, "'Course I'd rather be hung up by my thumbs and given electroshock therapy, too, so maybe that's not a huge compliment."

I laughed, appreciating his attempt to divert my thoughts.

"To answer your question, Levi programmed the GPS with coordinates for the entire area when we opened the business. He can track the car if needed. And I take good directions.''

"You take directions? Men don't take directions, it's a genetic thing. Directions must be one of those Delta Force tricks they taught you in army school, along with your communication skills and that ten-feet-tall swagger.'' Oh goody, I had my sharp tongue back. My best defense.

"Yeah. Army school,'' Eli laughed. "We're nearly there. You ready for this?''

"No. I'm not. But I'm here. Let's get it over with.''

Eli turned down an unlit, unmarked two-rut road. Three turns later, lights brightened the bare tree branches. Cop cars appeared. An ambulance. Men and women striding hard through an overgrown field, a small house in the center. I studied it as I pulled on my boots and my paper PPE coat.

It was brick, with a window on either side of the door, the front stoop no more than a small cement slab up two steps. No electric lines ran to the house. It was all darkness, wrapped in wavering shadows, the outside poorly lit by more of the huge klieg lights I remembered from the graveyard. A well-house made of curled, grayed plywood was nearby, its door hanging open on one hinge. A small gray hatchback was parked in the yard and crime scene techs were all over it. The Land Rover had been idling awhile, and Eli sat silently, letting me absorb the scene, letting me take my time. Maybe he could see the way my hands were trembling in the shadows of the dash. I started to open the door.

"Rhea?'' When I looked at him, slumped in the corner of the Land Rover, expression amused, Eli said, "Your lipstick's smeared and you have mustard on your chin.'' Taking one of the crumpled McDonalds' napkins, he wiped my mouth and held it up. Wine-tinted lipstick and mustard, all right. I studied it.

I was quivering as if a fine electric current ran through my skin. I really, really, *really* didn't want to go inside.

Eli pulled my bag from the floorboards and fished around, handing me the lipstick. "Put this on."

On the surface, it seemed a bit macabre to put on lipstick for a corpse viewing, but I took the tube and reapplied wine color. I was trying to avoid going into the house. Anything to avoid going into the house. Even lipstick. Heck, I'd have gone back to the batty–boy–poofter for another makeover to keep from going into the shadowed house. I twirled the stick back down and tossed it into my bag, took a deep breath, opened the truck door and headed into the clearing.

I noticed several double takes as I entered the house, and one, "Whoa, Doc. All doodied up. You got a hot date?" Someone else whistled. If the stench hadn't been so unbearable, I might have bantered back. But there was something dead in the little house. And I had to go look at it.

The house, bright with the heavy-duty lighting, was furnished in what Arlana would have referred to as Early American Garbage with a dash of Southern Filth tossed in. Some of the garbage looked as if it had been there for decades, and there were rebel flags painted on the walls, which were liberally smeared with excrement.

Two stackable plastic chairs and a similar round table were in the center of the front room, heaped with pizza boxes and fast-food bags, beer cans littering the floor beneath. A police scanner with a battery hookup sat on an overturned crate in a corner. A couch with no legs and ripped upholstery rested against one wall. Clothes were piled on it. Mostly women's. Shoes had been dumped in the corner. I stared. The quiver was back in my hands, moving swiftly into my spine and down my legs.

There were sandals, a brown boot and a green suede one. All sizes. Pumps, loafers, heels, one red stiletto with a five-inch spike. The pile of abandoned shoes said more clearly than anything else that women and girls had died here. I blinked back tears.

I wasn't made for this. I was made to put people back together again, not chase down bad guys and stand over evidence of death and destruction, weeping. I took a deep breath of the foul air. This was the last time I was acting as coroner's assistant. I simply couldn't take it. Didn't want to take it. Inside, part of me was howling, holding myself and rocking in pain, like Betty had howled back at the house where Wayne Edward Geter had shot and killed his foster father and wounded Anita. When I took a breath, it was ragged and coarse, and burned along my throat.

"She's in here, Doc."

I looked up from the pile of shoes, into Jim Ramsey's face. It was expressionless, shut down. Nothing there. Cop face. He was dressed in a white jumpsuit that covered his FBI suit, and paper booties that covered his dress shoes.

"You used me."

"Yes."

"Fine. I'm open game, thanks to being made special whatever to the coroner. But if you ever put Marisa into danger again, I'll find a way to hurt you. You understand?"

A slight smile creased his face. Conversationally, he asked, "You threatening an officer of the law?"

"Oh, yeah."

"Fine. I was out of line." Jim reached into his jumpsuit and inside his jacket pocket, pulled out a folded handkerchief. "Dab off your tears. It's messing up your makeup."

I dabbed. I hadn't known I was crying. A little plumy-looking color, a smear of black, marred his hanky.

"Keep it. I got hundreds."

I took a deep breath and handed the hanky back, anyway. "Dead body?"

"In here." He accepted the handkerchief, folded it and put into his pocket.

I followed him past other rooms, less well lit, flickering with shadows. A small kitchen had a brazier set up in the sink, and pans and pots were piled among the garbage. This room stank with a different kind of smell, chemical and harsh, a scent that tickled at the back of my throat. We passed a foul-smelling bathroom with no fixtures, only a hole in the floor that appeared to have been used as a toilet. We ended up in the back room.

She was on a table, spread-eagled. Tied at wrists and ankles to the table legs. The signature triangle was cut and burned into her abdomen. Crime scene people were everywhere. Cameras were snapping and flashing. Someone held a video camera. No one was talking. The profiler was standing to one side, just staring at the girl. His was the only expression not frozen in cop face. Not shut down. Not empty. He watched the girl with pity, curiosity, and some strange form of tenderness I couldn't name. His head tilted as he walked around her. Pulling a gloved hand from his jumpsuit pocket, he gently touched the girl's ankle.

I breathed in through my mouth. If he could do it, if he could look at this girl with compassion instead of horror and fear, then I could, too.

"What do you want me to do?" I asked Jim, my voice steady, almost calm.

"Pronounce her. We used GPS to track them to this location, but until we get the final word from the surveyors, we can't know for sure which of three counties we're in. We're asking coroners from Dawkins and two other counties to pronounce her and fill out paperwork. Then we'll use the one we need. The other two were closer in. They've gone."

"She's dead. I'll do the paperwork in the car." I looked up at Jim, turned my back on the girl on the table and walked out of the room. It seemed like yet another betrayal, and I sent a silent apology to her spirit, wherever she was.

"Thank you, Rhea." Jim had followed me.

I didn't look at him. For just a moment, his words held a touch of gentleness, and I couldn't stand to look at his face and not see the expression mirrored there. With my back still turned, I paused. "How's the chase going? Did you catch them yet?"

"No. We lost them." I looked up then. His face was like his voice when he said the words. Frozen. Dead and deadly.

"Mark's with the searchers, isn't he?"

"Yeah. He is. The task force is pretty much a tricounty pursuit now. He's heading the local team."

I nodded, stripped off my PPEs and left the little house. No one spoke to me as I exited. No one said anything until I was back in Eli's Land Rover. Without speaking, I spread out the paperwork and started filling in the blank spaces. Eli clicked on a reading light, a tiny spotlight that shined directly onto my lap. Lifted the papers and slid a clipboard beneath them. Said nothing. Just turned on the vehicle and its heater and let it blast me. When I was done, I climbed from the cab and found Jim Ramsey in the front room, digging through a pile of garbage with a crime scene tech at his elbow. I handed him the paperwork.

"Jim?"

"Yeah." He sounded distracted. Until I told him what I wanted. Then his gaze narrowed in on me, hard. "You're sure about this?"

"You want me to believe that you hadn't considered it before?"

"Stafford threatened to beat me to a pulp if I used you again."

"Mark isn't here, he's out chasing bad guys. Mark got me made assistant coroner. I want to bring the bad guys in, where you can get them, and I think I know how to do it." I stared hard, holding him with my eyes. "You going to help me?"

* * *

Standing beside the open passenger door, I pulled off the rubber boots, tossed them into the back and climbed in, slamming the door. The cab was still warm, but I was cold all through and shoved my sock-covered toes against the heating vent. Eli put the big vehicle in reverse and backed between two unmarked Crown Victorias and around, the headlights picking out the trail through the trees. We wound along the little rutted roads and suddenly the blacktop highway was before me. Nausea climbed up the back of my throat and I broke out in a sick sweat.

Letting down the window, I let cold fresh air blow in, taking away some of the smell that clung to me. Eli picked up speed, the tires loud on the asphalt. When I rolled up the window I was thoroughly frozen, but I felt better. "Mark used your toys for tracking the killers when they followed me, didn't he?"

"The task force used some of my equipment, yes," Eli said, his tone guarded.

"And you got to be part of the investigation because of that. Because I introduced you." I almost added, *I know you have ulterior motives. I just don't know what.* But I was getting smarter. I kept it to myself.

Eli's mouth quirked up slightly in the dim light. "Okay. I owe you. What do you want?"

"I want to hire you."

"Levi told me. He's working on it now."

"No. I want to hire *you*. Personally. To protect me."

"From what?"

"From the bad guys. Jim Ramsey is going to plant a little something in a certain reporter's ear, and when Anne Evans comes by, I'm giving an interview." I stared through the windshield at the dark earth, winter-deep fields, and gullies heavy with trees, at the occasional farmhouse, lights at the windows. "I'm telling the world about the cowards who are hurting these girls. I'm telling the world that I almost got them myself when they tailed my car. I'm going to imply that they are impotent and silly and jail bait. I'm hoping to make them come to me." The silence after my words was punctuated only by the sound of the Land Rover in the night.

"You're issuing a challenge. And you want me around to stop them when they come after you." He sounded amused. "Me, not Mark?"

Mark Stafford would have been screaming in rage about now. Comparisons again. But then, in his own way, Mark loved me and wanted to protect me. Eli might have wanted to have hot sweaty sex with me, but for some reason even that took a back seat, so to speak, to this investigation.

I took a painful breath, surely the first since I'd stood in front of the table where the girl had died. I itched to turn on music. Talk radio. Anything. I didn't. "Not exactly. When they come after me, I want you to kill them."

It was not until we were sitting at my kitchen table, Belle's body on my sock-clad feet, that we talked again. The dogs weren't protecting me from Eli anymore, but they sensed something was wrong and wanted to keep me safe from whatever it was.

Eli had picked up a six-pack of Michelob Amber Bock, a hunk of imported white cheese, crackers and a bottle of wine. I drank the chardonnay while he guzzled two beers in quick succession. Neither seemed to phase him. I was tipsy after about three swallows, but then, I'm a cheap drunk. One glass is all it takes to make me giggly, sleepy or morose, unlike my mother, who could down a fifth of Jack Daniels Black Label and still pass for sober.

Eli hadn't responded when I asked him to kill the bad guys. He had remained silent all the way home, miles of desolate countryside, and silence between us. When he spoke, his voice was soft, musing. "Maybe you didn't understand me. I'm in the security business. That's not the same thing as a killer for hire."

"That's what you said." I watched my hand turning my glass around and around on the old, scarred table. The wooden table had been in Miss DeeDee's attic, donated to make my rental house more cozy when I first moved in, before I signed the papers that made the house mine. And I kept the table after Miss DeeDee went to la-la land. That said something about me. The top needed refinishing. Almost as badly as the table the girl had died on. Had all of them died there? One-handed, I pulled the leather jacket closer. I still hadn't taken it off.

Choosing my words carefully, I said, "But you wanted in on this investigation from the first moment you heard about it. And I'm guessing there's some reason why. Something you haven't bothered to discuss in full." When Eli kept his eyes on his beer, his mouth closed tight, I continued. "You don't have to tell me. But let's just say that I feel you have ulterior motives. And I do, too.

"The police have to follow certain legal protocols if the bad guys come after me. They have to say and do certain things, like yelling 'Police,' and using handcuffs. As a private citizen, I could fire as soon as they enter my house."

Eli finally met my eyes. "But you don't want to shoot anyone. You want to hire it done."

"That makes me sound like a coward, doesn't it." The body on the table slashed into my memory like a flash-fire, searing hot. My fists clenched, nails digging into my flesh. "I want them hurt. Hurt bad." Tears prickled at the corners of my eyes. "I want this over. And I want the guys who tortured that dead girl." I took a breath that ached as it whispered along my throat. Her image was clear and detailed. "I want it as messy as it can get, I admit it, but barring taking up red-hot pokers, pinchers and knives, and going after them myself, dead is acceptable. Yes, I am a coward.''

''I don't know about cowardice, but perhaps you show a certain lack of conviction.'' His tone was dry, and when I looked into his eyes they were faintly amused, but not contemptuous. ''Okay. I may not pop them for fun, but I'll agree to protect you from the killers if they come after you.''

I nodded, and a tear slid down my cheek and fell. Landed on his jacket, near the zipper.

''What's Stafford going to say about this?''

I noted it was Stafford now, not *the boyfriend.* ''You like him, don't you?''

Eli laughed almost silently, once, but said nothing. Popped the top on a third beer.

''He threatened to beat Jim Ramsey to a pulp if I was used as bait again.''

''Good for him. Yeah, I like him.'' He drank, his throat moving in the dim light. ''You'd be safer with him. Doing it his way. Not sticking your neck out.''

I knew what he was saying. That I'd be safer with Mark in every way, not just today. And it was true. I smiled, my lips sad. ''Yeah. And I might lose him if I do this. If I put myself in danger to get these guys. We have this problem about police work and medicine and who's in charge of...stuff.'' Eli smiled at my lack of articulation. ''And I guess I'm walking into his domain and putting myself in danger and he isn't in control of the situation anymore.'' I nodded and sipped the wine. It soothed my tortured throat. ''I'd be safer doing nothing. But safety isn't all it's cracked up to be. It has its downsides, too.''

''Yes, it does.''

I stared into his eyes, watching the shadows move slowly through them. The silence between us was easy, companionable, without the heavy overtone of lust. "Have you ever been married?"

The silence that followed my question was too long, and when Eli answered, his voice held a strange tone I couldn't place. "Once. She died in Basra in the Gulf War."

I looked down at the leather bomber jacket, thinking. Wiped away the tear. It glistened on my knuckle before I smeared it on my jeans. "In the marketplace explosion?"

"No." When he said nothing else I just waited, watching his eyes as he watched me. "The bombing took out half of my reconnaissance team. There were just me and two others left, and one was injured. I had to get him out." The muscles in his jaw bunched and relaxed, bunched and relaxed. "I had to leave her. She had her family. She was supposed to be safe until I could get back in for her."

"She wasn't safe, was she?"

"No. Her brother had figured out who we were. He didn't like Shara being married to an infidel, especially an American. He turned her over to some...very nasty people. Three days later she died. Her brother sent me a picture of her body, hanging from a pole." No inflection in his voice, no sorrow, no grief. Nothing. He spoke as if it was ancient history.

Bad guys were everywhere, and women had no defense against them. And then I realized what he had meant when he said she'd died three days later. He meant they had kept her alive for three days. I was sure the captors weren't congenial hosts. Rather, they were likely similar to the bad guys I was hoping to bring to me. And I finally thought I understood what Eli had been hiding—his true motives for wanting in on this investigation.

The bad guys who killed his wife must have gotten away. He didn't get them. But he could get these guys. Right a few wrongs that needed righting. "Did you get the guys who did it?'' The silence stretched and I wasn't sure he was going to answer.

"At the time, my superiors thought it an unacceptable risk. I was sent elsewhere. Told to put it behind me.'' Eli drank a long pull from the bottle and held it up, looked at the liquid level against the light. Took another pull of beer before setting it down. "I retired before the Iraq Liberation War,'' he said, his tone indicating he might not agree with the designation. "But they called me up. I went back in with the first wave that hit Basra. Two of the sonsabitches were still running around torturing innocent women and children.'' His face was as giving as petrified wood. "Let's just say they didn't get a chance to surrender.'' Eli didn't look at me, and I closed my eyes a moment against his pain. "War's hell, ain't it?''

When I found my breath I said, "And you got home in one piece? Back to being a private citizen.''

"A piece of shrapnel took a hunk out of my arm. Took me out before the troops even reached Baghdad.'' He lifted his left arm. "After three surgeries it works fine, but looks like sh—looks bad.''

"How much to protect me?''

He named a price that was four times my monthly house payment. Without a word I went to my doctor bag and pulled out a checkbook, wrote him a check. "How long am I purchasing you for?''

"For as long as it takes.''

It seemed like a lot of money but I didn't think it was, not to him, not for what I was asking. I also had the feeling he might have done it for free, just for the chance to get close to the killers. "This is a cut-rate price, isn't it?''

"Call it a retainer.''

I handed him the check and he folded it once, tucked it into his back pocket without looking at it. I thought about Mark dumping me for what I was about to do. I thought about Miss Essie's passion statement. I thought about being alone for the rest of my life. "You said you wanted me without baggage. Is Shara baggage for you?"

"Shara died years ago. I'll always carry her with me. But she's buried."

"This is what you wanted from me all along, isn't it?"

His eyes took on a lazy gleam. He drank the last of the beer.

"You claimed it was medical help and attraction, but it wasn't." My brain screamed at the words. I ignored it. Sometimes my mouth knew just what to say.

"Oh, it was attraction, all right." His eyes traced a line from my eyes to my mouth, lingered a moment and moved down, across my jaw to my neck. "From the first time I laid eyes on you, when my mind was better occupied with Levi and business. It's still sex I want. But it became more." My pulse jumped as his eyes drifted lower before lifting and meeting mine. "Sex can take a number until the job is done."

Stoney jumped up on the table, tail moving in wide arcs as he paced to the chips, chose one and tossed it to the floor. With one lithe move he sprang from the table and pounced on the chip, crunching it under his paws. Settling down, he licked at the salt, his tongue silent, and ate the chip pieces, the sound like small bones cracking.

"That comment about you being a coward?"

I nodded and drank more of the wine to calm the pounding of my blood.

"I think you're one of the bravest people I've met in a long time. You haven't run from this and you could have. That enough information to chew on awhile?"

"Yes. Thank you."

"Go shower. I'll wait here, make sure you're safe. Then you get some sleep, and I'll be back in the morning. We'll go from there."

I nodded, too tired to speak, and moved to the bedroom, shedding the jacket as I went, draping it over the kitchen bar. I figured he'd take it with him when he left.

Sleep, he'd said. Yeah, right, with the nightmares I had for the first three hours when I tossed on the mattress. Nightmares about dead bodies and tortured victims. I woke a half-dozen times in the early hours, bathed in a cold sweat, trembling, my muscles cramped from sleep-fighting or sleep-running, paralyzed and desperate. I knew I could never live with the dreams. I'd be on massive doses of Prozac and Toradol if they didn't end soon.

Exhaustion finally knocked me under and kept me there. I slept like the dead. Well, maybe not quite, as I did wake when my alarm went off at nine, after less than the twelve uninterrupted hours I needed. I crawled out of bed, walked my full bladder awkwardly to the bathroom and minutes later pulled on Eli's sweats, which were handily piled in the corner. I called the dogs to me and left the house, stretching as I walked along the creek. The world was silent. Peaceful. When I started running, there was only the sound of my feet pounding and the dogs' breath matched with mine.

It took almost three miles before I blew away the cobwebs and reaffirmed what I wanted to do. I was going to make myself a target. And I was scared to death. Scared out of my wits. What wits I had left. By the time I was done with the five miles, I was laughing at my own subconscious jokes, jiving to the endorphins rushing through my system. I loved this! I could get down with it, to quote Arlana. I could do this. I'd help get the bastards who'd hurt those girls. In spite of Mark and with Eli to help me.

Mark was sitting on my back stoop when I walked up to my house after my cool-down stretching. His shades were tucked in his collar, his legs outstretched. He looked tired and worn and angry. I figured the tired and worn part was because of the bad guys. The angry part was because of me. The dogs were all over him, and after he gave them each one of the treats he always kept in his pocket, he pushed them out of his face so he could watch me.

Rather than speak with him, I took down the clothes that had been airing for the last few days and sniffed them. The smell of the graveyard was gone, even out of the down-filled coat. Rolling them under one arm, I walked to the stoop and stopped two feet away.

He studied me, taking in the clothes I wore. He had seen me in Eli's baggy black sweats. "Are you sleeping with him?"

It was so unexpected that I laughed, a sharp bark of sound. Belle and Pup barked with me, suddenly excited, and they bounded through the yard to chase each other in their complicated tag game. Mark's eyes narrowed. "No," I said. "I'm not sleeping with him. I'm still trying to decide what to do about you."

"And?"

"And you slept with a woman because you got ticked off with me. Until then I thought you were Galahad riding in on a white horse. After that, I started noticing that you were really more of a pain in the butt than a knight in shining armor."

Mark's lips twitched. "I do love a woman who speaks her mind."

"Even when I disagree with you? Because lately it seems that you get riled when I disagree. And I tend to disagree with you quite often."

He nodded, the motion slow and thoughtful. "I've been talking to Miss Essie. She tells me that happens in a relationship," he said. "First you have this overwhelming attraction where you see how similar you are." His eyes gleamed, clear in the sunshine peeking into the backyard through the bare trees. "Then all these little things that point out the differences start to crop up. Then, if you survive that part, there's a meeting of the minds. A true appreciation."

"And what about passion?"

"What about it?"

"When does passion come into the equation? That fire in the belly that makes you become someone you aren't, do things you wouldn't. Didn't she talk to you about that?"

His face closed off fractionally. "You telling me you don't feel passion for me?"

"I'm telling you I don't know what I feel for you. Every time we start to get close, something gets in the way. And this time she was a frosted blonde with perky boobs. And I don't know if I can trust you, Mark. And I'm hurt."

"I'm—"

"I'm sorry isn't enough. Not for this." I found that I was kneading the pile of dirty graveyard clothes. I stopped the frantic motion of my fingers.

"What is?" The tic was back beside his mouth. His hands clenched as if he might want to throttle me.

"I have no idea."

"I love you, Rhea. You're stubborn and hardheaded and opinionated and ornery. You're also good and kind and strong and the best person I've ever known. And now, according to Ramsey, you're getting ready to put yourself in danger and all I can think to do is lock you up somewhere safe until we get these guys. But I can't do that, can I? Not and have a chance with you."

"No. You can't. Your suggestion made me assistant coroner. It was your big idea. Now you're getting paid back for it. In spades. Frankly, you deserve it. But you can feed me. I'm starving."

He sighed and stood. "Go change. I'll take you to the bus station. Then I'll drive you to see Jim Ramsey. And my guess is, after that, Anne Evans will want to talk to you. And by tomorrow morning you'll be in danger again.''

''I've hired Eli to take care of me.''

''You what?'' He reared up and came half off the stoop before he stopped, and Belle raced forward, ready to play.

''You heard me. You can put me where you want to, set up all the outside stuff you need to, guns and people to watch the grounds.''

''Perimeter.''

''Whatever. But Eli will be with me inside. Because he won't have to think or act like a cop.''

The tic worsened. ''You doing this to punish me?''

No. But I didn't say that. ''Is it working?''

''Do you feel *passion* for him?''

I wasn't about to answer that one. ''You see, there's this problem with Eli. He doesn't want the same things I do. He wants sex and sex only. But only after he kills some people. And I'm more in the market for a one-woman man. Which you aren't either, it seems. Now, get out of my way, let me into my house and take me to eat. I'm starving.''

''Damn it, Rhea.'' But he moved off the little porch.

I took his place and unlocked the door. ''And if you have to cuss, you can go back to your cop buddies and do it there. I don't like it and I'm not listening to it.''

''This is insane.'' He raked a hand through his hair. It occurred to me that I had finally gotten him back for making me coroner. Point for me. If I was still keeping score.

I went inside and locked him out. Showered, combed my hair and put on fresh makeup, just the way the batty–boy–poofter had shown me, extra heavy on the eyes, less on the cheeks and lips. In clean starched jeans with a crease down the front, a starched white shirt with a clean bra underneath, a navy blazer and my country-girl western boots, I was ready to face the world. And I looked pretty darn good. So good I added little gold hoop earrings and pinned my gold lion pin to my blazer. But when I saw the leather bomber jacket on the counter and realized that Eli had left it for me, after all, I took it instead, the little lion pinned on the knit collar inside the leather one, peeking his nose out as if to scent the territory. Lastly, I shot a spray of my favorite perfume into the air and walked through it. I was ready for anything.

And then I called Marisa and Arlana and asked their help with my plan.

I went back outside and faced Mark Stafford. He had pulled his Jeep Cherokee around and was leaning across the hood, idly tossing a stick to Pup, who was bringing it back to him. I caught the stick and whipped it out of the air. "Maybe we needed to see if there was passion between us," I said baldly.

He stood slowly, dropping his hands, his eyes blistering me. "You're making me crazy. But damn, you look good."

"Thank you. Don't cuss. Feed me. And listen to what I have planned."

"Yes, ma'am." He smiled slightly. "Consider me your servant. You can call me Galahad."

25

GIVE MY STOMACH ROOM TO BREATHE

I didn't call him Galahad, but I did let him pay for breakfast, and I ate enough to choke a horse—biscuits, homemade preserves, honey, an omelette that draped off both sides of the plate, six slices of bacon and a pot of coffee all to myself. A full week's worth of cholesterol. If it took a few days to get the bad guys to come to me, then I wanted my last meal before I was forced to cook for myself to be satisfying. I had to unbutton my jeans beneath Eli's coat to make room for my bulging tummy but I wore a contented smile. Life seemed better with a full meal—calories, the drug of choice for most Americans.

Haden Fairweather joined us as I was taking my last bite. While Mark looked on with thunderclouds on his face, I shared my questions and thoughts with the bald, so-unheroic-looking little man. Got some really good ideas in return. We developed a rapport over coffee that excluded Mark and left him pretty well PO'd. I didn't care. Over the last cup of coffee, I called Eli and told him what the agenda was. He thought it all sounded like fun, and offered to bring a friend with some firepower. Which made Mark madder still, so I turned him down.

We drove uptown to the law enforcement center and I

walked into the inner sanctum of the LEC to meet with the task force gathered in an overcrowded room that smelled of burned coffee, male sweat, old cigar smoke and disapproval. When we arrived, Jim was telling the task force about his plan. There was general disagreement.

Some cops were saying I was a *civilian,* in a tone that said I was stupid and ineffectual. Some made *little woman* comments that truly made me mad. But I stood silent at the back of the room, hoping the men and women would get all the macho stuff off their chests. When they started repeating themselves, I stood up. My chair scudded back against the wall with a clatter, drawing all eyes to me as I made my way to the front.

"Let me tell you how I feel about this situation, ya'll." I pulled a folding chair to me, put a foot in it and leaned an elbow on a knee, very Mae West. Okay, it was to give my stomach room to breathe, but they didn't have to know that. "The killers already found me. The media made sure of that when they broadcast my name after Beata Geter was rescued. Then you helped it along when you let one of them follow me.

"Thanks to a certain law enforcement official, I'm a part of the legal community, which I guess makes me fair game, but you used me without asking me what I thought about it. Now I'm taking back my life. This time it's my choice, my decision, because whether you help or not, I'm doing this. But when someone's willing to be a reckless target, why not use her again?"

I looked around the room, meeting eyes, some bored, some speculative, some half-asleep. "Jim, has anyone spoken to Anne Evans?"

"Yeah. Someone spoke to her. Gave her the tip of her career. Are you going to be modest about your coup, when you chased down the bad guys and nearly caught them?" Jim was enjoying the sudden frowns in the room.

"I'm being modest. Make her think I made a mistake so she'll go to you guys for more information." I looked around the room. "With the help of Dr. Fairweather, Jim Ramsey and Mark Stafford, I'm giving an interview that should be calculated to bring the bad guys after me again, thinking I'm unprotected, stupid and ready for the taking. I'm also going to hint that I have a blond female and an African-American female with me on the premises."

I noticed that the cops were sitting up straight in their chairs, listening hard. I was going with bravado at the moment and it seemed to be working. "I'm not trying to do your jobs for you. Local law enforcement, with the help of the FBI, will run the operation. All I'm doing is making a target of myself. From the moment I speak with Anne Evans, I'll be at Stowe Farm, hoping you guys get a chance for some fun-and-games." Eli's words, but they seemed amused by it. All except Mark. He glowered. I grinned and gave a half salute to the law enforcement types as I left the room. General pandemonium followed me down the hall. They had an operation to plan, now that the lady civilian was done talking and out of the way.

Eli was waiting for me outside, the engine of his Land Rover rumbling. "Make a stop at the hospital?" I asked. "I need supplies"

Eli shifted into drive. "No problem."

The hospital was quiet when Eli and I let ourselves in through the back door at Intensive Care with my ID card. Eli flicked an index finger at the lock that secured the door. "Dark Ages technology. What do you guys do, rub sticks together to make fire? A ten-year-old could get through that lock."

"Hospitals are public buildings. It's pretty hard to keep the public out when family and visitors have the right to see patients 24–7."

"What about visiting hours?"

"You've got to be kidding. Try keeping people out of a hospital. They come and go at all hours."

"Are you trying to tell me that patients and family use this door?"

"No, not really. My point was more along the lines of why worry about this door, when anyone can come in through the front?"

Eli shook his head, disgusted. "If that lock is any indication of the hospital's after-hours security, your system is in dire need of an upgrade."

"Talk to administration about it. I'm just a contract doctor. A peon."

"Thought doctors had a God complex."

"Most do. I lost my M. Deity delusion in med school. I may tell you the story sometime."

"Dr. Rhea!" a voice interrupted.

I looked up at the excited voice to see Gloris.

"I'm so glad you came in." The plump nurse eyed Eli, checking him over, first in a professional manner, then in a more personal one as she assessed his presence with me. "I looked at the schedule today and you weren't listed. We got Charlie Denbrow back."

"You did? That's great. He must be on the mend."

"So they *said*." Her tone claimed otherwise as she studied Eli. "But he's got these sores and they won't even *guess* what they are down at Richland Memorial. *You* need to take a look."

I might never be able to shake Gloris's hero-worship. She seemed to think I should be involved in any case that looked unusual. "I'm not his doctor, Gloris," I said, as the nurse walked around to get a full 360-degree view of Eli, and I worked to prevent an amused grin. "That would be inappropriate."

"Statler said for you to take a look. Charlie's in room three. Who's this?"

"Eli Cordell," he said, smiling at Gloris, a smile that made me think of all things decadent. "I didn't have the pleasure when my brother was a patient here." He took her hand and held it between both of his.

Gloris almost staggered beneath the weight of his charm. "Oh my," she said, sticking a pinkie into her beehive, scratching delicately and shoving at the bleached mass to make sure it was still in place. "Oh my, yes. And I'm a married woman. I'm a married woman. I'm a married woman," she repeated, her tone not quite convinced, making me laugh. Eli had that effect on all women, it seemed, not just me. "And that makes you what, Mr. Eli Cordell? Are you married, too?" I sighed and went to room three, leaving Gloris—my self-appointed keeper—to grill Eli.

Charlie didn't look on the mend, he looked like death warmed over. His skin was flushed and pale in patches and his respiration was far too fast and shallow. There were vesicles all over his face, clustered around his mouth, nose and eyes, trailing down his neck, up under his ears and tracking down beneath his armpits. The worst site was his chin, where I had first seen the scratch. It was blistered over and seeping a thick, clear, slightly bloody liquid. The serous fluid from broken vesicles had stained the absorbent pads beneath him.

I pulled on gloves and lifted the sheet, checked his body. Vesicles clustered at his groin and the backs of his knees. And he was twitching slightly all over, as if his skin was crawling with ants, or as if his muscles were being shocked with low levels of electricity. He was groaning with pain.

The vesicles looked like some wildly out of control version of herpes. There was a saying in medicine: "When you hear hoofbeats in the night, don't go looking for zebras." But what if you were tracking hoofprints in the dirt and someone shouted, "Look! A herd of zebras!" Was I supposed to ignore the zebras?

"Gloris?" I called.

A moment later she stepped into the room. "He is so fine! Is he yours? That would show that cop Stafford a thing or two," she said, as if Eli were a toy I had purchased. I had to grin. Eli and I would be hot news in the county by nightfall, whether we really were or not.

"No. Not mine. A friend. He's interested in offering a security upgrade to administration." Not bad as extemporaneous white lies went. "You want to call up and see if Rolanda Higgenbotham is in?"

"I can do that. Is he really single?" She looked back over her shoulder, her blue-lined eyes speculative.

I laughed softly and shook my head at the inevitable. "He was married. He's a widower. And he's looking. Find him someone, if you know anyone who might be interested." I could have added *in a relationship that's mostly sexual,* but I didn't.

Gloris's eyes opened wide with incredulity. "Who *wouldn't* be interested? Question is, why aren't you laying a claim to him before he gets away? I thought things were over between you and Mark Stafford."

I had thought so, too. Mostly, I still did. "And get the reference lab's phone number. I want to call them on MODIS."

"Yeah, okay, Dr. Rhea. You sure?"

I knew the question was about Eli, not my request. I swallowed a sigh.

"I mean, this backwater county has a lot to offer, but men who look like that—all lean and mean, like they could digest steel for breakfast, keep the freezer stocked with wild game, swing through the trees on a vine and still have the energy to keep a nymphomaniac happy—ain't in great supply." Gloris had turned to catch another glimpse of Eli.

"You're married, Gloris. What would Elmer say?"

"I'm married to the man, not buried with him." She adjusted her uniform top, which today was covered with little locomotives, each with a little cloud hovering above the smokestack with cute sayings puffing out, like, "I think I can, I think I can," and "Nurses work up a head of steam," and "Nurses run on rails." She twitched the privacy curtain back to get a better view of Eli's backside.

"To use your term, Eli's fresh meat, Gloris. Set him up."

"Life is good," she said happily. "Trisha Singletary may need a new man about now! I'll buzz you in MODIS with the number. Mr. Cordell," she called, "you come with me now, while Dr. Rhea works. I'll get you in to Rolanda in a jiffy."

"You're abandoning me?" Eli asked me, as if that sixth sense produced on battlefields was setting off warnings in his head. Gloris in full takeover mode was reminiscent of a tank moving at full speed over desert terrain. Add a Southern woman's matchmaking skills to the mix and alarms might go off anywhere.

"Only for a few minutes. I'll find you in administration or back here shortly." When he didn't look the least relieved, I added with a malicious smile, "Don't worry. Gloris will take *real* good care of you. Your entire life will benefit by a few minutes spent with her."

"Oh, God, what have you done?" he said.

I waggled my fingers at him and headed toward the MODIS room as Gloris took his arm in predatory fingers and tugged him down the hall.

MODIS was an acronym for Medical Online Diagnostic Interface System, an intranet computer network of hospitals and labs, both private and public, education based and government based. It also had Internet access for research purposes. Locking myself into the dim room, I booted up the system, went to www.ask.com, and typed in a search for herpes. I found what I was looking for quickly.

Dr. Daniel S. Shapiro, director of clinical microbiology and molecular diagnostics laboratories at the Boston Medical Center, had a site devoted to zoonosis, infections transmitted from animals to humans. And rhesus macaques had their own version of monkey herpes.

I remembered the scratch on Charlie Denbrow's face beneath his beard, and the scratch on Ralph McMurphy's neck, both the initial sites of vesiclelike lesions. Scratches not made by a dog. But how about a monkey? How would they have gotten close to a macaque monkey, though? According to Shapiro's site, there were laws that prevented rhesus macaque monkeys from being used as pets, and they weren't often privately owned due to the danger from the herpes virus they carried. The monkeys were most commonly found in medical research facilities. I looked up testing for the monkey herpes and discovered that many times the virus gave false positives for human herpes simplex I and II, but not always.

Gloris rang me with the phone number to the reference lab in Charlotte, but I didn't think I needed it now. Charlie Denbrow's problem might be much worse than anything a local lab could prove or rule out.

Following links through the Internet system, I found photos of vesicles that matched exactly the ones on Charlie Denbrow, but nowhere did I see a human case study as severely infected as the cop. But then, I was looking for zebras, wasn't I?

I sat back, the information I was looking for bright on the screen as I put the few pieces I had into a puzzle pattern. Returning to MODIS, I gathered more information and minimized several screens to preserve the information I needed to make my point.

I picked up a pencil and tapped on the desk, the rubber

eraser making little patty-pat sounds. Mark was my best resource in local law enforcement, but he was notorious for withholding information from me, part of the long-standing competition between us. And with the way things were now, he might not listen to me at all. I would have to phrase this just right. A blitz of questions and information might get me the answer I needed fast. Finally I dropped the pencil and reached for the phone, dialed Mark's number at the LEC. After two misdirects and corrections he picked up.

"Captain Mark Stafford."

"Were Charlie Denbrow and Ralph McMurphy working undercover on a case involving illegal importation of exotic animals, specifically rhesus macaques?"

The silence on the other end was so telling I could have hung up without an answer.

After the uncomfortable pause, Mark asked, "Why would you ask that?" His tone was guarded and I could almost hear him thinking.

"Because Charlie and Ralph have something that looks like herpes, but Charlie tested negative for herpes simplex I and II. And rhesus macaques carry a version of herpes that can infect humans. It isn't diagnosed by standard testing."

"Is it dangerous?"

He hadn't said there were no macaques involved. *Bingo*. Now for the information barrage. "According to the Web site I'm looking at now, cercopithecine herpes virus, or B virus for short, is relatively harmless to the rhesus monkeys, but presents a different picture in human infection, where it can invade the central nervous system. And when that happens, patients often develop major complications and consequences to infection."

"English?" His voice was tight. Which meant that I was right, but that Mark couldn't tell me so, probably due to an ongoing undercover operation.

"Yes, it's dangerous. In humans, it's frequently fatal. It can be transmitted human-to-human by simple touch, which puts every health care worker in two hospitals at risk." When Mark said nothing, I added, "The only treatment is the prompt administration of acyclovir. That's the same drug used to treat human herpes infections."

"Can you test for it?"

"I can probably collect the samples, but I can't do the actual testing here. According to my info, the only lab in the U.S. with the expertise to perform B virus testing or to culture for the virus is at Georgia State University. I can reach them on MODIS but I have to have good reason to."

Mark said something that would cause his mother to pass out with horror. "I'll send McMurphy to the E.R. for testing. And a couple of other guys over the next few hours. Can you get Denbrow tested?"

"I can. And I can start the procedures for the nurses and techs and EMTs and family members, too."

"I need time. You can't—"

"There is no time, Mark. Not if it involves rhesus monkeys. It's *fatal*."

"I need two hours before you start calling in everyone in the county. Can you give me that long?" His tone said he expected me to argue or just say a flat no.

"This has to go to public health, infection control and DHEC at the state health level," I said. "Which means it will take longer than that to set things up here and in Georgia. There will be lots of red tape."

"Do it. And Rhea? Thanks." He hung up.

"You're welcome," I said to the dial tone.

I printed all the information on B virus I needed and made copies for Statler, Charlie's medical doctor, the E.R., the infection control nurse, and an extra copy for faxing to all the agencies that needed contacting. Then I made several phone calls. The first was to the Dawkins County Epi Call number. *Epi* was short for epidemiology. The Epi Call person carried a beeper at all times, as well as a special bag called the Epi Book Bag, with every conceivable contact number, every comprehensive procedure and protocol for any infectious disease scenario ever imagined or experienced. The hospital administration types and South Carolina State Department of Health and Environmental Control were next. I really made their day.

Then I called Georgia State University, where I tracked down the lab responsible for testing B virus, and put in an urgent request for the method of culture collection for cercopithecine herpes virus. I ordered a CT scan on Charlie Denbrow so his doctors could determine how much of his nervous system was compromised. Things didn't look good for Charlie.

And I called the pharmacy and let them know about the urgent need for acyclovir for several patients. Lastly, I called the surgeon and the physicians who would be responsible for treating the disease. If my hunch was right, they would start treatment immediately, even before positive test results were in.

If Charlie had B virus, it was late in the course of the disease for him to be helped by the acyclovir, but there was still hope. Even more hope for Ralph McMurphy and any others who'd had contact with the macaques. Health care workers who hadn't practiced proper contact precautions were in for a shock.

The only drawback to discovering a treatment for the men was Gloris. The last time I discovered something that proved helpful to a dying patient, she tried to give me an antique Indian motorcycle. I'd never be able to quell her adoration now. Finally, I closed up the MODIS system and found Eli, happy that the firestorm hitting the fan was not my responsibility.

26

KINDA QUIRKY AND GOTCHA

Eli braked and studied my house in the bright light. "I've decided it looks like you."

"Old and kinda weird?" I asked as he steered the SUV around back and checked out the grounds with restless eyes.

He laughed, his face doing that thing it did when he really smiled, looking younger, more vulnerable. "No. Kinda quirky." He glanced at me beneath his shades, teasing. "Cute. Like it's waiting for something to happen."

"I am not cute," I said, unbuckling my seat belt. He cut the engine.

His eyes were warm on me, too warm for my comfort or simple bodyguard interest. I felt my pulse speed up and looked away, which Eli found amusing.

When his cell phone rang faintly, I was relieved. Voice controlled and calm, he spoke a moment, ending with, "She is? Thanks."

He clicked off the phone, opened his door and stepped out. Bending into the cab, he said, "Anne Evans just turned off I-77. She'll be at the LEC in fifteen and we need to check your messages. Come on." He took my keys and opened my door, entered my house. The man was entirely too take-charge, but I couldn't gripe—I had paid for the services. The dogs followed, tails wagging happily. Looked like they had accepted Eli.

Inside, Eli moved through the house, checking it out, doing some security–guy thing. I freshened up in the bathroom, checked the batty–boy–poofter's makeup plan, and combed my hair. It still fell in perfect folds, far better than when I trimmed it with surgical scissors. I hoped to be interviewed today. I needed to look spiffy. After all my efforts to avoid the media, here I was throwing myself at them.

Sitting on the edge of the unmade bed, I removed Eli's bomber jacket and played my messages back. Found one from Anne Evans and took a deep breath. *Gotcha.*

Calling back the reporter, I caught her just about the time she should have reached the Law Enforcement Center for the day's briefing. "This is Rhea Lynch. You wanted to speak to me?" I asked.

"I hear from a source that you nearly caught the Triangle Killers."

I said nothing for a long moment, trying to remember what Haden Fairweather had said about lying, then I blew out a breath of air. Rule number one—be yourself. Rule number two—stick to the truth where possible. "You really are a bloodsucking media hound, aren't you?" Yep, that was following rule number one to the max.

Anne laughed. Not long ago, the reporter and I had had a conversation about media frenzies over anything that raised ratings. "I want to interview you. Will you talk to me?"

Eli came to the door, leaned a shoulder into the woodwork, watching.

"I don't want to be part of the media frenzy. And Mark Stafford tells me you came to my house. He had to run you off."

"I'll meet you anywhere you want."

I sighed again.

"Is it true you nearly caught the Triangle Killers?" she persisted.

"No. I didn't. But one of them… Look, Anne, are we off the record here?"

"If we need to be. But I'd rather interview you than have you just as a source."

"I don't know," I said, not asking for an off-the-record talk. "I don't want to make the evening news. I value my privacy. But at the same time, I've seen what those guys have done to the girls, and I want them stopped. So when I spotted one of them I did something stupid, hoping to catch him. I may have made law enforcement's job a lot harder than it should have been." I let a hint of indecision creep into my voice. Anne waited.

"Okay. Look, I'm on my way to stay a few days with my godchildren. You can meet me at the Stowe farm. You know where it is?"

"No. But I can find out."

"Two o'clock?"

"How about noon?" she said.

"Yeah, okay. But two things."

"What?"

"I get to see the finished article—"

"No can do."

I talked through her interruption. "—to make sure you protect my privacy and quote me right. And no photographers. Or no deal."

A slight hesitation followed. "I can't let you see the article. It's paper policy. But I'll read back your quotes for verification, and I'll read back your location as it will appear in the article. Only that."

"Done. I'm not asking for anything unfair. The article is yours. But I won't be misquoted and I won't have you tell the world where I live, though you can tell them about the farm. That's okay. That's the deal, take it or leave it.''

"Noon. I'll be there. No photographers. Thanks.'' The connection was severed. I dialed Arlana and then Marisa to tell them the schedule.

When I finished, I looked at Eli in the doorway. Our eyes met and held. One shoulder was against the jamb, his thumbs in his jeans, fingers dangling over the buttons. His eyes were hooded in the dim light. "Are you going with me to the farm for the interview?" I asked.

"Yes."

"And then?"

"I'll see Marisa and the twins deposited safely in a hotel with the nanny," Eli said, "and the old lady and her teenagers, too. Then I'll be back at the farm with you."

"And hope they come to us."

Though he didn't move, I could feel the instant heat from him. "Working," he agreed. "All business."

I was suddenly aware of the unmade bed, the sheets rumpled beneath me, the dim light from the closed shades. I stood up fast.

His lips quirked. "Talk to me about Stafford. I get the impression that things are a bit more platonic than he might want."

"Platonic," I laughed. "Yeah, platonic describes it well enough. I didn't see him for four months. Things have been…platonic." I wasn't in the mood to try and explain why Mark and I had never slept together. I wasn't sure I understood why myself anymore.

Eli said nothing.

I moved away from the bed as if it could blaze into flame. Maybe it would.

Eli uncurled from the doorway and crossed to me. Palms on my shoulders, he pushed me back to the wall, hands braced on either side of my head. I could smell mint on his breath. A strange smile touched his lips, as if he was putting two and two together. "The boyfriend went somewhere else."

My heart clenched. "Yeah."

His lips touched mine once and pulled back enough to focus on me. "He's a fool," he murmured. "But much as I want you, I'm not interested in being revenge sex."

My brows went up. I hadn't known there was such a thing. It sounded icky.

But Eli wasn't through and he seemed uncertain about something as he scanned my face. "If we do this, we do it, just you and me. No baggage." It almost sounded like a question. But he seemed to make up his mind. Stepping away and whirling me like a dance partner, he turned me to my closet. "Speaking of baggage, pack." He swatted me on the backside. "Time to move."

Less than a half hour later, I tossed a bag of clothes and essentials into my car along with my medical bag, and climbed in after them. I mentally ticked off the things I had arranged. Mark would pick up the dogs and keep them at his house across the street until this was over. Hotels had been lined up for my friends' protection. Cops would be bunking down at my place in case the bad guys misunderstood my location, and also at Miss Essie's. Inside, Arlana was changing sheets and moving boxes around in the unused bedroom, making space where a mattress could be put on the floor, and fussing about how it was nearly Christmas and I didn't have a tree or any trimmings and how I was a heathen.

Across the creek, Miss Essie was changing sheets and grumbling about how that nanny woman was going to be in the same hotel with her, while cops were to be in *her* house touching *her* things. Miss Essie was also talking to God about how I was taking over and rearranging their lives to suit some demented plan to stop bad guys. But the bad guys were the ones who took Shaniqua and Elorie and Natasha, so she didn't grumble loudly or long. They had all agreed to move. They would all be safe. Mark was putting a guard at each house. And I would have Eli.

I started my car, watching Eli step from the stoop and walk to his Land Rover. Arlana hung her head out the kitchen door, watching him move.

Head cocking to the side, she checked out Eli, with special attention to his butt, and made a face that said, "Oh my. *Nice.*" A half grin in place, she gave me a thumbs-up in approval. And then her brows lowered and she glanced back inside, no doubt thinking of the unmade bed. A speculative gleam entered her greenish eyes. I rolled my own eyes at her, gunned the motor and reversed down the drive.

As I pulled away, the wheel sliding through my hands, she stepped out the back door and pointed to me, mouthing, "We got to talk." I nodded. Yeah. If the bad guys came to me as I hoped, I would need to talk to somebody. Soon.

For now, I was ready for most anything. Even Anne Evans.

27

SWEET BOOGER AND GUNS

Miz Auberta showed Anne Evans into the room beneath the back stairs where I waited, Marisa at the desk behind me, trying to look as if she was doing bills. Auntie Maude sat on the couch with Arlana and me. Eli was out of sight, prowling, checking out the house, making plans. We all stood when Anne entered, smiling the uncomfortable smiles of women in the presence of the press.

After introductions, Auntie Maude lifted the babies from the floor where they were crawling in different directions, replete with milk from a recent feeding, happy, heavy-eyed and ready for nappy changing. "I shall take these little ankle-biters upstairs," she said from the doorway. "Miss Marisa, I'll be in my room should you need me, dear. Miss Rhea, Miss Arlana. A pleasure to make your acquaintance, Miss Evans."

"Auntie Maude," and "Miz Maude," we murmured back respectively.

"Well, let's get started," Anne said brightly, looking around at us. "Are you all staying here?"

Sticking to the truth as much as possible, I said, "Yes. We're friends. Marisa since grade school. Arlana for the last year."

"We'll all be here for the next three days. It's safer for women to stick together till they catch the Triangle Killers," Arlana said, sounding as if she had rehearsed the line. "My little place is too dangerous. Well, Marisa, you said something about wanting to get lunch started?"

"Yes. We'll be in the kitchen, if you need us. Would you like tea?"

"Iced, not hot, if you have it," I said.

"That would be wonderful," Anne said. "The same for me, thank you."

"I decided to stay at the farm until the killers are caught," I added, driving the point home, "because Marisa fits the profile of what the killers are looking for. And so does Arlana. So we're all staying here for the next few days because it's safe. I spent maybe a dozen summers at the farm while growing up, and it's the safest place I know." I was babbling, so I shut up and looked expectantly at Anne. She opened a spiral notebook and smiled pleasantly, as if she knew I was hoping to get the farm's location mentioned in the article and was pretending not to. A female James Bond, I wasn't. And then the bloodsucking began.

It went on for two hours. By the time it was over, my stomach was growling unhappily, I was exhausted, and I was trying to stop my mouth from making sarcastic comments that wouldn't have helped my cause at all. I couldn't have been any more blatant about hoping Anne would mention the farm in the article. I took her on a tour of the grounds, the barn, telling her little snippets of my past, things Risa and I had done as kids.

Twice as we walked I saw a shape move in the distance as Eli kept a watch on the surrounding scenery and the two of us. Not that Anne Evans was a threat, but Eli had gone into commando mode at some point, turning half-paranoid and a little hyped. Paranoid and hyped was good.

Finally her little notebook snapped closed, and Anne left. I trudged back to the house, scuffing my boots in the gravel as her car wended its way down the drive. Eli met me halfway. "That seemed to go well," he said neutrally, correctly reading my expression.

I groaned and stopped, looked back at the horizon, fields and wooded hills rising behind the barn. "She wants to do a feature on me later. I think she wanted to call it 'Beautiful Doctor Takes on the Rural South." I sounded disgusted.

"And?"

"It's the batty–boy–poofter's fault," I said. All because of the makeup. Because I sure as heck wasn't beautiful. Too tall, too skinny, too dark—my mother's words the few times she'd sobered up enough to try to make me into a proper Southern belle.

"Say what?" Eli was laughing.

"Never mind. For now, she'll call me and read my quotes. It'll make the front page sidebar, whatever that means, titled Local Doctor Battles Triangle Killers."

"That means you'll have your fifteen seconds of fame."

"Well, whoop-de-dang-doo."

Eli laughed outright. "You're hungry again. I can hear your stomach growl from here."

"A gentleman would have pretended not to notice," I said wryly, remembering his "nipply" comment. "I thought all officers were gentlemen."

"Being blind and deaf isn't being a gentleman." He lounged against the deck railing, his holster exposed where his jacket was pushed back. The weapon's stock was black and its barrel looked about two feet long. A mega handgun, not meant for a fast draw, but for stopping power.

"Yeah. I'm hungry," I said. "Let's eat before Miz Auberta leaves and we have to eat my cooking. I'll likely poison us both." Eli seemed to think I was joking. I just led the way back to the kitchen and the pot of stew Miz Auberta had burbling on the stove.

By four, Marisa, the twins and Auntie Maude were ready to be transported by Eli to the hotel. Miss Essie was already ensconced on a different floor and had called Arlana with orders to make a trip to the Bi-Lo for a chicken, vegetables, butter, milk, biscuit makings and salt. Miss Essie was acting as if this was a type of punishment. I was hoping this time of unpleasant living conditions would drive her and Auntie Maude into making friends. Well, a girl can hope.

And suddenly I was alone, the empty Stowe farmhouse silent around me. I had forgotten to bring my CD collection. Marisa had a nice selection of children's tunes, but listening to *Cinderella* or *Beauty and the Beast* didn't appeal. Feeling itchy, I pulled on an old pair of jeans and grabbed the bomber jacket, an intrinsic part of my wardrobe these days, and headed to the barn.

Once there, I found a padded saddle, the kind that is mostly saddle blanket, and asked Malachi to pick out a quiet, placid mare for me. He put the soft saddle away. Instead he chose Jesup, the horse that had been healed by the chiropractor, and a youth's cutting saddle. He boosted me up. The saddle fit tight around my backside, which was a good thing, but this bay horse was bigger than I remembered them being, back when I spent summers on the farm with Marisa. I stared at the ground, about two feet too far below me.

"You'll be fine, Rhea. Jesup is the calmest thing I got now that his back is fixed."

"How about your dog? You asked the chiropractor to look at him."

"Sweet Booger is prancing around like he's lost ten years," he said as he worked around me, adjusting the bridle and saddle.

Sweet Booger? Yuck. The high cantle molded to my backside and the horn support to my thighs in front, effectively holding me in place. I scooted around a bit, finding the stirrup length perfect. Malachi had always had a good eye.

"You don't got the little .32 pistol, in case of roving packs of dogs, do you?" There was censure in his voice. "They took down a foal last spring."

"Guilty. You know how I feel about guns, Malachi."

He disappeared into the dark recesses of the barn and returned with a small holster, handed it up to me. "It goes around your waist. Six shot. Should be enough to scare off most dogs. But you'll have to hold Jesup real strong. He ain't been gun-tested recently."

I strapped on the holster, the small weapon reversed on my left hip, gun butt to the front for easy drawing. "The path to the stream still there?" I asked. When Malachi affirmed that it was, I said, "I'll be up along the road, then back to the stream."

He held up an orange vest to me, one with reflective strips across the front and back. "Put it on when you hit the woods. It's hunting season. Land is posted against hunters, but no sense taking chances. Jesup neck reins, and he's five gaited. Likes the rack best if you've a mind to some steady speed." He held up a straw cowboy hat, too. "Sun's out. You'll get burned."

"Thanks, Malachi. I appreciate it." I put the hat on my head, adjusted the tilt so I could see easily under the brim.

With a slight tap of my heels, Jesup and I moved out into the meager heat of the December sun, my legs warmed by the barrel of his chest, the ancient, half-familiar smells of horse and fallow fields strong in my nostrils, the scents of my youth. At a slow walk, we took the old path beside the drive to the front of the property. The pea-gravel of the lane was impossible for shod horses, as small rocks getting stuck in their shoes would make them lame. The path was overgrown, barely visible as a depression where grass grew thinner.

The sun quickly became a warm blanket through the leather coat, and I found the customary slump acquired by trail riders in the saddle, shoulders dropped, back slightly bowed. The straw cowboy hat was perfect for keeping the sun off my face, offering a bit of shadow. After ten minutes, I shrugged out of the bomber jacket and tied it to the saddle with a strip of leather that was knotted there for that purpose. I couldn't remember the name of the strip. Lariat? No, that was a rope. Tether sounded too pedestrian.

Jesup was everything Malachi had said—gentle, easy to guide with just a touch of the reins to his neck. Placid, with a comfortable gait.

I slipped the orange vest over my shoulders and turned Jesup to the right, along the white fence beside the road. As we entered the woods, the cool returned, but I kept the vest on and the jacket tied with the lanyards—tickled that I remembered the right term. Clicking to Jesup, I added a little tap of my heels. He moved into a jarring trot, which would ruin my chiropractic adjustment, but with a little encouragement, he slid into the rack, a slow, four-beat gait I could tolerate all day long.

"Good boy," I murmured. "This is nice." His ears flicked back, his neck bowed and tail lifted, as if this was fun for him, too. It was like being in a rocking chair. Lulling and relaxing.

The sun dappled the ground, shining through the denuded branches onto the leaf- and pine-needle-strewn earth. The air was fresh, scented with conifers and late fall heat. Relaxing totally, I let the path and the horse decide where I was going. We passed an abandoned campsite littered with beer cans, discarded paper and trash, some of which looked like porn. I didn't look too closely. The remains of a deer carcass hung from a low branch, the meat too fresh to smell of rot, the entrails left to draw flies in a gully nearby. The gutted carcass reminded me of the girl tied to the table. I blinked away the image.

Sloppy hunters had been camping as recently as last night. The campfire still had a strong smell, and the garbage hadn't been disturbed by scavengers. There were two packages tied high in the branches of an oak. Signs of tent pegs. I'd have to tell Malachi he'd had squatters. He'd get the place cleaned up, and would run off the interlopers if they were still on the property.

For a moment, I considered the possibility that the campers had been the Triangle Killers, but that would be a big-mama of a coincidence. So I moved on, down the open slope toward the creek. Paused while Jesup relieved himself in an aromatic moment. Swiped away an old spiderweb that crossed the path. And then let the big horse find his way to the creek with delicate steps between the boulders.

Jesup drank his fill while I watched a hawk soar, listened to bird calls and wished Marisa were with me riding as we had as kids. She had always filled the quiet of the outdoors with chatter or with her own silence, the kind that took up space. Even with her injury, she could still do that, take up space with the presence of her spirit.

The stream was a meandering trickle because of the drought, little more than a muddy depression between the rocks and boulders that marked its course. It moved in the sluggish cool as if it, too, felt the winter that was still trying to descend on us. Winter in South Carolina was a six-week affair, mostly in January and February, the weeks broken up by spells of pleasant weather. Despite the cold snap the night the triangle graveyard was discovered, the season hadn't really arrived.

Jesup pricked his ears and turned unexpectedly, lurching back to the bank. I heard hoofbeats and saw a horse moving fast through the distant trees. I was surprised to see a second one on its heels. The squatters? I hadn't seen any signs of horses—no scattered lumps of manure, hoofprints, overgrazed foliage.

Clicking softly to Jesup, I turned him along the creek and upstream to a place where larger boulders would allow us to be hidden but still have a view. My heart sped up, and I took a firm grip on the reins with one hand and drew the little .32 just in case, hoping Jesup would be quiet. I had no desire to be accosted by drunken hunters in a place they considered their private preserve.

28

A MIND OF HER OWN AND HORSE, FOR *HOWDY*

Mark and Eli, mounted on horses, moved into view, their voices sounding down the slope to the creek on the cool air. My breath blew out quietly. Feeling stupid, I reholstered the gun.

"Too lucky to be Deacon and his pal," Eli said.

"More like hunters. The land is posted but that never stops some people."

"What size game do you take here?"

"I took down a two-hundred-fifty-five-pound buck last year. We used to get bigger kills, but the drought for the last five years has hurt them. I've been seeing some hundred-twenty pounders, and does a lot smaller, like that illegal one they shot for last night's supper and left hanging." The men were on the mares from Stowe Farm, their jeans-clad legs tight on the animals' sides. The mares had been ridden a lot harder than Jesup, and were sweat-dark around the saddles. Mark pivoted his dun-colored mount in a tight circle, his eyes behind his shades on the ground. Eli came into view behind him, wearing a long-sleeved T-shirt without a jacket, exposing his holstered gun.

The men looked relaxed with one another, bonding again over guns and hunting. I wasn't sure how I felt about their growing friendship. It made me kind of itchy—a fancy psychological term. Dr. Phil and Dear Abby would be impressed.

"I've got a stand on my farm overlooking the power line, with a couple acres seeded with alfalfa and rye and turnips," Mark said. "You're welcome to join me sometime. You see where the tracks went?"

"She always this independent? This way." They turned their mares upstream toward me. Jesup nickered. The mares' ears went up. Eli looked around, his eyes behind his shades on the surrounding terrain. Both men wore almost-identical sunglasses. Cute.

"Idiot used to run at night. Got shot at one time. Nearly got burned to death the last time." My eyes narrowed at the description of me as an idiot. I might act like one sometimes, and running at night wasn't the brightest thing I had ever done, but hearing Mark use the I-word with another person was enough to make me steam.

"She's got a mind of her own." Eli sounded amused, half-proud. "She must be just ahead. The mares scent her mount. How'd she nearly get burned to death?"

"I didn't burn to death," I said, tapping Jesup and urging him into view. "Not that it's any of your business. I took care of myself quite well, in fact." My voice rose. "Can't a girl have a few minutes of alone time before the fireworks start, without you following me like I'm—I'm—" I stopped and sighed. I sounded cross. Okay, bitchy. Jesup and I wove between two close-set boulders.

A gun blasted nearby.

I jerked. Jesup jumped. The mares half reared, crashing into each other. The impact made them wild; their ears went flat. Jesup half bucked his way out of the tight space between the huge rocks. I gripped the reins and held on to the horn. Tightened my legs around his barrel. When he did a little hop, as if to rear, I flattened myself to his neck and pulled the reins down on either side. "Easy, boy."

The blast echoed. Shotgun? My mind classified the sound from long-ago lessons. No. Hunting rifle.

Mark and Eli had their weapons in hand before the blast faded. Eyes rolling, the horses danced hard.

"Which way?" Mark asked.

"Ahead. You take Rhea. I'll see." Eli flung himself from the saddle and let the reins drop.

Mark grabbed them before they hit the ground. The mares pranced, alert, snorting. Eli turned away from the stream, back along the path and up the other side, crouching. Jesup jerked toward the barn, wanting home and oats, water and quiet. I struggled with him, boot heels shoved low to keep my feet in the stirrups.

A second blast sounded. Eli's mare bucked and kicked out while still in the air. Mark dropped her reins and the brown mare kicked away as he fought his own mount. Jesup heaved, hopped once, but held his place, feet planted wide, nostrils extended and blowing. I was talking to him, nonsense words. I should have leaned forward and covered Jesup's eyes to calm him, but that would have meant letting go of the reins. Not in this lifetime.

"There room for two horses in the boulders ahead?" Mark asked gruffly, his voice low.

"Yeah." I turned the horse into the rocks. Jesup didn't like the place where he had just hidden, and balked. I slapped him with the reins, and he bolted forward, into the crevasse. Somehow I held on. Malachi's last riding lesson had been nearly twenty years ago, but some muscle memory remained.

There were no more shots. Mark herded his mare into the tight place. Jesup flattened his ears. "No," I said, and swatted them with the flat of my hand. He looked back at me, his eyes narrowed. Okay, I wasn't exactly the horse whisperer.

"What?"

"Nothing." I must have spoken out loud. Dangerous habit. Jesup moved over and the dun mare slid in. Jesup butted her with his nose and she slid her muzzle along his neck—horse for "Howdy." Still prancing, they moved in the close quarters. Minutes passed. The horses calmed, stomped a few times to fight flies, swished tails rhythmically.

Mark's phone rang. Left-handed, he found the phone, reins looped tightly. Hitting Talk, he said, "Stafford. Yeah? Well, that's typical. It's safe for her? On our way. Your horse is a goner, though. Took off like greased lightning." He laughed at the response and put the cell in his pocket. "Eli says one drunk hunter shot another one, about a hundred yards up the trail."

"I don't have my bag."

Mark turned and looked at me in my orange vest, white shirt and jeans. "I didn't know you rode. You look good on horseback."

So did he, snug in the saddle, hands firm on the reins, but I didn't say that. "Learned here in the summers with Marisa."

"You do country real good." His eyes slid over me, the statement branding home. Words he'd once said to me in better times. "Let's go."

Reining sharply, he pulled the mare's head out and guided her between the rocks. Jesup seemed content to follow. "I don't have my bag," I said again.

Mark put away his weapon and fished for his phone. Punched numbers. After a long minute during which we rode up a sharp incline to the path on the far side of the creek, he said, "Malachi? Stafford. Call 9-1-1 and get an ambulance and a rescue squad unit up to the main road, okay? We got a couple drunks up here and one shot the other. You may need to guide rescue to the creek, so meet them. Yeah. Hunters. You got a cell phone? Number?'' Mark repeated it back. ''Got it. Where are we, Rhea?''

''Up the logging road from the boulders where Risa and I used to camp as kids.''

Mark repeated my statement and said, ''Don't know. We'll call back and tell you.''

''Why didn't you call 9-1-1?'' I asked.

''All I know is I'm near a creek on the Stowe Farm. There are about seven. Malachi can give exact directions.''

''I don't have my bag,'' I repeated.

''You said that. Does it make a difference?''

''Only in whether the guy'll die or not.''

Mark laughed at my tone and glanced back. ''You're better than the nothing he'd have if you weren't here. It's his lucky day.''

The man was under a tree, sitting with his back against the trunk. I ripped off the orange vest and slid to the ground, my legs stiff, my back very unhappy. I leaned against Jesup's shoulder and he craned his head back to look at me. If horses can be amused, he was. Dropping the hat over the horn and handing the reins to Mark, I moved away from Jesup. My back went into spasm and I caught my breath, but it passed. Gingerly, I walked to the fallen hunter.

Even from five feet away, he reeked of beer. He had taken a hit in the lower right quadrant, beside his hip, near his groin. Eli was bent over him, shirtless, tanned back bowed. Blood stained the hunter's camouflage. A second hunter moved closer, hands on his knees.

''He gonna be all right?'' the second man asked. ''I swear I didn't mean to shoot him.'' He spat, brown juice spewing to the side. Mark approached, muttering something, and shoved him face-first against another tree. Moving with economical grace, he grabbed the man's wrists and clicked handcuffs on him, then pushed him to the ground, prone, while reciting a quick Miranda. Then he joined Eli and me, a look of satisfaction on his face. It always did a man good to subdue another. He-man stuff.

Eli's Delta Force medic training had kicked in and his T-shirt was folded, pressed to the man's wound. His leather holster was slung across his spine, straps dangling. The patient was moaning, grunting, pushing away Eli's ministrations.

"Get his hands," I directed Mark. "Entrance and exit?" I asked Eli.

"Both. This side is the exit, big as my fist. Round caught the bowel. Entrance at the back, minimal bleeding." There was a first-aid kit open on the ground beside the injured hunter, its contents scattered.

I knelt in the pine needles beside him. I smelled the sickly raw smell of bowel, which, when released into the abdominal cavity, provided enough bacteria to kill a mule. Mark pulled the patient's hands to the ground from behind and secured them there, the tree between him and the victim.

"I swear I didn't mean to shoot him," the other hunter said again, his mouth pressed in the dirt.

"Shut up," we all said. In unison. It was kinda funny, and Mark and I laughed. Eli's brows went up, that half-amused look in his eyes. I got another whiff of bowel and knew the enteric bacteria was already leaking into the patient's system. The victim groaned and squirmed and gasped as pain writhed through his abdomen. I wished I had morphine for him. Bowel wounds were reputed to be torture.

"There was a package of sterile four-by-fours in the hunter's first-aid kit. I used that, then added the shirt." Eli glanced up at me. "I was worried about staph, until I smelled the bowel. Figured it didn't matter so much."

I picked up the torn sterile paper. It was old and cracked, no longer sterile. The paper had been broken in three places long before Eli had ripped it. But it was too late to move the gauze, even if I had anything sterile to use instead. If a clot was started on the unclean gauze, it was better than no clot on sterile cloth. Or so I hoped. Bleeding first, infection worries later.

The patient gagged and Mark caught his head, tilted it to the side. We eased him to the ground beside the tree. Mark came around and knelt, ready to fight the hands away from Eli's makeshift bandage.

Blood had soaked through Eli's shirt. The layered cloth wasn't enough. Blood seeped around the edges and dripped off the victim's side.

"Mark? I need your shirt." I looked over at the second hunter. "You got anything clean?"

He was bearded with a five-day growth, and I could smell him from here. I'd bet he hadn't bagged any game whose capture required skill, stealth or being upwind from prey. His smell was enough to cure meat.

"Never mind," I said. Cloth scraped and Mark tossed his shirts to me before he resecured the victim's arms. I folded them and added them to the pile beneath Eli's hands. We had no gloves. Blood was flowing freely over Eli's skin. I grimaced.

"Any way you can ask for an HIV to be done on this guy?" he asked, reading my mind.

"I ain't gay," the patient said. I looked at him, seeing his face for the first time. Shades of *Deliverance,* with this guy playing the one who liked pretty mouths. I wouldn't put money on any claim he made.

"Yeah. I can arrange that," I said.

Long minutes passed. I had no equipment. Nothing. I

hated it when I was useless. Eli was doing the work. I could have gone home.

In the distance I heard the faint sound of a siren. My fingertips itched. Something about sirens… Cops, scanners. And radios. Speculatively, I looked at Mark, the corner of one eye visible at the edge of his shades. "Can you get it mentioned over the scanner that I'm at the farm? With an African-American girl and a blonde? That I discovered the hunter? Maybe that I thought it was one of the killers or something."

He shook his head at me, not liking my plan. Eli grinned; clearly he thought it was great. If you're going to be bait, be bait all the way.

"Stafford!" a voice called from far off. It echoed like the gunshots.

Putting the patient's hands in mine, Mark stood and moved to the horses he had tied a little distance away. Help was here. Mounting the mare, he looped Jesup's reins around the saddle horn and rode out of the clearing, leading my horse.

I looked up at Eli. He was looking at me. The fallen man lay between us, groaning and writhing.

"I like Stafford," he said at last.

"Yeah." I paused. "So do I."

"I tried to arrange backup, but the guy couldn't make it. Previous engagement. Stafford'll be in the house with us. It'll give you a chance to talk." I looked away from his eyes, with the feeling he was about to spring something on me. I was right. "He told me about Skye. About the baby and the paternity suit and the man he killed."

"Great. You're another one." When his brows raised in question, I said, "Another man who makes my decisions for me. Like ordering for me at McDonalds and at IHOP. I'm a big girl, and knowing what I want to eat and how to live my life is something I've been doing for a long time."

Eli grinned and looked down at his hands.

"It's not remotely funny," I said. "This is my problem." I tapped my chest hard three times to drive the point home. Even I could hear the exasperation in my voice. "*My* choice. Besides, talking with Mark is counterproductive. He just does whatever he wants to in the first place."

"Like you?" I glared at him and Eli laughed. "Seems we all three have that characteristic." He smiled, his eyes not involved. "You still have feelings for him."

"I have feelings for my mother, too, but she's dead. Feelings don't always die when it's convenient, but that doesn't mean you still have a relationship to save."

"You can't work things out with your mother. You can with Stafford."

Suddenly it hit me and I rocked back on my heels. "You set this up, didn't you? You made sure your backup couldn't make it so Mark would have to be in the house with us."

"I'm not a Pollyanna. I still want you. But I like the guy. And as I said once or twice before, no baggage."

I wanted to curse. Instead I stood and strode down the path to the approaching horses, my feet stomping. All the men in my life wanted to live it for me. Tension thrummed through my veins like hot lava rolling downhill. Behind me, I could hear Eli laughing softly. I kicked a rock and sent it flying. It felt good to see it go, hear it ricochet off a tree.

Coming up from the creekbed on horseback, Malachi led a short cavalcade comprised of the rescue squad, two EMS guys in uniform with an oversize EMS utility toolbox balanced on the horse between them, and two cops. The cops were talking into their radios, and Mark was answering back, his eyes on me at the top of the hill. He was doing what I had asked. Making me a bigger target.

The EMS guys were out of shape. Tony weighed in at

close to 350, with a belly like a tractor tire hanging over his belt, and George had been eating hard to catch up with him. The rescue squad guys were not much better, but were slender enough to ride the small horses Malachi had saddled. As we walked, I filled them in.

"High caliber rifle shot, in and out, lower right quadrant. Probable bowel involvement. Bleeding not controlled, but attempts made with makeshift pads and pressure. I want two large bore IVs with Ringer's Lactate, O2 and transport ASAP."

"Yes, ma'am," Tony huffed.

"And we need to talk about an exercise program, Tony. You look like you might blow out your heart here."

"Feels like it, too," he said, reaching level ground. Bending over, hands on knees to let his belly drop between his arms, he moaned, "Oh, man. Oh, Jesus, Lord. I got to lose this weight."

I took the reins of the horse carrying the EMS kit and ran ahead, pulling the horse by its bridle. By the time the rescuers caught up, I was sitting beside the hunter with the kit open, gloves on my hands and an IV ready to start. "See if you can peel back the top layers of that bandage and put some fresh on it. Get me a blood pressure. And see that Eli has some sterile water to clean up."

"Yes, ma'am, Dr. Lynch," George said, wrapping the pressure cuff around the hunter's none-to-clean upper arm. Tony dropped beside him and started cutting away the patient's clothes, exposing a fish-white belly smeared with blood.

Twenty minutes later, the gunshot victim was trussed up on a stretcher, both entrance and exit wounds secured with pressure bandages, two IVs going. He was stable, but the inevitable surgery, peritonitis, post-operative infection and rehab would be difficult to manage. I stood with a dripping Eli as he wiped sterile irrigation fluid off his arms and torso.

The extra rescue squad hands lifted and carried the patient toward the creek, Tony and George behind. Mark walked with them, the prisoner—still whining about the terrible accident and asking to borrow chewing tobacco—ahead of him.

Glancing back once, Mark said, "Get Rhea to the house. I'll be back as soon as possible. I'll be coming in overland. Will call on the cell. If they want her and they heard…"

Eli nodded. "I'll take care of her."

As the sounds faded in the distance, I looked at Eli, not bothering to hide my anger. He just grinned. He was leaning against a tree, his bomber jacket on, his bare chest exposed between the open zipper, legs separate, one knee bent in a characteristic pose.

Without speaking, I went to Jesup and untied his reins, grabbed the saddle horn and shoved a foot in the stirrup. As I started to pull myself up, Eli's hands gripped my bottom and shoved. I was in the saddle, and instantly Eli was on the horse behind me. I hadn't even seen him swing up.

Reaching around me, he took the reins, pulled me against his chest and urged Jesup toward the trail. His skin was like an open furnace at my back. He secured the straw hat across the horn, gathered me closer and headed down the trail. I said nothing, seeing only his arm around my waist, bare below the cuff of the jacket, dark hair curled against brown skin.

"Something about a woman wearing a gun. Sexy," he said into my ear, deliberately provocative.

Words tumbled out of my mouth. "You're a real pain in the butt, you know that?"

Eli found my comment and my continued temper highly amusing. His laughter echoed.

We rode through the woods as silence settled on us, Eli holding me tightly against him. I could feel his holster and the butt of his gun at my left shoulder blade. "You might as well relax. It's a long ride back to the house, and I won't harm the horse just to end your misery."

"I could walk." I sounded petulant even to me.

"No." He was amused. Highly amused.

I didn't like dumb women and I was acting dumb. Night was falling; it was growing colder. His arms felt warm. The rhythm of the horse was soothing. I figured good feelings might be in short supply for a while. So I relaxed against him, snuggling into the leather jacket, into his warm skin.

When we moved out of the protective trees into the open, Eli pulled out his gun, checked to see that the safety was on, and rested his wrist across the saddle horn, the huge weapon pointed far to the side. With his body wrapped around me, we rode slowly back to the house.

The farmhouse was dark in the distance, the barn a shadow. Usually the ground lights and a security light near the barn were on, but tonight nothing was illuminated. To the far side of the drive, horses ran and kicked, snorting, pawing the air. Jesup's ears pricked eagerly and he whinnied, the sound vibrating along my legs as he picked up his pace, heading to the barn and food.

I put it together. Malachi had let the horses into the east pasture. It made sense. That was the least likely direction from which to approach the house. There was Prosperity Creek to the east, which meant getting wet to cross, and nothing but land that hadn't been farmed in thirty years. No logging roads. No way to make approaching from this direction easy. All the other points of the compass were simpler. Hence the horses were safer to the east.

We clip-clopped up to the barn, and Eli holstered his weapon and handed me down to a waiting Malachi. My legs were wobbly and I leaned against the horse, who was snuffling the stablehand, his big nose in Malachi's chest. I hadn't been on horseback in years and my muscles were stiffening. It was all that bucking when the gunshots had scared the horses. Eli swung down beside me, lithe and loose in the darkness. Show-off.

"You stay here at night?" he asked Malachi.

"Usually. I got a room over the barn, take meals in the house." Malachi grasped the reins. "Stafford told me what you got planned. I'll take care of the horse. You get her into the house and safe. Then, 'less you need another pair of eyes in the barn, I'm going into town to my sister's place."

"That might be best," Eli said. "We'll have eyes staked out on the hill there—" he pointed "—and across the front road in a hunter's stand."

"There's a month's worth of hay stored in the barn, and more covered in the back field. I'd appreciate it if you don't burn down my barn or shoot any of my horses."

"That's the plan." Eli grinned, that half quirk that didn't reach his eyes.

"I'll be back at sunup to feed the stock."

"Make it sunup-thirty and you won't get shot."

Malachi grunted and flipped a stirrup over Jesup's back to loosen the girth. Eli took my hand and propelled me to the house, drawing off the belted .32 as he hauled me around like so much horse feed. "Pull off your boots while I check out the house. There's a big tub with whirlpool jets in the master suite. You can wash and relax all at the same time." He shoved me forward, a hand at the small of my back.

"You're as bossy as Mark. Maybe bossier. Are all men this impossible?" I sat on the top step and started working on my boots. Wordless, Eli walked away.

29

YOU KNOW. ARMY SCHOOL.

"Place is clear," he said moments later. "I turned on the lamp in the master bath. It needs to stay on." I stood and walked past him into the house, up the back stairs and into the master suite. Shut the door and clicked the lock. My overnight bag and medical bag had been set on Marisa's bed, the dark-blue-and-lavender coverlet folded at the foot of the mattress, light blue blanket turned down to expose freshly ironed, dark blue sheets, a tone-on-tone stripe. Who in heck ironed sheets? One night and they were wrinkled.

I stripped and put my dirty clothes over the back of a chair to air the horse scent out of them. The chair was a floral in navy and grape, with matching ottoman and a lavender afghan tossed over it. The bedroom was all shades of blue and lavender, soft and warm and feminine, the blue almost the color of Marisa's eyes. I recognized Arlana's work.

Naked, I made my way to the bath and turned on the water in the tub. I wasn't much of a tub person, preferring the expediency of a shower, but I was really starting to stiffen up. And my back, strained in the moments of fear at the creek, was in spasm. Marisa had all sorts of bottles around the tub. I added some oil that smelled like almonds and some bubble bath from a matching container. A blue towel had been left folded on the small table by the tub, along with two matching washcloths and a blue terry-cloth robe. Guest stuff. Marisa, being her thoughtful self. At my house, guests often had to ask for towels, and were lucky if there were clean ones in the house.

I stepped over the tub's rim, slid down into the water, the porcelain cold at my strained back. As the hot water rose, I relaxed and sank deep into the warmth. The moment the water was over the jets, I flipped them on. Water rushed at me, hot rotating surges. I adjusted the placement of one at my back to the muscle in spasm and leaned into it. When the water was almost to the tub's top, I turned it off and closed my eyes. Soothed, feeling pampered, I think I fell asleep.

"The door stays unlocked."

I nearly slid under, then almost came up out of the water. Eli stood leaning in the doorway. "What?" I asked.

"The doors. They stay open and unlocked. At all times."

"How'd you get in here?" I slumped back under the water, feeling a heat rise in me that had nothing to do with the bath.

"I'm good at stuff like that." He lifted a brow. "You know. Army school. Keep it unlocked." Turning, he left the room, pulling the door closed.

"I'm good at stuff like that," I mimicked to my painted toenails, peeking out at the top of the bubbles, trying for macho and not succeeding. *"You know. Army school.* Well, whoop-de-dang-doo." Sarcastic as all get-out.

I stayed in the tub for an hour, adding water as needed to replace that siphoned off by the overflow valve. The oil was soothing to my skin, the bubbles cleansing, the aroma relaxing, and I could get used to the jets. When I had money to redo my bath, I might add a whirlpool. And maybe I'd rip out the old tile and change the color to this wonderful shade of blue. My bath was ecru, Arlana's fancy name for beige. By either name, compared to this it was pretty dull.

After the bath, I shoved my bags to the floor, crawled onto the bed and under the sheets, pulling the terry-cloth robe around me. Lying in the dark, I was asleep in minutes.

At 2:12 a.m. I woke and lay still, placing myself. I was in Marisa's bed. Two men were looking after me, neither one making my life easier. I stretched slowly, finding that my back was better. Sore, but not about to charley horse. In the dark, I rose, found my bag and pulled on clean underwear, a pair of sweats and clean socks, and wrapped the robe back around me against the chill. Calling softly down the stairs to avoid getting shot, I descended, feet searching in the dark, hands gripping the rails.

Mark was standing at the back window, silhouetted by moonlight. "You must be hungry," he said, not turning around. When I agreed, he said, "There's a bowl of soup in the fridge. The light's off inside, so you'll have to feel. You can nuke it. Crackers are on the table."

I opened the fridge and felt around until I touched the chilled rim of a bowl and lifted it to the microwave. The light was off in it, too. Nothing to create night blindness. I heated the soup, and when it was steaming, I sat at the table, my feet in the chair Indian-yogi-style, the robe tucked under them. A napkin holder was an outline in the center of the table and I grabbed a handful, tucking one into my collar, one at my lap and one in my left hand. I figured I'd be messy in the dark. Crackers were near the napkins, and I crumbled a half-dozen into the soup.

As I slurped, identifying homemade chicken noodle, Mark roamed, moving from window to window, front of the house to back. I figured Eli was asleep. What was this, first watch or second watch? I laughed at the thought. It was very 007.

"What's funny?"

"This whole thing. You two and me in here in this house waiting for the bad guys."

He didn't respond to that. Instead, he made another circuit. "How's your back? Eli says you've been having trouble."

I shrugged, realized he couldn't see the gesture, and said, "The bath helped. It never healed right. It spasms sometimes when I overdo it. I overdid."

"Are you in love with him?"

I paused, spoon in midair. "Eli? No. I'm not looking to fall in love. I figure I'd just get hurt again."

"I never meant to hurt you."

I looked around in the dark. His voice was beside me one time and behind me the next. I couldn't spot him. His steps were silent. I went back to the soup, spilling a little on me in the dark. "Do you understand why you hurt me?" I asked.

"Sure. It's obvious."

"You think?"

"Enlighten me, then." There was humor in his tone. Humor was good. It was better than frustration or bitterness.

I talked while I ate. "John Micheaux and I were together for four years, lived together for three during our residency. We had plans to be contract physicians, working in various hospitals around the world for five years or so. We had a real strong longing to spend time in New Zealand and Australia. Then, if we wanted kids, we would have kids. Settle in Charleston, with another house at the Emerald Coast on the Florida panhandle, and a cabin in the Blue Ridge Mountains. It was all planned out. And then his uncle died and his father crooked his finger. And John took a job in the family clinic. Just like that. Our plans were trash. And to make matters worse, he expected me to live with it and not have feelings about it.''

''I'm sorry.'' Mark's voice came from the front of the house.

''Me, too. We were good together.'' I crumbled more crackers into the soup. ''Anyway, when I got over being mad and sat down and analyzed it, I understood it wasn't the first time he had done that, rearranged our lives without asking me. It was a pattern. And I didn't want to live that way, without control over my life.''

''Your mother had forced that on you since you were a kid.''

''Don't psychoanalyze me.''

''You denying it?''

''No. I'm not. Life with Tammy was a bitch.'' My spoon clinked against the ironstone. Bowl empty, belly full. Mission accomplished. I sat back.

''So you came here, to Dawkins County.''

''To lick my wounds,'' I acknowledged. ''And because it might be possible to get medical school paid off by the government if I stayed here two years.''

''Go on.'' He was close, not more than two feet away.

''Can you get me some milk?''

Mark moved, found a glass, opened the fridge. A rush of cold air swept out. I heard the sound of pouring. The door shut. The glass settled beside my bowl. I took it and drank. Perfect with a bowl of soup and crackers. I took another cracker and chipped away at it with my teeth. They were club crackers, my favorite, buttery and rich. ''And so I settled here and met you, and dated a bit. Still talked to John on the phone.''

''I didn't know that.''

''It wasn't any of your business. You and I weren't exclusive. Weren't sleeping together. Weren't planning a future together.''

"Go on," he said from the window, voice tight. He hadn't liked what I said. Tough. Silhouetted, he moved from the window over the sink to the window by the door. Still silent.

"Things were getting pretty good between you and me, though. I was content, which I hadn't been in a long time."

"And then John called and you planned a trip to the mountains together for two weeks. Camping, in the middle of winter." His voice was bitter.

I knew that trip had hurt him. But John had been my fiancé. I had issues to work out with him. Probably still had issues to work out with John. "John liked to camp. And I needed to see if anything was left to salvage. If I still had feelings for him."

"And you went."

"I went. And knew after two days that though I still had feelings, the feelings would never make us work together. John wanted things I didn't. He wanted kids right away. He wanted to stay in Charleston with the social whirl he had grown up with, the friends he had grown up with. He wanted me to make up with the Grande Dame.''

"Your grandmother."

"Yeah. That's not gonna happen. She had money and assets that could have made my life easier, kept me from going hungry when I was a child, paid for clothes and necessities. She gave us nothing. Maybe she had reasons for disowning Tammy—my mother had problems you wouldn't believe. But the old woman had no reason to let me suffer." I knew he heard the bitterness in my voice and I didn't care. "John had lied to me all those years in Chicago, making plans he didn't intend to keep. And I didn't share his real dreams."

"And now Marisa needs you and you still haven't traveled."

"Yeah, but it was my decision. And the future is open and free. If she marries Cowboy, I can still travel. Get settled where I want, when I want."

"So what about us?"

"We have some of the same problems John and I did. We don't talk. We don't plan. You don't even know that I'm not sure I want kids."

"I do now."

"And?"

"And I know. I get to think about what that means."

"And you want to make my decisions for me."

"Yep. 'Cause you do the fool-damnedest things. But I can learn. Like tonight. I don't really need you here. I could have bundled you up and taken you off the property. How would they ever know? But I wanted you here, where I could take care of you. See you. Talk to you." His voice had moved up behind me. His hand encircled my neck, caressing. I leaned my head against him. "If it's the last time I ever get to do those things, then I want the time with you. Selfish, right?"

I smiled in the dark. Relaxed into the soothing kneading of his hands.

"Did you know I have a place in the mountains north of Asheville?"

I opened my eyes wide. "No, I didn't."

"The Stafford Place. Used to belong to my mother's cousin, my second cousin. When the family line died out, it came to me. The western half of a mountain. The sunsets are spectacular. The place is pretty rustic. No electricity. No indoor plumbing. Rough-hewn log walls. Big fireplace and wood-burning stove for heat." His hands had massaged below my collarbones and down the collar of my shirt to my shoulder blades. No farther. A Beau in a world of Bubbas.

"I understand why you slept with Skye," I said.

His hands stopped, resting warm on my skin.

"I'm not sure I can put it into words, and it still hurts, but I understand."

"Yeah?" he whispered.

"We weren't together then. You didn't know if you wanted me or not. Loving me was too hard. And she was easy. Available. She stirred something in you. So you took what was offered."

His bent, his lips pressed to my scalp. "I'm sorry."

"I know."

"I love you."

"I know that, too."

"I can learn to talk. To share my dreams with you. My hopes. I— Don't move. Stay put." He slid from behind me to the door. I saw him lift something over his head, standing there, still as stone, tension coursing through him like a live wire. A moment later there was a click and he said, "Eli? Company. Dirt bike."

His cell phone rang, the tone muted. "Yeah, I see it. Which way? Okay, notify backup. We're rolling." It chimed again as he ended the call. "Yeah. Really? Well, aren't they smart. They're coming from the back, too. I'll pass the word." He dialed two numbers, saying the same thing each time. "Front and back. Repeat, front and back. Both are on dirt bikes. It's a go." He wasn't using the police radio. It would keep the bad guys from knowing anything, should they have access to law enforcement frequencies.

"Where's Rhea?" Eli's voice came from the stairs.

"Kitchen table. She was hungry."

"What's the plan?" I asked.

"It's fluid. Has to be," Mark said. "We weren't sure if

both would come, or if they'd be together. On foot, in the van or on the bikes.''

"Upstairs, Rhea. It's safer," Eli said, materializing out of the darkness, gripping my upper arm and half lifting me.

I let him move me to the stairs, but when he gave me a gentle shove, I took only one step, stopping when he turned and moved to the front of the house. I sat on the bottom step, curled my arms around my knees and leaned out so I could see the front and the back of the house. If someone started shooting, I'd head up fast, but I wanted to see as long as possible.

"Front has a radio," Eli said.

"Back does, too."

I recognized that Eli and Mark were wearing night vision goggles of some kind, their heads shaped like space monster helmets from a fifties film. Eli's toys?

"Organized little critters," Eli said. "Backup?"

"Agents and deputies. A chopper just took off from the Dawkins airfield, ETA two minutes, should we need 'em. Ground crew are moving in, but they know to run dark and silent till we give the word."

"The closer your bad guys get, the better. They get away on foot and it'll be like last time."

"Back has stopped," Mark said. "He's putting the bike down by the dock."

"Get-away vehicle?"

"Sounds right."

"Thought they were gonna take her with them," Eli said, his tone conversational. As if he wasn't talking about my kidnapping and death by slow torture.

"Profiler said that was the most likely scenario. Looks like he was wrong. They plan to do her here and run. Fast and dirty. Either that, or the green van's parked close by. We still haven't found it."

I opened my mouth to breathe silently, gripping my

knees tightly. This was what Mark did every day. Let the bad guys get close enough for him to stop and arrest them. My heart was pounding so hard it hurt. Sweat soaked into my sweatshirt. It clung to my back, as if it was the middle of summer instead of the dark of December. I shivered in the cold, pulled the robe closer.

"Front has reached the house," Eli said softly. "He's at the door. Ski mask and dark clothes." I heard a soft metallic sound and a scrape, as if someone was trying the knob, inspecting the lock. A moment later Eli added, "He's moving around back."

I saw Eli shift with the man outside the house, from window to window, around to the kitchen at the back.

"Not checking windows," Eli said, "just walking."

"They're coming in together," Mark said, so softly I scarcely heard. Soft clicks sounded as the men checked their weapons.

"My guy stopped. Near the electric and telephone connections."

Sitting in the dark, I heard the refrigerator stop. Felt, more than saw, the faint illumination from the master bath upstairs go out.

"Good thing we live in the twenty-first century," Mark said.

Eli chuckled. I understood, too. Cell phones and radios, night vision equipment, flashlights and helicopters—all the cool stuff that make being a cop so much fun. Boys and their toys. I felt a sharp pain in one wrist and realized that I had dug my nails into the skin. I took a deep breath and forced relaxation into me.

I heard soft footsteps on the deck out back. An almost inaudible click from the kitchen. Mark said something into his radio, too soft to hear.

Out of the dark, framed in the panes of glass at the back

door, I saw a darker shape approach. Stealthy. Silent. Another one. They huddled at the door. Glass shattered.

I jumped, my heart in my mouth. I was rocking slightly in the safety of the stairs. Nausea gripped me. I swallowed hard, breathed slower, fighting the feel of acid in the back of my throat.

A lock clicked. The door opened. I watched as two forms entered. Mark and Eli were nowhere to be seen. Where were they?

The door clicked shut.

A blinding light wrenched me from the dark. An instant vision, a snapshot on my lids. Too bright. Searing. Outside of time. Mark and Eli behind the bar and doorway, night vision goggles dangling down their backs. Weapons drawn. Aimed at targets in the center of the kitchen. Two men, dark all over, crouched in shock.

"Police! Get down. Get down. Police!"

Movement exploded. As one, the strange men separated, flying apart, one toward the bar and the other to the doorway. Shouting. Cursing. Something smashed. The room went black. I lurched. Jerked back, up two stairs. Breath frozen.

Sounds of struggle, flesh hitting flesh. Furniture being overturned. Crushed. Pottery and glass rolling, breaking. A siren in the distance. A gunshot so close I saw the flash as the weapon discharged.

Another. A huge boom. A cannon so loud it stunned me.

I turned and raced for the top of the stairs on all fours. Tripping on the robe. Falling, banging my knees. Hearing the battle. Another gunshot. A different gun. Then the cannon again, surely Eli's weapon. Someone screamed. A window crashed and broke. I heard something fall with a muffled thud.

"Damn!"

"I got this one. You okay?"

"Yes!"

"Get the other one! Go! Go go go go!"

Feet pounded. I found Marisa's bedroom and scooted around on my bottom. The robe came off and I left it on the floor. My fingers touched my medical bag, cool and solid in the dark. "Airway, breathing, circulation," I was whispering, calling on the triple icons of emergency treatment. "Airway, breathing, circulation."

Sitting on the floor, I opened the bag. Pulled it to my lap. Felt in the dark for my stuff. Sterile bandages. Tape.

"Rhea!"

It was Eli, shouting. A light came on below. A flashlight, shining up the stairs.

"You can come down now. One's with me. Stafford's gone after the other one. My guy's hit. He's bleeding like a son of a gun. Get down here."

On wobbly knees, I stood and followed the light to the stairs and down. Into the kitchen. The site of battle.

30

The blazing flashlight was harsh in the stygian darkness, picking out the overturned table and a broken chair. A shattered bowl and napkin holder, crackers and paper napkins strewn like tossed playing cards. Lying in the middle of them was a man in a spreading pool of too-bright blood.

His legs kicked hard, smearing the gore. He was grunting. Little soft sounds of pain and disbelief. I pulled in a breath that ached deep inside me. This was the man who had kidnapped so many girls. Tortured them. Murdered them.

I could turn around and go back upstairs. I could let him die. I could. Perhaps I should. I blinked. I could smell the stench of the triangle grave. See the grisly body tied to the table in the old house. See Beata's eyes, pleading and wounded.

He deserved to die. He deserved to die in agony and pain like his victims. This was the man I wanted dead.

"It should be safe. I got his weapon, but be careful."

"I need more light," I said, my eyes glued to the thrashing form.

"This is it. One of them busted the other flash." Eli said, his voice now sounding almost bored. Sirens wailed into the kitchen from the open back door. Engines roared closer, tires spitting gravel. Red and blue lights glinted on the windows and on the broken glass shards on the floor.

Certain I was doing the wrong thing, I stepped closer and knelt in the dark, my knees just beyond the blood. Set down my bag. Opened it. "Shine the light on him." My voice sounded precise and cold and demanding. Eli moved the flash until the beam hit the man on the floor. Reaching out, I ripped off his ski mask.

Blue eyes stared back at me. Lips pulled in a rictus of pain. Uneven teeth were stained a tobacco brown, gums bright red, sickly pallor above, jagged beard below.

"Bitch," he spat at me. "Bitch whore."

"I've been called worse," I said, staring at his bright blue eyes. Laser blue. This was the killer. This was the man who had hurt Beata. Burned off patches of flesh. Skinned her for trophies. Deacon. His eyes blazed with hate. "I've been called worse by human beings," I said, "so hearing it from inbred, genetically warped, grotesque, bottom scum like you isn't a problem. If it hurts when I examine you, don't be surprised. Consider it part of my personal entertainment."

Blue lights and sirens filled the yard outside. I reached forward again and jerked at his blood-soaked shirt. Deacon cursed at me. There was a bullet hole in his abdomen about two centimeters off-center, just below his pierced navel. Blood flowed out, not an arterial pulse, but a steady venous stream. Cops shouted, the sound seeming far away, though they were in the yard.

Deacon's hand slashed out of the darkness and gripped my wrist, his fingers twisting hard. I stared at the dirty fingers and grimy skin holding me. There was dried blood beneath his nails.

"I really—really—want to see you dead," I whispered. "I saw what you did to those girls. I saw." I looked up from his hand to his face. Something less than human stared at me from his blue eyes.

"It was fun," he said softly. Smiling.

I jerked away.

Deacon twitched oddly. The light tried to follow the motion, but it missed. Eli held out a hand in the dark, gesturing for me to wait.

Voice calm as oiled water, Eli said, "Did a little prison time, didn't you, boy? Bet the cons used your ass like a dartboard."

With a roar, Deacon pitched himself at Eli. A glitter of something. Slashing.

"Eli!"

The two forms rolled through the blood, out of the beam of light. Into the dark. "Eli?" I whispered. I reached for the flash. Turned the beam on them as they fought and cursed.

In the darkness, the cannon boomed. I jumped hard, unable to breathe. Then another shot sounded.

"Eli?" I called, breathless, my voice wavering, lost beneath the blast concussion ringing in my ears.

Sudden light shot into the room. Voices almost lost in my abrupt deafness.

"Police! Put down the gun! Put down the gun! Police!"

"Get him down. Get his gun!"

"It's Doc! Dr. Lynch!"

"Don't shoot! Don't shoot. Civilians in here! I'm putting down the weapon. See!"

I looked across the broken body, saw Eli carefully set his weapon down on the floor. Raise his hands and lock them behind his head. Flashlight beams flickered back and forth wildly. One man backhanded Eli on the head. "Get down!"

"He's with me," I said calmly. "He's one of the good guys."

"Stafford went after the other one," Eli said, from the floor. "He needs backup."

"Stevens and Johnson, take two deputies to assist," Jim Ramsey said. "McDill, you hit that man again and I'll take it out of your backside. Better yet, I'll let him take it out of you. Rhea, you okay?"

I blinked. The motion seeming exaggerated, slow. A moment of dark and calm superimposed on the coarse brightness and scarlet gore. I lowered my arms, which had somehow gotten up over my head. I looked down. The pool of blood had widened. I was kneeling in the edge, the sweatpants soaking up the scarlet. A knife with a long, slightly curved blade, like a chef's boning knife, rested in the blood.

"Rhea?"

"I'm just dandy." My voice came from far away, sounding cool and detached and very in control. Very unlike the screaming maniac I was inside. "Is he dead?" A club cracker beside my knee seemed to pull the blood toward it, absorbing it suddenly. I thought of tomato soup, crushed crackers floating on top.

"He's dead," Eli said. His voice was cold and even. "Can I get up now, Ramsey?"

"Yeah. Leave the weapon. It's part of the crime scene."

Eli cursed, the words vicious. Above me in the dark, Ramsey continued to issue orders, call for medic, talk to dispatch on his radio. Cops milled around the scene. One stepped into the blood, tracked it out. Ramsey shouted at him. Foul cop-talk, earthy and coarse.

I found Eli's eyes as he stood, irises black in the darkness. "I'm sorry," I said, my voice rough as a rasp.

"For what?" he said, his own voice harsh. "I got what I wanted. I did the job you hired me to do." His body was stiff as he rose from the floor. Eli was covered in blood from rolling through it, wrestling with a killer. The wet stains were dark against his black clothing. "My client's still alive, I discovered the weapon he had hidden before he used it on her, and he's dead. I just wish I had gotten the other one, too."

I could almost hear Eli telling me about his wife, dead in Basra because he had left her there, supposedly safe. I hadn't been alone in wanting the killers dead.

I blinked again. Felt myself sway. Licked my dry lips. "I didn't mean for him to... For you to have to..." I shook my head, unable to clear it. "Not really, not...really. I just opened my mouth and the words fell out. I didn't mean to make him..." A tear overflowed and fell, landing in the blood with a splat. "Oh, God."

Eli sighed in the dark and I could almost hear the wry smile in his voice when he said, "Anyone ever tell you your mouth is gonna be the death of you?"

"My mother. Miss DeeDee. Miss Essie. Mark. You want the whole list or just the top ten?"

Eyes still on me, Eli asked, "Stafford's okay?"

"Got his guy and bringing him back now," a voice said from the doorway.

I quaked hard, my hands shaking, gorge rising, my eyes taking in the shadowed kitchen. Blood all over Risa's kitchen. Broken chairs. The fiber-optic Christmas tree, dark now, on its side in a corner. A dead man seeped in gore. Merry Christmas, Risa.

"You're kneeling in blood."

I looked down. Shuddered again, the nausea so strong I needed to spit. I swallowed down the foul taste. "I don't think I can stand." I sounded like a breathless little child, bewildered by the grown-up world.

Eli walked around the body and lifted me beneath the arms. "I'm taking her upstairs to change out of these clothes. You can have her pants for crime scene. And I'll change, too. Got a couple large evidence bags?"

Someone stuffed two bags into my hand. Somehow, I

closed my fingers on them. I could at least do that. "I'm gonna throw up," I said softly.

Eli balanced me on my feet. "You throw up on me and I'll turn you over my knee."

I giggled, a half-hysterical note, as harsh and bitter as charcoal. My legs gave way.

He caught me, cradled me beneath the knees and under the arms, carried me up the stairs in the dark. Unerringly, he entered the master suite and then the bath, settling me on the edge of the tub, feet dangling. I gripped the tub edge, feeling the vertigo return in the blackness.

There was sudden light as a match struck. I smelled sulfur as it blazed. Watched him in the faint glow. Smoke curled up around his hand. Abracadabra. Let there be light.

Eli lit two candles, then two more on the other side of the room. Blew out the match. "They'll get the lights back on pretty soon," he said. When I didn't answer, he took the evidence bag from my fingers and knelt at my feet. Pulled off my socks and dropped them in. Somehow, I had gotten my feet in the blood. "Pants," he said. Half lifting me with one arm, he steadied me as I hooked the elastic waist of the sweatpants and slid them down my hips.

"Look, Miss DeeDee. Clean underwear," I said, my voice sounding hollow. "No holes." And I laughed that awful laugh again. Had I really meant to make Deacon angry? Had I really meant to make Eli shoot him? I was a doctor. I put people back together again. It was what I did; it was who I was. But I had wanted Deacon dead. And he was.

This was the second man who had died because of me. Mark had killed one. Now Eli. The room tilted a moment before righting itself.

Eli turned me and set my feet in the tub, my rear on the rim. Turning on warm water, he handed me a washcloth and left the room for a moment. I stared at the cloth in my hand, at the water falling into the tub, a stream of white rain. *Oh. He wants me to wash.*

My body moved like it might break, forward, bending. My hand slid beneath the weighted wet heat. Pulled the cloth back to my legs. Washed. Again. Red ran down my legs and over my feet. Red lighter than the dark crimson of my toenails. Odd colored, nearly invisible against the navy tub. Eli returned, standing at my back to steady me as I washed until the blood was gone.

He wrapped a towel around my legs, lifted me out of the tub and into his arms. He was wearing clean black sweats and running shoes instead of his paramilitary combat clothes and a killer's blood. Sitting down on the toilet seat, he held me. And I cried. Face against his chest, I cried. Eli's warmth seeped into me. Soothing. Letting me weep. I couldn't have said why I cried. Not really. Part of me kept flashing on the sight of the body lying in the blood, and that part was fiercely glad Deacon was dead. Glad I didn't have to treat him. Glad he wouldn't hurt anyone else ever again. And my satisfaction horrified me.

Minutes later, Eli handed me a tissue and I blew my nose. He lifted me off his lap and set me back on the toilet seat. "Get dressed," he said, voice soft. "You have to call in a replacement to pronounce the man downstairs. And Mark may need help, too. And the cops will want to debrief you."

I said a bad word. Very distinctly. Eli laughed as though I had made a great joke. Then he placed my overnight bag on the floor beside me and left the room, shutting the door behind him. When I could, I stood and plundered for the jeans I had worn prior to the horseback riding excursion. Found them. Pulled them on. Added fresh socks. Sneakers. Pulled off the sweatshirt and added a bra, a navy tank and the starched white shirt I had worn to the Law Enforcement Center. It was wrinkled now, but I didn't care. I tied the sweatshirt around my waist and looked at myself in the mirror.

I had never taken off the makeup I had put on first thing in the morning. It was smeared and running and I could have played a pretty good ghoul in a movie. *Night of the Recent Dead.* I rummaged in the bag and found the little bottle of makeup remover and smeared it into my skin. Wiped it off with a tissue. Cleaned and toned my face like the batty–boy–poofter had shown me, and patted it dry. I was pale, but I was me. Taking a deep breath, I opened the door and left the bathroom. Descended the stairs to the war zone.

On my cell I made the necessary calls to get another coroner to the house for bagging-and-tagging. Called Miss Essie at the hotel and reassured her I was fine and she could go back to her house soon. She was grousing and wanted me to know just how put-upon she was. She seemed unconcerned that there had just been a gun battle in the Stowe farmhouse, and blood was all over the floor. "I got my own troubles. You clean it up," she said, as if the blood was solely a housekeeping problem. I called a sleepy Auntie Maude and told her everything was settled. I could hear a baby crying in the background, and wondered if it was my godson or goddaughter, but I didn't ask.

As I talked, deputies, crime scene techs, agents and even the sheriff worked around me, careful to preserve the actual bloody spot on the floor. All wanted to be part of the death, a macabre fellowship of law and blood. Lots of blood.

I was feeling lost and remote. Half dreaming. A sign of shock. A simple case of emotional shock. That was what was wrong with me.

Diagnosis made, I stood with my back to the carnage and watched out the window. A county electrical truck pulled up and an electrician went to work on the box at the side of the house. A telephone company repairman followed. Mark half guided, half shoved a dark form, the prisoner's hands cuffed behind him. Their shadows moved in a strange strobe of colored lights. I smelled cigarette smoke, exhaust and male sweat. Beneath it all, anger had its own scent, something that got under the skin and almost itched.

As Mark tried to get the man into the county car for transport to the jail, the prisoner whirled, head-butting Mark in the stomach. A second cop took the man down to his knees with a single blow from a nightstick. It was too far away for me to hear the crunch of bone and tendon. Mark stood and body-slammed the guy into the back seat. It still wasn't enough. I wanted more. I wanted him dead, too.

Not able to stand the direction of my own thoughts, I left the house and wandered to the dock where Marisa and I had sat the day she'd told me she liked being married. Since then everything had changed. Marisa had changed, wanted to have sex with Cowboy or marry him. Maybe both. I had changed. I had become this bloodthirsty woman who, deep down, wanted two men dead.

And who also wanted to punish Mark for sleeping with Skye. For being a man who was human and fallible. For embarrassing me in front of the county. Revenge. It was all suddenly so clear.

Voices faded into the night. I untied my sweatshirt and pulled it over my head against the chill.

Okay. That was it. I was angry because Mark had embarrassed me. I was making decisions that might affect me for the rest of my life because I was embarrassed.

Now that was stupid. Just plain dumb.

Boards rang hollowly beneath my feet. I settled on the dock over the placid water, knees bent, legs lifted, my arms around them. I hadn't bothered to bring a jacket. A cold breeze ruffled the pond, moving the surface like liquid black pearl. Behind me, the cops worked. After a while, lights flickered on as the county electrician successfully restored power to the house.

I was shivering, but I didn't want to go back inside. Inside, where my big mouth had helped kill a man. Would he have attacked with the knife had I kept my mouth shut and tried to treat him? Or would he have attacked Eli, anyway? Knowing he was about to be taken by the police, had he attacked to force Eli's hand? There was no way to know. I had wanted Deacon dead, and yet I didn't. I didn't like who I had become.

Boards vibrated beneath my nearly numb backside. "We need a statement, Rhea. I'm taking Eli in, too." Mark wasn't using his cop voice. He just sounded tired.

"Why is Eli going in?"

"Solicitor has to decide if he's to be charged."

I pivoted around on my bottom. Mark stood backlit by the barn lights at the edge of the short dock, hands in his pockets. "Eli had to shoot him because of my big mouth."

"Oh?"

I told Mark what I had said. I could have sworn he was grinning in the dark.

"You're shivering," he said.

"Did you hear what I just said?"

"I heard."

"And?"

"That's my Rhea-Rhea." And his voice was filled with a gentleness I had never heard before. Compassion, as if he knew exactly what I was feeling. And he loved me anyway.

I lifted my hands and let him pull me to my feet. His hand warm around mine, he led me to the transport car. Overhead, a news chopper roared, a light hitting the ground as early morning news footage was captured. I imagined the announcer's voice: "Early this morning, there was a gun battle in Dawkins County as police captured the infamous Triangle Killers.''

And then I remembered the Charlotte newspaper sidebar with my name in it, which mentioned that I was staying at the farm. Reporters would be all over me if I wasn't careful. And the really bad thing? I had done it to myself.

''Great. Just freaking great.''

There were news vans parked along the narrow blacktop road in front of the Stowe farm driveway, access blocked by a young deputy who was trying to look blasé about the cameras trained on him and the house beyond. As we drove past, I hid my face in Eli's shoulder to avoid the cameras and the lights bright enough to sear retinas. I could feel his chest shake with silent laughter, and I pinched him before I could stop myself. Once past, I scooted to my side of the seat and buckled myself in. Eli rubbed his stomach where I had pinched him. I really did have to learn some self-control. I wondered if there were exercises for that.

31

I FIGURED I'D SEDUCE YOU

The morning of the day after Deacon died dawned cool and dreary, with sterile clouds that only teased of rain, hiding the sun and holding in the earth's heat. I was in my bed beneath the down comforter, shades drawn, Belle on the bed with me, her head on the pillow beside mine, Stoney curled up on the other side of her, purring. Pup lay across the foot of the bed, his feet dream-running. There wasn't much room for me. It was perfect.

I had been awake for nearly an hour, lying in the dim light. There was no reason to get out of bed. I didn't have to work until 7:00 p.m. Didn't have to study anything. Didn't feel like running.

Pup sat up suddenly, ears alert. Belle followed suit a moment later, her head coming off the pillow, a low growl starting deep in her throat. She rose to a half crouch, claws digging into the comforter. I swiveled, feeling the pain in my back, and slowly set my feet on the cold floor.

I heard a lock click. The back door opened. Belle and Pup darted off the bed in full-alert mode, barking viciously for two seconds until they reached the door and their anger turned to excitement. They knew the intruder, whose voice was speaking to them in low tones. They led him into the house.

Standing, I checked to see that I was decent, and cautiously entered the brighter kitchen. Mark stood at the kitchen table emptying a bag of groceries—eggs, milk, whole-grain bread, bacon. He looked up when I entered. "Morning, sleepyhead. You going to sleep the day away?"

"I was thinking about it." Seeing him standing there looking so alive and awake made me aware that my teeth were wearing their usual early morning fuzzy socks and that my hair was likely standing up in a Caucasian rapper imitation. "You ever hear of knocking?"

"You might not have let me in if I knocked. I'm here to feed you breakfast."

I put two and two together. I was sleepy, so it took a second. "You used your key to get in here."

"Yep. You got a problem with that? How do you like your eggs?"

"Scrambled. And I don't know," I said, answering his questions in reverse order. "Why are you here? Besides breakfast."

He turned on the gas stove and set an omelette pan on one burner, a small frying pan on another, adding oil to one. He found a bowl and broke six eggs, poured a little milk into them and whisked the mixture to a froth. Measuring out grounds, he started coffee. I waited. Finally he said, "We have things to talk over. Things to decide. And I finally realized that if I leave it up to you to make the first move, I could lose you to Eli Cordell." Mark grinned sourly without looking up. "Then I'd have to shoot him, and that'd be a pain, because I really like the guy. And gunshots are predictably sloppy. Blood. Guts or brain or both on the walls. Press all over. Court. Jail. Years in prison."

Into another pan he lay strips of bacon. Reaching over

the stove, he found my toaster and plugged it in, dropped pieces of bread into it. "So I told Eli to get lost, that you were mine. He said I should feed you. He gave me some other advice I might consider, too." The smell of bacon reached me and my stomach started rumbling. Without a word I turned and went back to my room, brushed my teeth, washed my face and dressed in jeans and a red oversize sweatshirt. Thick socks on my cold feet.

Looking in the bathroom mirror I saw death dug up, warmed over slightly and left to go bad. Though I thought about it, I didn't put on makeup. For some reason I wanted Mark to see me as I really was most mornings, sheet wrinkles, sleepy eyes and all. The smell of breakfast pulled me to the kitchen. I was nervous about what kind of advice Eli Cordell may have given Mark about me.

As I entered, he resumed speaking as though I hadn't left. "So I decided it was time to court you proper. Breakfast seemed like a good start. Then a couple of days in the mountains, just you and me in the old Stafford cabin. Maybe get snowed in. Sit." He nodded to the table and I sat at one of two places set with my good china. I wondered if he intended to wash dishes, too, or if that part of courting would be left to me.

"At some point in the scenario, I figured I'd seduce you."

I smiled down at my plate. Put my napkin in my lap. Wondered a little at the soft warmth I felt at his words.

He dumped a huge portion of eggs onto the plate in front of me. Bacon followed a moment later. Toast. Coffee. I sipped and it was delicious, freshly ground, dark roasted. Maybe a hearty Arabica. I added sugar and cream.

Mark milled at the stove. Over his shoulder he said, "I'm in love with you, Rhea Lynch. In love with your courage, your strength, your independence, your love of life." He glanced at me as he walked closer again. "And with your big mouth." Still serving me, he spooned grits beside the eggs. I hadn't seen him make grits, but they looked like the microwave kind. Soggy. Mark scooped a huge serving of butter onto them, so at least he knew how to disguise the nuked taste properly. He stacked toast on the side, one tip in the grits, one in the eggs.

"I love the fact that you're a bad housekeeper, dress like a tomboy and work awful hours in a job that's dangerous and exhausting because you love it and the people you serve. I love the competition between us, and the fact we need to work at not being so competitive. Working at things is what makes relationships grow. I have that on the finest of Miss Essie's authority." He stepped behind me and placed a single kiss on the top of my head. His arms encircled me, his chin in my hair. Somewhere in the long list of things Mark loved, I had started to cry. God, I hated crying. It was for sissies.

His voice lowered. "I love the fact that we need to work at finding the fire that was there between us when we first met, before things and people got in the way of it. Remember that?"

I wrapped my arms around Mark's as he continued. "I love the fact that you can take care of yourself. I love the fact that you saved Belle in that awful fire. Did I ever tell you that? How proud I was that you had the physical and mental strength to pick up that eighty or hundred pound dog, sling her over your shoulders and carry her and yourself to safety. That you were quick-witted enough to think where to go. That you kept your cool in an emergency that could easily have resulted in your deaths. I love you. Just you. Not your lineage with the Rheaburns, not your potential as a money-maker, not just your body, though that's a hard thing to say, because loving your body is something I've looked forward to for a long time. I want to grow old with you, Rhea Lynch. Have kids, if that's what you decide, or live to our eighties or nineties alone, if it isn't. I want to marry you. Now eat.''

All I could do was nod, since there was no way I was going to talk through the lump in my throat. I wiped my face free of tears, took a breath that shuddered though my chest, and sipped coffee as Mark settled beside me. Some coffee made its way to my stomach, easing the pain in my throat. And because he didn't look at me as he dug into the feast he had prepared, I was able to join in. Mark made a pretty creditable breakfast. I couldn't help but wonder what else he did well that I didn't know about yet. Maybe it was time to find out.

Epilogue

Change comes to all of us—change of jobs, addresses, lovers, friends, thought processes, beliefs and hopes. A strong person deals with the changes, rocks with the waves, bends with the winds, all that pseudo-psychobabble garbage. Dr. Phil and Dear Abby stuff. Me? I guess I'm getting pretty good at change. In some ways, I'm even starting to expect it, like it, roll with the punches. Yeah, right.

I sat on the mountaintop, arms wrapped around my knees, the wind howling, encircling the sheltered place I sat, the first snowstorm of the Christmas season slamming onto the leaves and bare ground near me, beating the earth with the force of its crystal anger, as if the flakes were determined to take the world back to an ice age where they ruled and man was less than nothing.

The sun was a golden haze behind the furious clouds, setting behind the next mountain, impotent and weak against the storm and coming night. I'd have to start back soon or risk being stuck in the small cleft of rock until Mark came and found me. I didn't like being the little lady needing to be rescued. But still I sat. I had some thinking to do. Some deciding to do, as Miss Essie had said when I phoned to tell her Mark and I were leaving for a few days. 'Course, she was always telling me I had some deciding to do, when most times it was just easier to let things be, easier to let things work out on their own.

I was lazy. No doubt about it. I was being lazy now, and

I could almost feel Miss Essie's worry over the miles. But lazy or not, things were working out just fine.

Four days before Christmas, we had driven north and west, into the North Carolina mountains. The Appalachians weren't high by Rocky Mountain standards, most peaks less than five thousand feet. But the sense of isolation was just as extreme, just as rich. The feeling of being a little closer to God just the same.

Far below me, a herd of sheep ran in their ungainly wobble down a trail to safety. To the side three horses ran, tails high, legs lifted in excitement, steam blowing behind them. The scent of wood smoke reached me, whipped up from the chimney in the Stafford cabin. Snow blinded me for an instant and I hugged my knees tighter. Still waiting.

With the wind making its mournful sound I didn't hear him, but I looked up just as he came up the path, dark hair blowing in the wind, green eyes alight. Laughter in the depths. I loved that laughter. Loved the way his eyes lit when he saw me sitting there, in the shelter of the rock. Loved the way he strode silently and sat behind me, arms wrapped around me, legs making a V around my body, sharing the warmth. I loved the smell of him. The way he sighed into my ear as he looked out over the valley and into the coming storm. Loved the way his hands interlaced with mine as if by instinct or decades of long practice.

Maybe I should tell Mark sometime. That I love him. Like tonight, by the light of the oil lamps, curled beneath the handmade quilts and the new down comforter. Yeah. Maybe I should. Maybe I would.

MIRABooks.com

We've got the lowdown on your favorite author!

☆ Read an excerpt of your favorite author's newest book

☆ Check out her bio

☆ Talk to her in our Discussion Forums

☆ Read interviews, diaries, and more

☆ Find her current bestseller, and even her backlist titles

All this and more available at

www.MiraBooks.com

If you enjoyed what you just read,
then we've got an offer you can't resist!

Take 2
bestselling novels FREE!
Plus get a FREE surprise gift!

Clip this page and mail it to The Best of the Best™

IN U.S.A.	IN CANADA
3010 Walden Ave.	P.O. Box 609
P.O. Box 1867	Fort Erie, Ontario
Buffalo, N.Y. 14240-1867	L2A 5X3

YES! Please send me 2 free Best of the Best™ novels and my free surprise gift. After receiving them, if I don't wish to receive anymore, I can return the shipping statement marked cancel. If I don't cancel, I will receive 4 brand-new novels every month, before they're available in stores! In the U.S.A., bill me at the bargain price of $4.74 plus 25¢ shipping and handling per book and applicable sales tax, if any*. In Canada, bill me at the bargain price of $5.24 plus 25¢ shipping and handling per book and applicable taxes**. That's the complete price and a savings of over 20% off the cover prices—what a great deal! I understand that accepting the 2 free books and gift places me under no obligation ever to buy any books. I can always return a shipment and cancel at any time. Even if I never buy another The Best of the Best™ book, the 2 free books and gift are mine to keep forever.

185 MDN DNWF
385 MDN DNWG

Name	(PLEASE PRINT)	
Address	Apt.#	
City	State/Prov.	Zip/Postal Code

* Terms and prices subject to change without notice. Sales tax applicable in N.Y.
** Canadian residents will be charged applicable provincial taxes and GST.
All orders subject to approval. Offer limited to one per household and not valid to current The Best of the Best™ subscribers.
® are registered trademarks of Harlequin Enterprises Limited.

BOB02-R   ©1998 Harlequin Enterprises Limited

By the bestselling author of
THE OTHER TWIN
and *STAR LIGHT, STAR BRIGHT*

KATHERINE STONE

ANOTHER MAN'S SON

Sam Collier was leading a quiet life—until the day he learned the shocking news: Ian Collier, the man who abandoned him when he was four, is dead.

The man he believed to be his father...

Sam returns to Ian's house in Seattle, a place he hasn't seen in thirty-two years, and meets Kathleen Cahill, the woman Ian had planned to marry. Within weeks, Sam's fallen in love with her. And then Kathleen tells him she's pregnant. With his baby——or Ian Collier's?

"Stone's high-quality romance ranks right up there with those of Nora Roberts, Kay Hooper and Iris Johansen."
—*Booklist* on *Thief of Hearts*

*Available the first week of January 2004
wherever books are sold!*

GWEN HUNTER

66916	PRESCRIBED DANGER	___ $6.50 U.S.	___ $7.99 CAN.
66803	DELAYED DIAGNOSIS	___ $5.99 U.S.	___ $6.99 CAN.
66669	DEADLY REMEDY	___ $6.50 U.S.	___ $7.99 CAN.

(limited quantities available)

TOTAL AMOUNT	$_____
POSTAGE & HANDLING	$_____
($1.00 for one book; 50¢ for each additional)	
APPLICABLE TAXES*	$_____
TOTAL PAYABLE	$_____
(check or money order—please do not send cash)	

To order, complete this form and send it, along with a check or money order for the total above, payable to MIRA Books®, to: **In the U.S.:** 3010 Walden Avenue, P.O. Box 9077, Buffalo, NY 14269-9077; **In Canada:** P.O. Box 636, Fort Erie, Ontario L2A 5X3.

Name:_____
Address:_____ City:_____
State/Prov.:_____ Zip/Postal Code:_____
Account Number (if applicable):_____
075 CSAS

  *New York residents remit applicable sales taxes.
   Canadian residents remit applicable GST and provincial taxes.

MIRA®